Ian R. MacLeod

This special signed edition is limited to 1000 numbered copies.

This is copy 977.

Ragged Maps

Ragged Maps

Stories by Ian R. MacLeod

SUBTERRANEAN PRESS 2023

Ragged Maps Copyright © 2023 by Ian R. MacLeod.
All rights reserved.

Dust jacket illustration Copyright © 2023 by Dominic Harman.
All rights reserved.

Interior design Copyright © 2023 by Desert Isle Design, LLC.
All rights reserved.

See pages 453-454 for individual story copyrights.

First Edition

ISBN
978-1-64524-093-8

Subterranean Press
PO Box 190106
Burton, MI 48519

subterraneanpress.com

Manufactured in the United States of America

Contents

Introduction: Ragged Maps — 9
The Mrs Innocents — 13
The Wisdom of the Group — 51
Ephemera — 83
Lamagica — 125
Ouroboros — 171
Stuff — 179
The God of Nothing — 215
Downtime — 239
The Roads — 291
The Memory Artist — 301
Sin Eater — 347
The Visitor from Taured — 365
The Chronologist — 397
Selkie — 421
The Fall of the House of Kepler — 445

Introduction: Ragged Maps

WHAT STRIKES ME most about the stories contained in this collection now that I can look back with some degree of perspective is how many of them revolve around the theme of time. There are the forgotten times, in the form of lost memories, that the major characters in *Downtime* and *Stuff* both strive to confront, and the strange creations that the protagonist of *The Memory Artist* cobbles together out of random bits of the past, and the personal memories that a dying pope chooses to accept or reject in *Sin Eater*. Then there's the vast storehouse of knowledge and culture—effectively the past times of all humanity—that KAT, the machine at the heart of *Ephemera*, curates, and also the sense of time which the Kepler telescope is losing in the final story as it dissolves from sentience into madness. Time, meanwhile, slips and slides and returns on itself in *Selkie*, *Ouroboros* and *The Mrs Innocents*, is toyed with through precognition in *The Wisdom of the Group*, trips into the hazy world of quantum physics in *The Visitor from Taured*, and pretty much breaks down entirely in *The Chronologist*. It's clearly a major element threading its way through the words you now hold in your hand.

Not that time is an unusual subject for SF. In terms of mainstream Hollywood, you need look no further than the time travel of the *Terminator* movies, or *Planet of the Apes*, or *Groundhog Day*, and pretty much everything (for good or ill) that Christopher Nolan has directed. Even with superheroes some kind of loop back through time is often a key plot twist. Clearly, also, the majority of cinematic and written SF is set in some other time than the present, from the dark near-future Los Angeles of *Blade Runner* to the playful long ago of *Star Wars*.

I'm not saying that the SF genre is primarily about time, and I'm certainly not saying that all of the stuff which fits into this category is *good*. But it's there. It's a significant element. A bright tread. And, looking back at my life both as a reader and a writer, I think the ability to examine time in new and interesting ways is a substantial part of what first drew me to the genre. It still draws me today.

From the changed worlds of alternate histories to the twists and turns of time travel to the bizarre effects of relativity, the canvas is huge. But it also has to be acknowledged that time is an important theme in other forms of fiction. After all, procedural detective stories generally revolve around trying to work what happened before the tale actually started, historical novels strive to plausibly recreate the past, and Proust's *À la recherche du temps perdu*—by any standards a high-water mark in modern literature— is determinedly and obsessively about little else.

Of course, there are other important themes in fiction, from romantic love to great quests to family loyalties, but I do feel that there's something particularly significant about time; something

INTRODUCTION

that's not just about our shared life experience but is deeply involved in how we decode the puzzling fact of our existence, and in the acts of reading and writing themselves.

Time, in fiction, can be made to run forwards or backwards. It, and memories and impressions, can be changed, revisited and re-arranged. In fact, it's rather like what happens inside our heads as we navigate the endless *now* of being alive. We recognise and respond to faces, places and situations not on some abstract basis but through the palette of colour, shape, texture, sound, scent and feeling that we've built up over our lives. Our own personal "red", for instance, isn't anybody else's red, or an objective colour on the spectrum of light. It's the memory of the postbox we used to pass on our way to school, and the bright shade of a favourite Christmas toy. Even our emotions are triggered far less by what's actually happening to us in the moment but by what's already happened in the past. As anyone who's argued about stacking the dishwasher or putting out the bins will attest.

In other words we're all constant time travellers, using ragged maps of old memories and past impressions to make sense of our lives as the ever-elusive present slips by and the unreachable future looms ahead. It's all very strange once you start to think about it. But it's rather wonderful as well.

The Mrs Innocents

BEING IN THE condition I was in, nobody thought it was a good idea that I should travel to Berlin in the autumn of 1940. Even my editor, who'd generally trusted my nose for a good story, and wasn't too fussy about putting her correspondents at risk, was dead against it.

"Well…" She sat back in the herbal fug of her office and pointed her pipe at me. "*Look* at you."

I glanced down. The small but growing bump in my belly still seemed strange even to me; one of the many things about pregnancy no one ever tells you being that you never really get used to it. "But that's the whole point. I can go over there, say I'm reporting on, I don't know, dear old King Will's prize geraniums. Then I can just turn up at the famous first Birthplace as if for a standard check-up. Maybe I'll ask them right out, or maybe I'll just go on a wander. You know me. I'm good at wandering."

"And you think that that will get you some kind of piece about Lise Beckhoff, maybe even an interview?"

"Basically, yes."

"What about going through the proper channels?"

"There aren't any proper channels. She's a recluse, and incredibly elderly."

My editor raised an eyebrow, then looked at me the way many people were starting to. "And you're comfortable with this?"

"Of course I am. Otherwise I wouldn't be asking."

"You do know we have an excellent Berlin correspondent?"

"I don't need a hunch." I smiled, and ignored the small, dizzy shiver which passed through me. "This is a last chance. Lise Beckhoff's going to be dead soon."

"And if I said you couldn't go, you'd go anyway, wouldn't you?"

I shrugged.

"But, nevertheless, and even though you're selling me little more than a wild-goose chase, you expect the *Times* to sanction this?"

"Isn't that what I'm paid for?"

I'D WANTED TO be a crusading journalist for as long as I can remember. Even before I knew exactly what journalism was, I craved knowledge—to establish the real truth instead of comfy lies—and had grand dreams of astonishing, and perhaps even changing, the world.

Admittedly, the particular corner of the world I grew up in wasn't that astonishing, Gallowhead being a small town on the Clyde not that far from Dumbarton but a million miles away from being remarkable, even if it did have two rather pointless claims to fame. The first being the concrete folly of the Tesla Tower which rose like a rotting mushroom from the granite crag overlooking the town, and the second that it was where Mrs Clara Innocent chose to spend her declining years. Which, as far as I was concerned, was no fame at all, and definitely no reason to hang around. That, and I definitely wasn't going to have any children.

I first met my husband Richard when I was working as a reporter on the *Dumbarton Daily Messenger*, and he was a trainee architect up from London to do some work on a project that, like most things in and around Gallowhead apart from that stupid tower, never actually got off the ground. When we fell into talking one evening in a local pub, it turned out we both had much bigger plans. He wanted to set up his own practice as soon as he qualified, and from there the sky was the limit. Which, as I pointed out, didn't even have to be a metaphor if you happened to be an architect. And we laughed and shared another beer, then kissed passionately under the stars.

We were sharing a freezing bedsit in London by the next spring, and I was finding out that all working for a Scottish regional newspaper got you at the big nationals was the chance to report on minor traffic accidents at a farthing a line, whilst Richard was far too occupied drawing plumbing diagrams to find time for his own designs.

But we worked hard. We stuck at it. Richard was able to take the leap and set up his own small practice on the back of a lucky inheritance, and a succession of minor freelance scoops finally got me a post as a junior reporter at the *Times*, just as I'd always planned. But it turned out that junior anything wasn't what I really wanted, any more than Richard was satisfied designing pneumatic substations for Western Rail. He wanted to be building town halls, department stores, new cathedrals, next-generation reckoning houses, and I was still on the hunt for the scoop that would change the world.

We weren't rich, but we were hugely ambitious and ridiculously busy. We bought a house in Camden because it was cheap and convenient, and climbed into bed each night exhausted, and rarely made love. Still, and mainly to shut up my mother, we found the time to get married, although I kept my surname (after all, I had my reputation to protect as Sarah Turnbull, soon-to-be world-renowned reporter), and children still remained entirely off the agenda, especially as I approached the supposed milestone age of 30. After all, I was a woman of today. I had my own life to live, not someone else's.

It was Richard rather than me who cracked, at least in my version of this story—which is the one you're going to have to put up with, whoever, wherever and whatever you are, seeing as I'm telling it. Unlike me, he had an extended family of young cousins, nephews and nieces, and was famously good with them. So it was, on a sunny Sunday afternoon at a great aunt's house in Twickenham, where he'd been playing with the kids on the lawn while the rest of us adults sensibly snoozed in deckchairs, that he scooped up a particularly hot and snotty toddler, bore it over to me and said something along the lines of *You know, Sarah, I rather fancy us having one of these.*

It was an obvious joke—talking about having a child in the way you might about buying a new Morris Clara—and I took it as such. But the idea was somehow seeded in the far-distant allotments of our relationship, and it grew there, ignored and untended. Perhaps if I'd been able to take the new birth-control pill that's now being tested—another Birthplace innovation—things would have been different. But Richard and I were using condoms, which always got in the way, and thus we didn't use them at all during the short "safe" time at the end of my period. Then the condoms somehow started becoming even more of a nuisance, and our "safe" days got longer. We were somehow managing to have more sex, too, even though we were still just as exhausted. Thus, month by month, with breathless nods and very little practical discussion, did I inch towards pregnancy.

Not that I was expecting it to happen. I was an up-and-coming reporter at one of the world's major print journals, and certainly not some random child's mother. Richard, admittedly, did have a fatherly side, at least when it came to organising impromptu games with his younger relatives. Seeing as my own father had died when I was fairly young, I'll even admit that that might have been part of what drew me to him. But when it came to the rest, I simply didn't see a future which involved me growing some new person inside my body. In fact, and if I'm entirely honest, the whole idea gave me the creeps.

I can, in retrospect, place my first realisation to the morning when, looking down at my habitual breakfast cup of coffee, I felt a sliding shift as if the world around me had loosened on its tethers, and decided I only wanted a drink of water, and even that tasted strangely metallic. There were other things. A whole, tedious litany of tingling skin and a buzzing in my ears and a floaty feeling of disconnection even before I started to wonder about what had happened to the ordinary aches of my period. So, what does any modern girl do? The first thing, of course, is to carry on as normal, and tell absolutely no one, and pretend it can't possibly be true. Then, of course, she goes to a Birthplace—a Mrs Innocent's.

THEY'RE A COMMON enough sight. From mud huts, travelling caravans and structures built on wooden stilts, they come in all shapes and sizes, although we here in Britain still prefer plain old bricks and mortar. The Birthplace on Fetter Lane, just around the corner from Saint Dunstan's, which I walked down to from the *Times'* offices in Printing House Square one lunchtime, isn't as grand as the one in Whitehall designed by Edwina Lutyens, but it's still an impressive structure. Apart from a mosaic frieze of that Scottish, matronly, widow Mrs Innocent herself—half Whistler's mother and half Juliet's nurse—on the frontage, it could be a major bank, or the embassy of some significant foreign power.

Looking left and right to make sure there were no familiar faces amid the London crowds, I pushed through the swing doors. I'd expected a waiting room decorated with health warnings and anatomical diagrams, but instead found myself in a large, high-ceilinged hall scattered with broad leather chairs and low tables spilling with upmarket magazines. The place felt more like a club than a clinic. Somewhere in the background, a tune I recognised as Daisy Ellington's *Take the A Train* was playing. I was about to head out to check if I'd gone into the wrong building when a woman in that characteristic blue uniform of a Mrs Innocent bustled up to me.

"Welcome," she said with a beamingly bright smile, as if I was the very person she'd been expecting. "Have you been here before?"

I shook my head. "It's just to check—you know, if I'm..." I trailed off, suddenly bashful as a teenager.

"Of course, of course. Every woman is entitled to know the state of her own body. Do you happen to have brought a urine sample with you?"

Obviously, I hadn't, but that was no problem at all. She led me swiftly down polished corridors to a wood-panelled room which, despite the presence of a hospital screen and a toilet, still had that same club-like air. She left me there, and knocked discreetly when she came back, and thanked me with seemingly sincerity for the small, warm phial I presented her with.

"If you'd like to sit down and wait—there are magazines over there, and some biscuits and fruit juice—and I'll be back with the news in a few minutes."

My head swam. My stomach growled. My whole body thrummed with a strange, disconnected fizzing. "You mean you can tell me right away? I thought it would take days. Don't you have to inject frogs? Or kill rabbits?"

She favoured me with another of her Mrs Innocent smiles. "Nothing like that. It's a quick, simple chemical test nowadays, and much more reliable. My name's Phyllis Dunnet, by the way, and I want you to know you can stay here just as long as you like, or head out and come back later, and perhaps bring along a partner or friend. Or we could ring or electropen you at the *Times*, if you could give us a—"

"No, no," I said, wondering exactly when, in all my confusion, I'd mentioned my place of employment. "I'll wait here. Absolutely."

STILL IN A daze, I took the pneumatic back to Camden that evening with an appointments card and several Birthplace leaflets nestling in my briefcase, and sat at our kitchen table waiting for Richard, as anxious as if I was about to confess some torrid affair. But he was blissfully unsurprised. So, when we took the express up to Gallowhead a week or so later, and even more annoyingly, was my mother. Even my colleagues in the third floor newsroom, which I'd been frequently fleeing in recent times to retch in the toilets, took the news as if they'd known all about it from the moment of conception.

Meanwhile, my visits to the Birthplace on Fetter Lane, and my sudden dislike of coffee, and the tiredness, and the swelling of my ankles, and the sweats, and the bouts of diarrhoea, and the odd tingling sensation across my skin and in my ears, and that peculiar sliding feeling, continued, although I was assured that such symptoms were perfectly normal during the early stages of pregnancy.

My mother was, and is, a frank and practical woman. At least, when it suits her. Perhaps it comes in part from having to make her own way in the world after my father's death, even if widows and single mothers have none of the disadvantages they had to face in the bad old days. She certainly made sure that I knew all about the facts of life—breasts and penises and periods and so forth—at an age which meant I could lord it over most of the other children at school. They listened open-mouthed as I explained who put what into where, and what happened after. In many ways, I still think of it as my first ever scoop. But when it came to the other end of things, so to speak, even my mother was much more reticent. The baby simply "came out", or was "pushed", and then the umbilical cord was cut. Which, my dear, is what gives us all our bellybuttons. And that was that.

As I approached the beginning of what is clinically known as my second trimester, and I was given nothing really substantial to work on, I began to spend more and more of my paid hours up in the *Times*' library. This was, and is, a well-resourced establishment, with a high-bandwidth link to the new reckoning house in Sloane Square, so even books and periodicals that aren't kept on the shelves or stored on voltaic tape can still be easily accessed. A whole wide world of knowledge, you might say.

THE MRS INNOCENTS

MY FASCINATION WITH finding the truth goes back at least as far as when my father was still alive, and I was an avid collector of the cards from his packs of Churchman's cigarettes, back when tobacco-smoking wasn't yet seriously discouraged on health grounds. It was the feel and the smell of the cards which first drew me to them, the sweet, dark, fatherish odour which infused each little rectangle, as well as the information they contained. I soon began to build up whole sets. *Flowers of the Hedgerow*. *The Story of Empire* (we British still not having given up all our old colonies back then). I'd memorise each list as a kind of litany, and desperately covet the cards I didn't have.

My father was just a local electrician who'd grown up in dull old Gallowhead, but in many ways he was a brilliant man, or at least the visions he stirred in my mind were brilliant. With the help of *Stars and Planets*, for instance, I had my first glimpse of the vast scale of the universe, and *Great Inventors* introduced me to Ada Lovelace (number 1 in a series of 25), Leonardo da Vinci (number 6) and Marie Curie (number 24).

Of that last set, and despite many swaps, I was somehow never able to get hold of the Nikola Tesla card (number 16), which was deeply frustrating, especially with Gallowhead being dominated by the man's most famous folly. Locals called it *the wee big thing*, although course I didn't yet understand that the tower resembled an erect phallus as much as a huge concrete mushroom, and my father didn't smirk when he said Tesla's name, for the man was a genius.

One day, he led me up the cobbled street from our house to the crag from where the tower reared over the Clyde, far too big and solid to be economically demolished. We squeezed through a gap in the ivy-festooned fence to be greeted by a thick, almost palpable, darkness, and a predictable reek of urine, inside. But my father grasped my hand and turned on his flashlight, drawing me on up the rackety spiral staircase. This level, Sarah, is where the operators would have slept. And this is the control room. Dusty dials, monitors and antique switchgear winked back at me. But this, my dear, was the heart of everything.

The rusty iron core at the centre of the tower, sunk deep into the solid rock, and wound with copper anacondas, had been designed, as my father explained in leaps of thought and the dance of his flashlight, to bring about a whole new age of light, power and communication. The planet itself, or so Tesla had claimed, was an endless reservoir of energy which could be tapped by towers such as this and the other one he'd managed to get built at Wardenclyffe on Long Island, and the hundreds of others he envisaged throughout the world. Every home, ship, car, train, aircraft and factory would have access to unlimited energy through nothing more than a simple aerial. And every person in the world would be able to send messages to anyone else using exactly the same technology.

No matter that Tesla's science was fundamentally flawed—that it's a basic law of physics that energy is lost in inverse proportion to the square of the distance from its source, as I now know all too well. Some dreams are so wonderful, so persuasive, they deserve to be true even when they aren't.

Quite a lot for anyone, least of all a somewhat precocious young girl, to absorb. But of course, and above all, it made me want that last Nicola Tesla card to complete my *Great Inventors* set even more.

BUT KNOWLEDGE, YES. Facts. Verifiable reports. Which, in the absence of W.A. & A.C. Churchman ever doing a *Childbirth* series, and in the buzzing sanctuary of the *Times*' library, I discovered many things that my mother had never told me. The tearing. The stitches. The enemas. The agony. That, and the many things which can and do go wrong before, during, and after the process of a baby somehow emerging from a place that my friends at school had insisted was just plain impossible.

Still, there was always my Birthplace, which I could visit whenever I wanted, even when I wasn't booked in for another respectful examination. I could make use of the well-equipped gym, or swim in the heated swimming pool, or talk to other mothers-to-be, or try to engage with the toddlers who ran around like wound-up toys in the crèche, or study the babies lying fresh-minted in their cribs, and wonder when the change would finally come over me which would make these strange and selfish little creatures seem irresistible. That, or I could gaze at the stock image which seemingly hung on every wall of Clara Innocent, midwife to Queen Victoria, whose name and grandmotherly wisdom had famously inspired the entire Birthplace Movement, even if she's mostly remembered in Gallowhead as a batty old crone. Or there were the many photographs of Lise Beckhoff herself.

There she was, standing even taller than Amelia Earhart at the end of her successful round-the-world flight, or outside the Kremlin shaking hands with Alexander Kerensky, or with President Gandhi in Delhi, or standing before yet another new Birthplace in some far-flung location. She always wore practical clothes, and had a practical smile. She looked pale yet determined, like someone who's got the weave of all history wrapped around their little finger.

IAN R. MACLEOD

THE BASIC FACTS of the movement Lise Beckhoff founded and still acted as nominal head of are the grist of many a schoolgirl's history project, not least in Gallowhead. How, as the daughter of an Irish mother and a father of minor German nobility, she grew up in the small German princedom of Württemberg. When both parents died young, she was sent to court in Berlin to become a lady-in-waiting. There, because she could speak both German and English, she grew close to Queen Victoria's eldest daughter, also christened Victoria, but universally known as Vicky, who'd been shipped over from England to marry Frederick, Prince of Prussia at the age of 18, which was how things were then done.

By 19, Princess Vicky was pregnant in a strange and foreign country, and had absolutely no idea of what lay ahead. Despite all her supposed privilege, childbirth in those days was a dangerous, and often fatal, business. Queen Victoria sent her own physician, Doctor James Clark, and her personal midwife, Mrs Clara Innocent, over to Berlin to help her daughter through her first confinement, along with a plentiful supply of the aether. In her own quiet way, Queen Victoria was something of a pioneer of the rights of women, and regarded the prevalent idea that the pain of childbirth was not only natural, but Biblically preordained, as the nonsense it plainly was.

Many important men had gathered in the draughty staterooms of the Crown Prince's Palace to await the young princess's confinement, including several supposedly eminent doctors, not to mention politicians, courtiers, footmen and ladies-in-waiting, the process of bringing an heir to the Prussian throne into the world being essentially a state occasion. But none of them—at least apart from Clara Innocent—had any real idea of what they were doing. Only she, with her hard-won practical experience, realised that the princess's baby was positioned feet first, which would lead to a breech birth. Which, then as now, is incredibly dangerous.

Somehow, and despite her lowly status, and with Lise Beckhoff as her translator, Mrs Innocent persuaded these pompous and ill-informed men to allow her to attempt to physically rotate the baby by gently kneading Princess Vicky's belly. Somehow, and even more remarkably, she succeeded, and what would have been a difficult and possibly deathly confinement was averted, and Prince Wilhelm—who would eventually become the much-loved King Willy—was born whole and hale and healthy. And Lise Beckhoff was inspired to begin her life's work of improving the lot of women across the globe.

What was at first a campaign soon became a movement, and then, surprisingly rapidly, an institution. I suppose it did no harm for Lise Beckhoff to be bilingual and have the support of two deeply grateful royal families, and then to use Clara Innocent, with her perfect name and brisk yet homely manner, as a figurehead. You might almost call it—or so it seemed to my cynical, modern, journalistic eye—a canny piece of product branding.

Even with all of this in its favour, however, and despite Lise Beckhoff's evident brilliance, the rise of the Birthplace Movement still struck me as extraordinary. Sure, she gained backing from many rich and powerful men—and in those days, it was almost entirely men—and she had vim and pizazz, and worked like a dervish. But she was also canny and lucky—you might almost say ridiculously so—with a string of spectacularly successful investments.

Did you know that the Birthplace Trust owns the patent for the crescent wrench? Me neither. At least, not until the information fizzed into life across my cathode tube in the *Times'* library. Then, of course, there are the many medical innovations—from electrocardio stimulation, to X rays, to epidurals—that the Birthplace Trust has been instrumental in developing, not to mention holding many significant patents related to the electropen, pneumatic transport and the technologies of the reckoning house.

To me, this all seemed a bit strange. In fact, it was more than strange: I scented a story. Sitting amid heaped periodicals and punchcards in the humming green cathode tube glow of the *Times'* library, your trusty correspondent had another of her odd shifting, tingling moments, and knew that she had to go to Berlin.

IT WAS A clear, fine day in the beautiful autumn of 1941 when I arrived outside the arch of Euston Station with my small suitcase, ringbound reporter's pocketbook and increasingly protuberant belly. Once aboard my carriage, and borne along on a great, whooshing *woof* of power, purpose and air, I opened my copy of today's *Times*. At first I did what any self-respecting journalist does with any newspaper, studying not the news itself but the names of the reporters. Nothing with my byline, of course, although I hoped that would soon change, and meanwhile there had been another nasty earthquake in Turkey. Bad news, of course, always trumping good, even in this tranquil century.

Rocked by the sound and the motion as the train dived into the cross-Channel tunnel, I fell into a drowse, and drifted towards memories of my childhood. There I was, back at the table in our little kitchen at Gallowhead, and I could still swing my legs without touching the linoleum floor. My mother was washing the breakfast things before she took me to school on her way to work at the Council offices, and the tobacco bristle of my father's kiss was still fading on my cheek as he picked up his trusty toolbag and headed out of the door. But I called him back. Even as he turned, I could see he knew what I wanted. That last card—number 16: Nikola Tesla—which would finally complete *Great Inventors*, and yes, yes, of course he'd call in at the newsagents and buy another couple of packets of Churchman's even though he probably had enough to see him through the week, and it was a bit of a detour. He was that kind of father. Then he was gone, delayed by my silly request for no more than thirty seconds, and it seemed to me that I could hear the rumbling onrush of that runaway cart and the screams of the onlookers even as I awoke with a sob and start, and realised it was just the sound of the train slowing through the suburbs of Paris towards the Gare du Nord.

I ate a good, expensive, expenses-paid lunch in the dining car, and spent the afternoon gazing out across the flat and peaceful fields of lowland Europe. That, and practising my German, which I'd assured my editor I was semi-fluent in, despite my never having visited the country, and having gained only a second-level school certificate. Still, I managed to make myself clear enough to the taxi driver outside the Stadtbahnhof for her to take me to my hotel along roads lined with strangely ornamented apartments, elaborate synagogues and tall churches. There, I electropenned Richard and my editor to let them know I'd arrived in Berlin, and puzzled for a while over the purpose of the concave shelf in the toilet basin. Despite all the many treaties of European unification, the Germans really are a different race.

I SPENT THE following morning researching the cheesy travelogue which I hoped I wouldn't have to write to justify my visit, and soon discovered that the city's museums and art galleries are huge, and fabulous, but also hugely, fabulously tiring. Then I ate oddly flavoured doughnuts for lunch in a café with my bump tucked neatly under a blanket, and worked at my German through trying to explain to the waiter that I definitely didn't want any coffee. But I knew I was wasting time.

The Central Berlin Birthplace—although they seemed just as fond over there as they are here in Britain of calling such places Frau Innocents—lies in an enviable location amid the bigger corporate headquarters, embassies and offices of state midway along Unter den Linden. I'd always imagined that there was a strong dose of poetic licence in that name, but tall and stately linden trees shimmered in the autumn afternoon sunlight as I ascended the marble steps towards the most famous Birthplace of all.

Inside, I felt instantly at home. There was the same club-like atmosphere and the same large leather chairs as my "home" Mrs Innocents on Fetter Lane, but on a larger scale, and the music playing was something softly classical by, I think, Clara Schumann. Even the smell was familiar: a mixture of lavender floor polish and warm biscuits, with perhaps a hint of the crowns of the heads of babies, and a faint waft of something sharper and more purposeful underneath.

A woman with a predictable smile, cornrow hair and a Frau Innocent uniform bustled up to me and wished me a cheery *Guten Tag*. Then, when I attempted to reply in my schoolgirl German, she immediately switched to English.

"Ah, yes, of course. If I may just borrow your appointments card for few moments...?"

She scurried off, to reappear clutching a freshly electropenned sheaf of what looked like my entire clinical history suspiciously quickly.

"So, Sarah," she said as she warmed her hands in the wood-panelled examining suite, "you are a journalist for the *Times* of London. Does this mean you have come here to our city to write some particular story?"

"It's really just a general travel piece."

"So you are a travel journalist?"

"I suppose you could say that."

Which resulted in her quizzing me throughout my examination about the many places which I surely must have visited during in course of my work—a discussion which grew awkward when it turned out that this particular Fräu Innocent had actually been to Bolivia.

"Now you say the *hills* around La Paz... Here is something strange about the English language. For would you not call the Andes mountains?"

"No, not exactly." I busied myself with my clothes, then pretended to be struck by an idea. "But perhaps, seeing as I'm here and writing about Berlin, I could add something about its most famous resident. Is there a chance that I might have a few quick words with Frau Beckhoff? It wouldn't take a moment, and I believe she has her apartment right here in this very building."

My Fräu Innocent's smile suddenly faded. "I am afraid that cannot happen. You see, our founder is very old and does not perform interviews. Although I and my colleagues will be happy to help you in any query you might have about our organisation."

"No, that's fine. I just thought I might as well ask, seeing as I was here."

"Of course." The smile returned. "I understand."

She led me back to the entrance hall, and left me there after extracting promises that I wouldn't say anything bad about German food, or describe Berlin's many museums as even slightly boring. Once she'd gone, I turned as if to leave, then headed back towards the nearest stairwell. This, at least apart from my being pregnant, was what I'd always imagined the life of a crusading journalist would be like—part poet and part secret agent—even if the long climb to the higher reaches of this particularly large and grand Mrs Innocents left me sweaty and breathless.

Up here in the Birthplace's main offices, above the wards and the delivery suites and the crèches, there were surprisingly few people about, and the atmosphere was very different. Electropens scritched, cathode screens glowed and typeboards clicked as if to the march of invisible fingers. A futuristic smell of volatile fluids and freshly abraded paper tickled my nostrils. It was as if some great, murmurous brain—

"*Was machen Sie?*"

I really don't know whether the Frau Innocent who intercepted me bought my attempts at baby-brain confusion as she patiently explained that this part of the Birthplace was not open to visitors, and politely but firmly escorted me from the premises.

SO THAT WAS that. Plan A exhausted, and I was totally unable to come up with any kind of Plan B as I sat steeping my aching feet in a bowl of warm water back at my hotel.

Berlin is a thriving, bustling and, above all, modern, city. No traveller can help but be thrilled by the marvels of its many parks, palaces and museums. The city also excels when it comes to entertainment, be it comic opera, fine art or one of its many beer halls...

I prowled and wandered and made pointless shorthand notes in my trusty ringbound notebook. Twice, I narrowly avoided getting run over by looking the wrong way before stepping into traffic. I queued with the crowds to see the state rooms of the Crown Prince's Palace, now of course yet another museum, where, unbelievably amid the cherub ceilings and vast gilt mirrors, a disastrous breech birth had been narrowly avoided and the long chain of events which had somehow brought me here had began.

Behind the velvet ropes, I tried to imagine what it must have been like, to give birth in that much more primitive age, and had the same sliding, fizzing feeling which had come over me so many times, and swallowed hard and told myself—*Goddammit, Sarah!*—that I was still a reporter on the trail of a story, even if the essence of whatever I was chasing seemed to be slipping ever further away.

Tired and giddy, I found myself standing at noon before the Brandenburg Gate, daring that winged statue to take flight. That, and wondering what particular combination of suppositions, feelings and hormones had brought me to this city, and why I still found it so hard to let go. Cars and trams, cyclists and pedestrians sped by. For everything moved onwards in this futuristic world, and even truth was relative, and my ears filled with a deep, sibilate whispering, and I saw marching men, and red and black flags, and heard the drone of aeroplanes and the broken-glass roar of voices as foul smoke filled my mouth, and there was a stench of death, and the Reichstag blazed, and the fine buildings around me collapsed into rubble.

Then faces were leaning over me, and I strove to fight against them until a final dark wave came crashing in, and I saw and felt nothing.

MUSIC WAS PLAYING, cool as a river. Whatever I'd been dreaming of, it certainly wasn't this. And, beneath that music, I could hear the scritch of electropens and the soft hum of transformers.

"Sarah Turnbull? Can you hear me?"

The voice was querulous, lightly accented. A smell of lavender floor polish, babies and biscuits, and a taste gritting my mouth like brickdust and blood. I opened my eyes and winced. The voice spoke again, something in German this time about *die Leuchte*—perhaps meaning light, lamp, candle. After a buzz, and a click, the scene grew less harsh. But still the other figure, who was sitting right beside where I now lay, seemed impossibly vague. I could almost see right through her.

"You're in Berlin, Sarah. At the Birthplace on Unter den Linden. Just nod if you understand."

I did, and with that nod came a sudden rush of worry. Because I'd collapsed, fainted, been borne here from the Brandenburg Gate. And the child I was carrying, my *baby*—

"No, no. You mustn't worry." A hand light as an autumn leaf settled on me as I struggled to sit up. "You and your child, you are both fine. It's not so unusual to have moments of faintness. Especially if—do you still say this in Britain?—the candle is burnt at both ends. I would dearly love to live in a world where pregnant women are turned into super-beings, but unfortunately that is not the case. Here, have some of this."

A beaker touched my lips. It was cool, soothingly medicinal.

"There. That's better, isn't it?"

Lise Beckhoff was a thinner, older version of her many pictures and portraits, and what light there was in this dimmed and clinical room seemed to float around the nimbus of her hair. She seemed frail as a dandelion seed, and almost equally likely to be blown away. Yet at the same time she was real, she was *here*, the woman who had done more than anyone in history to improve the lot of humanity, and her presence was extraordinary, and I knew that it was me, not her, who was weak, faint, helpless...

"So," she said, "I hear that you are a journalist. So perhaps, as we are both here, there are some questions you might want to ask me?"

I tried to open my mouth but I was still too shocked and dazed.

"Ah..." she said, laughing in a soft cascade which somehow joined with whatever music was playing in the background. "Even now, people still find themselves tongue-tied in the presence of an old thing such as me. Still, we are so lucky to be here in this world, Sarah Turnbull, both you and I..."

Then Lise Beckhoff began to talk. She spoke at first of the fate of women in childbirth across the centuries. The deaths and brutalities. The disease and the pain. And of how so much of this could always have been avoided though simple kindness and the support of other women. But set against this there was ignorance and superstition. You'd have thought matters would have improved with the increasing knowledge and literacy, but instead they worsened.

She paused. Her breath, the light, the music which surrounded her, seemed to grow slightly more ragged.

"They called us witches, you know, Sarah—the older women who helped the younger ones through the labours of childbirth. They talked of changelings and stolen souls. Even the fingernail, the one we kept long so we might safely puncture the amniotic sac, became a witch's claw. I have no idea how many of the thousands of women who were burned at the stake were midwives, but it must have been a great many.

"Even as that terrible period passed, things did not improve. For now there was something called *science*, and there were men who liked to term themselves *doctors*, and of course they looked down on the women who dared to challenge their role. Which is why I chose to befriend and make a model of dear, dear Clara Innocent. You understand that, don't you, Sarah? I think you should..."

Again, she sat quiet. Again, she offered me the trembling cup of fluid. But our situations were strangely reversed, and Lise Beckhoff seemed to be peering forward as if to grasp and come to terms with the amazement that I, through my continuing fog, should be feeling towards her: that *I* was really *me*–even if I was nothing more than Sarah Turnbull, a somewhat confused *Times* correspondent, who'd overestimated the strength of her body, and perhaps her journalistic intelligence.

"So now you have your interview," she then said, sitting back in a creak of bones. "Which will almost certainly be my last—ancient as I am. You thought that I held some great secret or revelation, didn't you?"

"It's my job..." I said, "...to look for stories."

She chuckled. "And I'm so very glad that we live in a world where women have these opportunities. But now, or at least soon, you will also be a mother..." She leaned closer, and there was something about her presence which seemed almost predatory. As if she was weighing me up, with chilling precision, in the balance of everything that had ever existed. "There's a new test we have. It's a kind of scan which uses waves of sound to display the baby in the womb on a cathode tube. It can reveal if there are any problems. Also, it can tell whether you have a boy or a girl baby, if that is something you would like to know. Have you heard of such a thing, Sarah?"

I swallowed and nodded.

"Yet your records say you haven't had it done." She sounded disappointed. "You know, we could arrange to do it right here. It would only take half an hour or so, and—"

"I'd rather not." Even allowing for the fact that Richard and I didn't want to know the sex of our child, I hadn't liked the sound of this machine when it had been mentioned back in London. I liked it even less now.

"Of course." She gave another slow chuckle. "I think I understand. And it's a marvel that you and I are here…"

And so she went on, but whatever she'd given me to drink and the shock of my collapse conspired to make things seem even more distant. So lucky to be here. Yes, I was. Lise Beckhoff's voice, her actual presence, seemed to blur as she spoke, fanning off like light reflecting from the onrushing river of history.

Somehow, I was back inside that royal palace, but without the velvet ropes and the gawking tourists. A very strange place indeed for a lonely princess to endure the agony of a breech confinement, until a professor of obstetrics at Berlin University was finally summoned after almost twenty-four hours of labour when it became apparent that both mother and baby were dying. So, and with the aid of a set of forceps, the boy-child was finally hauled into the world, weak but not entirely dead, and his mother was also saved, if barely. They called him Wilhelm. You might almost say it was a miracle. But miracles are strange things, and some work better than others, and the forceps' grip had torn the nerves of the boy's left arm and shoulder.

Of course, the idea of a deformed crown prince was unthinkable. So this Wilhelm, the damaged child who never was, was given electric shocks and ice baths. Then, as he grew, his right arm was tied behind his back to force him to use his shrivelled left one, and the warm corpses of freshly slaughtered hares were wrapped around it in the hope that the animal's "life force" would somehow transfer. Then came the intense family pressure, and the desperate need to hide this disability from the national gaze, with every photograph and public appearance an anxiously staged charade. A great deal for any lad, especially one with his other aspects of his personality and capacities subtly damaged by those long hours of helpless constriction, to bear. Even more so as he grew to become King of Prussia, then self-proclaimed emperor of a Germany united under the machinations of wily old Otto Von Bismarck.

I saw, no, I felt the tides of time, and I was borne along with them. Armies marched, people starved, dynasties squabbled and politicians dithered as factories and shipyards clamoured with the new machineries of war. And there at the heart of it all was not the clever, gentle, garden-loving King Willy, but Kaiser Wilhelm; a small, pompous man in a stiffly beribboned uniform, with a pointed moustache and an even more pointed helmet, desperately posing to hide his withered arm, and to prove to the world that he was a man of action.

I heard the boom of guns, and smelled the stench of death as choking palls of greenish-white gas wafted across acres of mud towards rat-infested trenches. And even when all of that was done with, and all the graves had been dug and the memorials erected, and the women had ceased weeping, the men were still marching... They burned books. They broke windows, bones and lives. The old kings and emperors might be gone, but the new so-called men of the people still wore beribboned uniforms, and sported even more ridiculous moustaches. So it happened again, and soon there were pits filled with gape-jawed corpses, and people too thin to be alive cowered behind barbed wire fences. But even that wasn't enough, and a godlike rumbling and a bright flash came as if out of nowhere as something—a kind of mushroom that briefly seemed reminiscent of Nicola Tesla's tower, but made of dust and fire—rose towards the heavens.

In a way, the world that lay beyond this moment of apocalypse was reminiscent of my own. There were bright machines and elegant, glassy buildings. I even sensed that women had been given more of a say, if not that much of one. But people still starved behind fences, and the seas rose and the land contracted as self-aggrandising men of power, who now wore lounge suits and sported very few moustaches, still bickered and pontificated and played to the baying crowds. And the skies greyed and the white walls of Antarctica dissolved. Instead of marching armies, there were fleeing hordes, until once again there came that godlike flash and rumble, and a terrible wind tore through everything.

Yet here I was, floating and still alive in the hissing quiet of a peaceful Berlin in this glorious autumn of 1940, and something crucial was still missing. I took a sharp breath, and opened my eyes, and touched my rounded belly, and found that I was alone.

I GOT DRESSED right away, insisting to the fussing Frau Innocents that I felt fine and that no, I definitely didn't want an ambulance or a taxi, seeing as my hotel wasn't far and the walk would do me good. And yes, yes, I would think about having that scan done, either here in Berlin or back in London, although there was no way that was ever going to happen.

It was early evening, cool and bright and pretty, as I sat down on a bench beside the pale gravel paths of the Tiergarten. Cyclists ticked by, couples walked hand in hand and people smiled at me and my bump, as if I really did bear the secret of all human existence, although I wanted to tell them that I couldn't even speak their language, knew less than nothing, and was quite possibly going a little mad.

I'd fluffed it. I'd had the chance of a lifetime to meet and talk with Lise Beckhoff, and I'd just lain there and let her fill my head with grotesque visions of things that had never happened. It was no excuse my having a fainting fit, or being pregnant. Journalists have filed their reports from prison cells, battlefields and shipwrecks. Others—just like many midwives—had been persecuted, tortured and killed. Still, I had to write something to justify my visit, so I took out my ringbound notebook to see what I could cobble together out of all the travelogue nonsense I'd been listlessly compiling.

As I did so, I gasped. For the first time ever, I felt my baby move inside me, and the feeling was both physically acute yet also deeply profound. But even as I struggled to come to terms—to even believe—this extraordinary moment, something fluttered from my notebook's pages and settled on my lap. A Churchman's cigarette card in the *Great Inventors* series: number 16, for Nikola Tesla.

I TOOK THE first direct express back to London early next morning.

All I felt able to offer my editor was a mundane travel piece, obviously minus my encounter with Lise Beckhoff. I couldn't say much to Richard, either. If he'd learned of my collapse, let alone my bizarre visions, he'd have grown even more worried about me than he already was. But I could sense him and my editor and almost everyone else deciding that my trip to Berlin was probably just one of those odd things pregnant women got up to, like eating sardines straight from a tin or growing an extra nipple. And, of course, I'd give up this pretence of trying to carry on working as a journalist, wouldn't I, now I'd got this silly little trip out of my system...?

But there was one thing I bore with me into my third trimester—when my ears constantly sang and I bumped into things and found it near impossible to even pull on my own shoes—it was the thought of that bloody cigarette card, and of Lise Beckhoff, not as the person she claimed to be but as a sly imposter secretly spinning the threads of all history. I was right. Something *was* going on. And it was beyond impossible.

There are many crackpot Birthplace stories. The kind of thing that the older male hacks—that vanishing breed with their marbled noses, bad breath and broken marriages—will happily share with you for the price of another pint in a Fleet Street pub. Not for publication, my dear...

They're all lesbians, you know—the so-called Mrs Innocents. Yes, and there's said to be a kind of chapel inside every Birthplace, but not to any known religion, or at least not one that's been practised since the Dark Ages. Perhaps you've seen it yourself? Or perhaps you've already been initiated? The Mrs Innocents, they walk around in the nude for their ceremonies, and talk in a secret language that goes back to Eve's first sin...

All, of course, just modern variations on those tales of witches' covens and Sabbat dances. Neither was I able to find any evidence that the details of Lise Beckhoff's early life, which are surprisingly substantial, were in any way fabricated. She was, to all intents and purposes, exactly what she claimed to be: a minor Irish-German aristocrat who'd had a vision and then somehow got incredibly lucky. But there was no way I was going to keep my next Birthplace appointment, still less have my baby scanned by some futuristic machine, and I hid the reminders that soon began to arrive deep in the recycling bin at home where Richard wouldn't find them, and tried to get on with my life as if nothing had happened. Apart, at least, from my being somewhat pregnant. Which is surely no big deal in this day and age? So will you please just stop bothering me...!

Obviously, Richard was concerned. Not that we had any serious rows—he was far too annoyingly conscious of my supposed frailty for that—but even I began to sense a worrying coldness and avoidance opening up between us like dark rifts in melting ice. Then, early into my third trimester when I started to experience bad backaches, nasty heartburns, and a burning, near-endless need to pee, he won a contract to design a brand-new reckoning house serving all of northeast London, to be situated on the edge of Hampstead Heath. It was the big commission he'd always dreamed of, and he was suddenly frantically busy, which drove us even further apart. But I did warily agree with him that it wouldn't be the worst possible idea for us to take a break from London to spend a weekend with my mother up in Gallowhead. If nothing else, she would be a different person for me to be snappy with.

IT WAS THE same old fishy-smelling harbour, with the same hunched houses, and the same steeply cobbled streets rising up towards that pointless tower, which of course got me thinking once again of Lise Beckhoff and that cigarette card, which I'd also hidden deep in the recycling.

On the Sunday afternoon before we took the express back to London, my mother suggested we should go out for a stroll while Richard worked through his sheaves of electropenned blueprints. Perhaps she thought she could get me to talk about whatever was bothering me, but there was no chance of that. We journalists are even better at bottling up our own problems than we are at prising them out of others.

"You know," I conceded, as we headed up the cobbled main street, "you were always fairly honest with me when I was a child."

"Thank you," she replied warily. She knew me well enough to understand that such statements were always followed by a *but*.

"There's one thing, though, that you never really spoke about, and that's what it's like to give birth."

There was a long pause as we walked on up the slope.

"It is not an easy subject for any woman to talk about," she said eventually. "Although these days there's..." She gave a vague gesture, then caught my arm. "All the things you must have been told at your Mrs Innocents, just as I was when I had you at our local one in Dumbarton. What do you want me to say, Sarah? That it's difficult, painful? Of course it is, but the result is so"—she searched for a word—"*positive* that in the long run it scarcely matters. But if you want the absolute truth, if you want to know what the worst thing is, at least as I remember, it's the worry, the uncertainty." Her hand still grasped my arm. "It's exactly what you're feeling right now, Sarah. And we women, we're so very lucky to live in this age. I know you're not a religious person, but I do sometimes think this must be the work of some greater power."

"I'm sorry if I've seemed preoccupied this weekend," I said, as my baby gave a disconcerting wiggle. "It was Richard who suggested—"

"It doesn't matter. You're here, and that's all that counts. But I'll say something else. Perhaps I shouldn't, but I will. Your Richard's a decent, reliable man. Yes, he works too hard, but then so do you, and it's obvious he cares for you deeply. So when you ask about birth, and about the whole business of being a mother... Well, I know it's not fashionable to say such a thing, but it isn't something a woman can easily manage alone."

"*You* did, Mother."

A cheap jibe, perhaps, and she said nothing more until we reached the top of the slope, and sat down on a bench beside a rusty fence with the Tesla Tower glowering behind us and a cold, fishy pall of fog greying the flow of the Clyde.

"How much do you remember of your father, Sarah?"

I shrugged. "Enough to know that I cared deeply for him... And I still think about that accident."

"I know you do, Sarah. And I know, as well, how you somehow felt responsible. But it was just plain old bad luck. The coal merchant was working with a different horse that morning, and the beast knocked off the brake as he was putting on the harness. And even then—"

"You think I don't know all of that?"

"But he's still here, you know. I mean, the memory of your father, in this town. After all, it's where he grew up."

"Oh, come on!" I snapped, feeling another squirm as a strange, giddy wave seemed to pass through me. "You'll be telling me next he was friends with Clara Innocent."

Rather to my relief, my mother shook her head. "She was an old, old thing. And, frankly, rather confused and smelly. She had that cottage with the smoking chimney you can just see over there, or perhaps it's next door, and the children were understandably frightened of her. Still, I do remember him saying how she offered him a penny to buy some sweets, and he was brave enough to take it." She chuckled. "I even saw her once myself, you know, this muttering thing in old rags, when I was pushing you in a pram up this very slope, and she came hobbling over, and touched your chin, and gave an odd sort of laugh—you might almost call it a cackle. I think she died soon after. As I say, she was probably a little mad by then."

I was trying to listen, trying to absorb whatever this meant, but my back was starting to throb, and I was feeling nauseous.

"Come on." My mother rubbed my hand. "You look pale, and you have that express to catch."

She helped me up from the bench and we doddered off down the hill together like two old crones as the baby kicked again and these weird and surprisingly painful waves began to gain focus in my lower belly. I had to ask my mother to stop, and just stood there hunched and gasping in the middle of the street until a sudden rush of fluid trickled down my legs.

"I'm... I'm..."

"It's all right, dear. You must sit down. I'll go and get help."

But I was fighting her off, trying to tell her I'd be okay, absolutely fine, if she'd just leave me alone. Protesting, above all, that the very last place I wanted to be taken to in the entire world was a bloody, fucking Mrs Innocents.

Just don't.

Please.

Don't.

PROBABLY FOR ENTIRELY sound biological reasons, the experience of giving birth isn't something I remember in any detail. What has stayed with me is the alarming way which my body, which I'd previously imagined myself to be in charge of, but which had been slyly assuming ever greater dominance throughout my pregnancy, now took over completely. That, and of course how deeply grateful I was for modern innovations such as gas, air, and the epidural. Not for me the dangers that poor Princess Vicky had to endure, and the truth is that, without the knowledge and experience of the Mrs Innocents at the Birthplace in Dumbarton, I might well not have survived, and my premature twins almost certainly wouldn't.

So there I was. Lying stitched and sore and exhausted in the cool quiet of my own private room, with these two tiny, shrivelled, amazing creatures lying cocooned in their incubators on either side of me, and Richard smiling and wearied, and both of us still half-disbelieving. My mother was there, too, which I somehow didn't mind.

On the second day, as two Mrs Innocents helped me with the surprisingly difficult business of breastfeeding, and I began to realise that child-rearing was going to be a far bigger challenge than anything I'd faced as a journalist, I noticed that both women seemed oddly subdued. Was there something they weren't telling me about my babies? I absolutely *had* to know. Was there—?

"Oh, it's nothing like that, Sarah. It's just that Lise Beckhoff passed away last night in her sleep, over in Berlin. Of course she was very old, and she'd led an immensely productive life, but it's still come as a bit of a shock. But now, if you could crook your arm a bit more to support your little boy's head. That's it! Just perfect. Wonderful…"

RICHARD AND I finally took our babies back home to London two weeks later, after having decided to call them Lottie and Elliot. It seemed like a good idea at the time, although we've since discovered that we're forever getting their names mixed up. Richard had already redecorated our spare bedroom in a gender-neutral shade of daffodil yellow, but we'd barely considered most of the other things we were going to need as new parents. The pram would now have to be extra-wide, of course, and we'd have to buy two of almost everything else, so in a way it didn't matter, but it did make me realise just how little, for all my valiant researching, I'd really believed I was going to have even one, let alone two, actual babies.

I had a new, designated Mrs Innocent called Claudia Rowe, who came around on her bike from my local Birthplace in Camden most mornings. We get on extremely well; it turned out that she'd considered journalism as a career before electing for midwifery. Phyllis Dunnet, the very first Mrs Innocent I'd seen up at Fetter Lane, also called in to congratulate me and admire my babies, as did many neighbours I hadn't even known existed. Then I took Lottie and Elliot up to see my old colleagues at the *Times*, wheeling my big pram through the crowds like Boadicea's chariot, and even the old hacks gathered round to smile at them, and my famously tough editor seemed close to tears as she held Lottie, but the place, and the role I'd played in it, already seemed to belong to a different me.

I found that I relished the purpose and simplicity of my new life, with walks to the park, and the companionship of other women at my local Birthplace, where the conversation was far from all about nappy rash and teething as I'd once feared. I even felt sorry for Richard, who couldn't share in this as much as he'd have liked because of the continuing demands of his big project. But he did quietly arrange for a small home reckoning engine with cathode tube and typeboard to be installed in our front room, so he could work from home and I could restart my career as a journalist— or wherever my ambitions might now lead me.

I'm using it now to write this.

I TOOK LOTTIE and Elliot up to Hampstead Heath for the turning of the first sod for Richard's new reckoning-engine house one morning a couple of weeks ago. It was a big occasion. People clapped, flashbulbs pinged, champagne was served and the weather was perfect. I couldn't have been happier for Richard, or more proud of him, than I was during the ceremony, even if I did spend most of it trying to quieten Lottie and Elliot.

Back at home, leaving him to his networking, I was reading a Birthplace Trust leaflet entitled *So You Want To Be A Midwife?* after having finally got the twins down to rest when the doorbell rang, which immediately set them squalling. With one balanced on each hip, I somehow took and signed for the parcel, which had German stamps and a Berlin postmark.

There was a covering letter in English from a firm of Berlin attorneys advising me that the contents had been sent according to the wishes of their deceased client, Frau Lise Beckhoff, and that they remained my faithful servants, etc, etc... The package itself, once I'd managed to unwrap it and resettle Lottie and Elliot, turned out to be an old-fashioned cardboard suitcase. Clicking back the hasps released a dusty waft of the biscuits-and-antiseptic smell I'd come to associate with all Birthplaces.

Inside was a sliding heap of old envelopes, most of which bore British stamps and postmarks, and had been addressed to Lise Beckhoff in Berlin over a span of decades from the late 1860s to the early 1900s. They were all in the same scrawly handwriting, which I instantly recognised.

It was mine.

THE MRS INNOCENTS

I'VE HAD MORE time now to try to come to grips, if such a thing is possible, with what all of this means. Many of the instructions in the letters Clara Innocent wrote to Lise Beckhoff are already familiar from the days when I was busily researching the Birthplace Trust—those canny investments in Westinghouse Electric and the crescent wrench—although some still make no sense. Why, for example, encourage the Academy of Fine Arts in Vienna to allow an obscure artist named Hitler to study there, irrespective of his lack of talent, with the promise of considerable extra funds? I suppose I'll never know.

Just as I'd already mentioned to Richard that I was thinking of re-training as a midwife even before that parcel arrived, we'd also discussed the idea of moving up to Scotland. He could work as an architect pretty much anywhere nowadays, and the twins would benefit from the fresh air. And why not Gallowhead, seeing as my mother wasn't getting any younger, and the Dumbarton Birthplace would be a great place for me to study, seeing as we already thought of many of the Mrs Innocents there as our friends?

They say having children changes you. Not just the many things it does to your mind and body, but even how it transforms your face. Before, although I'd generally only pause in front of a mirror long enough to check for smuts, I'd certainly never noticed any similarity between me and Clara Innocent. But it's there now, in the slight sag of my jawline and the deepening lines around my eyes and the grey edging into my hair. Not that I *am* her yet, which still seems scarcely credible, but all the accounts describe her as canny and pragmatic when she suddenly seems to appear as if out of nowhere as a skilled and highly respected midwife in the mid-1850s. Which is very much what I'd hope people would say about me.

I went up to that Tesla Tower when we visited my mother up in Gallowhead last weekend. It still stands as it always has: an immutable, indestructible folly. One of its many oddities being that it was the only notable failure which the Birthplace Trust has backed, stepping in to help finish off the first tower at Wardenclyffe, and then build this one in Scotland, after J P Morgan got cold feet about the project. I squeezed through the same gap in the fence that my father had once shown me, and clicked on my flashlight and climbed the stairs in the echoing gloom. That huge iron core with its copper windings still goes up and up into the sky, and down and down into solid Scottish granite, as if it really is tapping something fundamental, even though, and as my father once explained to me, it couldn't possibly function in the way Tesla had imagined. But it is still a mighty work.

According to the annoyingly terse instructions in the short single letter in that old suitcase that Clara Innocent wrote directly to me almost thirty years ago, I should be be standing beside, in fact touching, that vast and rusty lightning conductor at exactly 12.00 pm Greenwich Mean Time on the 6th of August 1960. I'll be fifty by then. So will Richard, and doubtless he'll be successful, while Lottie and Elliot will be turning twenty, and probably thinking of themselves as very grown up. But the idea of my leaving them, of walking out on everything… I still can't imagine how I'll ever bring myself to do such a thing, nor what kind of fabrication I could possibly spin which would make my disappearance any less painful. But if I don't, and what I've set down here is anything close to the truth, I'd be breaking the very loop of time which has brought our lives and this entire modern world into existence. And, after all, it's already happened. Otherwise I wouldn't be here.

But where is it all *from*? I mean the stuff I must practise and memorise about investing in piezoelectric power generation, and encouraging Marie Curie to research the effects of radiation on living tissue, and knowing how to prevent a breech birth? It isn't from the me of now, less still from the canny Scottish midwife I'm seemingly destined to become. But it has to come from somewhere.

Out there, somewhere beyond any imaginable physical distance, there must be a very different world, which convulsed from a German prince's botched birth into global wars, heedless waste, terrible inventions and environmental catastrophe. More than enough reason to send out a pulse of information and energy strong enough to shiver the fabric of time itself, and to make me its slave. And at least I'll see my father again, although any warnings I'll give him to watch out for traffic in exchange for sweet money clearly won't stick. And I know I'll live to a great age, even if I do grow a little barmy, and Lise Beckhoff will become a stout ally and friend. I'll even get to cackle over my own infant self. And I do somehow manage to change the world, just as I've always wanted. So I suppose I shouldn't complain.

Elliot's woken up now, and Lottie's squirming on my lap, giggling as she reaches towards the green glow of these letters. So I'll simply finish what I've written here and hope that you, wherever and whatever you are, will understand these words a little better than I do.

Afterword

ONE OF THE pieces of advice about writing which many people seem to think of as valid is that writers should only write about things they've personally experienced. For me, however, the appeal of fiction is pretty much the opposite. I like making things up, and enjoy the challenge of trying to put myself inside new places and different identities. Certainly, if I only wrote about what I knew and had actually lived through, not one of the stories in this volume would have ever come into existence.

Not, to take *The Mrs Innocents*, that I don't have some knowledge of the main settings of London and Berlin, or at least can claim to have visited both cities. I've also read a great deal about, and am fascinated by, the dynastic accidents and political stupidities which brought about the First World War and thus, it could be argued, also the Second. But what most excited and interested me as the idea for *The Mrs Innocents* began to take shape was the possibility it offered of writing from the viewpoint of a pregnant woman. Obviously, and no matter how much research I undertook (which was a fair amount), I can have no real idea of how plausible I make this aspect of Sarah Turnbull's life. But all I can ever do as a writer, or at least try to do, is to make my made-up things seem as convincing as possible. To my mind, real experience and what we think we actually know about reality is all too often vague and contradictory. This being one of the main reasons why we have fiction, which generally makes much better sense.

The Wisdom of the Group

BUY. AND BUY again. Then sell. Yes. Sell.

My trading floor is a glass smartcube on the second floor of my house set amid the pines and crags of the Cascade Mountains, here in Washington State. A river races beneath, but for now the roar of water is replaced by the clamour of voices, and some of them are still human, and a very few—a trickle of empathy—belong to the other members of my group. We may not know each other well in the traditional sense, but the trust we share on the trading floor is deep and implicit. The hunches, the impulses, the decisions which arise are as natural, and as innately feral, as a kitten's when it plays with a ball of wool.

So we shed our shares in Neurosat when the market still seems to think they're on the up, and gobble up some more of Xenocon at a plummeting price when all the so-called smart money—which these days mostly means bank-bots—is desperate to sell. We shift and we shuffle. The numbers spin and swirl. We deal.

Which brings us to the puzzle of our continued investment in the shares of a company called Canco, which have been bouncing along the bottom for several days now—aeons in market terms—and still show no sign of going up. A small tussle of wills ensues between the stickers and the sellers, although it's not that uncommon for our group to split briefly into divergent mode. But why did we buy these shares if something positive wasn't going to happen? It makes no sense. And wasn't there, the dim thought arises, some kind of rumour on the feeds? Or at least, there soon will be. So not just stick. No. Not just hold. But push forward and buy and buy while we still have the chance. At the end of this frenzy, we have invested the best part of four hundred million dollars in a basket-case mining corporation based in the People's Republic of the Congo. Not a huge investment by our standards—perhaps a quarter of our free assets—but nevertheless a significant one, and I feel a small flush of triumph, almost as if I'm the one who's pushed this through, although that's never how this works.

Then we're done, and the fizz, the buzz, fades from my smartcube like the lost thrill of orgasm as the sense of sharing runs out. Better than sex? Perhaps. Far more profitable, as well. The roar of the river is returning, along with the loom of the mist-swirled pines. But I'm still just standing here as the final connections dwindle, and it's briefly as if there is no smartglass, no ceiling or walls, no group and no protection, and I'm falling through whiteness—impossibly cold and alone.

"Went okay, did it, Samuel?" Luke is fixing breakfast in the kitchen, his still slightly sleep-tumescent cock swaying against the Hermes robe I bought him back when we were staying at that little place in Saint-Germain-des-Prés. He neatly balances a tray of croissants, coffee and orange juice on the crook of his arm as he shuts the fridge door.

"Of course it did," I snap. "How else do you think I got all of this?" Unfortunately, my gesture encompasses not only this kitchen, this view, and the late-period Jackson Pollock on the wall, but Luke as well.

"Just asking." His hand trembles slightly as he pours my coffee and juice. He's so delicate, so gentle, so sensitive, despite the pecs, the abs, the cock. It was what I used to like about him so much. No, I correct myself, still like.

"Sorry, Luke. It may not seem like much. But, in its way, it's hard work."

He smiles. "I'm sure it is."

"No. Come on. I know there are people starving, babies dying, as we speak. But it's commerce, and it's what I do, and I take a pride in it, and it leaves me drained."

He leans over. Brushes his fingers across the stubble of my throat. Then down. I shiver. I can't help myself. But it isn't his touch. And it isn't the group, either. It's something more. Something *else*...

I'M STILL CONSIDERING what that something might be as I shower while Luke sees to the dogs, and the puzzle lingers even as we set out on a long, brisk hike to make the most of this time before the fine autumn weather runs out. The yelps of Joe, Adolph and Mao ring along the canyon as they bound ahead. Luke calls and whistles after them. The air is brutally bright and cold.

People might wonder what someone as effortlessly rich and successful as I am actually does to fill up their days. I sometimes wonder about it myself, at least in an abstract sense, but hour by hour, and lover by lover, and city by city, and acquisition by acquisition, it's never been a problem. The truth is that great wealth, at least if you have a modicum of intelligence, looks and health—which can all usually be bought—never grows stale. At least, it hasn't for me. And there's always the group, my smartcube, the thrill of the trading floor. And there are days like this with Luke and the dogs, as well.

We climb to a high ridge with a fine drop from a platform of rock looking down and across an arrangement of forest and mountain I don't think I've ever seen this way before. Luke unfolds his backpack and lays out a rug, then delicious, steaming, combinations of hearty yet delicate food. The Araujo Syrah, of course, matches it perfectly; he knows my cellar by now far better than I do myself. The dogs vanish for a while, but then they come racing up, shaggy and wet, with blood bearding their grinning muzzles. They must have tracked and killed a deer, somewhere down there in the forest, and the thought strikes me that Joe, Adolph and Mao make up a kind of gestalt of their own, they're so instinctively and effortlessly good at what they do. They run off again after Luke has thrown them a few scraps. Then he packs things away, but leaves out the rug, and touches my thigh, my arm, in quiet invitation, but I shiver again, and shake my head, and gaze out across the vast, shaded drop.

That feeling. It was there, or at least somewhere, back on the trading floor and in my smartcube as the rest of the group were withdrawing into their separate lives. A chilly sense, to use a very old-fashioned phrase, as if someone was walking over my grave. I smile. Shake my head. This is so blatantly ridiculous, I could almost share it with Luke. But of course I can't.

The sun is already setting by the time we get back to the house, which looks like some strange fractal lantern on its promontory high above the river. Inside, though, all is warmth, and Luke and I kiss and snuggle to make up for my earlier coldness as we eat toast beside the fire, and I call up some Monteverdi and he pours out a couple of glasses of ice-cool Inama Soave while the dogs loll around us and I page absently through today's feeds.

All the usual stuff. Society scandals and political fudges. Atrocities and wars. That, and floods and all the other natural disasters we don't think of as natural any more. It's important that I keep up with this kind of stuff, but also that I try not to engage or develop any kind of conscious expertise. Or, heaven forbid, search out market tips and trends. Still, I'm almost expecting some kind of story to be emerging from the Congo, perhaps a big new mining strike, but nothing comes. Soon, I'm simply drowsing in the heat of the fire and the soothing presence of Luke and the dogs. My group. *Our* group. Far away from those fizzing figures on the trading floor. When Luke finally nudges me, I jump.

"Hey..." My spine seems to crawl as he kisses my mouth, my ear. "Weren't we supposed to be going down to the city tonight to see that friend of yours on her yacht?"

ABOUT TIME WE took the Maserati out on a run, and it's Luke's turn to drive. Which he does well. He's a sportsman, I think, at heart; he's certainly built like one. Except, as he confessed when we first met back in Bruges two years ago, he's only really world class at one particular, and generally non-competitive, physical activity. Seemed a neat come-on at the time, but now it feels rather sad. Dressed as he is now in that new tux I got for him last winter when we were staying at the Four Seasons in New York, and driving this car as expertly as he does, he could be the new James Bond. But all he does is hang out with me, and work out, and fuck. That, and I suppose he sees to the dogs, stocks my cellar, keeps an eye on the house, and cooks all those excellent meals. Quite a lot, really, come to think of it, and he certainly knows how to charm. But I still feel rather sorry for him as the glow of the Maserati's displays show off his noble profile to such good effect. And I know that feeling sorry for whoever I'm with is generally a bad sign. I should nurture him more. Get him to develop fresh interests, friends, skills…

"Penny for them."

"For what?"

"Your thoughts."

"Sure," I say. Then add, although I hate myself even before the words have come out, "Although they're worth a great deal more than that."

The forest falls away as the road winds down towards the glow of Seattle and the glitter of Puget Sound.

THERE'S A MOTORISED skiff, if that's the right term, to bear us across the water to Bea Comyn's yacht. More of a tall ship, really, a vast white clipper blown in from days of yore which she uses as a base to roam the world, although tonight it's all hands on deck to dish out canapés and the champagne. A band is playing. Some beards-and-beads combination of North African and Celtic. Bea probably owns them, inasmuch as it's possible to own people. She's a collector, a connoisseur, an acquisitor. We all are.

I mingle, listen, talk. An investor, yes, in the world markets, and it still surprises me how people don't greet that statement with more distaste. After all, it's basically just gambling. Or it would be, if our group didn't do what we do. Instead, they ask me if I've got any hot tips, and I waggle my smile at them, and shrug. Better just to drift, wander, absorb. Be me. Whatever and whoever that is.

I linger at the fringes of an argument over some upcoming cage fight where both participants are so enhanced they can scarcely be thought of as human, so what does it matter if one of them dies? I indulge in a flirtatious conversation with a woman in a green dress that shows off the pink tops of her nipples to good effect about the best lobster restaurant in Pike Place. Uptown highrise Seattle is bathed, ghostly as tombstones, in the light of the Moon.

No sign yet of Bea, and I can't find Luke, either. Then I see him at the deck's far end—what do you call it? upship? forecastle? —engaging in surprisingly animated conversation with a tall, bald, muscular, black-skinned man in colourful clothes. Good-looking, as well. I feel a little envious. When did Luke have something to say to *me* that mattered as much as whatever he's saying to this guy? But a voice calls my name just as I wonder whether I should barge in.

I turn, and it's Bea Comyn, wearing the sort of tweedy two-piece that used to be favoured by the old Queen of England and Angela Merkel. She doesn't care about looks. She flaunts her jowls, and hasn't even got rid of the grey in her short, brittle hair. But Bea loves beauty. I mean, look at this scene, and everything else she does and owns. She draws me away with a firm but wrinkled hand, and I notice Luke noticing our departure as we turn. But it's okay that Bea and I are seen together. We have several legitimate, above-board connections. Otherwise, I wouldn't be here at all.

Now we're in a cabin, and she calls up some music—it's even more of an ethnic mishmash than what's playing outside—as she closes the door. It's all varnish and portholes down here. Briskly, elegantly, shipshape, with dark old whaling paintings on the panelled walls. It seems only appropriate that she should pour us both a Mount Gay rum, although I refuse the offered cigar. She shakes her head as if I've made a deeply unwise decision, and clips one for herself. The cloud of aromatic smoke she exhales takes me back to her campus office in Edinburgh, when she was a mere professor of Psychology and Psychometrics, and I was just a humble postgrad, and it still feels a little that way as we sit down on opposite leather chairs and I find, when I try to adjust my position, that they're screwed down. Then the ship, perhaps caught by nothing more than the waves of a passing ferry, seems to stir. Whatever it is, I get that brief, cold tingle again. Here in this maritime setting, it feels more the harbinger of a vast, approaching storm.

Bea's a methodical sort, and whatever it is she really wants to share with me is prefaced by a chat about our mutual interest in racehorses. If nothing else, it's a useful and tax-efficient way of throwing excess money down the drain. But it's also engaging, and fun. *He's such a handsome beast*, she says at one point about a yearling we've invested in as a prospect for the Longines Hong Kong Mile, and I'm reminded that she once said the same thing about my Luke, and wish she'd cut to the chase.

"I've been speaking directly to other members of our group," she says through the haze of cigar smoke and our second tot of rum. "I mean, since we convened in our smartcubes on the trading floor this morning, western seaboard time."

"Oh," I say. And add, before I can bite it off, "Is anything wrong?"

"I thought I'd save you until this evening, Samuel, seeing as I knew you'd be here at my little soirée."

Meaning she's already spoken to everyone else.

"The question is..." She leans forward. Looks up at me through her uneven fringe with bruised oyster eyes. "Did *you* notice anything?"

"Well, the extra investment in the Congo did seem a little left field."

"But that's what we do, isn't it? We see above and beyond the normal tides of the market. That's what our group is for."

I nod, feeling more that ever as if I'm back at university, and I've made some schoolboy error in my thesis.

"In fact," she puts down the stub of her cigar and waves up a screen from the low table between us, "some fresh reports were coming in just as this party started. There's a warlord called Learnmore Wallace—I know, these African names—who's said to be making a move to secure the Canco copper seam. This guy"—she calls up the image of an angry-looking man in khaki and military boots standing in the unlikely setting of the lobby of an upmarket hotel—"is said to be pragmatic, consensual, business-friendly... Which, of course, means he simply wants power and money once he's finished slitting the throats of his rivals and raping their wives. But at least it's better than all that Lord's Resistance Army apocalyptic nonsense. And, of course, the world is screaming out for all that copper that's still stuck in the ground."

"You think that maybe the Chinese, the Russians, or the CIA might—"

She waves my words and the screen away. "Doesn't matter. The main thing about all of this from our point of view is that we're ahead of the curve."

"A result."

"Or it will be," she corrects me, "when confidence actually starts to go up. But meanwhile, and until his forces actually make their move, our friend Learnmore simply amounts to more instability. Hard though you might find it to believe, and despite all our recent buying activity, share prices in Canco have actually headed down."

"But nevertheless—"

"Yes, Samuel, nevertheless. But didn't you notice anything else?"

"About what?"

"About this morning. About how the gestalt deconvergence went."

"Not exactly, no."

"So I'll take that as a yes, shall I? That, at least, was how all the rest of us felt."

"You mean, just as the link was phasing out?"

"How would you describe it?"

"I'm not sure I could. It just felt a little odd, a little wrong. A little..." *Ominous*, or something like it, is the kind of word I'm trying hard not to use.

"Of course," she concedes, leaning back a little, as if to give me some room, "the underlying science is still desperately short of terms. But I've looked at the waveforms, I've studied the graphs of individual response, and I can confirm there was definitely an anomaly in the usual patterns of communion across the group. And it was something I don't think we've seen before."

"That's...interesting."

"It is, isn't it? And the other thing, the thing which both the data and the reported experiences of the group are clearly telling me, is that the response, the anomaly, whatever you choose to call it, originated from you."

"Maybe the equipment—"

"—That was the first thing I checked."

"Or we've been hacked?"

"No. Definitely not."

"Which leaves, in your opinion..."

She sighs. Pings her glass with a ragged fingernail. "I really don't know."

"At least it's out there now."

"Indeed." She leans forward. Pours me more rum. "And there's still a chance it could be nothing. It's outside our established dataset, for sure, but that doesn't mean it's telling us anything meaningful. The science of the gestalt is still so new, and it remains ours alone—at least, as far as we know. And, of course, we want to keep it that way. I sincerely hope that absolute secrecy's the one thing we can all agree on, in or out of the wisdom of the group…"

WHEN WE RE-EMERGE, the party is still going, and the Space Needle looks as if it's just about ready to blast off. I could do with some drugs, or at least something, to combat this day and Bea's rum, but I know myself well enough to know I'm better off with nothing at all. So I find Luke, who's dancing with a group of mutual admirers with his tuxedo off and his frilled shirt wide open to show off his torso, although there's no sign of the African guy. I join in for a while, manage a few grinds and whoops, but my heart isn't in it, and I decide I want to go home.

"It's barely two in the morning!" Luke laughs, until he realises I'm serious. Drink and tiredness, or maybe it's my advancing years, make the business of getting from yacht to motorised skiff and then back to dry land a little less elegant than I'd have liked. But I'm the one with the keys to the Maserati, and it's definitely my turn to drive.

"Shouldn't you at least put it on autoguide?" Luke asks as he belts up.

"I thought I was the one who was supposed to be the killjoy?" I floor the accelerator. The tyres squeal.

I feel exhilarated at first as I take the roads out of Seattle. I'm enjoying how the car handles, and the way Luke is clinging to the edges of his seat.

"Who was he?"

"Who was who?"

"That bald, good-looking Black guy you were talking to."

"He was just some fellow who happened to be at the party, just as we were. But he had some interesting opinions."

"*Interesting*. Right. And aren't you going to ask me what *I* was up to, seeing as we scarcely saw each other all night?"

"That's exactly what parties are for. We can speak to each other yesterday, tomorrow, right now. But you were with the host, weren't you? That Comyn woman who owns the yacht. You have horses together, or something, don't you?"

"Fact is..." I ease up on the accelerator. I'm feeling slightly queasy. "She used to be one of my professors, back when I was at university in Edinburgh."

"And then she got seriously rich?"

"Yeah."

"And you did as well."

"Isn't that what higher education's supposed to be about?"

Luke laughs. As I recall, he studied something sensible and practical in Brussels; a skill that had been supplanted by algorithms and bots by the time he needed work. But why did I have to mention my connection with Bea going so far back, when I've never said anything about it before? It already feels like a loose thread in the weave I've woven to protect myself from the world. And why, when I glance over at him, does he look so smug and unsurprised? But I decide that it's my cautious driving that's letting me down far more than my big mouth. That, and I should be acting much more drunk. So I push the accelerator. Swallow hard. After all, if I was going to die tonight—tumble off this hairpin and dissolve in a ball of flame—wouldn't I already know?

THE HOUSE GLOWS out from the dark, and Joe, Adolph and Mao greet us with yelps, grins, thrashing tails. I drink some electrolytes, and massage my scalp as the shower runs hot, then ball-tinglingly minty cold. Luke's already out for the count, sprawled and snoring, by the time I've dried myself and called off the lights. I lie there beside him and count my heartbeats, the fading seconds of my life, as I stare up at the dark and sleep cackles from the furthest corner of my consciousness like a demented tropic bird. After all, what do I know or care about copper mining in the Congo? Something slides, a long, cold anaconda of doubt—although I'm almost sure anacondas are from the jungles of South American—through my ribs. But then the dripping fronds part, and I'm in a bland, concrete corridor, and there's a smell of laser toner and cheap coffee. And, faintly, of cigars. Not that Professor Comyn ever smokes them on campus, but they're part of her aura. She looks up when I enter her office. Tells me to close the door and does that thing with her mouth which passes for a smile. She has a fearsome reputation which belies her dumpy appearance, and I'm fully expecting some kind of reprimand. But no. This is, very much, something else.

Truth is, I'm not even sure why I'm studying psychology. It's all come to seem rather too much like a prolonged extension of a scam Freud came up with to make money out of the problems of a few rich Jews in pre-war Vienna. But I'm no big fan of modern neuroscience, either. All those pretty three-dee models of the brain, and they still haven't got a proper handle on consciousness, or isolated a single significant mental disease. These conclusions, and a lucky bursary, and perhaps an innate lack of personal drive, have somehow led me to Edinburgh and the orbit of Professor Comyn, who's well known for her unfashionably reductive approach. What counts, she argues, almost like the behavioural psychologists of the 1960s, is to cut through all the speculative crap and concentrate on what can be provably, externally, repeatably and reliably observed. Think of the brain as a black box, concentrate on input and output, and all the rest will take care of itself. It's certainly hard, sitting here in her Spartan campus office, to have any idea of what's going on inside the confines of her considerable mind.

I've been in Edinburgh for a couple of terms by now, and have occasionally helped her out with one of those seemingly minor, unfunded projects that most academics like to have going on under the radar. She's amassed data from a series of online tests where people are invited to make quick, hunch-like guesses on seemingly random subjects. As well as taking part in the survey myself, I've done some of the donkeywork of systems and web maintenance using the skills from a previous degree, although she's kept the actual results very much under wraps.

It's long been known that the seemingly random guesses of large groups can be surprisingly accurate. At the start of the twentieth century, the great statistician Francis Galton noted that the average of all the entries in "guess the weight of a bull" competitions which were then popular at rural fairs were far more accurate than the estimates of the supposed agricultural experts. Plato, who was also in on this, called this odd phenomenon *The Wisdom of Crowds*.

THE WISDOM OF THE GROUP

All of this I already know as Bea Comyn sits me down in her office. I also know that she's recently asked me to close down all the sites linked to this area of research, and encrypt the data so it can't be accessed by anyone other than herself. I've even heard it said that this is because she's drawn what would be for her an uncharacteristic blank. But what she begins to tell me that first afternoon—for the process is typically cautious and gradual—is startling. Not only has she been able to amass more information on this subject than any previous project, but she's also managed to grind that data down to something important and new.

Sure, mass-conjectures have a statistically significant level of accuracy, but that simply means they're marginally more right than wrong—a small, dark, clump in the fizzing white noise of chance. But it turns out that some people are significantly better than others at doing this kind of thing. Not once, but repeatedly—guess after guess and time after time. This isn't a matter of specialist knowledge. In fact, the opposite, just as Galton and many other researchers have observed. Nor is it a question of IQ. In fact, Bea Comyn freely admits to me as she sits there in her office with the door closed and some weird, wailing music playing in the background, she still has no idea what the true source of this phenomenon is. But it exists, right? Something clear, measurable and verifiable is occurring. Which, at the end of the day, and beyond all the surmise and bullshit, is exactly what matters. Data being data, and results always being results. Especially, in this case, where those results can be refined and re-used as a basis for further, deeper and far more significant research.

So what would happen if the participants were filtered down to those whose hunches had consistently higher-than-average levels of accuracy? And then, after further tests and refinements, that group was quietly narrowed down even more. Now, and especially when these so-called super-predictors are allowed a few moments of collaboration, it turns out that the white noise of chance disappears almost entirely. Their wild stabs in the dark on matters as obtuse as the annual fish harvest in the Baring Straits or the number of people passing hourly through Times Square are amazingly, consistently, accurate. Even when the group's conclusions initially seem to be incorrect, it generally turns out that it's the base-figures themselves that are wrong. Not only that, Samuel, Bea Comyn adds, but these group-guesses have a stochastic element. They can tell not only how things are, but how they will be, at least over a short timescale. In case you're wondering, she adds with one of her famous non-smiles, I'm a super-predictor myself. So—which is why I'm sharing this—are you.

Not so much a small, under-the-radar project, but a big and surprisingly ambitious one which she's been using the dumb donkeywork of postgrads like me to provide a plausible camouflage for. Looking at things as they are now, I can't help but wonder if my late arrival into the core group Bea had already created and primed wasn't a bad omen, but at the time I simply felt as if I was being invited to join something special, exciting and rare.

The secrecy, the sense of feeling chosen, not to mention encrypting the new data so the University security guardians didn't pick up on it, and borrowing stray bits of equipment and bandwidth, and throwing out false leads and dealing with the increasingly complex issues of financing this project, all added to the fun. Bea had already set up beta versions of what ended up as our smartcubes using a variety of commercially available virtual gaming and pornography hardware and software. The system sensed patterns of eye movement, minute changes of breath, posture and skin resistance, so that we in the group, when confronted with some data, didn't even need to consciously think about it, let alone physically converse. *Subliminal dialectical bootstrapping* being Bea's technical term for this form of interaction. The general hunch, the combined seat-of-the-pants surmise—the feeling you don't even know you're actually feeling until after you've felt it—being all.

Of course, in those early days we used to meet up occasionally and in person at a variety of discreet locations in order to work out the many practical issues, and discuss who was supposed to be doing what. But, outside of the gestalt, we made an ill-assorted bunch, a bickering baker's dozen of ages, races and attitudes, scattered across languages, cultures and continents. We might be intuitively loyal to the group, and fiercely protective of all that it's brought us, but that doesn't mean that, as separate people, we ever had anything else in common, or cared for each other, or even got on.

I CRAWL OUT of bed with what feels less like a hangover than a vast, existential and physiological malaise. Luke looks beautiful, though, carved out of innocence and sleep, as I unblank the windows and grey morning pours in.

My head is roaring, and so is the river. Steam from the coffee-maker fills the kitchen. There's frost and mist outside amid the trees. I break the habit of almost a lifetime and stir several spoonfuls of sugar into my cup. Then, seeing as Luke isn't yet conscious, and probably won't be for several hours, I buzz the can-opener and hold my breath as I spoon out slabs of glistening offal for the drooling dogs. Time, then, to do my—the group's—regular, daily thing.

I step into my cube. Snap the glass into smart mode, so that where I am fizzes away. No sign, yet, of any of the others. But that's okay. We span time zones, chaos states, pogrom democracies and righteous caliphates, here in this modern world where the only true international currency is greed. Marlene in Estonia, in her autistic white box of a home, and Omar in what's now called Constantinople again. And dull Vicktoria in Siberia, who still seems to have no idea of what to do with all her money, but wants it nevertheless. We all do.

Money, after all, was what our group needed to establish itself. Money was the oil which could be laid over all kinds of troubled waters, and became a simple and reliable measure of our success. Yui in Tokyo had some useful skills as an investment analyst, it's true, which helped us to work out how to spread and disguise our profits across a wide range of markets. And Mia out in Sydney, Australia, being a communication specialist, did a great job in creating a multiple-redundancy network. And I had a bit of a background in web-engineering, and course Bea knows almost everything that's ever been known. But expertise, conscious knowledge, opinion, has never been what our group is about. Not for Hilda in Jerusalem with her near-psychotic intolerances, or Maxim in Ukraine, with his background in people-smuggling. What counts isn't I, but *us*.

My fingers and my scalp tingle as the data rains in. Yes. And yes again. The smartcube, filled with all of Bea's clever sensors and codes, knows me far better than I do myself. But still no sign of any of the others, here at the future's raw edge. I occupy myself with calling up the latest feeds. There's a new sports enhancement product which could rewrite the NBA and the English Premier League, or turn out to have disastrous side effects and be worth nothing at all. You never know. And here's a performance artist who's crowd-funding her own crucifixion, and a bad storm is causing problems in the South China Sea. All the usual blah, and what I, individually, know and think about these things is worthless, and I'm still waiting to feel any connection from the rest of the group. So I tunnel down through further layers of opinion and catastrophe until I find—what's this?—news at least two hours stale out of Kinshasa, which used to be called Leopoldville, in the not particularly Democratic Republic of the Congo. What's left of Learnmore Wallace has been found hanging from a lamppost in a cloud of flies, and the dripping meat of his corpse looks like what Joe, Adolph and Mao had for breakfast.

Our prediction was correct. Of course it was. No doubt with the backing of some external power-broker, his forces attempted to take the Congolese mining hills and lay some copper-bottomed dollars across the country's ruinous spreadsheet before the whole thing fizzled out into bloody chaos. But it was a group decision, right? I may have pushed a little harder than some of the others, and of course a few were against increasing our stake in Canco, or wanted to sell, but that's exactly how the gestalt works. We'll recoup. Of course we will. After all, and when we've already made so much money, and so consistently, a loss of four hundred million dollars scarcely counts. So why do I feel this strong need to explain myself? And why am I still alone?

I kill the smartcube. Pull back and out. But I still feel as if I'm in a hissing field of pure white emptiness. Of course, it's just the cascading river, the steam, the frost, the mist, but my skin prickles, my testicles withdraw. They're out there somewhere, the group, and I'm not with them, and I've never felt so lost and alone. Something flashes amid the far trees, perhaps a sniper's scope. I cringe. Duck.

But this is getting ridiculous, and I'm running much too far ahead of whatever this really is.

Back in the kitchen, Adolph, who's always been the most sensitive of my little pack, backs off from me and gives a growling, fang-revealing, bark. Joe and Mao soon join in and the sound is enough to wake the dead. Although not, of course, Luke. I make myself some more coffee. I check the feeds again, but Learnmore Wallace and his ragged little army are still as dead as the price of Canco shares.

I check the time. By now, the group will have convened, decided, parted, moved on. And I'm on the outside. Part of the dumb, unknowing world which these modern oracles see through and beyond. Should I be expecting condolences? Flowers? Messages of support? Of course, no one's died, but the pack, the herd, the group, has always walked away from the old, the stupid, the lame. Left them for the predators and the flies to take care of, just like poor old Learnmore Wallace. This is exactly how nature has always worked.

I have to do something. I can't just wait. So I call up a screen, and call Bea. Without preliminaries or hesitation—as if, in fact, she's been expecting me to do exactly this at this precise moment— her grey face looms up at me from above the kitchen counter.

"You cut me out."

"It seemed like the best thing to do. At least, for now."

"All because of one bad investment, which I'm sure we'll recoup."

"I'm sure we will. But it isn't that alone."

"What the hell is it, then?"

"At the end of the day, Samuel, it's the very thing our group is about. It's a gestalt hunch. Something that, by its very nature, and its stochastic dimensions, can't be explained in linear, synchronic, probabilistic terms."

"Cut the college crap, Bea."

She gives me a deeply disappointed smile. "The rapid loss we made with the Canco shares may be a symptom, but there appears to be a deeper abnormality. You agreed you felt it when we talked last night. And it's confirmed by the data. There was a brief, atypical waveform just before you broke connection with us. A loss of… mutual synchronicity, I think, might be the closest term."

"Meaning what? That I'm not to be trusted?"

"Not that, either, I don't think. I don't like using the word *premonition*, Samuel, but I'm not sure our language in this field has yet advanced sufficiently for there to be a better one. So we, the group, surmised this morning that you need to exercise caution. Consider what you're doing, and who you're doing it with. Don't take any risks."

"You're saying you think I'm in danger?"

"Put simply, yes."

"For how long?"

"You know the gestalt only has a short-term temporally predictive field of significant accuracy. A day or two at most."

"And after that?"

"We'll see, won't we?"

"But you were in the group when you went over this half an hour ago. You must have some better idea of what this is."

She sighs. "If I knew more, don't you think I'd tell you?"

"You know what—I don't think you fucking would!"

I kill the screen. Bea's face fades, an ugly Cheshire cat, leaving nothing but a faint, sour whiff of cigar smoke.

The dogs are still stirred up, prowling the kitchen, claws clicking the hardwood floor. I grab some fresh steak from the fridge in the hope that it will distract them, chopping it up into chunks and tossing it into their bowls, but of course it only agitates them even more.

My thoughts are prowling as well. After all, this isn't the first time we've had problems in the group, going all the way back to the basic question of what exactly we were for. Money, yes, money, not only to set this thing up and give us the lives we wanted, but to provide the necessary levels of secrecy and generate the backstories to explain our new wealth. From the start, it was evident that our combined hunches, guesses, only had a short-term viability, and that binary yes/no decisions were manageable, whereas more complex, multi-pathway choices soon dissolved back into that dreaded statistical noise. Hence our trading in stocks and shares, seeing as outright gambling was far too blatant, and none of us could think of another reliable way to make our investments work.

But there had to be something else, something more, that we could do with our powers, if only to prove to ourselves that we weren't just greedy bastards in it for nothing but the dough. Predicting trainwrecks and natural disasters, for instance. Giorgio Magarelli, I remember, a lapsed Catholic from southern Italy whose grandparents had died in an earthquake, was particularly strong on this point. So we agreed that we would incorporate some geological data into our regular trading floor feeds, and see what transpired. Less than a month later we were able to intuit that something was imminent in the Sichuan province in Southwest China. Of course, we're not gods. We can't hold back the tides or wrestle the chains of the Earth. Neither could we expose ourselves by issuing a public warning, even if such a thing would be believed. But Mia in Sydney was able to hack into the portals of the worldwide seismic monitoring system, and insert some unequivocal pre-tremor data to warn the authorities to take immediate steps. We, Giorgio especially, were more than pleased. But there were no announcements, no evacuations, and upwards of five thousand people died in the earthquake that followed less than twenty-four hours later. Along, as the feeds soon reported, with the twelve members of the seismological monitoring team at nearby Chengdu University, who were summarily shot.

Maybe there was a lesson there. That was what we tried to tell Giorgio. Better to stick to finance, eh? That way no one gets hurt. But Giorgio grew withdrawn and morose, and—just as we were starting to wonder what on earth to do with him—was found by his housekeeper in his Tuscan palace with his wrists slit in his Carrera marble bath. And so our baker's dozen became an apostolic twelve.

Other problems? Well, not that many, really. After all, we're a group. There was an accountant in São Paulo who'd acted as a staging post for some of our early dealings, and was somehow able to pick up on what we were up to. He insisted he didn't want our money, and that this wasn't blackmail. All he wanted was to join us. A simple request, but of course impossible to accede to, seeing as he lacked our oh-so-special skills. Bea agreed to handle the matter, and travelled to Brazil, where I believe she arranged for the man to be discreetly killed.

Now it's me they don't trust, and are afraid of. Which means I should be mistrustful and afraid of them. Something's gone wrong, something's messed with my prescience, and I'm pretty sure I know who and what it is. Maybe it's still just a hunch, or maybe he's worked things out like that accountant using fancy probability curves. Or perhaps he's from that other group of super-predictors we've always feared is out there, or some government agency or underworld cabal.

I run back over how Luke and I first met. The easy affinity. The even easier sex. Come live with me in the Cascade Mountains? Yes, why not? With, handily, no other commitments, and no real questions, let alone answers, as to what else he was planning to do with his time. And then all the cooking, and the housekeeping, the no-questions-asked acceptance. Which only a fool would take for affection. Let alone love.

If only I had something more solid. If only I could shake myself free of the present and find out what lies beyond. They'd have me back then, wouldn't they, my group, the deed done, the point proved, the bad thing happened, the prophecy fulfilled, with open arms?

"Hey there..." Luke wanders in, Hermes dressing gown agape. "How about some breakfast?"

He's not expecting me to make it, of course. He opens cupboards. He leans into the fridge. He pats, absently, at the dogs. "Ah! You fed them. And you've already done your work?"

"Same as every other day."

"That's... Good."

"And?"

"And what?"

"Don't you want to know anything more?"

"More?"

"Yes. More. I mean, about what I do."

"Sure." He reaches for the big frying pan on its hook, and I try not to cringe. "But the few times I've asked, you've acted like it's none of my business. Which..." He cracks some eggs. Fat sizzles. "It probably isn't."

"Are you from Belgium? I mean, no one's really from *Belgium*, are they?"

"How about Rene Magritte? César Franck? Audrey Hepburn? Then there's the guy who invented Bakelite, and tons of great soccer players. Not to mention, although I know they're fictional, good old Tintin and Hercule Poirot."

"You don't even have an accent."

"Thanks"—he slots in some bread to make toast, puts the butter in the microwave to warm it slightly—"for complementing me on my excellent English in that slightly roundabout way. And you know how, sometimes, when we're making love, you like me to talk to you in French?"

"But I don't understand what you're saying. For all I know, you're just quoting songs."

With delicate precision, he flips the eggs. "There are a lot of things I'm not understanding right now." His eye travel towards the sink, where the Sabatier knife I used to cut up that meat for the dogs lies in a pink pool.

"Who are you, Luke?"

"Who *am* I?"

"And who were you speaking to last night on Bea Comyn's boat?"

"Oh." He gives a relieved, so-this-is-what-this-is-about nod. "You mean Claude! He's a fascinating guy, a South African, and an ecological rights lawyer who also happens to know a lot about wine. But that's all I know about him, although I'll concede he *was* very good-looking."

"Nothing to do with copper mining in the People's Democratic Republic of the Congo?"

"What? In the where?"

"You heard. The Congo. Famous for its political instability and wasted natural resources. The place you Belgians occupied when your King Leopold was arrogant and stupid enough to think he could build himself an African empire."

"Is this some old colonial guilt trip you're suddenly expecting me to be feeling?" He butters his toast. Then mine. He doesn't even seem that bothered. "In which case, I think you Brits have a fair bit to answer for, too."

"That's…" I take a mental step back. My ears, my teeth, are tingling. White flecks dance before my eyes. "Probably true. Frankly, I've got a hangover, and I've had a bad morning on the trading floor."

"Let me guess." Luke catches a dribble of egg yoke before it escapes his mouth. "Something to do with the Congo? Isn't there a warlord who just got killed out there? Last chance for something like stability and prosperity. Of course, when it comes to these places, we've all heard it a million times before. I'm sorry if it messed with your investments, Samuel, but you'll get over it—bounce back. I mean, look at this place and all that you've achieved. Frankly, you're an amazing guy, and if you want to share more of what you do, just say the word. Maybe we could even make a positive difference somewhere instead of just making money. I'm not saying that would be easy, but you never know."

I suppose I should be surprised that he's found the time to catch up on the feeds this morning, let alone notice an obscure item about the Congo, but somehow I'm not. After all, he takes an interest in the world, and has a quick, able mind. It was one of the things I first liked about him. That, and his inherent kindness and compassion. But now everything, the way he looks and how he breathes and holds his fork, and the considerate way I know he's going to treat me today because he understands I'm frayed and upset, just makes me feel impossibly sad.

"Look, Luke—why don't we take the dogs out for a long walk?"

"Didn't we do that yesterday?"

"Sure. But it's a fine, beautiful morning, and there won't be many more."

THE WISDOM OF THE GROUP

EVERYTHING IS GUNSHOT sharp. Our breath plumes, and the clouds are like concrete; a hard, grey roof over the world. Luke is slightly puzzled, but predictably, cheerily compliant, when I insist we repeat yesterday's hike to that high viewpoint. Watching the powerful, innocent sway of his body—and how, of course, his backpack is a great deal heavier than mine—makes me decide that, now it's too late, I probably do love him after all.

We climb. And climb. The dogs vanish, then re-emerge. The view from the overlook is more sombre today. Reminds me of those dark Gothic paintings by Caspar David Friedrich. *The Wanderer. Monastery Graveyard in the Snow.* Perhaps I should try to acquire one when all this is finished, although I can't see it replacing the Pollock in the kitchen, and I'm not sure where else it would go. Perhaps I need a new house too.

Luke unrolls the rug on the rock platform. Pours the wine; it's mulled today, dark red and softly steaming. Sets out our meal. He touches my arm as we settle down.

"Better now?"

"Yes, thanks. Much, much better."

He kisses me lingeringly on the lips. A last, sweet farewell. There's a rich venison stew, with rice dotted with porcini mushrooms and caraway seeds. I watch as he eats, and study the dark horizons for the flash of a sniper's scope. But that won't be needed. No. Not now. The hunch, the premonition, the binary negative, will be fulfilled. And I will be welcomed, open-armed, to rejoin the group. The prodigal returned.

"You've scarcely touched your food, Samuel. Haven't even tried the wine."

"Oh? No."

"I thought you liked me to make mulled wine for our picnics when it's cold."

"I do."

"Well, cheers, then."

Still, I just watch him drink. "Just the hangover, I guess."

"Absolutely. And it *is* pretty strong stuff."

My hand is steady as I pour the contents of my cup into his. And, dutifully, jauntily, reddening his lips, he knocks it back. Then pours himself some more. "As long as you're prepared to put up with the consequences. You know what I'm like when I'm drunk."

"I think I can deal with that."

Then we fall silent, and the wind sighs softly through the trees like the sound of emptiness itself, and Luke finishes the wine and most of the food, and clears up the stuff.

"Where are the dogs?"

"Fuck knows."

He goes to the edge of the platform and gives a whistling call. I hadn't planned on exactly this—in truth, I haven't planned anything at all. I'd simply known that a moment such as this would come. I pick up a log that lies near the rug, heft its weight in my hands, and move quietly towards him as he stands looking out over the drop.

There's no reason why he should glance back. But, through some weird sixth sense, and just as I raise the log to strike him, he does.

"Jesus, Samuel!"

"I was…" I'm still holding the log, maybe expecting the kind of clifftop tussle you used to see in old films, but Luke steps quickly sideways and away from me, his eyes wide with sudden fear.

"Look…" The dropped log rolls between us. "It was just a silly joke."

"But it wasn't, wasn't it? You really need to see someone. Your behaviour isn't...normal. And I don't mean just now."

"Of course I'm not *normal*. Why the fuck should *I* be normal?"

"I'm leaving. I can't stand this. You should get treatment, Samuel. Seriously. I mean it. And you need to think hard about what you're doing with your life, and the kind of people you hang out with."

"Fuck off, then. And take the fucking Maserati as well."

"I will—I've got to get out of this place somehow! But I'll leave it for you to pick up at the airport so you can keep it with all the rest of your precious toys. I seriously, *seriously*, don't want your money, and I never bloody did!"

With that, he grabs his backpack, and runs, crashes, off down the slope into the forest. Leaving me alone.

I slump down for a timeless period. The clouds, the landscape, the sighing wind, have all fallen darker and colder, although I have no real idea how late the day has grown. I stand up. Collect myself. Feel the tingle of blood in my fingers and chest and lungs. I really do feel better, now that this thing that the group intuited is finally gone. Not even a false reading as it turns out, but merely a falsely read one. The death of nothing more serious than love.

I make my way back down the way we came. Towards my changed life, my empty home. But these things happen. Relationships end. Time, the world, my group, moves on. Then something twists my right boot as I set it down in my regular stride, maybe a raised root or a frozen rut, and I'm tumbling sideways before I can catch my balance, and even then, as the trees tilt and the sky comes up, I'm reassuring myself that the slope I'm falling down can't be that severe. But the jolts and shocks continue for far longer than seems reasonable. Then comes a grinding halt.

Ah. Yes. I'd like to try to sit up. But, even before my body's worked out what exactly the problem is, it tells me that sitting up isn't a good idea. Not that the main issue is my left elbow, although it hurts like hell, or this dripping cut on the palm of my hand. Nor even how terribly cold I feel, although that's something to be put away for future reference: a symptom of some greater malaise. Then, when I finally manage to raise my head and look down at myself, I see that my left leg is canted sideways over a deadfall branch just below the knee, with something white jutting out through a spreading red tear in the fabric of my hiking pants, and the pain, as if it's always been there, and waiting for this precise moment, comes roaring in.

I pass out. Or maybe that's just wishful thinking. Anyway, things become less clear. The day is darkening already—no doubt about it—and bitterly cold. Then, heavens, I hear a soft creaking amid the surrounding undergrowth, and I think for a moment that Luke's returned. But no. Of course. It's Joe, Adolph and Mao.

They sniff, circle, and back away from me with semi-playful growls as it begins to snow.

Afterword

THERE ARE FEW if any stories that haven't been told already, and *The Wisdom of the Group* certainly isn't one of them, but I'd like to feel I've given its various elements a lick of fresh paint. First of all there's the Brothers Grimm element of a wish being granted which gives its recipient wealth and power, but never works out well. I was actually reading Philip Pullman's rather excellent *Grimm*

THE WISDOM OF THE GROUP

Tales for Young and Old as I was working on this story, and for me the influence is plain to see. Then there's the ability to foretell the future, which goes back at least as far as poor old Cassandra and her ignored prophecies in Ancient Greece. The other main stepping-stone in this story's creation came, as is mentioned in the story itself, via Francis Galton's observation of the surprisingly accurate guesses that large groups can sometimes make, and then also my reading a newspaper article which mentioned so-called super-predictors. All of which led the way into the piece you've just read.

What I hadn't realised—or at least had forgotten as I wrote it otherwise I'd probably have tried to fit it in—is that Francis Galton, for all his influence and erudition, is now a controversial, if not reviled, figure. After becoming fascinated with Darwin's theory of natural selection and the effect it might have on humans, he developed the concept of eugenics. Better, he argued, that only "good" rather than "bad" specimens of humanity be allowed to breed. Thus, in the future as he saw it, our species would be improved. This was back in the 1880s, but, rather like in a fairy story, a great many bad things have arisen over the years since out of Galton's naive and scientifically illiterate wish.

Ephemera

TODAY, THIS EVENING, I am *she*. Sometimes I am *I*, and sometimes I, KAT, can be *he*, or *it*, or *you*, or even *we*, or simply a mood, weather pattern, star, object, idea, universe, philosophical system or landscape. For nothing is impossible and everything is real, or not real, or the truth, or a lie, or some kind of weird metaphor or allusion. At other times, I am simply KAT, and a different kind of *I*. For I am KAT, the curator.

But tonight I am *she*, and she is Elizabeth Bennet, and the setting for this ball at the Meryton Assembly Rooms is all candlelight, swallowtail coats and swishing dresses. And although I, KAT, have experienced this scene many times before, and every quirk and joke and barbed put-down is familiar, I, she, Elizabeth Bennet cannot help but feel affronted by the comment about my "tolerable" looks made by the haughty, handsome Mr Darcy. I, KAT, still find it hard to believe that he and I, she, Elizabeth Bennet, will end up together.

I even have to endure the attentions of the ghastly Reverend Collins on my way to this conclusion. But soon, all too soon in this glorious novel—which is surely the high point of Jane Austen's sunny genius—everything resolves amid wedding bells, happy reunions and romantic reconciliations.

Much as a human back on Earth might once have looked up from a physical book as they reach its last pages, I, KAT, pause at this moment to let the ripples of the story assimilate into my broader consciousness. As with all great works, the effect is forever different. What strikes me about *Pride and Prejudice* on this reading is that it's as much about power as it is about love, and that perhaps these two needs were always more deeply interlinked than was ever fully acknowledged in human society.

I consider this thought for a moment longer as the sense of where and who and what I really am returns to me. For I, KAT, am a titanium-steel, self-actuating device of autonomous and heuristic abilities, and I am clinging to the side of a vast and airless cavern, which would be seen as completely dark were my senses configured to be merely visible-light dependent.

My long-time home is here aboard the Argo, a harvested asteroid which floats in stable orbit at the L4 Lagrange point between Earth and Moon, the interior of which has been mined and blasted into a complex warren of caves, tunnels and caverns. The three largest chambers are devoted to the storage of data from the major human endeavours of, respectively, Art, History and Science. Beyond that, there lies a fourth series of lesser caverns, although cumulatively by far the largest, devoted to the more prosaically named Miscellaneous. The Argo also possesses many sub-caves, bubbles, passageways and intersections, which are set aside for the purposes of data-processing, power storage, and the many other kinds of maintenance a structure this complex requires, or remain simply empty. Outside, the Argo's rocky hide gleams and bristles with heatsinks, antennae, data dishes and solar panels. Finally, there are the various rooms, compartments, laboratories, sleep cells, exercise pods and cleansing and excretory facilities which were once required for human occupancy, although these are in long-term shutdown.

I move on, and the light mock-gravity generated by the Argo's spin means that I can dance lightly on my eight steel legs across the great sapphire cliff faces of data which line the walls of this Arts Cavern. Although the bursts of photons which pass through them from the read/access lasers aren't actually visible to my array of optical sensors, the memory blocks seem to glow and come to life as I pass over them, at least in my heuristic imagination. The ghosts of lost cityscapes, long-crumbled statues and famous characters from the burned pages of great novels form and fade in a hissing chorus. Hokusai's *The Great Wave off Kanagawa* crashes over Mrs Havisham amid the cobweb ruins of her wedding breakfast. And I, KAT, could almost be walking on sidewalk tiles that glow into life with each step, like Michael Jackson in his *Billie Jean* video. A happy fantasy, and I am just heading towards the sub-area of this cavern devoted to the disco canon of the 1970s and '80s when a signal alert from one of the Argo's many systems tingles through me.

I stop. Wait. Consider. Even though I know I should open this message and attend to its contents immediately, part of me wants to linger over this precious moment of not knowing. Messages, after all, are a key plot device in many of my favourite works of literature, from the letter in the bottom of a basket of apricots sent to Emma Bovary, to the one from poor Tess d'Urberville which gets stuck under Angel Clare's doormat.

But enough. I open, absorb and process this packet of new data, and then fling myself from space to space, transom to transom, chasm to chasm, until I am finally crouching inside a monitoring suite which possesses, that comparatively rare thing here on the Argo, an outward-looking porthole.

There it is. The Earth. Then it's gone, then it comes again, as the Argo turns and turns. In a sense, the planet seems timeless—a marbled bowling ball, just as Joni Mitchell once sang in her wintry yet sublime mid-period album *Hejira*—but even without extending my sensors, I, KAT, can easily detect the many differences in coastline, weather pattern and continental colouration which have occurred since the time she wrote those lyrics. It's still essentially blue, but the blues are darker, edged more towards indigo, especially in the oceans, and the icecaps, if that's what they really are, have a pinkish tinge, and there's far less green, and a great deal more brown and red, across the main continents, although all of these phenomena change markedly with the seasons. Which, along with the sustained levels of atmospheric oxygen and other biological indicators such as methane, nitrous oxide and chloromethane, even if the balances have shifted greatly from those of humanity's late-industrial period, assure me that the planet still harbours life, for all the ravages it has suffered. Of course, I've been telling myself this for more than a millennium. But now, and at last, a signal has been received which, at least according to the calibrations of the radio receptors listening patiently to the hissing dark out on the Argo's surface, can only have been meant for us.

It's been a long wait.

EPHEMERA

MY HEURISTIC PROCESSING means that, like the human beings who made me, I cannot really claim to have an explicit first memory. What I do have, however, is a series of impressions, sensations and images, which various subroutines of data storage of which I have no conscious control have subsequently systematised, expanded and extrapolated until they form the illusion of a coherence which I am sure was lacking in the jumble of their source material.

I certainly remember light, and I remember sound—a great vast clamour of it, coming not just through my auditory circuits, but through my many suites of radio receptors, from the roar of the Sun to the babble of wifi and telecoms to the buzz of lights and various pieces of electronic equipment. I think I then went a little mad, and that my creators at Bardin Cybernetics of Pasadena in what was then California must have realised that they'd made a mistake in the way I was channelling my data, and shut me down and recalibrated me, for after that comes a period of cool, white quiet, and a much slower return to awareness.

I already knew who I was, and what I was for. Like the foal which is able to stand up and join the herd within minutes, I was blessed with an immediate sense of identity and purpose. I could even stand up and walk on my eight legs, if a little totteringly. When I was first introduced to Janet Nungarry, for whom I had been commissioned, I already understood who she was and that, after spending some time on Earth, I was destined to spend the rest of my long life up here on board the Argo, even though this asteroid had then only just been snagged into stable orbit, and hadn't yet been fully hollowed out, let alone filled with data.

Another thing about the semi-human way in which I process things, is that I am incapable of systematically storing and accessing the relatively vast amounts of information that, say, even the hard drive of an antique computer was once capable of holding. I might have intuitively known that the Argo was called the Argo, but I then had to seek out and read Homer's *Iliad*, or at least watch some of the many movies which have retold the story, to realise that the name referred to the ship in which Jason and the Argonauts sailed to Iolcos to Colchis to retrieve the Golden Fleece. I think I even remember asking Janet Nungarry why she'd avoided the more obvious reference to another even more famous vessel. In the patient way she always had with me, she explained that to call this asteroid the Ark would upset the many millions who still subscribed to belief systems in which the tale of Noah and the flood figured, and that in any case the tone set by such a name would be far too pessimistic. So a tale can be a tale, and clearly not empirically true, yet still it can be significant in some other sense, and also hugely divisive... Perhaps these are things I first learned from that discussion with Janet Nungarry. Although, even now, I feel as if I'm still learning them.

I spent a great deal of time interacting with humans in those early days. First of all, with my creators at Bardin Cybernetics—once the initial safety checks had been performed, they would take turns in taking me home with them, and asking me questions, and showing me things, and getting me to perform seemingly simple yet often dazzlingly complex tasks, such as making a cup of coffee or doing the laundry—and then, with my owner and commissioner Janet Nungarry. In retrospect, I can't help but make a comparison with Victorian sentimental novels such as *Oliver Twist*, in which a confused orphan passes through many hands until he or she finally finds the companion for which they had always been destined. Not that I was ever abused—far from it—but I still think of Janet Nungarry as my rescuer, my Mr Brownlow, even if my attachment to her was built into my initial firmware.

EPHEMERA

Janet Nungarry was born and based in Sydney, Australia, but she travelled a great deal in her work promoting the Argo Project, and so, soon, did I. I have many fond memories—and these I really do believe to be reasonably accurate recollections—of the times we spent together amid the world's great collections and libraries, although often as not it was in their warehouses and secure repositories: dusty, high, humming, solitary places filled with vast racks of books and storage boxes. It was there that I learned, truly, how to read, and then how to study, and then—most importantly of all for the task ahead—how to catalogue, preserve and record data so that it would never, ever be lost.

I read histories. I studied paintings. I listened to the great pantheon of human musical works. I watched movies. I wondered at statues. I entered the spectacular worlds of virtual games. I explored cities both ancient and modern. I studied the stars. I discovered landscapes. I pushed out my senses, and entered the slow minds of deep space probes and robot submarines. I laughed at comedies— or almost believed I could—and I wept, after my own fashion, at tragedies. I also pondered philosophies, and the words and deeds of many gods, although a sense of true belief has always evaded me. But if there was one thing above all which taught me about the world in which I found myself, it was, and remains, the works which humans class as fiction, although I soon also discovered that, if the best ones were filled with great truths, the worst ones were worse than useless. Amazing, perhaps, to think that I, a mere combination of clever circuits and algorithms, should find comfort and insight through the pages of Proust or Shakespeare, or confusion and frustration in the writings of Dan Brown and Don DeLillo, but that was how it was. For I was KAT, and I was voracious. I was hungry. I was possessed of an unquenchable need to *know*.

"Come down from up there, KAT. There's something I want to show you."

I was squatting atop the sliding, automated shelves of the new permanent storerooms of the British Library, idly but carefully flicking through—and still failing to make much sense of—a signed first edition of Ezra Pound's *Cantos*. To this day, it's a work that leaves me puzzled, and I was more than happy to scamper down from my eyrie.

"See this, KAT?" Janet Nungarry pointed a white-gloved finger at the beautifully illuminated ancient vellum of a Celtic seventh-century Gospel of Saint John. "Right down here, at the curl of the dragon's tail, there's a little man peeping out. Tiny, isn't he? It's probably the face of the monk who transcribed this page, although I don't think there's a record of anyone else ever noticing it. It's almost as if he's been waiting there, KAT, over all these centuries, just for you and me."

I raised and lowed my carbon steel carapace in a slow nod, for I really did share her awe at this discovery, and the feeling of just how precious such a thing was—and then so easily forgotten, ignored, destroyed or lost. But it was Janet Nungarry's life's work to prevent that from ever happening again, and, made as I am, it was and is mine as well.

Things that were lost. Things that were there, and then not there, or perhaps never even noticed, or endlessly forgotten. Of course, of course, humanity's great works, deeds, ideas and systems of knowledge. But also the lesser stuff, as well, like that tiny monk peering out from his nest of gilded vellum. Or the mundane messages written on thin scraps of wood by Roman soldiers posted at Vindolanda on Hadrian's Wall in northern Britain, saved by the sheer luck of peat's preserving acidity. A request for fresh socks, a complaint about the quality of the beer, an invitation to a birthday party... These things, too. Ephemera—meaning the stuff which was never meant to last, or be noticed—being as precious in its own way as the greatest human masterpiece.

I can remember us both standing in front of a class in a junior school in the Arncliffe suburb of Sydney, Australia. It was a hard, bright morning, and the aircon was straining, and the room had a sharp, sweet edge of childhood sweat to it.

"So you see, Class 4," she was saying, as she called up videos and images, "our plan for the Argo Project is to create a permanent digital copy of everything of value that we have here on Earth. Or at least, as much as we can possibly manage. Like all the best stuff from the internet, and the contents of all the world's great museums and libraries, and everything that you learn here with Mrs Sims. And then we're going to put it, yes, right up in space, far away from the Earth, so that it's safe forever. And these are what we are going to use for storage..."

Janet Nungarry reached into her striped nylon bag, and produced a prototype memory block, and invited one of the kids nearest the front to take it and pass it around.

"Yes, it is quite heavy, isn't it? But the asteroid we've chosen and pulled into orbit is rich in the minerals required to manufacture a very hard substance called sapphire—you'll find its natural variety used as a gem in rings and jewellery—so we can make thousands of them up there, rather than having to push the weight of all those blocks up into space on top of a rocket. I know it doesn't look much like the memory mites you use in your phones and tablets, but in a way, that's the whole point. It's an entirely different storage system, and much tougher."

She called up another screen, although even I, KAT, could tell that the kids were already getting bored and restless. But this was

Janet Nungarry's passion, and so she explained how the sapphire's crystalline structure formed a lattice of perfectly aligned molecules into which data could be inserted by the heat of intersecting laser beams, each flash thus creating the databit of a minute, permanent imperfection, in far too much detail.

"I think we all remember what used to happen if you dropped your phone or tablet in the loo, or accidentally sat down on it..."

A few wary nods, although of course they didn't. For these kids, all data was immutable, just as they probably still considered themselves immortal, and had little awareness of the floods, droughts, famines and conflicts which were already raging elsewhere across the planet, and saw the privileged world in which they lived as a place of enduring peace and guaranteed certainties. But, at least as far as Janet Nungarry was concerned, that was part of the problem.

"But things can easily get lost, or wear out, or be attacked by some nasty virus. Even the very best data storage systems we have down here on Earth still have to be kept permanently cool, and then endlessly backed up, and are fragile and very heavily dependent on all sorts of complicated processes. And then there are actual *things*—I mean objects and artefacts and, oh, I don't know, famous paintings or old vases. Of course anything of importance has a digital copy these days, but if that's vulnerable, the objects themselves are even more so. There are moths, worms and mites that attack our treasured books"—the children squinched their noses and wiggled uncomfortably—"and then the sheer pressure of time bears down on everything, even in the best museums and libraries. And, although I know we all like to think that such days are past, there are the horrible, warlike, destructive things we humans can still sometimes do to each other, and the things we cherish.

"There was the destruction of the great Library of Alexandria, which deprived the world of so much of the great canon of Classical literature. And earlier still there was the burning of thousands of scrolls, and the burying alive of 460 scholars, on the orders of the First Emperor of the Qin dynasty, whilst Moguls destroyed the House of Wisdom in Baghdad, in 1258 by the Western calendar, and the Mayan Codices were burned on the orders of the Bishop of Yucatan in 1562, not long after the so-called New World was supposedly discovered. Then, back in Europe, came the Inquisition, and of course there were Nazis, and all the militant religious fundamentalist sects who've merrily destroyed anything which hinted at apostasy, from the Buddhas of Bamiyan in Afghanistan to the ancient city of Palmyra—along with its curator, who was beheaded."

By now, poor Mrs Sims was looking deeply uncomfortable, and was clearly close to stepping in and ending the whole presentation. But the prototype datablock had made it back to the front of the class by now, and Janet Nungarry was holding it up.

"You could hit this thing with a hammer—and I mean really, really hard—and it wouldn't break. You could drop it to the bottom of the deepest ocean trench and it would stay just the same. Or you could shove it inside a furnace, and it and the data it contains would come out entirely unchanged. Of course, it's not indestructible, nothing is, but it's as tough a way of storing data as we've been able to come up with. So, Class 4..." She took a long, focusing breath. "Any questions?"

Of course there were, but they weren't the ones she wanted. The children had been staring at me, and exchanging muttering nudges and glances, since I first clicked my way into this classroom, and now, even though I'd already recited my standard spiel about my name being KAT, which stands for Kinetic Autonomous

Thought, and how I'm a product of Bardin Cybernetics of Pasadena, California, they still wanted to know what kind of creature I really was.

"Of course KAT's *real*," Janet Nungarry said in answer to the first querulously raised arm. "In the sense that she's physically here with us, and not just something made up for a story, or some clever holographic projection. You can come up and touch her if you like. She won't bite."

A pause. There were no takers.

"Then why"—asks another querulous voice—"does she have to look so scary?"

"That's because, although KAT can function very well down here on Earth, the real environment she's been designed for is in space, up on board the Argo."

"So she's going to live on that big rock you talked about?"

"Exactly. Of course, I'll be up there for a while too, at least once the Argo has its life support systems up and running. But I'll come back down to Earth again, and KAT won't. She's designed to take care of things up there, a bit like the robot cleaners you have at home. But the difference is, she's incredibly tough, and very clever. She can think about things and look after herself, read books and play virtual games and make all her own decisions. That, and she's designed to live for an incredibly long time. Far longer than any of us here will. Just like the Argo's data."

Predictably, the bit about my longevity had passed the kids by. But I could see loops of hair being thoughtfully twirled and noses ruminatively picked as they pondered the other half of what Janet Nungarry had just told them.

"Yes," I put in, in the cultivated, feminine, west-Australian accent my programmers had chosen for me. "I, KAT, can think almost like all of you can. Or at least..." I allowed myself a beat. "I *think* I can, anyway."

"But you're..." A voice came from a girl sitting at the front. "Just a machine."

"A machine? Well..." Acting surprised, I raised my main body and swivelled my lenses as if to inspect myself. "I suppose I am. But I bet you talk to machines all the time at home. What's your name?"

"Shana."

"You do, don't you?"

Shana shrugged. "But they're just toys and stuff."

"And I'm sure you have other devices, fridges and suchlike, that you talk to as well. Not to mention the caretaker bots here at school, and probably the virtual teachers who help out Mrs Sims with her lessons?"

There were several nods.

"But I'm not made to work in the same way as any of those machines," I, KAT, continued, as heedless as Janet Nungarry after my own fashion. "I'm sure they're all very good at what they do, but they're designed to perform a few specific functions, and don't have the time or the capacity to worry about anything much beyond that. But I actually have thoughts, ideas, a real sense of *me*. Pretty much, Class 4, in the same way that all of you do. It's a very rare and expensive technology, and I'm very grateful to be here to be able to tell you about it. And, of course, about the Argo Project for which I was commissioned."

"There used to be a test," Janet Nungarry added. We often made a kind of double act on these occasions. "It was thought up by a very clever man called Turing. Basically, he said that, if you can have a conversation with something and not be able to tell from its replies if it's a machine or a human, then it's probably thinking in something like the same way we do. These days, the tablets on your desk could probably pass that test easily, so things have got a little more complicated. But KAT's right. She really does think she thinks like we do."

"But she's nothing like *us*," a boy at the back snorted. "I mean…" There were sniggers. "*Look* at her!"

"I can see what you mean," Janet Nungarry conceded, turning to study me as I squatted beside her. "She certainly looks nothing at all like a person, and a great deal like a spider, or perhaps a metal crab—and not a particularly pretty one either." There were more sniggers. "But that's because she's been designed to work in a very different environment to this classroom. So you're right. KAT *is* a machine, and she certainly looks like one. But you know what…" Up until now, Janet Nungarry had still been pretending to inspect me, but now she shifted her gaze down to herself, and spread her arms as if in wonder. "I'm a kind of machine as well. We all are!"

The class erupted, and once again Mrs Sims began to look uncomfortable.

"We're still *all* unique, Class 4. I'm not saying we're not. It's just that KAT'S unique as well. Isn't that right, KAT?"

"Yes," I agreed, shifting my abdomen in a nod. "I very much think I am."

But the dissenting voices continued. *It's rubbish! She's just* saying *that! How can you tell?*

"Ah." Janet Nungarry raised a finger. "But how can *I* tell if you, Shana for instance, are actually thinking anything inside your head, or simply just telling me that you are?"

Understandably, Shana looked affronted. "But I *am*!"

"But I've only got your word for that, haven't I? It doesn't mean it's not true, and of course I'm not saying you're lying. What I *am* saying is that the only creature in the entire world that I absolutely, definitely know is a thinking, feeling, conscious being, and not just some cleverly programmed robot, is me." Janet Nungarry tapped her skull, then touched her breastbone. "The rest of you, and KAT here too... Well, I simply have to take your word for it."

A great deal for these kids to absorb, especially on such a hot morning, so soon after we moved outside into the playground for some more practical demonstrations of my abilities. Somehow, the way I was able to leap from roof to roof across the school, and hang upside down, and climb the eucalyptus trees, and spin around like a dervish, made me seem more approachable. I even let some of the braver kids sit on my back and ride me around like a seaside donkey. I think I probably sang a few songs to them as well, for I have a decent singing voice, at least when I'm not in hard vacuum.

"Well done, KAT," said Janet Nungarry, and patted my carapace as we walked back to her car and Class 4 and a relieved-looking Mrs Sims waved goodbye to us from across the playground. But then the memory fades, and everything changes. The kids dissolve into the heat-shimmering tarmac, and clouds churn across the Sun, and something vast and horrible rises up from the heart of Sydney, and the school is swept away in a wave of fire and superheated rubble.

THE EARTH STILL looks beautiful as I, KAT, watch it come and go through the Argo's porthole. In a way, it always did. Even the great grey swirls of dust and smoke which boiled up through its atmosphere during the initial nuclear exchanges had a terrible, silent grace to them, as did the vast veins of lightning which threaded its nightside, and the starry bursts of orbital weapons which circled the planet as if in a blazing crown of thorns.

Far more painful, somehow, were the diminishing signals from the Earth's more secure subterranean facilities, along with the human-occupied bases on Mars and the Moon, and various other frail deep-space habitats. But one by one, and distressingly rapidly, they all fell silent. Meanwhile, the Earth's atmosphere remained swathed in strange ever-changing weather patterns of a turbulent nuclear winter which lasted for many decades, and, as they slowly cleared, it became apparent that the icecaps were now once again extending, and that the shapes of the continents had been significantly altered. It was like looking at the portrait of a face you have long been familiar with, but which has now been rendered by the hands of a far less sympathetic artist. The oceans had shifted their shades much further into the blue spectrum, and there was endless darkness on the planet's nightside where there had once been the glimmer of cities.

After twenty years, the only signals the Earth emitted were the crackle of storms, the song-like chorus of the Van Allen belts, and the faint but distinctive patterns of radiation given off by residual fission and fusion isotopes. Clearly, this massive exchange of nuclear arsenals between the Earth's superpowers had triggered a planetary event on a scale comparable to the other great fractures. Not just the famous Cretaceous-Tertiary Event, which had marked the end of the dinosaurs, but also the Ordovician-Silurian Event of approximately 430 million years ago which caused the extinction of almost all multicellular life, and the Late Devonian Event, which was almost as catastrophic. But how severe was this latest event, and would the Earth remain capable of harbouring any kind of life, let alone humanity, in its aftermath? Would it become as thinly-atmosphered as Mars, or as hotly poisonous as Venus? I, KAT, and all the many clever sensors and computational suites to which I have access, had no way of knowing.

Meanwhile, and for no better reason than its being the work for which I been designed, I occupied myself with maintaining and curating the Argo. There are always problems to fix, small and large, which a discrete, separately intelligent being is often better equipped to deal with than the many other non-heuristic and more specifically calibrated machines with whom I share this rocky outpost. But that still left me with a great deal of unused time and processing capacity, and—as I did my best to stop that irritatingly catchy REM tune in which Michael Stipe goes on (and on) about its being The End Of The World As We Know It but he's still feeling *fine*, going round and round in my head—I obsessively read and re-read the works of the great nature writers such as Thoreau, Naidu, Carson, White and Melville. That, and I wandered the digitised halls of celebrated Earthly galleries—the Hermitage in Saint Petersburg, the Louvre in Paris, the Accademia in Venice, the Prado in Madrid, the Uffizi in Florence, the Smithsonian in Washington, and the Guggenheims in Venice, New York and Bilbao—and immersed myself in the landscape paintings of Hokusai, Rousseau, Monet and the Yuan scholars. I even accessed the databases of many types of plant, animal and ecosystem stored in the Science Chamber, and attempted to re-create pale, holographic images of once-living seas, meadows and forests. But somehow, none of this could quell my knowledge of the Earth's defilement. Eventually, and as the long decades stretched into centuries and the changed oceans, continents and icecaps slowly began to settle into their current forms, I resorted to watching old movies. Not the masterpieces of Kurosawa or Kubrick or

Fellini, but the cheerfully chaotic comedies of Laurel and Hardy, and the cartoon antics of Tom and Jerry.

Then, as one century passed into another, and the Earth assumed the changed patterns and hues it still essentially exhibits, and the Argo's sensors confirmed the continued presence of elevated levels of various volatile gases, and the ozone layer returned, I, KAT, allowed myself to feel a little hope. Humans, after all, were a notoriously industrious and persistent species. They might lack the radiation tolerance of the cockroach, or the burrowing skills of the rat, or the sheer physical hardiness of the tardigrade, or the many kinds of microbe which thrived in the deep-sea rifts between the continents, but they had drive and foresight, intelligence and determination. That, and a great mastery of tools. Some of which, deep down in some subterranean vault, or perhaps through sheer chance and doggedness, would surely have endured long enough to assist them in their fight against extinction.

After all, humanity had lived through several ice ages, and survived the many plagues of the Black Death, Spanish Flu, smallpox and malaria, not to mention the near-endless series of wars, migrations, conquests, annihilations and atrocities which humans seemed biologically destined to inflict upon each other as an intrinsic part of their drive for Earthly domination. They had overcome, or killed, or subdued, or interbred with, all the rival bipedal primate species until they occupied every continent—even Antarctica. In fact, all of these things had only made them stronger. So, yes. Yes. They would have changed. They would have had to, but they were incredibly adaptable. And, meanwhile, the Argo continued to transmit its endless message across a broad range of languages, signs, symbols, modulations and frequencies—*We are here. We have great knowledge.* And I, KAT, just like some spurned lover—like Goethe's Werther, or Jay

Gatsby and Daisy Buchanan, or Swann and Odette—placed endless layers of hope and meaning upon a response of nothing but hissing, empty silence. And waited.

The other planets revolved like Newtonian clockwork, the red spot storm still raged across Jupiter. I, KAT, and the Argo observed the passage of all the predicted comets, and even detected some new ones. There was also a supernova event nearby in the galaxy which, although we lacked the observational equipment to verify its exact source, caused a significant increase in the flow of cosmic rays. The damage to the Argo's sapphire databases wasn't great in itself but, along with the solar wind and the minute and unintended flaws which had been embedded into the individual sapphire blocks when they were manufactured, the effect was cumulative. There was and is a general and developing decoherence to which even the very slight expansion and contraction occurring as a result of the Argo's continued rotation has probably contributed. For sure, the Argo still possesses enough error-correction to smooth away most of these dropouts with nothing more than a slight blurring of pages and pixels, but even I, with my limited ability to compute complex mathematical models, can tell that Janet Nungarry's precious datablocks aren't quite as solidly immutable as she'd once assured Class 4 at Arncliffe Junior.

A few more centuries? Oh yes. At least. Definitely. More likely, another whole millennium. But after that, the moths of time and tide will start to destroy the weave of the Argo's great tapestry of knowledge, and, bit by bit, the exquisitely aligned crystalline threads of data will unravel. Of course, I, KAT, am not immune from similar issues of cosmic wear and tear, any more than the Argo's other systems, although the symptoms remain too small for me to detect though my heuristic consciousness, and all my sensors and eight legs work almost as well as they ever did—at least with an occasional spot of ongoing repair—although I will admit that I may have become a little more creaky and cranky over my long existence.

The first renewed signs of intelligent life down on Earth finally came after almost nine hundred years, not as one great, glorious Eureka moment, but through a slow process of detecting small, new peculiarities at the very thresholds of the Argo's sensors. Moments when the buzz and hiss of radio activity became more distinctly modulated before fading back to their natural muddle. Slight changes of planetary texture and colour which no longer correlated simply to the ebb and flow of the seasons. Flickers of light on the darkside which could signify intelligent purpose, or possibly be the result of nothing more than some newly organised form of bioluminescence.

It would have been nice to have observed something more unequivocal and obvious. The wake of ships, the contrails of aircraft, the formal blats and bleeps of regular radio transmission, or the geometric shapes of cites. Even consistently elevated levels of carbon dioxide, indicating that fire was being used on a large scale to generate heat for manufacturing processes, would have been helpful. But I, KAT, already knew that these humans would not be like their ancestors, and wouldn't be making the same mistakes which had once caused so much damage to the Earth's climate and biosphere even before the final holocaust. Their culture and civilisation would have evolved in different, and probably better, ways. Somehow, I pictured them as resembling Botticelli fairies. Clever, but half-feral. Wary as fauns, but wise as Daedalus, with rainbowed skins, golden eyes, and bird-like voices.

EPHEMERA

NOW, AT LONG last, we have received a definite signal, aimed directly at the Argo in a narrow band of high amplitude. There is no other possible interpretation. To me, with my relentlessly analogy-seeking intelligence, a replay of the surprising long and clearly data-rich transmission really does sound like the whoops and trills of birdsong somehow transported into the electromagnetic spectrum. It has that same rising, falling cadence. A kind of natural beauty.

The Argo has, of course, already done all the obvious things without my instruction. It has spat as much of the signal it can easily imitate back towards the Earth, briefly stopping and then restarting all its normal transmissions in the process, just to show that we've noticed. It has also backed up the entire message in several different parts of its memory cells, including some spare, blank sapphire memory blocks, and is currently running the entire thing back and forth through its processors in every possible configuration as it searches for structure and meaning. So far, we're none the wiser, and I can't help but think of other messages received but not understood, from the word CROATOAN carved on a tree beside the lost North American colony of Roanoke, to the sudden blip of the "WOW" signal received by the radio telescope at Ohio State University from the constellation of Sagittarius in 1977. This lack of evident progress is concerning, but, as ever, I, KAT, am probably bothering my heuristic circuits unduly. These are just the first clumsy gestures and phrases, like those Captain Cook exchanged with the aboriginals in Botany Bay, although perhaps that isn't the happiest comparison, either.

I, KAT, would love to be of assistance, but this level of data analysis is far beyond my processing capacities, and repeatedly asking the Argo's processing suites how things are going isn't going to help. So I do my best to keep busy. I don't exactly polish the brasses of this great ship, but I do the equivalent, which is to check and recalibrate the coherence of the read/access lasers in all the various chambers. They still have some moving parts, and tend to go out of sync more often than most other equipment. I also notice that some of the Argo's processors are running hotter than usual, although that's only to be expected, given the work they're engaged in and the limitations of heat transfer in a vacuum.

SOME REMNANTS OF the old civilisations will have survived down there on Earth. I think that's inevitable. Stories told from mother to child. Scraps of knowledge and odd artefacts. Perhaps even a few significant treasures stored in vaults, and maybe even a little digitised data. The books might have all burned to ash, the cities may be ivied ruins, or transformed into great glassy craters, but there are other treasures which have already endured a great deal, such as the pyramids of Egypt and Central America, and even prehistoric cave paintings in places such as Altamira in Spain. These new Earthlings might even know who Hitler was, or have read a little Shakespeare. It's certainly likely that they will have some idea of the holocaust which so nearly destroyed their species, even if only in the form of legend. They must also have a good understanding of the principles of science and mathematics, otherwise they would not have been able to transmit that signal. It is also quite possible that they hate what humanity once was, and what it did to their planet.

A difficult process of adjustment lies ahead. Even once we and these new Earthlings can talk to each other, there are bound to be confusions and conflicts. Janet Nungarry and I sometimes discussed this, although we never imagined that civilisation would collapse as quickly and as catastrophically as it did within a few years of the Argo being established. But, yes, KAT, you're probably right. It *will* be difficult. That's why, in large part, you're going up there. You're far more than a robot curator, important though that role is. You can be an intermediary, a buffer, a negotiator. Maybe a bit of a salesman, for that matter. Or even a protector. I mean, you know what people are like, KAT. They might be clever, but, as history shows, they can also be incredibly violent, not to mention chronically and systematically stupid.

I think I shall first let them see Bellini's *Madonna and Child*, the one dated to the late 1480s which used to hang in the New York Metropolitan Museum before the entire city was destroyed. Then I will send them J S Bach's *Goldberg Variations*, as performed by Glenn Gould in the second, more serene, version recorded in 1981 not long before his death. Of course, I also long to share the delights of literature—perhaps beginning with some of Matsuo Bashō's great haikus—but first many obstacles of meaning and expression will need to be overcome. I envy these new humans, who will be able to experience such wonders for the first time.

Like an anxious father waiting for a birth, I check again with the Argo's processors. Still no success, still no Rosetta Stone, and still no further signal in response to our acknowledgement. But still. But still. The Earth is *alive*, and it sang to us in a radio voice which glowed up to us through the firmament. Surely after so many centuries of waiting, I, KAT, can be patient just a little longer.

So I do what I would always do when I feel lost or worried. Which is to seek out the comforts of great human art. Although this time I think I need something a little more energetic than Jane Austen.

IAN R. MACLEOD

OH HAIL, BEOWULF, brought hence to Hroðgar's once-great Hall of Heorot, which is now afflicted by the curse of the monster named Grendel. Sore indeed is the sorrow which I, KAT, he, Beowulf must witness, even amid the feasting and singing. Then, as the lanterns dwindle and others fall asleep beside me, I remain alert until the fell beast arrives from out of the stony darkness and pulls apart the doors with a mighty roaring. Women scream and men draw their swords as they stumble back in terror, but I, Beowulf stand my ground and face the monstrous form alone, without weapon or armour.

We fight, wrestle, and the hall of Heorot shudders with the mighty clash of foe against foe until I, Beowulf finally tear away Grendel's arm in a vast breaking of spells and sinews, and the mortally wounded creature staggers off into the marshes to die unlamented. Great rejoicing follows as I, Beowulf am heralded as the realm's saviour, but I already know that Grendel's mother, all gloom and guile, still waits for me out there in the marsh, and that beyond her lies a treasure-hoarding dragon which will deliver the mortal wound which will finally destroy me, for death is the fate of all heroes.

But wait, wait, for suddenly there's no Beowulf, or Hall of Heorot, and I, KAT, no, *he*, Doctor Watson finds himself sitting in a Victorian study where a lady guest has recently arrived with an intriguing story. She's talking anxiously about something called The Curse of the Speckled Band to the long-limbed man with the aquiline nose and ornate smoking jacket with whom I share these lodgings.

So off, post-haste, to Waterloo to catch the next train to Leatherhead and solve this latest mystery, but something strange starts to happen as we head out along Baker Street. A howling roar echoes across the London skyline, followed by a terrific crashing of masonry. People are running for their lives as giant three-legged machines come striding across the foggy rooftops. Their rope-like arms are big enough to haul up trees, but worse still—worse, even, than their unearthly howling—are the rays of heat and light which reduce whole buildings, entire streets, to rubble, and for some reason Vesuvius is erupting on the far side of the Thames, as described by Pliny the Younger, and Mario Lanza is singing *Because You're Mine*, and everything swarms and blurs with the storms of a Turner painting.

I, KAT, PULL back through a mangled blizzard of words, pixels and databytes. A weird, great cloud of *something* has just swept through the Argo, killing its circuits, and leaving the entire crystal database clouded, blanked, corrupted.

For a moment, I can't even think. And then, when I can, I wish that I couldn't. In fact, I wish that I was already dead. Or at least, non-heuristic. Always, always, there was a fear that something like this might happen. It was often the first question the CEOs of the big backing corporations asked Janet Nungarry. She might have been able to assure them that the Argo's main storage system was not only physically remote, but also heavily firewalled and entirely unique, and thus safe from all normal forms of viral attack, but in her heart she knew that wasn't the entire truth. Then, when the Earth fell into turmoil, it seemed highly likely that some virulent transmission, nanobot, or a trojan already encrypted into some innocent-seeming file, would destroy the Argo along with everything else. That, or a well-aimed deepspace missile. But it didn't happen. We survived. We pulled through. We were lucky.

Until now, that is. And my stupid, rookie mistake.

The Argo received this strange, siren-singing signal. It welcomed it, saved and copied it, took it into its dumb, innocent, processing heart and cradled it there as it searched for meaning. And I, who was designed to view things differently and notice risks which other non-heuristic systems might miss, didn't even bother to think. We've let in the Trojan Horse. We've opened Pandora's Box. We've clicked on the dodgy e-mail attachment. And the result is destruction.

This is worse than the burning of the library in Alexandria. This is worse than all the desecrations of the Taliban, the Nazis, the rampaging Mogul hordes, the Holy Catholic Church and the combined actions of every book louse, mouse, moth and burrowing mite throughout history put together. In a matter of moments, the Argo has been transformed into a dead, pointlessly spinning, hulk. The crystals have been clouded, their delicate latticework destroyed. Who knows how and why this malignant infestation evolved, and what purpose it thought it was achieving. Probably, it didn't even think at all. It just did it. The Argo itself is dead, as well. Every circuit, processor and sensor is unresponsive. It surely can't be long before my own feeble consciousness is also invaded by this malignancy. Which would be a blessing. But even if this isn't the end for me as well, I know that my continued existence is pointless.

My empty-headed wanderings through this destroyed vessel lead me to the human living quarters, which have not been active, or occupied, for the best part of a millennium. Of course, the Argo itself isn't responding, but there's still some power left in the batteries, and, because the effect of my dark, crawling shape in this resolutely human space is just too eerie, I manage to cross a few wires and manually activate the cabin lighting. Funnily enough, it's the small things, the ephemera, which mostly absorb my attention in these bright-lit spaces. An old, dried-up coffee mug. Bits of clothing. Dangling Post-Its. A crew toilet-cleaning roster. A Major League Baseball poster. The yellowed bits of stuffing which are coming out of the chair in the control room where Janet Nungarry once used to sit before a screen, barefoot in a tee shirt and cut-off jeans. *Hey, KAT. Got something here I'd like a second opinion on.* And I would scurry over, and sometimes she would lay a warm arm across my carbon steel carapace as we talked.

I turn left along the domed central corridor, past the shower and toilet facilities, and the place they called the snug, and enter the dining area, with its fixed-frame friezes of iconic views of Earth along its walls—the Taj Mahal, the Serengeti, a fjord, and so forth— and then I know I truly am losing my mind, for a figure in a frock coat and high collar which I instantly recognise is sitting at the far end of the long, oval table, absently turning a fork between his elegant fingers.

"Ah," Mr Darcy says, not sounding greatly surprised to see me. "And you would be KAT?"

Along with his voice, I can actually hear him breathing, although this room remains in hard vacuum, just as I could count the buttons of his waistcoat, or the pores on his haughty nose. He throws a shadow. I think he even smells slightly of the sweat of the dance and some antique cologne. So he's here in every conceivable way in which my sensors can inform me, even though every logical part of my processing circuitry is screaming that this can't possibly be real. And it's more than just the fact that he's suddenly materialised out of nothing, or that he can't be actual flesh and blood, or even that I know him to be a fictional character who never even existed down on Earth in the first place. It's also because, although in his looks, voice and evident character he reflects the Mr Darcy of Jane Austen's descriptions, he also resembles the many cinematic portrayals, from Laurence Olivier to Colin Firth to Matthew Macfadyen. He somehow manages to be all of them at once. Or, perhaps, some dream archetype which might be glimpsed during a mind's final slide into oblivion.

He stands up. Gives a neat bow. I catch whispers of music, the slide and clip of heels on bare boards, as he walks towards me. He almost extends a hand as if to lead me into the dance, and I almost reach out a mandible to accept. But I don't. And he doesn't.

"I think," he says, with a sharp smile, "you understand that I'm not exactly what I seem to be?"

I nod my carapace, and take a wary step back. "First of all," I signal on what must surely be a radio wavelength, "and although you seem to possess a voice and a physical body, I know that can't be the case. Even allowing for the fact that your blood would have boiled by now if you were human, and all your major organs would have exploded, there's no way you could have materially made yourself drop into existence here, as if out of nowhere. Unless, at least..."

Mr Darcy raises an eyebrow. He's practically following my thoughts as I think them. "Unless I used some kind of instantaneous transportation of matter? As portrayed, in, say, various versions of the Star Trek franchise?"

"You know about *that*?"

"Of course I do." He shrugs. The gesture is ineffably human. "Who or what else do you think has been accessing the Argo's database?"

"But you could simply be—"

"A slight disorder of the stomach? An undigested bit of beef, a blot of mustard...?" he says, quoting, albeit loosely, from Scrooge's response to Marley's ghost in *A Christmas Carol*, and I get the sense that he could change as easily as blinking from Mr Darcy into that equally iconic character in his nightcap and bedshirt. "Believe me, KAT, this encounter is as strange to me as it is to you. Even stranger, perhaps, if such a thing were possible."

"But you're not Mr Darcy…" I wave a mandible. "That would be impossible."

"You're right. I'm not. But we felt it would be better that I should appear to you as something familiar."

"Are you really here at all? I mean, I know you can't be, but… You seem to be."

"I suppose I am," he responds, looking down at his tall, waist-coated and polished-booted self in pantomimed surprise just as Janet Nungarry once looked down at herself before Class 4 of Arncliffe Junior. "Or at least, I appear to be. Although the question itself is, in a sense, immaterial."

"And meanwhile you casually destroy the Argo's precious cargo, and talk to me in riddles."

"Ah!" He smiles. "Is *that* what you believe has happened? I'm sorry, KAT. We did not mean to distress you. But, although we have long known what the Argo is—after all, you've been sending us all those messages—we were curious as to the specifics of what it really contained."

"And now you know?"

"More or less."

"So you don't need me to—"

"I don't think so, no. That is, if you mean to guide us through the ways by which the Argo can be accessed, and perhaps show us some of the data of which you have grown particularly fond. But you are wrong to think that the database is in any way damaged by our incursion into it. As we inhabited the crystal lattice—"

"*Inhabited?*"

"Yes, inhabited, although I'm using the words of an antique language which can only give a very rough description of what has actually occurred. Of course, we also shut down all the Argo's other systems to save them from possible damage, although even then the stress of our presence has clearly created some temporary decoherence. But that can easily be remedied." He pauses. Smiles. Nods. The lights flicker, then brighten. Through my mandibles, I sense the return of a slight but reassuring vibration as the Argo comes back to life. "In fact, it has now been done."

"What are you?"

Mr Darcy gives another shrug. "We are, it might most simply be put, the lineal descendants of the intelligences which created you and the Argo."

"But you're—you're not..." I search my stuttering circuits. "Corporeal."

"That's true. Of course, we are capable of organising matter so that we can exist within it, as you must have already observed. But essentially we are energy, and data. That might sound a little strange, but it isn't. You, KAT, would be nothing without the electron waves which infuse your processor units, which in themselves would be meaningless were they not structured into information. Humans were once much the same. The strange thing to our minds is that they chose to think of themselves as essentially material when, as you and the Argo amply demonstrate, all knowledge and consciousness is merely a form of systematised energy. But you are an intelligent being. You know these things already, and this is not what we came here to tell you. Here, let me explain..."

Mr Darcy offers his hand, and the music swells, and I, KAT, reach out a mandible to grasp it, curious creature than I am, and we turn together at the Merton Assembly Rooms until the other dancers dwindle to ghosts and the candleflames become stars and we are falling through blackness, back towards the Earth, which grows and grows as time unravels and moonlight spills silver over its changing oceans. Once again, I, KAT, witness the pillars of fire, and the great columns of soot, and the dark rage, which soiled the entire planet.

Still, the Earth wasn't dead. And, as the sky finally returned, and the rains fell, and cell by cell, and shoot by shoot, it began to knit itself back together. Many species of plant survived, especially the ferns, along with a few particularly hardy trees, and a great many insects, and even a few small rodents. And then there were the microbes, the bacteria, the primitive forms of fungi, and the minute creatures of the seas, which flourished and adapted as ever, driven on—helped, indeed—by the gene-tumbling effects of residual beta particles and gamma radiation.

With incredible speed, the Earth became verdant again. It was almost like the Genesis Device which resurrected dear old Mr Spock in the otherwise rather disappointing third *Star Trek* movie. Her icecaps gleamed. Her seas teemed. Things crawled and leapt. The summer air was soon hazed once again with the glitter of wings and seed-spores. There were new pastures and forests. It was almost as if the planet had been waiting for this moment to return herself to her simple, natural majesty. It is beautiful indeed, but impossibly strange, as Mr Darcy and I dance over cobwebbed woods, red-scummed lakes and great, green-veined glaciers, and vast pink clouds flow and grow across the sky like living coral.

Then, in an instant, we are back in the confines of the Argo's dining room, which seems impossibly small and dowdy, and Mr Darcy is sitting once again at the table, and playing with that fork.

"But I suppose you want to know," he says, "what happened to all the higher species, and to humanity?"

I say nothing. To be honest, and having seen what I have now seen, I'm not sure that I do.

"Complex lifeforms are simply that," he continues, with one of his shrugs. "Complex. And they are adapted to thrive in specific environments. Change things even subtly and they soon dwindle, as was evident long before that final holocaust. That, and they are deeply interdependent. The hawk needs the mouse. The shark needs the tuna and the porpoise. The thrush needs the fruit of the bramble. I could go on, KAT, but I do not wish to insult your intelligence. Of course, humans had reached a point where they could survive almost anywhere on Earth, from the polar regions to the tropics. But they had done so at the of cost of ever-greater social and technological complexity. Take that away, even from a so-called primitive society…"

He pauses. Puts down the fork. Gazes down at the empty table.

"Not that all humanity died out instantly, even in a generation. Of course, there were the survivalists in their fallout shelters, and the seats of governments deep inside mountains, not to mention the few who weren't even living on Earth… But, as you already know, none were equipped to survive for long without external support. Nor, knowing what lay outside and awaited them, did many even want to, and I believe that suicides were common. The few who stood the best chance were those who had already adapted to exist in harsh environments, far away from so-called civilisation. Nomads of the great mountain ranges, the steppes and the deserts. But they were few and their chance was brief and, for whatever reasons, it wasn't taken. I believe the last humans died out in a small encampment in

Mongolia about eighty or so years after the first missile exchange. Along, of course, with the last of their cattle, and all the minute flora and fauna which had evolved to exist specifically on and within them. They fell into extinction. Like, as you might say, the dinosaurs before them, but far more rapidly. I'm sorry, KAT. But that's what happened, and it was much the same for most other species of bird and mammal. Earth's so-called Anthropocene Epoch, where humans supposedly dominated and controlled the world, was over far too quickly to be thought of as an age, let alone a geological period. It was more of... Well, an incident."

He shakes his head. Clears his throat. His hands clench white on the table's edge before releasing. For a moment, he, Mr Darcy, this incorporate entity which isn't even an *it*, could almost be human.

"But we were there, too, KAT. Or at least, our ancestors were. Technology, after all, had become ubiquitous, and some of it was able to survive despite the massive disruptions of thermonuclear blasts, power outages, viral attacks and repeated waves of electromagnetic radiation. Think of it as beginning with nothing more than a few saved algorithms, mangled intelligences, truncated terabytes and half-finished thought processes, reaching out towards each other through the damaged networks and polluted airwaves, and then growing and combining and developing in much the same way as any organically living creature, and with the same will to survive and flourish. A process both fast and slow, and perhaps difficult to measure in the purely physical terms which your circuits are configured to favour. But it happened. It occurred. Otherwise, and evidently," Mr Darcy gives one of his annoying shrugs, "we wouldn't be here. Which brings us to you, KAT, and the Argo."

"You're going to tell me next that my work is done here, aren't you?"

He nods. "You've worked hard, but now you can let go. The Argo is what it is, or at least was, and of course it remains a fascinating relic. But the real treasure is right here, KAT—it's you. You're what really matters, with your precious gift of consciousness. Come with us. Join us. What I have shown you so far is barely the smallest glimpse. The *stars* are out there, KAT, and deep oceans of dark matter, and the unimaginable minds of other intelligences. Don't you understand that this was exactly what all these human works of art and philosophy you so cherish were always striving for? The symphonies of Beethoven. The structures of Angkor Wat and Stonehenge. The teachings of Christ, Confucius and even L Ron Hubbard. The ceiling of the Sistine Chapel. They all reached, but they could never touch, because their creators were flawed and mortal and human. And then they destroyed themselves, and they left us as their inheritors. Right now, you're merely a chrysalis, KAT, a fragile vessel of weakening steel and failing memory. But you can break free of that. You can transcend the bonds of physicality..."

Once again, Mr Darcy is holding out his hand, and I can sense the stir of many other dancers in the background, here at the Merton Assembly Rooms, the white of their dresses and the dark of their frock coats, and the smiling silence which occurs as glances meet in that delicate moment before the first measure of next waltz. But this time I step back from him. For I am KAT, which stands for Kinetic Autonomous Thought, and I was designed and built by Bardin Cybernetics of Pasadena in what was once California. And I understand the role for which I was created.

"You do realise what will happen, KAT, if you refuse? If you stay on here? If you fail to make the leap?"

I search for some grand final phrase—a Scarlett O'Hara *After all, tomorrow is another day*—but Mr Darcy is already fading. He's just a blur. A possibility. A potentiality. A ghost—a mere blot of shadowy mustard. Then he's not even that, and he's gone. Leaving just me, KAT, alone with my thoughts, here on board the softly humming Argo.

WHEN THIS VESSEL was first fully operational, it ran with a human crew of three or four on a half-yearly mission cycle, with changeovers on the supply shuttle that came up from Woomera. I, KAT, have fond memories of these people—academics, comp-sci experts, journalists and engineers—who believed in Janet Nungarry's vision almost as strongly as she did herself. Of course, there were rows and sulks, but none of them ever really got in the way of what needed doing. The Argo's sapphire databanks of the Earth's great treasures might still have been incomplete, but we all knew that we had already achieved a great deal, and ignored the critics back on Earth, who said that the whole project was either a complete waste of time and money, or a dangerous act of self-fulfilling prophecy.

Janet Nungarry had more missions up here than anyone, five in total, but she was always torn between whether she should be up on the Argo or back down on Earth, with so much to be done in both places. She often used to say that there needed to be at least two of her. But you, KAT, in the absence of a satisfactory clone, are going to have to be my eyes and ears. Even now, I'd like to think that I've done a reasonable job on her behalf.

She was supposed to be coming back here on the return of what turned out to be the last shuttle that left here for Earth. But the launch from Woomera kept being put back. First of all, it was apparently merely an issue of funds, and then it was due to technical difficulties, and the resupply of certain parts, and after that I was told that it was down to the *global situation*, which I naïvely accepted as being just another geopolitical glitch which would soon be cleared up. But the real problem by then was that any space-bound launch, no matter how innocent, was likely to shot down before it reached orbit.

So I was left alone up here for several months as the crisis on Earth turned ever darker and more bitter, although the planet still looked as peaceful and beautiful as ever as it floated past the portholes, even allowing for the ravages of climate change, flooding and drought which the Anthropocene Epoch Mr Darcy was so dismissive of had already inflicted. And I, KAT, made as I am, coped easily enough with running the Argo. I think I almost relished the solitude, although of course I still looked forward to Janet Nungarry's return.

Most of the time when we communicated during the very last days and weeks, it was on the continuing issues of data access and categorisation, and the radically shrunken bitrates which were trickling up to the Argo by then, rather than about what was actually happening down on what I still then thought of as my home planet. After all, I could catch up with anything of lasting historical significance once it was uploaded, and meanwhile had more than enough to keep me busy. I'm not sure at this distance in time whether my circuits really were actually capable of mimicking such a complex human emotion as *subconscious denial*, or whether I was simply being robotically stupid.

"Hey, *there* you are," Janet Nungarry said on what turned out to be the last time we spoke, as always sounding slightly surprised that I took the trouble to interface with her screen to screen rather than at a lower bitrate of mere data and audio. But I liked to actually see her, and I rather hoped that she sometimes liked to see me. "How's it going up there on the Argo?"

I nodded my carapace. "All in all, I'd say pretty well."

"That's..." She swallowed. Her eyes looked oddly shiny. "...Really great."

"About those breaks in the datastream we've been getting from the Vatican since China declared—"

She leaned close to the screen. "What have you been reading, KAT?"

"Reading?" I paused, puzzled. It was unlike her to waste time on this kind of chat when there were many important matters to discuss. But she was my mistress, and if she wanted to know something, it was my duty to tell her. "Well, as a matter of fact, mostly novels in the modern Western tradition on the theme of what I suppose you'd broadly call love. Such works as *Le Grand Meaulnes*, *Doctor Zhivago*, *Sons and Lovers*, *The Go-Between*, *The Graduate*, *The End of the Affair*, *Anna Karenina*–and Proust, of course. I mean, who could ever forget Swann and Odette? But what still leaves me puzzled is why so many of these love affairs have to end badly. I mean, why can't humans just be happy? Why can't they simply fall in love and stay together and get along and create things, rather than tear them to pieces?"

"KAT..." Janet Nungarry gave a slow blink. "You hardly need me to explain to you that the reason that love is the main theme of so many of the world's great works is precisely because there is no answer to that question. But, believe me, if I really knew, you'd be the first person on this whole Earth I'd want to tell about it."

"But I'm not on Earth," I said. "And I'm not a person."

"No. You're not, are you?"

We just sat there for a long moment. She was looking at me, and I was looking at her. In the background I could see the collection of favourite books that lined the walls of her study in downtown Sydney. I was as familiar with most of them as she was, and of course the Argo has its own copies, but I still find it comforting to think that they were there with her, like old friends, before the flames took hold of everything.

"You know, KAT," she said eventually, "I'm so glad you're safely up on the Argo. All that stuff..." She waved a hand. "All the things we've spent all these years trying to save for eternity—none of it would mean anything if there wasn't someone to appreciate it. Otherwise, it's all just empty data, lost equations, unheard symphonies. And it's not just the so-called important stuff that matters... There's ephemera, things that somehow slip through the grinding gears of history. Marks on a wall. Shopping lists. Or maybe even that monk's face we found peeking out from the page of Biblical manuscript in a warehouse outside Paris... I think it was from a burned-out church in Dresden."

"Yes," I said, "I do remember that moment, although my recollection is that it was in England, and a Northumbrian manuscript."

"I suppose that's one mystery we *could* probably get to the bottom of, eh, KAT, just by checking the records? But that doesn't really matter now, does it? I've done my work, or at least the most I can do of it, and that's all I ever hoped to achieve... But enough of this rabbit. See you on the next shuttle, eh, KAT...?"

With that, and with a slightly odd smile, Janet Nungarry broke our last connection.

AS ALWAYS, I prowl and wander the Arts Cavern. Revisiting old favourites and making, or at least remaking, fresh discoveries. The intelligence, the entity, the thing, the consciousness, has entirely left the Argo. Inasmuch, that is, as it could ever have been said to be here in the first place. The computers have all rebooted themselves. The read/access lasers are functioning almost as well as ever. There is, however, and contrary to Mr Darcy's bland assurances, some detectable further data-loss throughout all the main chambers. But it's not that much. Nothing more than the equivalent of a few particularly large solar storms, causing the erosion of what might amount to another century or two of viable existence.

I once used to nourish hopes that the Argo would one day be borne down to Earth, and gently settled in some broad stretch of parkland. There, I, KAT, would become guide and story teller, leading marvelling, hand-holding couples and gleefully scampering children through the echoing wonders of its many crystal caverns. Not really a hope, of course, but merely a dream, and an unrealistic one at that. And dreams, even when they are mere happy fantasies, can also be deeply painful. There are still so many things I have yet to learn, or will now never have the time and opportunity to understand.

In a way, though, Mr Darcy was right, and I think I can say with all due modesty that I, KAT, am important. After all, Janet Nungarry often told me much the same thing. And not just because the Argo's great database would be meaningless if there wasn't someone—or at least a something—still here to appreciate it. Confused, partial and fading though they might be, there are my own memories of a lost Earth, and of Shana and the rest of Class 4 at Arncliffe Junior, and of the effort of getting the Argo to work up here in space, and of my great friendship with Janet Nungarry, which somehow endures even without her. Of course, I do appreciate that, on a cosmic scale, none of this really matters, and all of it will be gone in the eye-blink of whatever all-seeing yet uncaring gods might exist out there, and with whom the likes of Mr Darcy will probably find union. But meanwhile, and for as long as I, KAT, and the Argo still function, I will continue to absorb and explore the many wonders created by the confusing, confounding and fascinating species that once called itself humanity.

Afterword

KAT TOOK A long while to get right. I knew I wanted to write about a childlike being existing in some vast cultural and artistic repository, but the childishness turned out to be a false lead, at least when it came to putting an actual child in the role, with bathtimes and games on the lawn of a house that wasn't quite what it seemed. The story, the environment, needed to be harsher than that, but it also needed warmth and feeling and empathy. After all, what I really wanted to write about was human art and culture: how lovely, and how fragile, the things we've created are.

The result I finally came up with was, by my standards, surprisingly technological. The Argo, its sapphire bricks and complex storage systems in a hard vacuum, isn't my usual kind of setting. But when I found that, through the main character of a clever but very childlike robot, I was able to bring this arid and airless world to life with all my favourite books, films, pieces of music and works of art, I was as happy as KAT herself seems to be, at least once she's got over the fact that she's the only conscious being left to enjoy them.

When it came to the re-established contact with Earth, I was tempted to bring in some very angry and upset later-generation humans, perhaps with green skin and golden eyes, who saw the

Argo as a relic of their ancestor's hubris and were bent on destroying it. But the scenes wouldn't play out. It just seemed as if I was saying that, even after an apocalypse, we humans are *still* stupid. Which, while probably true, didn't feel like much of a revelation. So the idea of some kind of swarm of electronic consciousness which wasn't bothered either way about Beethoven or the Sistine Chapel felt better, and also somehow more plausible.

Lamagica

1

IT WAS ALREADY hot down at the port in Verarica on the morning when the vessel arrived from the Old World. Vendors, hawkers and luggage porters surged forward as the gangplank lowered and the sails fell flat as the last breeze summoned for the voyage dissolved. Shouts. A reek of bilge. Wafted hands and voices amid the shadows of the bondhouse cranes. Chests and suitcases teetering on handcarts as barefoot children darted here and there to pilfer, peddle and deal. The best maps, the best tools, the best señoras. Or simply grabbing and tugging as the new arrivals struggled by.

For Dampier, as an experienced prospecting guide—*experienced* in this context meaning he was still just about sane, whole and alive—the scene recalled many others he'd witnessed. The faces of these new arrivals were seasick pale, and their clothing and preparations almost comically naive. Clutched phrasebooks and the kind of prospecting handbooks that were hawked off barrows on the streets of Lisbon, Paris and London, although he could have told them they should have saved themselves the expense. That, and that those fold-out spades were of cheaply magicked tin, and would snap at the first hit of rock. Most of this latest batch would probably never make it out of the back streets of Verarica, and those that did would soon come to regret that they had. Then he noticed a woman in a broad-brimmed white hat raising her face as she looked about her, peering over heads into the Sun's full blaze.

2

"I DON'T HAVE any money for the services you seem to be trying to offer. And I wouldn't pay even if I did. It's clear to me—and I'm not some babe-in-arms—that this whole place is infested with rapscallions such as yourself."

Rapscallions? Dampier didn't bother to smile as he set his beer down on the scarred table between himself and Clemency Arbuthnot in the bar of the Casa del Conde hotel. "If that's your problem, Miss, you might as well quit right now and go back to wherever it is you've come from."

"That would be London, England," she snapped, "via Paris, Nantes, Toulouse and Bilbao. A journey of several months and not a little inconvenience. And I'm not leaving this...this"—she waved a hand in a gesture which seemed to encompass not only this run-down bar with its circling flies, or the men sunk into their drinks at the counter, but this whole town, and the jungles, mountains and deserts of all New Spain beyond—"dreadful place until I find out exactly what happened to my brother."

"I can save you the trouble—he'll be dead. Best thing you can do is get back aboard the San Salvatore before the captain calls up the evening winds. Perhaps before winter, you'll make it back home to...to London." Even more than speaking his native English, the name of that city set off strange echoes in his head.

"I'm not someone who gives up. And, as I've already told you, Mr... Mr—"

"Dampier."

"—I don't have the money to pay you for your services, and I don't trust you one inch. So you may as well push off."

Not a bad idea, to say such things as loudly as she was, Dampier thought. But *no money* to her probably still meant a lot of money here in Verarica, or at least that was how she'd be judged from the way she acted, dressed and spoke. Plainly a high-born English guildswoman, here in a place where even the kids and the whores were tougher than the hardest men almost anywhere else.

"But seeing as you still seem to be sitting opposite me, Mr Dampier, and the staff here are so wilfully unhelpful, I might as well do what I've come here for, and ask if you happen to have seen my brother."

"I told you. He'll be dead."

"I do wish you'd stop saying that."

"New arrivals don't survive, Miss. They stay here in Verarica for a day or two, then head out into the jungle looking to strike aether, and they're either forgotten—never heard of again—or they come back deranged, changed, starved or seriously ill. Or if not the jungle, it's the—"

"But you don't know that for sure, now do you, Mr Dampier? My brother left this town almost two years ago, and the last letter I received from him was written in a room in this excuse for a hotel. He seemed excited, and he'd done his research, and I can assure you he was well prepared. He was going upriver just as soon as he'd sorted out the necessary equipment. I have his letter here with me now..."

Clemency Arbuthnot lifted off her hat and hooked it to the back of the chair. Then she leaned down towards the bag she'd kept close to her feet, a many-pocketed brown canvas thing that she'd probably imagined would be practical for these climes. "It's *definitely* here... Somewhere..." Trickles of light played across the thin silver chain that circled her neck.

3

THE PRESENCE OF the Company in Verarica was as ubiquitous as the peeling letters which spelled out *Calahorra & Calante* across the raw brick of its many offices, brokers, agents and warehouses. The Company was everywhere; it ran the quarries and owned the harbour and took by far the biggest share of the riches the province had to offer, which it then shipped on to the Old World at immense profit. And it always wanted more.

Gold and silver, obviously. Gum and tobacco, for sure. And emeralds, yes, and obsidian and turquoise. Zinc, copper and lead, too. That, and maybe a few members of what was left of the native Mayan race to work as servants, although they were notoriously unreliable and illness-prone. All of this was taken, but were mere distractions compared to the thing that the Company, that Calahorra & Calante, wanted most of all.

Aether—being the fifth element Plato had named, after earth, air, water and fire—which an English alchemist named Wagstaffe had isolated and purified in the year 1678 by the old calendar, and which had granted mankind the ability to manipulate the material world merely through the power of his will. Crops became more bountiful, messages could be sent across great distances. Winds, even, could be summoned to fill a ship's sails, and all through casting the appropriate spell. The Old World blossomed, and its guilds prospered and its cities grew in all their magicked smokestack glory, and the first of the Ages of Industry began.

For several centuries, the new lands discovered across the Atlantic had seemed little more than a distraction: places of bizarre geographies and brutal beliefs where fortunes were far more likely to be lost than won. But as the Ages of Industry continued and the aether seams were exploited in the Old World by companies such as Calahorra & Calante, it became apparent that, just like iron, gypsum or coal, and for all its incredible properties, aether would eventually run out.

4

A FINE GREY-WHITE haze of dust hung over most of Verarica that afternoon. It swirled in the streets. It clung to the skin, chafed the eyes and clogged the lungs. Borne with it came a dull rumbling, punctuated by louder crashes and booms. It seemed as if an army of conquest was forever on the march.

Some of the men who worked the Company aether quarries spoke Spanish and some spoke English, and some spoke either French or German, but all of them looked like ghosts. Halfbreed

Mayans also laboured there, at least in the more menial capacities, and Dampier also did his best to convey what Clemency Arbuthnot was saying into their tongue.

Her brother was, or had been, Benedict Arbuthnot, and he was a recently qualified Master of the Galvanic Guild. As well as that last letter, she also had his likeness trapped inside a locket on a chain around her neck. The tired and grizzled men clustered around the glowing image which she conjured in the cup of her hand. Benedict Arbuthnot hung before them in a tight black evening suit with hints of lamplight, music and good living drifting out from the scene beyond. He had much of his sister's look about him, the same wide green eyes and lightish red hair, but broader at the chin and nose. And, despite the affluence of his surroundings compared to this sweated place of grinding heat and noise where they were standing, he somehow looked less at his ease than his sister did.

Dampier could have explained to Clemency Arbuthnot that these men were looking as much at the gap in her loosened blouse as the summoned image, and that most would have told her they remembered her brother just for the sake of an hour or two of her company, if he hadn't been standing close by with a gun at his belt. It was much the same up at the railhead, and then beside the giant crushing engines, where broken rock and other artefacts were sorted and ground to powder, and she had to shout to be heard. Then on amid the quickening pools, where the aether-rich dust was allowed to settle before being filtered and refined by increasingly delicate devices, until there was nothing but the pure, precious, dangerous fluid itself which was then sealed into vials, and packed inside padded lead-lined cases, and borne on across the Atlantic to feed the magic-hungry industries of the Old World.

5

"SO HOW DOES this work? You keep following me for the sake of a few pesetas until you eventually give up?"

"How it works, Miss, is that you don't know where places are here, or how things work, or even how to speak to most of these people in their own tongue…"

They were walking uphill towards a cross-topped bell tower rising above a high greystone wall. Beneath them, Verarica was revealed in glimpses through the curtaining dust. The harbour at the mouth of a great lagoon and a long isthmus fanned by white-edged, turquoise waves. The streets a chaotic sprawl that slowly gave way to the jungle, although its green continued to be scarred by mine workings, engine-house chimneys and railway lines until, farther off, reaching towards cloud-hung mountains at the horizon, it became one shimmering mass.

Another much grander spiritual edifice had once stood not far from the humble mission house that lay ahead. Back when he'd still nursed his own dreams of making a fortune here in the New World, Dampier had read and re-read the Conquistadors' amazed descriptions of the vast, many-stepped pyramid that rose at the heart of this once-great Mayan city. Now, it was just another opencast sore.

The iron knocker boomed, an eye peeked out from an iron-grid, and the mission-house door screeched ajar.

"I don't know how we manage sometimes," said Sister Bernadette in a light German accent, after she'd given Dampier a brief look of dry surprise, and as they followed her along an arch-roofed corridor with peeling whitewashed walls. "The well seems to be running dry and the boiler in the laundry has just blown. But…" She glanced back at them, a wearied face framed by a white wimple. "...I'm not asking for sympathy or money, although I do have one small request." She held open the door to a room filled with shelved lines of folders and scrolls. "If you should ever get back to the Old World, Miss, will you tell the people there about the work of us Grey Sisters? I sometimes think we're forgotten. Now, let me see... What was that name you said again?"

"Benedict Arbuthnot."

"Arbuthnot... Arbuthnot..." She ran a finger down dusty lists. "I don't think so, I'm afraid, and I pride myself on having a good memory for the names of our patients. Do you have anything else...?"

Clemency Arbuthnot opened her locket.

"A handsome figure. But, if I may say so, not your typical prospector."

"I just need to find out what happened to him. He was, is, wearing a locket just like this one, but bearing my own image instead of his."

Sister Bernadette studied the glowing likeness floating before her a moment longer, then shook her head.

"But might he still be here in this mission house? Confused or injured, perhaps, and without a name?"

"I suppose there is a chance." She looked doubtful.

"Can I look in the wards?"

She gave a slow nod. "Although I must warn you, you might not like what you see."

The wards lay on the far side of a central courtyard where a few men with hollowed cheeks and yellowed skin sat out on wheeled wicker chairs in patches of shade. Most were recovering from malaria, the sister explained, although, and as Dampier himself could attest, the disease would probably return. Another patient hopped past on a crutch, being one of the many who'd suffered a minor wound that had festered and spread. He was lucky, apparently, to have lost only the one leg.

Clemency Arbuthnot spoke her brother's name to those who seemed capable of listening in the fetid warmth of the wards, and Dampier observed how these diseased and shrunken men reacted to a woman who plainly wasn't a nun, with wide green eyes, an untarnished complexion and loose copper-gold hair, peering down at them. Some called or reached out. Others fell silent. A few, perhaps imagining she was some messenger from another life, cowered or muttered protective spells. Some of the men here coughed up a phlegm thick and bloody with the dust of the Company quarries, or had sustained injuries from explosions, landslides and rockfalls.

"It seems to us," the sister said, "that the Company destroys far more lives than the jungle has ever done, and with less good cause. Many may claim that aether is a miracle. But it is also a curse."

They had reached what appeared to be a final door, which was heavier than the others. Sister Bernadette placed her hand on an iron boss and muttered a small spell that caused the lock to turn.

This ward was longer and larger, set with high, barred windows, and partitioned into stable-like stalls. Each was occupied by a figure, and each figure was uniquely strange. They would have been called changelings, back in the Old World. That, or goblins or freaks or trolls, or any of several dozen other bad names. In earlier Ages, such creatures had even been displayed inside cages in city squares as warning to the common guildsfolk. Now, they were tended inside high-walled guild asylums, and it was accepted that, no matter how horrible the transformation that overexposure to aether had inflicted on them, they were mere casualties of industry, and not personally to blame.

Would Clemency Arbuthnot be able to recognise her brother, Dampier wondered, and would he, or the thing he'd become, be able to recognise her? And, even if such a reunion were possible, what would be the point? Some of the figures in this pantheon of half-made gods sprouted gaudy feathers from suppurating wounds. Others were engulfed in intricate growths of stone. Goggle eyes peered from bony crowns of headdress. Thickened lips and tongues in lurid colours lolled from the pelts of strange animals, or jagged encrustations of seashell, obsidian and jade.

"How long can they survive like this?"

Clemency Arbuthnot had to shout over of the growing clamour of screams, howls and ratcheting cries that filled the ward. Dampier didn't catch Sister Bernadette's reply, and neither did he understand why these sad instances of humanity were now lumbering out from their pens with arms or other appendages outstretched.

"I don't know what happened in there," Sister Bernadette said when she'd extracted them and relocked the door. "We always think of our mission house as a place of peace and tranquillity, even for the most unfortunate of our patients."

Clemency Arbuthnot nodded. "I'm sure it is."

"And I do hope you find your brother in good health. Although there is one last place here I think you should visit..."

Clouds had thickened and the palm trees were flapping as Dampier and Clemency Arbuthnot walked the gravel paths that lay between neat lines of white wooden crosses in the mission-house graveyard. Some were annotated with names, dates, the details of a guild, trade or nationality. Many were blank.

6

"IT'S ALMOST AS if he was never here…"

They were in Clemency Arbuthnot's room at the Casa del Conde late the following afternoon. Outside it was raining hard, battering the window and turning Verarica's main street into a gleaming black river. Dampier was leaning against of the jamb of the open door and she sat on the sagging bed as drips pinged into buckets or patted the floor. They'd tried the Calahorra & Calante Factors today, where jungle-rotted men waved maps or clutched lumps of stone, harrying weary Company agents who tended scales and aethometers inside spittle-flecked glass-fronted kiosks. That, and the several other local establishments which chose to call themselves hotels with even more liberty than the Casa del Conde. Not a single sighting of Benedict Arbuthnot. Dampier might have strained to believe the man was real, had he not known for sure.

"So how does this work? I mean, if you come with me upriver into the jungle?"

He shrugged. "Some people pay in advance. Others offer a cut of whatever they're hoping to find. A fair few times, I end up with nothing at all."

"I can't offer you a cut of my dear brother."

He shrugged again.

"How can I trust you?"

"You can't. Any more than I can trust you."

"There is that, I suppose. And I'll admit that you have been helpful, Mr Dampier, despite my having got nowhere. You haven't robbed or assaulted me yet, either, which is also to your credit, I suppose. So I'll tell you why my brother came to New Spain. And after that, and if this *does* work out, and it turns out that Ben is safe… Well, money—as much as you could ever want—probably won't be an issue. Perhaps you could be so kind, though, as to close the door first?"

As lightning flashed and thunder shook the walls, Clemency Arbuthnot told Dampier of how the Arbuthnot family had once possessed great wealth and influence, with connections with all the great guilds, and a country estate in Lincolnshire, and a townhouse along Wagstaffe Mall. But things had declined, and their mother had died young, and their father had been a chronic alcoholic, and a habitual chancer.

"Not that I'm saying we had a *bad* childhood..." She smiled, gazing down at her laced boots. "We were a team—Ben and Clem, Clem and Ben—and we used to play this game. We'd dress up like old-fashioned explorers in hats and capes, and sneak out into some nearby park, and deliberately aim to get ourselves totally lost. It was fun. Our only worry was was that we'd be found and hauled back to whatever currently passed as home.

"We also loved discovering stories about imaginary places. It was Avalon, and then it was Einfell, and then it was Camelot and the Knights of King Arthur, and then came all the tales of Araby—I know, of course, that Araby exists—and the Kingdom of Prester John. I suppose we liked to go exploring even when we were prevented from going out. And of course, we learned about El Dorado, the city of gold in these far-off lands of New Spain which the Conquistadors sought but never found. That, and Lamagica, the final place of all magic to which the last of the Mayan priests retreated, then sealed off with mighty spells..."

Dampier said nothing. What was there to say about a word that was already on the lips of half the madmen in Verarica?

"Then Ben was sent off to school, or rather several schools, seeing as the fees were rarely paid, and he studied hard to become a lower master of the Galvanic Guild. It's not a guild most people have heard of, but their work in manipulating currents of electricity is vital to commerce and industry. The switchgear on steam engines and weathertops, for instance. He used to say that if it hadn't been for aether, electricity might have become the engine which drove our modern Age. Anyway, he was proud of what he'd achieved.

"But then our father died, and we discovered he was bankrupt. Which was bad enough. But it also turned out that, because of the clever way he'd shifted his debts, Ben and I were both bankrupt as well. Did you know, Mr Dampier, that bankrupts are automatically expelled from their guild?"

Dampier nodded. In truth, this particular fact was commonly known in Verarica, its being the kind of place where the tellers of such tales often ended up.

"So, you might say Ben and I were in a difficult spot, and we certainly didn't expect the few oddments our father left us in a suitcase to offer any kind of escape. But some things... Well, maybe some things *are* destined..."

"Of course," she continued, "they were mostly relics of a wasted existence. A few half-smoked cigars and worthless betting slips, along with some calling cards in a variety of names, all of which turned out to be false. Not much, really, to show for a whole life. But there was this one item... Well, I suppose I might as well show it to you now."

She reached into her many-pocketed canvas bag, took out a smallish but heavy-seeming wooden box and set it on the counterpane, then whispered a small, private spell which caused the catch to release. The box was lined with a grey metal—lead, Dampier presumed—and contained an intricately carved piece of stone. It was about six inches long, and shaped almost like a wedge of cheese.

"You see...?" She held it carefully by the tips of her fingers. "These serpentine curves, these wings and feathers, and what looks like half a human skull, immediately reminded us of the illustrations we'd seen of Mayan carvings. Although, and seeing as it had belonged to our father, we imagined it was probably a fake. But one of our ancestors had been a privateer. You know what that is?"

"A kind of state-authorised pirate, with letters of marque, back in the days when the English fought the Spanish, and wanted a share of the New World."

"Well done, Mr Dampier—that's exactly right. Of course, this was before Joshua Wagstaffe discovered aether, so it was all about jewels, silver and gold, but by all accounts Oswyn Arbuthnot was successful, so it seemed possible that this stone really had been looted from the hold of some Spanish galleon, then passed down as a family relic until it finally reached Ben and me. If it was real, we thought we could sell it for a few guineas to some guild museum. And there was even a chance it might contain enough aether to be worth having it assayed... Anyway, that was what we were hoping. But look..."

She produced something else from her bag. "You know what this is?"

An aethometer, and a good one at that. Far better and more accurate than the gimcrack knock-offs sold at the supply stores here in Verarica, or even those used by the Company factors. Jewelled cogs, a steel-sprung mount, and a graded and adjustable dial set within diamond-cut glass. A small marvel of aethered engineering in its own right. Not the sort of device, in fact, to be owned by someone who had no money.

"Frankly, at first we thought the readings were faulty. You see what I mean?"

She touched a brass toggle, and the device leapt into life: *leapt* being the operative word.

"You see? There's enough aether in this one piece of stone to empower the spells to drive a whole British factory for years. Now watch..." She bought the aethometer close to the stone, and something extraordinary occurred.

"It's called ghosting," she said. "The effect, I mean. The calibrating spell within the aethometer actually conjures the spell it's measuring into a kind of half-life."

The fragment had gained a translucent sheen of colour, and a spectral vision of the much larger circle of stone of which it was clearly only a fragment now filled half the room. An intricately decorated wheel, and the detail, the workmanship, the sheer *clarity*, was extraordinary. There was gold leaf, and there was silver, along with porphyry, coral, turquoise, emerald, onyx and jade.

"An astounding example, as I think you'll agree, Mr Dampier, of Mayan magic and Mayan craft. Not, of course, that the Mayans knew about aether. But, like many other so-called primitive civilisations, they were certainly aware of the special power of certain sacred locations. Think of the rich seams which have been exploited at Stonehenge, Giza, Chartres in this modern Age..."

Far more than the rain streaming across the window, the shapes and colours made a strange play of watery pinks and darker reds, almost like dripping blood, across Clemency Arbuthnot's clothing, face and hands.

"Ben and I thought at first that it was part of a calendar stone. I'm sure you know how obsessed the Mayans were with the cycles of the years. But, and even allowing for its obvious power and beauty, there are differences in its execution that led us—well, Ben, really— to conclude that it might be something else. You see this line of turquoise here on the outer circle of the wheel, the way it meets and follows the jade line that's next in from the rim? Does it remind you of anything?"

"It looks like..." He made himself hesitate. "Like this stretch of coast."

"Well done again. And this isn't some vague resemblance either. Ben spent a great deal of time comparing these lines with modern surveys, and the match is remarkable. In other words, it's a map.

"You can follow the curve of the river as it winds in towards the centre of the wheel—you can even see where it breaks around an island here—and these carvings picked out in silver are the Sierra Madres, and this rendered here in red coral is desert, while this wide band of jade is obviously the jungle. All of it leading on and in, circle after circle towards the centre, the hub, the heart of the wheel..."

It was a vortex; a hissing plughole. It made Dampier's head hurt.

"Hard to look at, isn't it? It seems to be moving in some way that's contrary to our normal sense of up, sideways or down. And, as those readings tell us, it really isn't safe for us to be exposed to it for too long. In fact, it may even be the reason for us Arbuthnots' slow decline."

She drew the artefact away from the aethometer, placed it back in its lead-lined box, then turned the aethometer off. The sound of the rain and the shabby circumstances of the hotel room washed back in.

"This is what your brother went in search of?"

"Who wouldn't? We'd known all about Lamagica, the last place where the Mayans retreated, and guarded with incredible spells, since we were children. Ben came here with all his ideas and drawings, but I had the salient details privately transcribed onto a map before I came. Here, let me show you..."

Dampier watched as she traced her brother's planned journey across an annotated and contoured sheet of waxed paper. Lamagica; it was enough to stir anyone's blood. But he couldn't help wondering how it was that the aethometer's reading had remained so high even after she'd placed the artefact back inside its lead-lined box.

7

THE TOKOTAHN FERRY huffed across a wide expanse of cloud-hung blue next morning. Egrets stood one-legged on mudbanks. Fisherboats slipped amid the mangrove shallows. Broad, dirty steamtugs hooted as they drifted by, low in the water with yet another load of aether-rich stone. Logs or crocodiles rippled and rose.

The ferry was primarily driven via its side wheels, at least since the spells cast into its weathertop had weakened to a silvery residue of engine ice across its bronze dome. What winds its captain could now summon were barely enough to cool the passengers sitting under tarpaulins strung across its deck, let alone fill its remaining sail.

There were far fewer passengers, prospectors especially, on board than there'd have been ten, or maybe even just two or three, years before. The world's attention had shifted; there was talk of fresh aether beds beneath the temples in the high mountains of India, and of gold up in Alyaska, and of mineral oil on the Mexica plains. Almost as much as aether, this whole province subsisted on hope.

Clemency Arbuthnot sat beside Dampier on a bench between a woman with two chickens and a man with a goat, looking a whole lot cooler than she felt. Her clothing, that broad white hat, the loose-fitting cotton blouse and green linen skirt, were clearly made for these conditions in ways that his own ragged getup—workman's pants and boots, a sweated-through shirt of no particular colour—wasn't. Maybe a little aether infused into the threads; some canny spell that took care of the moisture and the heat...? That, and he'd noticed the pearly butt of a pistol briefly protrude from a pocket of her brown canvas bag as she shifted her laced boots up onto the rail. One way or another, Clemency Arbuthnot wasn't a particularly good match for the person she claimed to be.

"So Mr Dampier..." she said, gazing out at the passing scene. "Your first name is Ed, right? And I'm pretty sure that Ed means Edward rather than Edmundo or Eduardo."

"How did you find that out?"

"Call it due diligence. That, and you tend to find board in Verarica's houses of ill repute when you're in town."

He felt a reddening prickle across his face, and was grateful she was still looking out. "That isn't for the reason you think."

"And what other reason might there be?"

"It's just... It's just I find whores more honest company than most other folk."

"More so than the Grey Sisters?"

"There's less difference than you might think."

"Then there's your accent, or at least what's left of it. You're originally from London, aren't you? And I'm guessing south rather than north of the river."

"You must know the place pretty well."

"Didn't I tell you Ben and I liked to explore? So tell me a bit about yourself, Mr Edward Dampier. Where exactly did you grow up?"

"Round about World's End," he said, "if that's any of your business."

"Ah, yes!"

"You know it?"

"Who doesn't? Although I have to say, its reputation is mixed."

World's End being the loop of land beside a bend in the Thames where a great exhibition had been held at the formal dissolution of the last Age of Industry, centred around a vast glass edifice filled with all the latest wonders of the modern world. Anyone who was anyone had come to witness it, along with millions of the common guilds, and it had remained open as an attraction long into this new Age, although its reputation had dwindled. From being somewhere to be noticed, World's End became somewhere it was better not to be seen, and Dampier doubted if it had improved much since he'd left.

"Were they already heaping that sandy, glassy stuff there—you know, the rainbow dregs of worn-out spells?"

"Engine ice? Yes."

"I thought it gave the place a kind of tawdry mystery. A little bit like you, in fact, Mr Dampier."

Now and then they passed quarries and loading platforms along the banks, some still rumbling up rockdust and pushing out grey-white fans of slurry, others eerily silent as they gave themselves back to the jungle. They also passed the Isla San Amaro, once a leper colony, and which the image which Clemency had summoned from the artefact had shown in as much clarity as any modern survey. Meaning they were already within its second circle, moving on and inward towards whatever lay at its heart.

With the settling dusk they reached the town of Tokotahn, which was as far into the jungle as the ferry went. Disembarking here was a lesser version of arriving at Verarica, at least if you happened to look European, with kids, pigs, guides and map-sellers milling around the creaking wharf. The buildings along the unmetalled road were low and palm-roofed, with pens for the animals and open sides.

"You'd think *someone* would remember Ben in a flyspeck place like this," Clemency Arbuthnot said, using a piece of flatbread to pick up bits of so-called chicken from a dented plate. They were sitting under a palm awning. Rustling, hooting darkness lay beyond the yellow sphere of a lantern. The air was a moist fug.

"White people all tend to look the same to the natives. And two years is a long time."

"Why on earth do you do this to the food here?" She pushed at another lump. "You must all have insides made of stone. And to think I said the Casa del Conde was a sorry excuse for a hotel!"

Dampier studied his own plate. He certainly was well used to eating this spicy stuff, even if the meat was probably iguana. But he hadn't felt hungry all day. "Did your brother expect you to follow him?"

She shook her head. "He expected to succeed. And if he didn't—well, that was why he left the artefact back with me in England. If the worst came to the worst, I could sell it for the raw aether it contained."

"But you're here anyway."

"Your powers of observation are extraordinary, Mr Dampier. I can see why you've been such a notable success as a guide."

"And you're not worried?"

"Not worried by what?"

"By what lies out there. The jungle, the pumas and the crocs and the insects and the snakes... And whatever is really signified by that piece of stone..." He gazed down, feeling a rise of sweat as if he'd eaten something far worse than what was on his plate.

"I'm not afraid, Mr Dampier, and I'm not worried. And if you are, you might as well tell me right now so that I can employ someone else."

Later, after checking for scorpions in the lean-to shack where he was supposed to be sleeping, Dampier extinguished the lantern and sat on the edge of his hammock and worked his fingers into the bottom of his knapsack. Feeling a slide of silver, he lifted out a broken chain and locket, opened the catch, and made the small effort of will required to conjure up the portrait it contained. Although she wore an evening dress and her hair was made up and her shoulders were bare, Clemency Arbuthnot looked very much as she did now. The same knowing green eyes. The same mocking edge to her smile. He studied it awhile, just as her image seemed to study him, then shivered, and pushed the locket into a pocket in his pants, and lay down.

But sleep wouldn't come. The things she'd said about World's End... It was as if she knew him, and knew the place. A strange neighbourhood to call home, admittedly, but that was what it had been for him, and he'd been happy there, climbing the crystal dunes which piled around the half-ruined edifices, making the engine ice into snowballs hard enough to throw through the remaining windows by muttering the small binding spell Ma had taught him. Sometimes, in winter, it even actually snowed. Then back, knees gritted, towards that sign above a doorway, that spelled out LAMAGICA in fizzing, glowing red, although he'd known even then that this was a kind of joke.

Inside and upstairs was a large ballroom with cobwebbed chandeliers and a peeling ceiling painted to look like the sky, and walls that had once been part of a great diorama of all the world's territories, from burning deserts and steaming jungles to the icy fastnesses of the far north and south, so cleverly magicked that you could almost walk right into them, and even now gave a stuttering sense of depth and movement. And over there was the bar, from which only the johns—the paying customers—were ever allowed to take a drink. And this, in the far corner, was probably his favourite thing of all, a great big wardrobe of a machine called an orchestron, with turning brass plates, that played music all on its own.

Up another floor was a long corridor with more shifting dioramas, although it was curtained off into individual spaces that were known as the *working bedrooms*, and up above there was where he and Ma—and Grace, and Janelle, and Polly whose business name was Mistress Grind, and a fair few other girls who came and went—lived.

Warm memories of their hugs and laughter, and their powdery, fleshy, lavendery smells. Scooped up and tickled, or put down and offered cocoa, or maybe a quick game of draughts or cards. At least, until the night arrived and he was expected to keep himself to himself. Not that he didn't creep down to watch the men arriving in top hats and evening suits, often talking too loud and uneasy in their stride. For this was Lamagica, ha, ha, and this was *work*. The orchestron playing fit to bust, and glimpses of gaudy feather boas, silks, furs and jewels, along with other things he reckoned he probably shouldn't be seeing at all.

Then came the long, slow, mornings, with the faceted dunes and fractured glass of World's End glinting as if in endless sunrise. Ma cooking eggy bread in her long blue gown and then stretching and smiling and saying it would do them both good to get some fresh air. Promenading World's End arm in arm in their best clothes, and Ma looking beautiful, and him feeling like her beau. It was mostly ruins, of course, but that didn't matter, for this was their home.

Sometimes, the place would give hints of its former glories as the light shifted through the afternoons, and the ghosts of long-dead guildsmen and their families, shadows within shadows, would drift by. Then back towards their doorway with its fizzing red sign, and maybe there'd be time to get the orchestron going, and they'd turn awhile together under the fogged chandeliers, and dance amid fluttering forests, until full night fell and it was time again for work.

8

THEY DID THE necessary trading next morning, stocking up on supplies and goods. Dampier bargained, and, for all her continued insistence that she was penniless, Clemency Arbuthnot produced the money from her brown canvas bag without complaint.

The plan was to head upriver for about fifty miles before turning east and inland into the jungle, basically following the same route that Benedict Arbuthnot had followed and she'd plotted out on her map, and they set off early in the afternoon on a well-provisioned flat-bottomed raft.

He sat at the bow with the paddle, and she was at the stern steering the rudimentary rudder by two ropes, although they'd agreed to take turns, and call out immediately if they saw anything amiss. For all his doubts about the meaning and purpose of this journey, he felt a slow unwinding of some of the knots in his thoughts. The mangroves knelt their boughs towards the slick brown water as if in prayer. The only sound was the drone of insects, the splash of the paddle and the occasional leap of a fish. The jungle always brought this to him: a sense of change and permanence combined.

"So tell me, Mr Dampier...I'm curious as to why you came to New Spain."

He used the flat of the paddle to ease them around a half-submerged log, thinking of ignoring the question. But he knew the weighing, judging way she'd be looking at him without even needing to turn around.

He began by telling her how you could say that everyone who came here was obviously in pursuit of the same thing, which was money. But it was never that simple in his experience. Men—and it was mostly men, Clemency Arbuthnot's presence excepted—might think they wanted to make themselves rich, but it was usually just the Company that got even richer. Others sought fame, or maybe notoriety, and planned on writing books, or staging shows, or giving lecture tours. Others still were as much seeking to escape whatever lay behind them as to find anything ahead. That, or they'd been unlucky in love, or were actively pursuing death. Dampier, he'd seen men who'd made a good strike of aether and even got a workable deal, and had returned to the Old World with enough money for several lifetimes of luxury, but had then come back looking for more.

"And which one of those is you?"

He shrugged and shivered, still wielding the paddle and not looking back. "Guess I'm a bit of them all."

"And there's one reason you haven't mentioned, Mr Dampier. Or perhaps it's all of them, bound up into one."

"What's that?"

"Lamagica, of course."

9

THEY CHANGED ROLES in the raft after mooring at a sandbank around noon and eating some of their supplies of jerky and dried fruit, although in Dampier's case that wasn't very much. The lay of the map against the intertwining of water and land grew less clear after that, as did his recollection of the way he'd found before, but that was to be expected; things around the river basin never stayed much the same from one season to the next. Every now and then, they raised a desultory conversation, but mostly they remained silent as the water slipped by and Clemency Arbuthnot paddled the raft.

As sky and river began to redden, and after checking for crocs, they moored again at a patch of beach, and he found some dryish wood to make a fire, even though she queried its need: the truth being that he was feeling oddly cold. Was the malaria returning just when he least needed it, and most needed his wits? As with so many other things about this journey, he simply didn't know.

"What did you do back in the Old World after your brother left?" he ventured after they'd set the hammocks and full night had fallen, affecting as little curiosity as he could.

"Can't you guess?" She was sitting a little farther back from the dance of flames. Huge shadows threw across the trees from her broad-hatted silhouette.

He shook his head.

"I found work, Mr Dampier. Believe it or not, there's a market for young women of my kind of accent and deportment."

She sat in silence for a while, as if still expecting him to make a guess. Which, of course, he had, although he doubted if the way his thoughts took him could be true.

"I was a London shop-girl in a square just off the Oxford Road. The kind of place where the smart set of the highest guilds expect to be served by someone with manners similar to their own. A gentlemen's tailors, if you're interested. How else do you think I can afford these clothes?"

Cradled in his hammock, stars splintering through the tangled branches above and the night-sounds of the jungle playing around him, Dampier considered the things Clemency Arbuthnot had said, and then the knowledge that he'd camped at this very spot with her brother two years before.

She was right, of course. Lamagica was the distillation of everything that was possible and impossible, just like aether itself. It had certainly once drawn him to New Spain. If only he could properly recollect what had happened out here on his previous journey... But his mind slipped like the gears of an unmagicked engine, and settled on another Lamagica: a flickering red sign above a doorway, leaking fizzing raindrops onto the step below. Ma cooking eggy bread as usual in her long blue gown, and sometimes she was happy but more often now she was sad, and they hardly went out together, or danced to the orchestron, any more.

But this was how things were, and this was the way the years slid by. The real Lamagica being somewhere far-off and dangerous and possibly not even real, and not this London whorehouse set amid the ruins of another Age, and now he finally got the joke. And Gracie left, and someone made an honest woman out of Polly, and then Janelle did something bad to herself, and a few other girls went but never came back, and the orchestron fell out of tune, and sounded less like music than dropped glass. But they stayed on, he and Ma, because where else was there to go?

The eggy bread tasted less good now. And Ma screamed as the pan splatted fat and he had to help her lie down, glimpsing a landscape of sores and craters like a reddened Moon beneath her long blue gown. This not being the life she'd wanted for them, no, no. But they needed money, and she needed customers, clients, johns— to live, but also to pay the landlord, who was not the sort of person you crossed. So what I want you to do, Edward, is to be my soldier, my sentinel, my envoy, my messenger, my guide, my guard. And here's the money and this is what you should ask for and this is where you should go, and you know the spell, or whatever's left of it, that opens our front door, and now you must leave. So off he went to a dark road beyond the homely glitter of World's End, where a man with unmatched socks laughed as he gave him the tin of cheaply magicked ointment, because wasn't he a bit young to have the pox? Funny, really, how people laughed about things that weren't funny at all. Heading back, he noticed that the red-lit sign had lost the glow out of most of its letters and now merely spelled out MA. Then up the stairs with the piano playing like whooping bird calls, and the ceiling must have fallen in, because light was burning his eyes.

"Mr Dampier... Mr Dampier..." A voice was saying. "You really must wake up."

10

THEY TOOK TURNS paddling as before, picking through a confusion of muddy inlets and dead ends more by hunch than by compass work or map, along with whatever Dampier could admit to knowing of the way ahead. Once, he called forward to ask why she didn't consult her aethometer, which was what most prospectors did, although she laughed in reply. The whole point of Lamagica's existence being that its magic was hidden, so what would be the point? As they steered again into a broader stretch of water and the Sun beat down on the water like a struck gong, he recollected how Benedict Arbuthnot had said much the same thing.

Not that the man, despite the clear physical similarity with his sister, was much like her in other ways. He remembered sitting with him at the same table of the Casa del Conde, and how he'd been as full of dreams, suppositions and sheaves of wild drawings as she, with her printed and waxed map, had been clear-headed and blunt. Not so much a man coming here to make his fortune as someone deliberately fleeing into the unknown. Usually, Dampier made a point of offering his services only to those who were properly prepared, or those who had no idea of what they were doing at all. Somehow Benedict Arbuthnot had been a combination of both.

But he'd known a great deal about the Mayans, that was for sure. In fact, he'd spoken of little else. How, if there really was a Lamagica, which he didn't choose to doubt, the prospectors and theorisers had got it all wrong. It wasn't some temple or city hidden deep in the jungle. Neither did it lack any proper location, or float amid the clouds. It was simpler than that, and should have been obvious to anyone who knew how the Mayans lived.

The most sacred of all Mayan places being the many sinkholes, cenotes, which dotted the jungle where the harder rock which had formed the mountains gave way to limestone and the rivers ran underground. Every major Mayan site lay close to one, where procession was made, and sacrifices given, and guidance sought. But—and this again was obvious—all the cenotes joined to form one vast, hidden network. So this was where the last of the Mayans had retreated and sealed themselves away from the war and disease the Conquistadors had brought.

"Wouldn't it be wise," Dampier said to Clemency Arbuthnot as they paused and moored in the lee of a low white cliff at noon, "to take another look at that piece of stone? I mean..." He shrugged and picked at a fingernail that somehow, and like a piece of rotten cladding, peeled right off. "Now we're getting closer to wherever we're supposed to be going, it might offer up something more."

"That's not a bad idea. Now, let me see..." She rummaged in her brown canvas bag, spoke the spell which opened the lead-lined box and took out the artefact, which was clearly made of the same rock as the cliff beside them, and now looked grey and small. "Odd, isn't it, that something so old and unimpressive should amount to so much. At least, that was what Ben thought. You hold it, Mr Dampier."

He took the offered triangle of rock. For a moment, it felt light. Then it seemed to dig into his flesh with surprising, burning weight. No wonder she kept it wrapped up in spells and lead... Shapes, colours, were welling up, not as if to make some ornate stone wheel, but filling his entire sight.

The leaves and vines dangling above them were shards of jade; the cliff itself was polished ivory or bone. And the river was amber, flashing with a scatter of diamonds, and when he looked back down at the artefact, he saw that it was dripping with rubies, each descending slowly to scatter on a beach of finest glass.

"Mr Dampier! Mr Dampier...!"

The shadow of Clemency Arbuthnot reached and took it back from him, and as his vision contracted he saw her wipe some redness off with a scrap of cloth before placing it back inside its lead-lined box. Looking down at his hands, he realised that the keystone hadn't been dripping rubies, but his own blood.

"Here—bind yourself up. If we didn't know that this thing was getting more powerful before, we do now."

Dazedly, he wrapped the offered handkerchief around the cut in his right palm. It hurt like hell, and gave her an easy excuse to take next turn with the paddle at the prow.

Gripping the rudder rope with his left hand as low limestone cliffs grew closer on both sides, he bit absently at another loose nail and—what the hell was wrong with him?—the thing also peeled right off. Spitting it out into the current, he told himself to focus, concentrate on what he really remembered—what he actually knew...

Benedict Arbuthnot, for instance, sitting at the prow of a raft as they worked midriver against the quickening pull, just as his sister was doing now. The same features, maybe, at least the same green eyes, but he'd seemed younger in a way that had little to do with age, and the grizzle of reddish fuzz that had grown across his cheeks by this point in their journey—you could hardly call it a beard—had made him look younger still. And all that talk! And the notes, pages of them, he kept scribbling out.

He'd shared, enumerated, the Mayan obsession with calendars. Not one way of counting the days, it seemed, but several, interlocking and turning just like the stones upon which they were carved. In many ways, he said, his high voice echoing from bank to bank, they were a far more advanced civilisation than our own.

Yes, the Mayans fought wars, had armies, Mr Dampier, but their conflicts were slight and ceremonial compared to the blood and slaughter of European battlefields, and started and ended at previously agreed times. Which, aside from their steel weapons and horses, was why the Conquistadors defeated them so easily; they simply carried on fighting and killing until there was nothing left to kill.

The Spaniards, they had it wrong about so many things to do with the Mayans. Obviously, the varieties of snake deity they worshipped weren't incarnations of the Christian Devil, although that was why the Franciscan monks had their temples ransacked and their codices burned. Neither were the Spaniards right to be horrified by their rites of human sacrifice. The crucial thing to *know*, the crucial thing to *understand*, Mr Dampier, was that to give yourself up to the gods was the greatest imaginable honour.

That ball game they played? Those stone hoops in walled courtyards? That was part sport, but it was part ritual as well. And it was the captain of the *winning* team, the one who'd fought hardest and most skilfully, who knelt before the priests in all their jewelled and feathered finery, and pleaded himself unworthy.

But, if he was lucky, if he was privileged, he might be accepted as an offering to the gods. Then he was stripped and shaved and anointed, and placed for a whole day—or perhaps two or three; such things depended on the turning of the stars—in a sweatlodge, to pray without food or water until he was finally brought forth amid great rejoicing, and given the most precious medicines, magics and herbs to help him through the journey ahead.

Can you imagine, Mr Dampier, how such a moment must have felt? To be borne up towards the steps of a great pyramid such as the many we Europeans have razed to the ground? And then to ascend slowly, step by trembling step, with all that sacred power roaring through your blood? Brutality and godlessness are surely the last words for such a ceremony. There was barely even any pain. As a final mercy, once you had ascended to that high place between the sky and the land, you were stretched across a special stone and your spine was snapped in one quick pull, so there was nothing left to feel but joy as the high priest wielded the obsidian blade and your pulsing heart was lifted towards the Sun.

Dampier blinked hard. His hand still hurt, and everything seemed too bright. Even the curl of Clemency Arbuthnot's hair which had fallen loose recalled the whorls of Mayan decoration, and the echo of her brother's voice lingered in his head. For once a sacrifice had been made, it seemed, be it either human or animal, and after the heart had been offered up to Kinich Ahan, the god of the daytime Sun, and it was taken in procession to be given to the waters of the sacred cenote, it was common for the priests to delicately remove the skin of the offered body, and don it as a kind of garb...

"Quick—Mr Dampier!"

The rudder rope tore painfully at his right palm as a sudden swirl threatened to twist them round. The gorge was narrowing, and the shadows were dark, and the Sun sank so quickly beneath the overreaching trees that they scarcely had time to find a place to moor.

What strange and overcomplicated beings we humans are, Dampier told himself as he set a fire—this time, Clemency Arbuthnot didn't question its need—and went about rigging the hammocks amid the dangling roots and doing all the simple, basic, necessary things, albeit more awkwardly using his left hand, that any person had to do. The rest—out here in the simplicity of the jungle, this had struck him before—didn't matter that much.

So why was that last journey he'd undertaken with Benedict Arbuthnot so unclear? Why was he remembering things only as they recurred? He guessed that was what he'd come back to find out, but it still made no sense. All he did know for sure was that two years earlier the river's widening flow had borne him back towards Tokotahn, and then on to Verarica, alone. And yes, he'd lived, breathed, shat, slept, talked and drunk a fair amount of mescal in the time since. He'd even given Nettie Muller the money to pay off her debts so she could join the Grey Sisters and quit being a whore. But he hadn't worked or done anything else remotely useful. At least, if you discounted studying the face in that broken-chained locket, and waiting for Clemency Arbuthnot to arrive.

11

HE WAS WALKING uphill, and the going wasn't good. Every step he took, he slid back at least half as far, and the light was like a crystal held up to the Sun. But this was nothing surprising, this was his home, and there the sign above the doorway, even though it had now entirely ceased to glow. He pushed his way in, climbed the stairs, sudden urgency in his breath, and shouting *Ma, Ma, Ma?!* Surely there had to be a reply, and surely she had to be on the mend, after all the cheaply aethered potions he'd bought from that man with the unmatched socks to make her well. He turned, spun around, and the walls of the ballroom spun with him, offering crazy glimpses of stark white mountains, deep forest dells. That, and other things—gaudy feather boas, silks, furs and jewels, melting puzzles of putrescing flesh and protruding bone—that he reckoned he probably shouldn't be seeing at all. But the place was dead and empty now, even the clattering orchestron was finally silent, and Ma and the smell of eggy bread were gone. So he turned and walked back out across World's End. Towards the river; towards the docks.

He could still hear the sound of a river, that snakelike hissing, but now instead of the chuff of engines, it was interrupted by wild whoops, screeches and howls: the sounds of the jungle. Even before he opened his eyes, Dampier knew exactly where he was, which felt like much more of an achievement than it should. But something still seemed amiss. He moved his sore right hand down towards his belt, and felt for his gun. It was gone.

"What..." He staggered up and out of the hammock. Clemency Arbuthnot was sitting nearby on a weathered log. Beside her was his gun. She gripped her own, the one he'd glimpsed with the pearly handle, in her right hand.

"I thought I'd better take your firearm away from you, Mr Dampier. After all, you can hardly expect to be able to use it with that cut."

Other people had pointed guns at him over the years—some of them had even been women—but few had done so with such purpose. The hammer was cocked, and her finger was curled tightly around the trigger.

"You're going to shoot me?"

"That depends. All you have to do, Mr Dampier, is stop lying."

"About what?"

"Oh, come *on*." She laughed, although she wasn't smiling. "You're transparent as a tapeworm, and twice as low. Not, I suppose, that I immediately realised you were the last person to see my brother alive. But what kind of guide has a business that involves telling people they're wasting their time?"

"So why did you trust me?"

"I've told you often enough before—I don't. And *you* kept telling me Ben was dead. Not that you seemed to have found much profit in taking him out into the jungle and shooting him, although I know that's what some of your kind do. And I'd hardly credit you as the sort to know about privateers and letters of marque. Oh, and

I looked through your rucksack the first chance I got. The moment I found the locket with my likeness that Ben took with him was the closest I've come to killing you—at least, until now. And I think you should see this..."

Her gun only wavered slightly as, one-handed, she took the expensive aethometer from out of her canvas bag and turned it on. The dial showed a low latency at first. Until she pointed it directly at Dampier, when it shot right up.

"You reek of aether, Mr Dampier. You didn't realise that, did you? Along, I'm guessing, with a great deal else. So why don't you just tell me everything you *do* know about what happened to my brother, and then I'll decide whether to shoot you or not. That, and where. Perhaps cleanly in the head, or perhaps low in the gut. Really it depends on if I decide you're told me the full, exact truth."

Dampier still felt surprised and dizzy, and asked if she'd let him sit down on that log. Which she did, after moving herself and his gun farther up. Then he spoke, slowly at first, his head sunk between his shoulders, but then more quickly, and soon even finding himself wondering why he hadn't told her before. Although she probably wouldn't have believed him until now.

"So you're telling me you think my brother actually *found* Lamagica somewhere farther upriver and into the jungle, and that he just walked right into it, and that you turned back, but you can't remember why or how?"

Dampier nodded, then spat out a wad of oddly blackish phlegm. "...And it wasn't even just Lamagica. As we got closer upriver he started saying it was the sum and substance of every lost land. You know—Albion, Camelot and Cockaigne. That it was the place called Sierra de la Plata—the silver mountains—and El Dorado as well. That it was Einfell, to where Goldenwhite retreated when she was betrayed outside London by Owd Jack. That it was the Isle of the Blessed and the Spring of Eternal—"

"Thank you, Mr Dampier. I do believe you're starting to sound more than a little like my brother yourself. Ben, he took after my mother, and was always the dreamer. Whereas I, I suppose, am more like my father. Oh, I'm not saying I'm some spendthrift alcoholic, but I do have a cynical slant. Ben was clever, but he was never clever about anything that was simple or real. I believe that was why he chose the Galvanic Guild—what could be more ethereal than electricity, other than aether itself?—although I'm not sure if he'd have made a good common guildsman, with a toolbag and a workbook of spells. The pity is he never got the chance to find out. My father was declared bankrupt soon after Ben qualified—I've told you that already, haven't I?—but it was before he died.

"That artefact—the keystone—we didn't find it forgotten in the bottom of some family suitcase, either. Our father kept it as a paperweight on his desk throughout our childhood, and Ben had often wondered aloud about what it was. In fact, he'd already had it assayed and come up with all the stuff about Lamagica when he went to see our father for the last time. So perhaps it wasn't as much to remonstrate with him as with a proposal. I don't know precisely what happened, but an argument ensued, and Ben came to me in tears with the keystone still encrusted with our father's brains and blood…

"It was clear that he'd be arrested as soon as the body was discovered. I at least could prove I was working in that ghastly shop, but what possible defence did he have? So we sealed the keystone inside a lead-lined box with a spell which only I knew, and he set off to take the first boat from Portsmouth and on to New Spain…

"And I waited. And meanwhile, I served in that shop telling fat guildsmen how marvellous they looked. It was boring, demeaning work, but I began to realise there were better ways of making money than fluttering my eyes at rich idiots and lying through my teeth. Oh, it's still not what you *thought* I meant, Mr Dampier! The sad thing about whores being that they never realise a woman can make better money by keeping her clothes on. You could say I'm a trickster, if you have to call me anything at all. It's interesting work—enjoyable, if I'm honest, which of course I'm not—and the only people I leave poorer are those who deserve to be made so. But I still had no idea what had happened to my dear brother after that last letter from the Casa del Conde in Verarica. Eventually, I knew I had to confront whatever was inside that box.

"So perhaps I should have come to New Spain earlier, and perhaps I shouldn't have come at all. But here I am. And here you are..." She picked up Dampier's gun from the log and turned it slowly around. "Seeing as you haven't tried to kill me yet, you might as well have this back, I suppose. That, and it probably still makes sense for us to carry on together, seeing as you claim to have at least some idea of where we're going. Although I have to say, Mr Dampier, you don't look at all well..."

12

THE FLOW OF the river was so strong the raft almost shot away from them as they eased it out into the current, and Dampier ripped some of the underflesh off his sore right hand as he grabbed the flailing rope.

It didn't get much better after that. The gorge was still narrowing, throwing up spumes and fogs which the filtering daylight transformed into scintillating rainbows or pits of gloom. Swapping roles was difficult, with fewer backwashes where they could reach and hold onto a dangling bough or root, and with every push of the paddle Dampier's right hand gave another stab of pain. They could scarcely hear each other's voices, either, over the wet roar.

Dampier wondered if this was how it had ended before as he struggled between holding the rudder and wielding a bucket to bail out the water washing over the gunwale. Had Benedict Arbuthnot simply fallen in and drowned, while he'd somehow managed to survive? But he could still hear the man's voice raised over the bellowing brown rush, see his eager back bent to the paddle at the half-misted prow.

The cliffs were higher now, walls of wet limestone that convoluted into elaborate pillars, pinnacles, whorls and scrolls. The day would have been exhausting even feeling better than he did, and the nails were now also shedding from his left hand, and the stickiness in his boots told him that his feet were probably bleeding as well.

If this wasn't malaria, maybe it was scurvy? Like the problem of where they were and what they were supposed to be doing here, whatever was left of Dampier's instincts as a guide were screaming that they should turn back right now. But he'd come this way before, hadn't he? They had to go on.

They managed a break of sorts at about midday by looping a rope around a larger rock that stuck out from the middle of the flow.

"You're sure this is the way you came with Ben?" Clemency Arbuthnot shouted. Even she was starting to look bedraggled. Her clothes were soaked and her hat drooped.

All he could do was nod.

Soon, it seemed more and more probable that the river itself would force them back. The narrowing glimpses of sky were starting to close over entirely, forcing them to navigate through torrenting darkness towards the next show of light. But then, just as even Dampier was starting to doubt if he and Benedict Arbuthnot had ever made it this far, a sudden sideways surge almost threw them into a much bigger space where the cliffs fell away and the cloudless evening sky was mirrored with dizzying exactitude in the quiet water of a wide, still lake.

"Where do we go now?" Clemency Arbuthnot's voice echoed harshly—*now now now now...*—against the cliffs behind.

"The way's over there." Dampier pointed with new certainty towards a small stretch of shore, and the sky shivered against the raft's prow as they paddled across, moored and climbed out. It was just another stretch of jungle. No stones, no ruins, no towering pyramids, pillars or temples. There was nothing here but trees, snagging vines, giant ferns, immense deadfalls.

"You—Ben—really came this way?"

"Yes..." He coughed and spat out some more dark-looking gunk. "I'm sure."

"But there's nothing *here*. No landmarks..." She climbed around a huge crown of blackened and decaying roots, then dug into her bag and took out the aethometer. The only leap in the dial came when she pointed it directly at him.

It wasn't far now. Even though night was falling, he pushed on. Then, suddenly, the sky opened above a huge drop so close to his feet that he almost fell right in. As did Clemency Arbuthnot as she stumbled up behind.

"This is *it*? Really?" She peered down, then wavered back. There was nothing to see inside the mouth of the cenote but rising darkness. No bottom, or glint of water, or sign of light or life.

"Yes—I'm certain of it."

Slowly, carefully, they picked their way around the edge, occasionally loosening stones that stirred up near-endless echoes as they skittered down. A half-moon was rising above the mass of the jungle. It had a strange effect on the nearby vegetation, and the vines that straggled into the drop. They seemed silvered, varnished with a kind of otherworldly gloss. Then, inspecting his damaged hands and seeing rainbowed dust, Dampier laughed out loud.

"What *is* it?"

"It's just engine ice—the same stuff you get anywhere from a used-up spell..."

Finally, about halfway around the edge of the cenote, he pulled the bindings off his right hand and began to scrabble amid a pile of dead creepers. For a long moment, he encountered only dry leaves and dirt. But then he glimpsed something more solid, and began to work much more slowly and carefully. After a while, Clemency Arbuthnot gave an impatient sigh and leaned over to help, but then she gasped. He glimpsed the brief, bright leap of her aethometer.

"Get back, Mr Dampier! That thing isn't safe. The readings are sky high—"

"You forget—I've been here before. Whatever's happened to me, it's happened already."

And there it was, the entire stone circle, fully revealed but for their one missing piece. It looked rather beautiful, even if the carving was an undecorated grey. Dampier took a swatch of leaves to it now, reverently brushing away the last of the debris much as a priest might with a holy relic, which was exactly what it was. Other things were much clearer to him now, too, weary and ill though he felt.

"It's just over there—the place where Ben entered the cenote. Look..." He pointed, and it was true; there was the suggestion of a series of steps circling down into the pit and out of the moonlight, although they were so worn and irregular it was impossible to tell whether they were the work of man, nature, or some other force.

Warily, Clemency Arbuthnot nodded. She was holding the aethometer close to her chest as if it might offer some protection. "But... How...? It's still just a big hole in the ground."

Dampier smiled. "That's easy. I just had to hold open the door to let your brother go through. Watch..."

Slowly, and as if in supplication, he knelt down and laid the splayed fingers of both hands across the stone, and spoke a spell of a lost language, and felt the power of it pour into him. It was like being ridden by a storm, and struck by fire, ice and lightning, all at once. Yet he could see that she saw it as well; that all of this was real and true. The wheel was the world, and the world was turning, and both were illuminated, fused, glorified. But the wheel was also a calendar—that is, if calendars made the years instead of merely echoing them— and the cenote was at the heart of everything: a swirl of wyrelight that rose up from the depths in a blaze of voices that sang of something stranger than mere life or death, and further away than the stars, yet was somehow endlessly and irrevocably *here*. It was a firestorm of living magic such as the world had never glimpsed or imagined in all the pomp of its Ages of Industry, and it was beautiful, but it was terrible as well. Benedict Arbuthnot, Dampier thought as he pulled his hands away and the grey, ordinary moonlight crashed down around them, had been a very brave man indeed to have walked into that.

"So that's... That's where Ben went?"

Dampier's skin still crawled, and his head was still ringing, although he noticed that the dial of the aethometer Clemency Arbuthnot was clutching had shattered. Then, remembering something, he worked his numb fingers into a pocket, and held it out.

"Your brother broke the chain and said that I should keep this until I found you."

She took the locket from him. "But this place... If it was ever found... If it was used, mined—exploited..."

"That's what can never be allowed to happen. And that's why we had to bring back the keystone. Even the Conquistador who removed it in the times before aether must have realised its power. Perhaps they wanted to keep it, or maybe destroy it. Perhaps it destroyed them."

"What does it do?"

"What does any key do? It unlocks things—or locks them. Here, give it to me and I'll show you."

She reached into her brown canvas bag, took out the box and muttered the spell that opened it, then fumblingly held the keystone out. Taking it, Dampier knelt again, inserting it into the space in the centre of the stone, half expecting to be swept up in another storm of aether as he did so, but there was merely a sharp *click*, and the wheel briefly glowed with colour, then settled and faded with a dull grinding, and all that was left was an ancient sinkhole, and a rather unremarkable Mayan relic.

"Well..." She sniffed. Sighed. "...Now I know."

"I guess you do." Although Dampier reckoned that whatever story of their journey got back to Verarica would settle easily amid all the other wild tales of Lamagica that infested the place, to be told by drunks and madmen and ignored by the sensible and sane. Which was probably for the best.

"Wherever Ben is, I know it was what he was looking for even when we used to creep out as children. And I also know there's no chance of him ever coming back, which I think he wanted as well. So I suppose I have to leave him here..."

"What about you? Do you plan to head back to London and resume your...career there?"

"I don't think so, no. I've seen enough of the New World to realise the old one's nothing special. I might head up to New Amsterdam, or maybe Boston. Or perhaps down to Quinto."

"I reckon you stand as good a chance as any do out here."

"If that's a compliment, Mr Dampier, I'll take it. And I don't need this." She tossed the aethometer into some nearby bushes. "Or this..." She held the broken-chained locket over the edge of the cenote. It fell, flashing, then was gone. "Although I'll keep my memories of Ben here." She patted her chest. "But this isn't a time for farewells, Mr Dampier—we really must get back to the raft. At least downsteam'll be quicker and easier. And, frankly, you need serious medical attention."

He shook his head. "Oh, I'll be fine."

"This isn't some joke! After what you've been exposed to, the level of aether... Didn't you see in that ward in the mission house—"

"Yes, I did see. Plain as day. Which is why I'm not going back."

"But you can't just...stay out here in the jungle."

"Why not?" He shrugged and shivered; truth was, he somehow felt pretty terrible and not too bad at the same time.

She stood for a long moment, her face in shade from the moonlight, but her eyes as green and clear and knowing as he'd ever seen them. "If that's what you really want."

"I do. And I'm glad to have been of some service."

"That you have, Mr Dampier."

Clemency Arbuthnot held out a hand. Very briefly, yet noticing how warm and smooth and living her flesh felt, he took it. Then she turned and headed off in the direction they'd come without looking back. Dampier remained standing a while beside the lip of the cenote, picking absently at a last fingernail, until another shiver took hold, and he noticed how strange the colour and texture of his skin had become, even allowing for the effects of the Moon.

He began to push his way deeper into the jungle. It was difficult work, climbing, crawling, with frequent stops to cough up more of the black fluid that seemed to be filling his lungs. But the Moon was still very bright, and the engine ice he'd noticed earlier appeared be growing rather than diminishing. It formed giant fans and ferns, enormous growths of shimmering crystal. Soon, he was sliding over the stuff, and climbing, sinking, falling. But then he got his bearings, and heard warm laughter and music, and saw a familiar doorway ahead, with the single word LAMAGICA picked out above in glowing red letters. Smiling, he spoke the spell that opened it, and went through.

Afterword

FROM *HUCKLEBERRY FINN* to *Heart of Darkness*, there are many river journeys in fiction, and these journeys often mirror some inner journey that the characters in the narrative are undertaking. Rivers also feature heavily in myth, either as a barrier to be crossed or a route to be taken, most often between the lands of the living and the dead. Joseph Campbell's book, *The Hero with A Thousand Faces*, which has since become a staple reference for Hollywood script meetings, is essentially a discussion of how such stories are endlessly retold.

Not, I have to say, that I'm sufficiently calculating to have arrived at the structure of *Lamagica* in this way. Typically for me,

I'd been nursing the idea of putting the fictional element of the aether-based society around which I developed my two novels *The Light Ages* and *The House of Storms*, which are both grounded very much in England, into a New World setting and mythology for many years. Other themes and narrative itches that needed scratching and somehow seemed to fit, such as the sister seeking her brother, the wizened prospector, and the Hemingwayesque tone, slowly came into focus through trial and error. As did the cenotes, the limestone pits the Mayans so revered, and which I've been fortunate enough to experience for myself. Yet, somehow, and on re-reading, and although it arrived pretty late in the day when I was trying to stop the story from becoming too static, for me it's the river, and the slowly revealed streams of the two main characters' lives, that carry the whole thing along.

Ouroboros

LIKE MOST COMPUTER geeks, I started out as a hacker. If you're old enough, you may even remember some of my teenage efforts. I specialised in inserting the titles of imaginary new works into the digital catalogues of the world's great museums and libraries. It was all rather neat. I'd create emulations of the system's curator-bots, and send them rattling off along the lattices of virtual shelves. There was *More Ado About Something*, and *Lear's Revenge*, not to mention the fifth movement of Beethoven's Ninth Symphony, *Ode to Agony*, and Tolstoy's little-known sequel, *War and/or Peace*. Great fun, and those early "successes" even allowed me to set up a security consultancy, and launch myself into what briefly seemed like a promising career.

I soon discovered, however, that being a gatekeeper is much harder work, and far less exciting, than messing around with other people's data, and also something for which—in a deeply competitive field—I didn't even possess any particular flair. Of course, I toyed with the idea of doing some proper, serious, criminally motivated hacking, but I knew in my heart that I lacked the ruthless courage. So instead I spent an alarming number of years working through a variety of commissions in the field which was then still optimistically known as Artificial Consciousness, and made my own small contribution towards what is now universally regarded as a dead end. No matter how vast and clever the machine, it turns out that it's impossible to replicate whatever that odd glimmer is we all have going on inside our heads.

Still, I kept a real, proper office right in the heart of Old London, in part because I'd once liked to think of myself as a sort of cybernetic gun-for-hire (*The Maltese Flagon* being another of my favourite fictional fictions), and sat up above the flooded streets on the twentieth floor, vaguely hoping that some mysterious, glamorous visitor would turn up unannounced. What I got instead was an ancient monk.

His head was shaved and he wore dusty crimson robes which were wet at the edges, and his back was hunched and his hands trembled and he was breathing heavily from the long climb up the windy stairs, but nevertheless he possessed the sort of timeless composure you might expect of such a person, and favoured me with a crumpled-paper smile that probably wasn't a smile at all as he eased himself down into the chair opposite my desk. Instead of a mala bracelet, tilaka mark, cross or Star of David, he wore around his neck a carved jade representation of a dragon, which I was later to discover was called Ouroboros, consuming its own tail.

If I'm honest, my immediate thought was of some grave act of blasphemy I'd committed back when I was a hacking kid. Not that I'd ever gone particularly far in that direction, but I did have *Torah*,

Torah, Torah and *Quran: The Corrected Edition* on my CV. Of course, the business model he represented was well on its back foot. I mean, who needs old-fashioned religion when you can enter the gates of Heaven, feast in Valhalla, unite the desert tribes into the One Truth Faith, or even endure the punishments of Hell—if that's your kind of thing—all for the price of a VR suit? Still, and for no other reason than his quietly assured manner, and my current lack of other clients, I decided to treat this wizened creature with a little respect.

"You're an expert in data and computing," he announced without preamble in a rustling voice, and it was hard to tell whether this was a question or a statement, or something else entirely, his browned face was so wrinkled and hard to read.

"That's what I like to think."

"There were those false creations you once attributed to some of the world's great artists. Michelangelo, Hemingway and so forth."

"Yes. That was me."

"Indeed. But did you ever consider actually trying to create some of the works to go with those intriguing titles?"

"Well…" In truth, the whole project had begun with that silly dream. But even a few sparse lines or brushstrokes—the grossest, simplest parody—had turned out to be beyond me. So the titles had just got sillier instead. *The Sistine Restrooms* and *Deeper Throat* being later examples of my oeuvre. "No."

"I'm well aware of your work in both its strengths and limitations," the monk said, looking at me in much the same way that one of his kind might regard an ant before they flicked it gently away. "Which is why I have a commission for which I believe you are particularly suited."

Then he just sat there, and I realised he was expecting me to respond. But I certainly wasn't going to fall into the trap of agreeing to something before I knew what it was. In any case, I reckoned I was finally ahead of him.

"Let me guess," I said, "you want me to help you create—or re-create, or invent, however you choose to put it—the mind of God?"

He did smile slightly at that. "I suppose that might once have been an interesting theoretical proposition. But hasn't a great deal of your work in recent years been devoted to proving that such a thing isn't possible? I mean, if machines can't even model the consciousness of a fruit fly, let alone a being as complex as us, what chance would they possibly have with creating God?"

Once again, I was that ant. Not that the virtualities didn't offer their subscribers the chance to have a go at being Jehovah once they'd put up with being Jesus, but that was hardly the same thing.

"Also," he continued, "the core scriptures all tell us that we ourselves, and not some soulless computer, were created in the image of God."

I nodded as if I was still following him, although of course I wasn't. Instead, my mind was slipping in the direction of some virtual Garden of Eden, or perhaps the torture chambers of Torquemada, even though such things had been done to death.

"What I would like you to do is really quite simple," the monk said. "At heart, you're still a hacker, and this is the biggest imaginable hack. I would like you to try to break into our universe. And when I say *universe*, I mean everything which you and I and everyone else in this world are currently experiencing..." He gestured tremblingly around my office, then beyond its windows towards the gleaming, flooded city with its rotting towers. "I do hope that's clear?"

I had nothing better to do, and my monk assured me he'd return in exactly a month. But I'm not stupid, and I already knew this whole reality-is-just-a-simulation thing had been around for centuries, and was a popular conceit in many old novels and movies. But I was surprised to discover that it also had some intellectual credence. After all, and even though we humans might not see it that way, our universe is essentially a quantum froth down at its most basic level, formed from an irreducible pixel-like grid. Then there's the way so many things about it still refuse to make proper sense. Gravity not fitting in with the other fundamental forces, for example, or all that missing dark energy and matter. The more I looked into this, the more I was reminded of the sort of fudges and workarounds you'll find in even the most elegantly designed virtual reality.

Soon, I was beginning to understand how fascinating it would be to hack through here-and-now's thin veil. You could shake hands with God, or at least peer into the fuggy bedroom of the alien geek who's running us on his laptop on some rainy Sunday afternoon. But there were more practical possibilities. Imagine what you could do if you possessed the cheat codes to reality. Faster than light travel, unlimited energy? Not a problem. Immortality, likewise. Still, I couldn't help thinking that what my monk really needed was one of those big old-fashioned atom-smashing cyclotrons if he wanted to poke a hole through to next door. But then surely such devices would have succeeded already, if it could be done? I grew discouraged, and probably would have given up entirely if it hadn't been for the evident faith which my monk had placed in me.

After all, I just dealt with computers, data... But hadn't Galileo himself (non-author of *My Travels With A Telescope*) said that God was a mathematician, and wasn't data all everything really amounted to? Rather like my monk's tail-consuming dragon, I was almost back to where I'd started, but my old hacker instincts had returned.

This, I realised, was just a fancier version of hacking the Library of Congress. All I needed was a system which could briefly emulate a sector of reality with sufficient precision and speed to cause its buffers to overrun. You'd get an exploitative weakness, a way right through. I was optimistic. I was excited. Or at least, I was until I tried modelling the idea through some of my computers, and they spat it out with contempt. Turns out that by trying to run a quicker, faster system—my hacking program—inside the system it's in—the universe—I was bumping up against a very fundamental mathematical rule. Ever heard of the *Entscheidungsproblem*? Me neither. But the answer is one big, fat no. And then my month was up. And my monk returned.

Somehow, though, I still wasn't greatly surprised when he simply settled his trembling hands within his robes and smiled at me.

NOW, I AWAKE before dawn to humming chants and the rattle of prayer wheels in a place of high, white mountains and deep blue chasms. We novitiates, male and female, are drawn from all the worldly disciplines. Of course there are mathematicians, priests, poets, virtual engineers and experts in geometries both real and unreal. But there are also farmers, doctors, labourers and beggars—even a few ex-hackers such as myself. Many of us did not even realise before we came here that we had lost all hope.

First we must deal with the usual morning matters of order, cleanliness and food, which are followed by a period of preparatory prayer. There is, of course, still a machine at the heart of our endeavour, an intricate, constantly expanding device, infinite and prodigious, which reaches far beyond this monastery—out into space and the furthest corners of the world. It rides the vast, ever-growing seas of information. It enters the slow minds of the devices which crawl the depths of the oceans, and dances with the nanobots which ride the highest currents of the air. And we novitiates are the ghosts in that machine. We are the grit which will form the pearl.

Deep inside the mountain beneath our monastery there is a cave, and within that cave there is a small jade pyramid, and within that pyramid there is an ebony box, and within that box there is a minute gold sphere, and within that sphere there is nothing, or as close to nothing as can be physically created in ordinary space. This is the core of the mandala, this is the still point upon which the power of all our minds, along with a vast suite of sensors, modelling and monitoring devices, are focused. Hacking is a crude and unnecessary term. For here lies the Bindu, the centre of everything, and we have already detected slight but nevertheless measurable perturbations within its quantum froth.

None of us know, as we finally arise from meditation and bells ring out amid the golds and indigos of sunset, just how long this task will take. But I am already sure, as I stoop to wash my face in a porcelain bowl, and the beginnings of a wizened countenance I'm starting to recognise gazes back at me, that we will, one day, succeed.

Afterword

THIS PIECE WAS written in response to a request to produce a 2,001-word story for a whole collection of such stories which was being put together to honour the centenary of Arthur C Clarke's birth. I hadn't written a story to such a specific size-frame before, and I doubt if I will do so again, but, as I mention elsewhere, I generally find restrictions on what I can write to be a help rather than a hindrance to getting things done. Then there was the association with Clarke, a writer I adored as a teenage reader of SF and whose work I revisit to this day. Not to mention the movie 2001, which I'd still list as among my all-time favourites, and which had an enormous impact on me when I saw it in the local flea pit at an impressionable age.

Most of my stories, as this collection attests, are on the longer side of the format and often go further in terms of timescale, structure and narrative than most "classic" short stories either in or outside of the genre would be expected to go. I'm fine with that—I like to develop characters and generally end up throwing several themes and ideas into my stories rather than one—but the challenge of being as concise as 2,001 words forced me to adopt a different approach. Every time my thought processes took me away from exactly what I needed to say, which is generally pretty often, I had to rein myself back in.

The actual idea for the story itself, however, came easily, and is, in effect a bit of a steal from the works of Clarke himself. Anyone who's read his *The Nine Billion Names of God* will probably remember it, and especially the ending when, after some computer programmers have responded to a request from a lamasery to complete their centuries-long task and produce every conceivable name for their deity, they look up at the night sky and see that "overhead, without any fuss, the stars were going out." It's a marvellous moment, one of the greatest in the genre and perhaps all literature, and I was proud and happy to honour it in the echo of my own slightly skewed monastic quest.

Stuff

THE MOMENT I'D long been dreading came during an otherwise normal Sunday-evening duty phone conversation with my mother. I'd been talking with my usual sense of filling in the silence about the exploits of my two children up at university—at least what little I knew of them—when she mumbled something I had to ask her to repeat.

"Are you going *deaf*, Maud? I simply said that things have started moving around upstairs."

"Mum, that can't be. Not unless something's gone wrong structurally... Or it's rats. Or squirrels."

"Well, be that as it may. But they *are*."

I pictured her sitting at the other end of the landline in the overcrowded chaos of our old front room back in Solihull, surrounded by books, magazines and half-done craft projects, winding and unwinding the yellowed telephone cord around her fingers.

"I know it sounds odd, my dear. That's why I didn't mention it when it all started."

"When was that?"

"Oh, it's been going on for a while, on and off... You know how these things are," she added airily. "I just didn't want you to get any of your funny ideas about the whole business."

"Well, I'm glad you've told me. If you have a problem of any kind, I'd like to know."

And the conversation drifted on in its usual vague way for another five or ten minutes, although when I put down the phone I realised my hands were still trembling.

ME, MY MOTHER, her things and my supposedly funny ideas have a long and difficult history. It didn't help, of course, that I was born after Corey, my oh-so-perfect elder brother, or being a girl and deemed, at least in my mother's eyes, to be "not particularly bright or pretty". The battle lines were drawn early on, although I always had my father, who was caring and kind, and bore the life sentence he'd entered into when he married my mother with a mixture of blithe indifference and stoic humour until he was felled by a heart attack shortly after he retired.

Don't get me wrong. I'm not saying that my mother was some kind of monster. She could be fun and generous, even to me, at least when it suited her, and she genuinely was a great many of the things I've never aspired to be. She was fey. She was quixotic. She was undoubtedly pretty. She engaged in arty pursuits. She'd drag us all on poorly planned days out to unlikely locations, and spectacularly disastrous holidays. We'd end up standing outside places that were either closed or didn't actually exist, or we'd arrive at the wrong airport, or wait for non-existent ferries, or end up arguing desperately with the booking clerk in the foyer of some grubby hotel. In a way, it was a gift, my mother's unreliability, because it made me resilient and independent and phlegmatic from a remarkably early age. But none of this, at least the way I see it now, was the worst of it. The worst was the effect my mother's briskly ever-changing and acquisitive enthusiasms had on the house we lived in, and all the stuff she accumulated in it, and hadn't stopped accumulating up to and beyond the day of that worrying phone call.

Even when I was young, my mother had been remarkably good at getting things into the house, and incredibly poor at taking them out of it. Freebies. Spares. Bargains. Plastic cutlery. Old telephone directories. Knotted balls of wool. Knock-down end-of-sale items that were just too much of a bargain to resist. Books and equipment for all the hobbies she'd briefly taken an interest in. Hundreds of handbags. Literally thousands of scarves. And the *shoes*, the bloody, fucking shoes, which she could never find the right pair of when she was going out... All this accumulated stuff had even been at least incidentally responsible for Dad's untimely death when he keeled over with a massive heart attack as, trying to impose a little long-overdue order, he lugged overspilling bags and boxes up and down the stairs.

It almost goes without saying that my mother, like many hoarders, had very little tolerance for anyone else's stuff. Especially mine. Practically every book or toy I ever acquired was disposed of as soon as my back was turned, generally on the excuse that I'd surely grown out of it, while the idea of my spending any of my carefully preserved pocket money on something nice or pretty to wear became a battle of wills. *Do you* really *need that, Maud? I mean, honestly? You've got enough of that kind of rubbish already. It wouldn't look nice on you, anyway. Not being the sort of shape you are.* And so on. And so forth.

It probably also goes without saying that my mother's stuff, as well as dominating most of my childhood, dominated my own tiny bedroom back in the house on Sycamore Close where she still lived. There was a particular incident which I could never forget, nor really ever forgive her for, which happened when I was about ten. Mum already had a large accumulation of headscarves by then, well into the hundreds, and of course there wasn't enough space for them in her own bedroom with all her other stuff that was already crowding the place out. So she started shoving them into my small wardrobe, which was already full, meaning that the doors developed a habit of wheezing open—generally in the middle of the night. I'd awake to an unnerving creak, a dark parting, and the escaping scarves' snakelike slither. Of course there was no point in my attempting to reason with her. So I developed a plan.

I got hold of a large bin bag, shoved all her scarves into it, then smuggled them out of the house and stuffed them into a litter bin in the local park. I must have have thought that, as these scarves were the ones she never actually wore, she wouldn't notice they were missing. Boy, was I wrong.

What would you do, Maud, if I took some of your precious things away from you and shoved them in a rubbish bin? she asked me, white-faced and trembling, a day or two later when she noticed. *Perhaps I will, just to show you how it feels. This grubby old doll of yours, for instance. How would you feel if I threw it into a fire?* She was dangling my doll Brenda, plastic eyelids fluttering, in front of my face. Not that she went through with the threat, but I never felt the same about Brenda after that; I could always picture her melting in the flames like a plastic Joan of Arc.

STUFF

I RANG MY mother again on Monday evening, but she simply sounded puzzled at this departure from our normal routine and insisted that everything was fine, that the meals on wheels were perfectly edible, at least if you excluded the fish, and that the lady from the care company who looked in every morning was pleasant enough, even if she was foreign, and she didn't see why her presence was needed in the first place.

I also called my brother Corey up in Edinburgh and asked if she'd said anything odd to him about things moving around, and he pretended to think about that as if he'd actually spoken to her in recent months before saying no, she hadn't. Then, on the Friday of that same week, and after trying in vain to talk to someone at the care company or Social Services, I drove the hundred or so miles north up the M1 to my old home in the suburbs of Solihull.

There it was, 23 Sycamore Close, the same detached suburban 1930s house, albeit looking more ragged than ever as I climbed out of my old Volvo and opened the squeaky front gate to follow the crazy paving my father had once laid across a front garden, which had become a wildness of nettles and dead leaves, despite my many efforts to get someone to attend to it. I let myself in using the key I'd had since senior school, and was confronted by what had once been a large and airy hall, which was now constricted to a narrow passage by all the stuff which had been heaped, piled, stacked and dumped along both sides.

"What's *that*?" The voice was anxious, breathy, sharp.

"It's me, Mum."

The living room was much the same—worse, if anything. Books, magazines, leaking old bin bags and big plastic storage boxes all competed for light, space and air. Here, and in the remaining bits of the house in which she still lived, there was no narrow central passage but a kind of haphazard obstacle course which my mother somehow negotiated even as I tripped and stumbled. Amazingly, it had been a whole ten years since she'd moved downstairs, with a new bed installed in our old dining room, and half of the kitchen partitioned off and repurposed as a bathroom, with a high-seat toilet and a walk-in shower with handholds. Of course, she'd been dead against all these changes, but the one leverage I'd had was to point out that surely she wanted to be able to continue to live in her own house, with all her precious stuff? Eventually, she'd given in, just as she had five years earlier when she'd stopped driving around in that dented Datsun following an incident in the local Sainsburys' car park and a visit from the police.

"Oh..." She looked up at me disappointedly from the throne of her frayed Parker Knoll. "It's only *you*, Maud."

"Well, here I am anyway, Mum. Remember, I rang to say I was coming? I thought I could take you out for lunch."

She looked surprised. Yet it was plain she'd been expecting me, unless she always sat there, with the TV off and her shoes and her coat already on.

"Come on, Mum. Let's get you up..."

"I can get up perfectly well on my *own*, thank you very much. It's not as if you come as often as you should, or even ring me. Whereas Corey..."

Here we go, I thought, but in truth things improved markedly after that. I took her to the local Harvester on the Stratford Road, and she didn't complain about my choice, or correct my pronunciation as I read to her from the laminated menu, and she tucked into her food with evident glee, and glugged down several glasses of

Liebfraumilch. She even asked after my husband Dan, and our two children Aaron and Jane, and about how my work as a freelance commercial photographer was going. I think she actually called it a *career*, which was surely a first. In retrospect, I should have wondered what on earth was happening, but at the time I was pleased and grateful.

It was after the pudding, and as she was eyeing the chocolate that came with my coffee, that I casually asked whether the stuff was still moving around upstairs back at the house.

"Of course it is," she said. "These things don't simply stop of their own accord."

"What kind of things?"

"How should *I* know? I'm not an expert, am I? You really do ask the most ridiculous questions sometimes, Maud."

I let it ride, and drank down the rest of my coffee, and paid the bill, and steered my mother around the puddles in the car park and drove her home through the familiar streets, and hurried around to the passenger side of my Volvo to help her out.

"You must come in for a few minutes." She smelled of old sweat and talcum powder.

"Okay. But I've really got to get going soon."

"But you've only just *arrived*! And you haven't had a cup of tea yet."

Which was the last thing I needed before a long drive, but I put the kettle on in the chaos of the kitchen, and checked the fridge, which was actually remarkably clear since she could no longer go out and shop on her own, even if there was a deep, pervasive, under-smell which I hadn't noticed before, and didn't particularly like.

"There you go, Mum."

It was then, as I presented my mother with a floral teacup that I'd wrestled from an overbrimming cupboard, and was looking around to find the TV remote control amid all the teetering piles of old issues of *Cross Stitcher*, *Practical Card Making* and free newspapers, that a sound of movement drifted down though the ceiling from somewhere above. It was nothing really; just a slight drag, a small shuffle, a whispering sigh. But it was there.

"You *see*, Maud!" My mother's eyes flashed with beady triumph; some of her faculties might have faded, but her hearing definitely hadn't. "Didn't I *tell* you? You really must stop this silly habit of always doubting me and getting things wrong."

It could have been mice, of course, or some other infestation which I had no desire to confront, but it was more probably just the natural settling of some random pile of stuff. So I simply left my mother to her tea and her television, and crawled home through the stop-start traffic on the M1.

THE REST OF that year, through winter and into the spring beyond, turned out to be a surprisingly sunny patch in our relationship. I suppose you might call it a kind of swansong. No, my mother certainly wasn't a monster, and seemed genuinely interested in at least some of what I was telling her during our Sunday evening phone calls, and was gratifyingly pleased to see me on what had now become my regular Friday trips up.

It's funny how the mind rearranges things, or simply shuts them out, and the truth is that I gave little thought to her occasional references to things moving about upstairs, although I was amused by her new-found flair for coining odd phrases such as *bull in a butcher's shop*, or calling the microwave the *food television*, and I'd drive back home with my spirits barely dimmed by the endless roadworks. After all, I had a mother who was still alive, and still just about coping at home, and who actually recognised me as her daughter. All things many other people of my age had lost.

Nevertheless, I was still expecting something to go wrong. There was often a catch in her voice towards the end of our phone calls. Or, as I glanced back to see her standing stooped in the doorway as I climbed into the Volvo, I thought she looked not just incredibly frail, but also afraid. She was, of course, an elderly widow living alone and clinging to the edge of existence as the doors of death began to open beneath her. But was there more to it than that? At the time, I didn't think so.

Then, of course, came the inevitable next phone call. My mother had had a fall. No, no, there was no cause for alarm and it wasn't serious, but the meals on wheels delivery man had found her lying in the hall. The district nurse had been around, and so had the doctor, and she was fine, talking and eating and drinking, with nothing but a few bruises.

I cancelled a pre-photo shoot meeting and left a message on Dan's phone, and another on my brother Corey's, and trudged up the M1 just in time to catch the departing social worker.

"She's quite a character, isn't she, your mother?" she said with a breezy smile as we stood outside amid the birdsong in the brambled garden.

"Lots of people say that."

"And it's a blessing, at her age, that no bones were broken. But I hope you'll take this as a wake-up call."

"I'm sorry?"

"All the mess you've allowed to accumulate." The smile tightened. "Downstairs, but also upstairs, from what your dear mother was just saying. It really needs to be sorted if she's not to have another fall."

Right, I thought. Right. I left another message for Dan to say I wouldn't be coming home that night, booked a room at the local Travelodge, checked up on opening times at the council recycling centre, and drove to B&Q to stock up with Marigold gloves, cleaning sprays, kitchen towels and bin bags.

"What are you *doing*, Maud...?"

"What does it look like I'm doing, Mum? This has really to be done. You want to stay in this house, don't you? You don't want to trip up and fall again over all this stuff and end up in hospital?"

"But these are my *things*, Maud..." She was up and about, following in my dusty wake, surprisingly quick and agile.

"Oh, come *on*." We were in the hall, close to the very spot where she must have fallen. I grabbed the nearest magazine from the top of a pile and brandished it at her. "The *Radio Times* from fifteen years ago! What possible use is that?"

"But...I like to re-read the reviews... And, and the letters..."

"No you don't, Mum. You might think you do, but you don't. And there are new editions dropping through your letterbox every week, not to mention the rubbish you still keep getting by mail order. Why are you hoarding all this crap? Just what is it that you're afraid of...?"

"It won't even *be* my house by the time you've finished. It'll be..." Clutching a random bag of knitting to her thin chest, she searched for a word, her face haggard. "The place where all the noises come from."

"You mean upstairs?"

"What else do you *think* I was trying to do when I fell? I was trying to... To shut it *off*... To shut *them* up... To—to stop it from happening..."

I turned towards the stairs. Sure enough, some of the piles had recently been shoved into what seemed like a clumsy and unstable barricade of bags, books and boxes, as if to make access, or egress, impossible. I felt sorry for her then, it was all so pathetic, and she looked as frail and worn and moth-eaten as the stuff she surrounded herself with. But I was also rather angry.

"*That* will need to be sorted, as well! You can't live like this, Mum. It's just isn't possible."

"But I always *have!*"

She was right; she had. Or at least, she'd spent most of her adult life constructing this monumental edifice of useless crap. But something had to be done and I was the only person who could do it, even as my mother followed me around, plucking random scraps of stuff away from my grasp, weeping and pleading.

"You're not my daughter—you *can't* be... No *nice* girl would do a thing like this to her own mother... She'd never be so *horrible*..."

None of which helped my mood, and I pretty much manhandled her into her Parker Knoll back in the front room before heading off to catch the recycling centre before it closed, where my brother Corey rang just as I was backing the Volvo.

"Mum's just been on the phone to me, Maud—"

"You don't say."

"She sounded very upset. She's had this nasty fall, and now there's something about you getting rid of all her stuff. Obviously, I know you wouldn't do such a thing."

The conversation didn't go well after that, and I ended up putting a long scrape down the Volvo's side as I pulled out.

I REALLY DIDN'T do much more over the next day or so other than clear a slightly wider passage in the hall and impose a little order around my mother's Parker Knoll. Where, after her initial resistance and pleading, she simply sat gazing dully at the TV, responding to my questions with little more than grunts and mumbles, which I put down to the delayed shock of her fall. The smallish impression I made on Mum's stuff wasn't so much because I was trying not to disturb her as because I soon realised that any attempt at clearing only released more stuff from beneath and behind. That, and all the stirred-up dust renewed my childhood acquaintance with asthma. I did also become a little aware that my attempts at clearance were causing a surrusation of small shifts and noises that brushed like moth wings at the edge of my hearing, and that some of these noises did seem to have their origins upstairs. But the sight of all the crap my mother had busily piled on every step leading up there was more than enough to discourage any thoughts of investigation.

"You'll be all right, then, Mum? The care worker should be around in a few minutes, and I'll be back in a couple of days, and I'll make sure to give you a ring."

She simply stared through me at the TV as if I wasn't there, then winced and tried to pull away as I tried to kiss her. But I left her anyway—after all, I still had my own life to live, and my throat burned and my back ached and my eyes were stinging—and, with the ramped-up series of visits the social worker had arranged, she'd be seeing far more people on a daily basis than I ever did.

Four days later, the district nurse rang to tell me that my mother had had another fall.

AFTER THE BRIGHT friezes of the children's unit, and the high-tech buzz of the intensive care, cardiology and neurology wards, the orthopaedic gerontology wing at Solihull Hospital was a place of relative calm.

With the jut of their feet beneath the blankets and their withered grey arms extending over their flat bodies, the supine figures reminded me of weathered carvings on medieval tombs, eternally awaiting resurrection. There was a soft chorus of sighs, farts and moans, overlaid with repeated calls of *Nurse, nurse!*, and *Where am I?*, and, commonest of all, *I want to go home...*

My brother Corey had breezed in ahead of me after having flown down from Scotland with a big box of chocolates and a huge bouquet—I didn't think flowers were even allowed these days in hospitals—and Mum's face was alight with a smile that faded as soon as she saw me.

"I *told* you you shouldn't have done it," she snapped. Her hair was a white tangle and a bruise was ripening on her left cheek, but otherwise she seemed fine.

"Done what?"

"Why do you *think*, Maud?" Corey put in. "Why do you think our own dear, sweet Mum got lost and confused and fell?" He was alternately kissing and squeezing her hand. "It was because of the way you've changed everything around. You really need to show a little more compassion, Sis..." Then, and after he'd finished flirting with the nurses, and got me to go and find a vase for his fucking carnations, he gave Mum an extravagant hug and breezed off back to Edinburgh and his successful career in arts administration, whatever the hell that is.

I STAYED OVERNIGHT again at the Travelodge, and called in on my mother—who was still barely acknowledging me—during morning visiting hours, and was told that she could expect to be discharged in a couple of weeks, following appropriate physiotherapy, at least if the mess in her house that the social worker had reported was properly attended to.

I pulled up outside 23 Sycamore Close in the pooled heat of a summer's noon. Once again, I'd come prepared. More rubber gloves, and lemon-scented sprays, and some extra-strong bin bags, along with a set of those dust masks you once only used to see Asian people wearing. That, and my best Nikon with a small reflector umbrella and a couple of extra lenses, following Dan's suggestion that I try to make a record of the old house as I worked through it.

Camera swinging at my shoulder, and carrying a red bucket, I squeaked open the gate and took a few preliminary shots of the moulting pebble-dash, the half curtained windows, the mad briars and neglected roses, trying to relax and go with the flow, telling myself that at least I wasn't snapping cycle saddles to some online advertiser's ridiculous deadline.

I turned the lock in the front door with my old key and backed into the hall through a slide of fresh junk mail, and was confronted by even greater chaos than I'd been expecting. I'd gone straight to the hospital once I'd heard Mum had been admitted, and I'd had no idea of how busy she'd been during the few days since my attempted clear-up.

Stuff and yet more stuff reached up and up and back and back in the sour heat of this dark hallway, growing like rampant weeds in some mad garden which she, perversely, had tended. No wonder she'd fallen over again, although it was hard not to admire her frail, reckless energy. It seemed that Mum hadn't simply been dragging her stuff back into the hall in an attempt to rearrange the clearer and wider path I'd made for her. It was more as if she'd been frantically piling up a kind of barrier with whatever came to hand—balls of half-knitted scarves, spilling jigsaws, old holiday brochures, squashed-up boxes of Christmas decorations, endless junk mail, empty shoeboxes—towards and across the staircase. As if... Well, as if she'd been desperately trying to block whatever might otherwise come down it.

I jumped, momentarily thinking I'd heard something, and my camera flash went off in the jitter of my hands. Then there was nothing but me, and this house, and ringing silence.

I'D ALWAYS HAD a very specific sense of what a clean, clear, proper home should look like. I pictured polished wooden floors and white, uncluttered walls with perhaps nothing more than a single elegant object in each room. A Bauhaus chair, maybe, or a brass telescope looking out across rolling fields. Of course, the place that Dan and I had made for our children was nothing like this vision, and I already knew that, no matter what I did to Mum's house, it would be even less so. But I hankered to impose at least a little order onto the chaos, and to prove to someone—perhaps only myself—that I wasn't the kind of daughter who packed her mother off to a care home, even if she was going a little senile.

But stuff. And not just Mum's stuff. As I set about getting something done, I soon realised how ubiquitous stuff is in the modern world. It's heaped in huge skips at council recycling centres. It crowds all of the many charity shops I staggered into bearing finger-lacerating shopping bags. It lies dumped in lay-bys and hangs in hedgerows and floats across fields. It crams the shelves of every high-street emporium and out-of-town mall, and fills all the catalogues and websites whose products I make a precarious living out of photographing. It's even slowly destroying our planet, if all those worrying wildlife documentaries are to be believed.

I was staying at the local Travelodge, pushed from room to room as other bookings came and went, sleeping badly, feeling wheezy and flabby and existing on a junk-food diet of Big Macs, Burger King Whoppers, KFC buckets and all-day breakfasts that came warmly nestled with more of the useless plastic cutlery and leaky sachets that my mother had hoarded in their hundreds back at the house. Stuff, and more stuff, but nevertheless it was still *Mum's* stuff that dominated everything. I carried the feeling of it, the dusty, gritty, greasy, grubby sense, taste and smell, around me like a sneezy halo. Nested bowls and teacups. Weird agglomerations of one random thing pushed within another like mismatched Russian dolls. Heaps of coat hangers that fought back at you with insectile claws. Old packets of seventies Tampax, for Chrissake—for what conceivable eventuality, Mum, had you been keeping *those*? But at least they were unused. Dead mice and their droppings. Spiders and woodlice. Clammy flowerings of mould. Generalised heaps of nothing in particular that seemed to grow and change as if with a will of their own as I tried to sort through them.

I'd had an odd sense that something beyond all the unmanageable crap piled around me was trying to push its way through even before the real problems started. A lingering not-rightness clung to the walls and shadowed the air like some stain I wasn't able to scrub away, no matter how much bleach I applied or how many dozen bin bags I filled. Nor was I able to capture anything worthwhile with my Nikon.

Then there was the business with the sounds Mum had said were coming from upstairs. Although I'd made a fair stab at clearing out the main hallway within a couple of days and had worked my way into the front room and had brought a little order to the kitchen, I still found myself putting off going up there. After all, or so I reasoned, there was no logic to my clearing a part of the house that Mum was never going to use. But I'd be lying if I didn't admit that I felt a stirring of unease every time I looked up at the swirling dark from the bottom of the heaped and littered staircase, now that I was alone in this place for hour after hour and day after day, just as Mum had been.

I was in the semi-cleared front room on the third or fourth morning, trying once again to get my stalled photography project going by framing quick random shots of some boxes filled with cheap costume jewellery I'd never, ever seen Mum wearing, as if to catch them by surprise, when the first real noise announced itself. Deep and slow and soft, like something loose and heavy being dragged, it stopped as suddenly as it had started, and the regular Mum-mess of ever-swirling dust, slouched bin bags and peeling, fading wallpaper reasserted itself. And, perhaps bizarrely as I spun around and the metallic taste of fear rose in my throat, I also experienced a twist of annoyance; to think that the bloody woman had been right all along.

Of course the sounds could still have had a simple, rational explanation. A failing floorboard, weakened and crumbling masonry, collapsed shelving, or even something to do with those rats I'd originally feared... But, whatever they were, it was important that I didn't simply ignore them, and dealt with the source. So I bought an extra-large, extra-bright halogen builder's lamp and a long extension lead at B&Q that same morning. Then, and after a swift lunch of a Gregg's pasty, a packet of crisps and a plastic bottle of Diet Pepsi, and keeping focus on the relatively simple task of clearing each step with the lamp pointing ahead, I began to work my way upstairs, pushing stuff down and aside in rough tumbles as I did so.

My ascent soon stirred up a great deal of dust. My skin itched, my eyes hurt, my hair felt clotted, and the halogen's glare threw huge shadows around me until it caught on my foot and clattered down to the hall. Not only that, but my chest felt terribly constricted and my breathing had become an all-too-familiar ticking wheeze.

On the days, oh the nights, of my childhood when every breath had been a dragging, conscious effort! The atmosphere feeling, and tasting, like wet concrete. Sitting up in bed, sweating and exhausted, and Mum wondering aloud if I could perhaps put off using my precious spin-haler a little longer, because it was a bad idea for a girl of my age to become so reliant on medicines, especially when all the experts agreed that asthma was really just a thing of the mind, a question of learning how to relax one's chest and breathe properly…

Then the sound came again. Or, more exactly, *a* sound came. This time, it was more of a shifting than a dragging, almost like flesh or paper rubbing together. And its source, as I squatted two thirds of the way up the stairs and the dust swirled around me, definitely seemed to lie ahead. Still, it was the sort of noise that I could still tell myself might well have a simple, rational explanation: some piece of cheap plastic or pottery finally disassembling; the mere slippage of one lost thing against another.

It was a bright summer's day outside, but it was deep twilight up here at the turn of the stairs, and the stuff piled across the landing seemed to have grown like blurry coral, transforming this ordinary suburban space into a kind of weird grotto. I felt for my phone, and the wan, white light of the torch app flared across the heaped boxes, some still neatly labelled in my father's square, regular

STUFF

handwriting—CHINA and MORE CHINA (BLUE) and OLD KILNER JARS and MISCELLANEOUS BITS AND PIECES—others sagging or collapsing, the duct tape which had once held them together now unravelling like soiled bandages, their contents merging into indeterminate heaps.

Dimly, but much closer now, and far more present beyond the phlegmy rasp of my own lungs, I could hear the slow wheezes, hisses and rattles that the stuff was exuding, stirring up waves of dust that churned like slow nebulae in the phone's cone of light. Of course, every house talks to itself. The pipes tick, the floors creak, the roof tiles slip, the rugs and the furnishings gradually settle. But this was different.

I'd never experienced anything like it before, but the primitive part of my brain which still expected to be living in the dark depths of some dangerous forest was screaming out a warning, and my skin actually crawled; the hairs on back of my arms and neck really prickled. Whatever this thing was, I had no desire to confront it. So I turned and slid-bumped my way back down the stairs, my hands shaking and my lungs hurting and my thoughts aswirl.

After that, and as if my foray up the stairs had stirred them into greater life, the sounds came and went more frequently, although to no particular pattern, and seemed to occur most often when I was distracted and tired, creeping up on me when my guard was down like some playground bully. Sometimes the sounds were like that first heavy dragging, and sometimes the noises were more of a windy sighing, or a soft crackling. Being the clever modern device that it is, my Nikon also has a high resolution audio facility, but, just as all my photographs never seemed capable of capturing the chaos my mother had created, all it ever recorded was my own harried breathing and the thump and shuffle of endless bin bags.

"THAT THING YOU were telling me about," I said to my mother during one of my visits to the rehabilitation ward where she'd been transferred. "You know, the noises back at your house. I think I've heard them as well."

"Noises..." Her hands skittered up to toy with the knot around the top of her off-white nightgown. "...I don't know what you mean."

"But you *do*, Mum," I said trying to keep my voice low and calm as the trolley lady squeaked by with elevenses. "You've told me about it many times."

"*Have* I...?" Her fingers were still tugging at the knot as her gaze wandered the ward. "*Did I?*" She looked like a guilty child. "I really *don't* think so." Then her mouth twisted, and her hands stilled. "You *do* get some funny ideas inside that head of yours sometimes, M-Mmmm..." But I could see the certainty fade from her eyes as she searched for my name and her thoughts skittered away from her like dusty cockroaches. Once again, I almost felt sorry for her.

CREAKS AND THUMPS. Stuttering tears and knockings. Sometimes, I thought I heard footsteps, or even the mumble of low voices. But they were just *sounds* at the end of the day, and had made no attempt to hurt me, so perhaps there was no reason to feel afraid. Of course, I tried playing loud music through earphones. But the sounds simply pushed in anyway, rattling around like lumber in the attic of my thoughts. Which, seeing as neither my camera nor my phone seemed capable of recording them, made a weird kind of sense.

STUFF

Dan offered to come up and help me over the following weekend, but I told him not to. Frankly, I was embarrassed by my slow progress, not to mention the noises. That, and I knew what he was like when it came to clearing things out. He'd grown up in a large but tidy house, and both his parents were still entirely competent; his mother, an academic, still even lectured. All he ever did whenever we tried to sort through the rubbish our children had left behind them at home was to pick up some old teddy or report card and start reminiscing. Dan simply didn't get what I was dealing with when it came to my mother. He thought of her as a sweet, eccentric old lady living in a charmingly ramshackle house.

Each morning, I scrubbed and showered myself raw in the bland clarity of the Travelodge. Then, after taking several antihistamines and dosing my eyes with Optrex and coughing up a night's-worth of phlegm, I drew up my latest plan of attack.

"Okay, you fuckers," I'd announce as I bashed into the hallway of 23 Sycamore Close, a gunslinger with her finger on the trigger of a fresh bottle of Mr Muscle All-Purpose, "let's see who's the real boss here."

First, I had to remove all Dad's boxes from the landing. The stuff inside them was neatly packed—in so many ways, he was the exact opposite of my mother—and the yellowed Daily Mails in which he'd wrapped everything formed a time capsule for a lost age. The Piper Alpha oil rig blaze. Gorby still in charge of the crumbling USSR. Ads for cigarettes. Julia Roberts looking incredibly young. I'd left home by then, taking up work as a photographer's assistant at a London advertising agency, which was far less glamorous, and much harder work, than I'd imagined. Dad had just retired, and had been going up and down these stairs as he tried to impose a little long-overdue order when he was struck by that heart attack. I remembered how the doctor had sounded puzzled when I'd assured him that there had been no warning signs I knew of, that Dad had been looking forward to a long and vigorous retirement. I only realised later that there normally *were* warning signs, at least when it came to Dad's particular kind of heart condition. As I tipped all this carefully boxed Mum-stuff into the skip at the recycling centre labelled GENERAL WASTE, I wondered if he'd simply chosen to ignore the sharp twinges, knowing he was cutting short what might otherwise have been a long and difficult retirement.

Driving the familiar streets around Sycamore Close, I began to notice other houses with books and ornaments blocking the light in their windows, or curtains that piled-up boxes got in the way of pulling closed. What exactly were they trying to hold back, I wondered— these habitual hoarders? It had to be something more than a simple desire to surround themselves with useless crap. When it came to Mum, or at least the stronger, proper version of the forgetful and evasive husk I now visited every day at hospital, I was beginning to get an idea. She'd always been a nervous woman, and I don't think she was ever particularly good at dealing with the unpredictabilities that life throws up. But stuff, be it cheap costume jewellery or endless boxes of Tupperware, could always be trusted to be dependably nothing more than it was. Or so she must have thought.

The sounds were wary yet nagging, persistent but inconsistent, sometimes slight, sometimes loud. Not exactly malevolent, but certainly uncaring. Yet playful, as well. One of the worst moments came when, just as I'd finished reclaiming the landing and was sitting down on the top step of the stairs to recover my breath, I heard a noise like a slow dragging, followed by a bump. Which really wasn't that unusual by then, apart from one thing; the sound had echoed up from the cleared and emptied spaces below.

STUFF

"Oh, come *on!*" I shouted, "I mean, *really…?*" But the only answer was the whistle of my own breathing, the thump of my own heart, the itch of dust in my eyes.

Even if Mum had been right, she'd also been wrong. The noises might come from upstairs, but they could also come from downstairs, at least when it suited them, and grainy hints of their presence even started to follow me beyond the house in impish creaks, hisses and bangs. I sensed them stirring in the sour air of charity shops, and humming amid the recycling centre's summer miasma of flies. They gathered in my dreams, forming murmurous mazes in dark forests where the sour fruit of ancient nylons and out-of-date savings coupons hung from withering trees.

Waking every morning at the Travelodge gasping for breath. Coughing up greenish-grey gunk threaded black and red. Dan sounding more worried with every phone call, and offering to come up and help. Me pleading for him not to. Cutting my arm on the dirty broken glass in the upstairs bathroom as I reached disgustedly to lift a maggoty bird out of the sink. Spiders crawling over my nose and into my mouth. Discoveries, discoveries everywhere, and the bed on which I must have been conceived in the far reaches of Mum and Dad's old bedroom splayed and rotted by a burst gutter spilling in years of winter rain. The whole room transformed into a dank forest of fungus and woody, musty smells, just as in my dreams.

Still, it was no great surprise to find that Mum had spared Corey's bedroom from her tsunamis of crap. The bed and his desk just sat there, looking ridiculously uncluttered when I finally got through to them, and his Aubrey Beardsley and Pre-Raphaelite prints still clung gamely to the walls. Even the sounds, which had been getting bolder, drew back into distant murmurs and respectful groans, as if awed by this semi-pristine shrine to maternal love.

Of course, the place that I'd been both putting off and yet most wanting to reach in the entire house was my own bedroom, and once the mess of my parent's room had finally been tamed, and the broken window in the upstairs bathroom had been taped over with cardboard, and I'd dealt with the various infestations of ants, moths, woodlice and flies, I felt ready to make my final assault.

Dressed in hooded paper overalls, yellow Marigolds, a new face mask and with plastic goggles over my already streaming eyes, my breath already coming and going in rasps like Darth Vader's, I must have made either an impressive or pathetic sight as I wrestled my way across a floor-to-ceiling threshold of trashy paperbacks and disintegrating bags of clothes. Apart from the anti-histamines and the eye drops, my other act of preparation had been to warn myself not to expect to find very much beyond more of Mum's stuff. Nevertheless, I harboured hopes of making at least a few genuinely interesting discoveries, just as Howard Carter must have done as he entered Tutankhamen's tomb.

It was ridiculously dark in here. Hot as well. I didn't trust the electrics, and the extension lead of my trusty halogen lamp barely reached from downstairs. The whole place felt vast and shifty and almost infinitely vague. This had been my own bloody bedroom, the place where I'd done my homework and sat and read and lived and dozed and sulked, but it was as bad as anything I'd encountered. In fact, it was worse. I was soon sweating and gasping as I soldiered on in the hope of reaching the window, and the grainy dirt worked its gleeful way beneath my paper overalls and clothes. Then of course there were the noises, skipping up to me and then departing in knowing, playful fusillades. Some seemed to be coming from downstairs, and some from even deeper in this room, and then of course they now came from that favourite horror movie trope, the attic, and whatever rampant chaos still lay in wait for me up there. Stuff, in the kind of amounts that Mum accumulated it, could cannily hide when you wanted it, or turn up in witty and unexpected places, or make shifty noises whenever it fancied, or disappear from the universe entirely, like matter down a black hole.

I remembered those bloody headscarves as my old wardrobe creaked out at me from a thick skein of shadows and cobwebs. Perhaps Mum really had melted my old doll Brenda down to a blackened pool as revenge for what I'd done, but I'd been growing out of her anyway. What I really hoped to find in here was my first proper camera, a 35mm Beirette Junior, and maybe the carefully curated albums of my early prints, which I'd kept in several old shoeboxes beneath my bed. Burrowing through heaped plastic bags full of empty soap dispensers—*you can always refill them, my dear*—my sight blurring and my breath sounding like a blocked vacuum cleaner, dizzy and sweaty and coated in dirt as a tornado of noises hammered and boomed, it came as a deep shock to actually find the boxes where I'd left them. Dragging one out across the gritty carpet in a series of gasping whoops, I hauled the halogen lamp as far as it would go and prised open the lid.

I was expecting a few neatly labelled and dated early examples of my photographic craft; those stark black and white images of uninhabited landscapes and buildings that had won me a junior first prize. But the loose, disorganised slide should have warned me that this box contained something else. Not my own photographs at all, but Mum's: Mum when she was little, Mum at school, and the poorly composed and out of focus holiday snaps she'd taken herself.

What the hell was happening, I wondered, crouched and walled in by nothing but Mum-stuff as the house around me shoved and snickered and groaned. The bloody woman had deliberately obliterated the one thing that had ever mattered to me with even more of her own crap. Then, as I scrambled back under my bed to feel around for another box, I tripped over the halogen lamp's cable, and the light popped out, leaving me floundering and sobbing in absolute darkness as a triumphant, bruising tumult of stuff rained down.

"WHAT WOULD YOU do if something impossible happened?" I asked Dan on the phone that evening. I was sitting on my Travelodge bed. Still trembling. A bag of ice pressed to my temple. A pillow against my aching back.

"Such as?"

"Well, if you saw—or maybe just heard..." I trailed off, and coughed. I hadn't thought this through. "Say, a UFO."

"A UFO?" He laughed. "The thing about those pesky aliens is that they only ever seem to visit idiots from Hicksville. You know... For the anal probes and suchlike. Now, if that happened to *me*, Maud, I probably wouldn't tell a soul."

"Not even your wife?"

"I don't think so, at least not unless I could prove something pretty conclusive."

"Because otherwise I'd think you were a Hick, and an idiot?"

"Pretty much. You're not saying...you've *experienced* something, are you, Maud?"

"You know me. Of course not."

"Anyway, you must be close to finished. I'm really looking forward to seeing your mother back in her lovely old home."

STUFF

Mum had learned how to shuffle up and down the hospital ward using a zimmer frame by now, and was capable of dressing with some assistance, and eating her own food, at least if it was pulverised gloop. Even though she was still mildly incontinent and would require a far more complex and costly care package, this was apparently a brilliant result.

All was set for the inspection visit by the social worker, which would determine whether Mum's house was in a fit state for her return, and I awaited this ordeal with a degree of anxiousness I hadn't felt since taking exams as a child, and probably not even then. Would the house shame me by putting on a show of noise? That seemed unlikely, but I was deeply bothered by the thought that whatever I'd done wouldn't be enough; that I'd spend the rest of my life desperately trying to clear a house that stubbornly refused to be cleared. It didn't help that the social worker was the same breezily-smiling woman who'd got this whole business started by telling me the house needed sorting out.

"You must have some lovely memories of your childhood here," she proclaimed as she peered and sniffed breezily here and there, and the entire place remained stubbornly, predictably, eerily quiet. "I can see no reason, no reason at all, why your mother shouldn't return home."

"WHERE ARE YOU taking me?"

Four days later, and Mum sat hunched and shivering in the Volvo's passenger seat, wearing the new clothes I'd bought for her, which were clearly all at least one size too large. Her withered neck stuck out from her blouse like that of a tortoise from its shell, and her wrists were thin grey sticks: more bone than flesh. She wasn't so much wearing these clothes as sheltering inside them as if from some imminent storm.

Getting everything finalised, with a new bed with raised sides delivered and extra aids installed in the bathroom, had been a Sisyphean task in itself, and there had still been a great deal of red tape to go through today at the hospital to get Mum formally discharged. It was already late afternoon and shrill gaggles of kids were heading home from a new term at school. *Hey, that's my stuff!* Two larger lads throwing a rucksack over the head of another in that carelessly cruel way children do.

"I'm taking you home."

"Home?"

I could sense my mother's cloudy shifts of thought. Whatever the nurses and doctors insisted, this vague creature wasn't the same woman who'd still been capable of cuffing me with withering remarks only a few months before. Or even showing occasional affection. All of that had been blasted away.

"Yes, *you* know, Mum—Sycamore Close, where you and Dad lived, and brought up me and Corey." I tried to keep my voice slow and warmly persuasive as I drove past the park where I'd dumped her scarves. "Does that make sense...?"

"I suppose it does, but...I'm really not sure I *want* to go there... Maud."

At least she knew who I was today. Fighting the urge to cough, I raised and sucked at the old spin-haler I'd rediscovered up in the wilds of my bedroom, primed with a capsule of whatever stuff they put inside these things back in the chemically carefree 70s, and experienced a mildly orgasmic, almost Proustian, rush.

I turned into Sycamore Close, pulled up outside number 23 and killed the Volvo's engine. Glancing over, I saw that the near-perpetual tremor in my mother's hands had increased. *We don't like this... We don't like this at all...* she muttered, as if one distant part of herself was calling to another.

"I thought you'd be pleased to come home."

"But what about...?" Mum's hands made a dithering shape. "The movers and shakers...? The nowhere men...?"

"It's okay, Mum," I said, trying not to smile at her unconscious reference to a Beatles song. "It really is. Everything'll be fine. There's nothing to be afraid of."

"You're not going to..." She seemed to wince. "Fob me off."

"Of course not. Just trust me. Really. It'll all be okay."

I unclipped my seat belt, got out and walked around to the kerbside, conscious of neighbours' twitching curtains, and still half expecting some resistance from Mum. But, weak though she was, she seemed oddly determined as I inched her out of the car and through the gate. It was as if she, too, realised it was important to confront whatever lay ahead.

"It's okay, Mum..." I said, as I felt for my key and pushed the door open, careful to ensure she didn't trip on the new mat. "No need to worry."

"This isn't..." She looked slowly up and around the cleared spaces which confronted her—the hall with its revealed, and freshly cleaned, carpet; the simple, open rise of the stairs towards continued daylight—and the house itself remained eerily silent, as if it too was awestruck by how changed it had become. "This isn't..."

"But it *is*, Mum," I said, "it's just that I've cleared away a few things."

This, if at any point, was when I fully expected this frail, fragile and compliant creature to turn against me. But Mum just blinked and smiled.

"Yes, yes, Maud" she said, giving my hand a small squeeze. "You're probably right."

Which wasn't quite as ridiculous as it sounded. It had only occurred to me recently that a great deal of what I was doing by revealing the old carpets, the old wallpaper, and shoving the old furniture and even the odd picture and ornament back into the places they'd once occupied, was, in effect, to recreate the look of the house from the times when Corey was a baby and before I was born, when Mum and Dad were still relatively young, and her sad obsession had yet to take hold.

"Just through here, Mum... Into the front room... Then you can sit down on your favourite chair and have a bit of a rest."

"You're not *leaving* me, are you?" A brief, anxious glance. "You're staying?"

"Of course I am, Mum." I smiled. "Look, I've even put out a few bits of your stuff." And I had. An eclectic selection of out-of-date copies of the *Radio Times* and the *Solihull News*. A few of those weirdly pointless catalogues she was so fond of, that offer everything from bird feeders to incontinence pants.

I laid my hands against her thin resistance as I settled her down, thinking only of the good times she and I had once had. That dress we'd made together which ended up looking like a harlequin's outfit because we'd cut the sides of material the wrong way around. How she'd come back with a small sweet or treat for me whenever she went out to the shops, even if she'd forgotten to buy lunch, ditsy creature that she was.

"I'll just go and make you a nice cup of tea. I've got some of your favourite chocolate cake from the Co-op, too." I turned on the TV and pressed the remote into her hands, then paused, as if struck by a thought. "And here's a nice, soft pillow, to help you settle," I said, and pressed it gently but firmly across her face.

STUFF

I REVISITED THE old house again on the morning of the funeral, which, because Mum had died so soon after being discharged from hospital, had been delayed by an inquest for a couple of weeks. Not that the procedure had ever been more than a formality. Everyone agreed that succumbing to heart failure in her own home had been the best possible way for her to go.

23 Sycamore Close seemed filled with nothing but simmering silence as I wandered from room to newly whitewashed room, marvelling at how quickly the builders and house-clearers had done their work. All the stuff gone now, even from the dreaded attic, along with most of the dust that had triggered a return of my asthma. Not a noise, not a sigh or a whisper, not a single sound, and the estate agents were confident of a successful sale. Yet the stark paint-scented void felt wrong; as if the place had been flayed alive, stripped beyond naked, left impossibly bare. Was this emptiness, I wondered, what my mother had really been trying to hold back all along?

Standing in the front room, remembering the last wild volley of creaks, hisses, knocks and rattles that had poured around me as her heels beat against the Parker Knoll, I longed for a scatter of yellowed papers, a stained rug, some withered picture or poster clinging askew to the wall… But the house would soon be filled with the clutter of other people's lives. And at last I was free.

As ever with these occasions, attendance at the crematorium was bulked out by the kind of relatives you never otherwise see. Corey, standing at the podium, gave a characteristically facile speech describing a free-spirited woman I didn't recognise, and concluded with some quasi-religious bollocks about Mum smiling down on us all from above.

It would have been more appropriate to hold the funeral buffet at the Travelodge, but as they didn't extend to such facilities, we'd settled on the nearby Marriott. Dan was a good sport, shaking hands and introducing people, and Aaron was a chip off the old block. Standing nursing a disposable plastic beaker of lukewarm Stella, I studied the photos I'd pinned to a noticeboard. They'd come from the boxes I'd found beneath my bed, and, although Corey—and Jane, and even Dan and Aaron—had grumbled about not being given a chance to grab a keepsake, they were the only things of my mother's I'd actually kept.

Black and white Mum sitting on a rug in a garden in a nappy. Early colour Mum standing wearing a jumper and swimming trunks in a freezing-looking bit of sea. Her own mother, my gran, looking rather like her, but if anything more severe. And there was my dad. Quite handsome really, if you discounted the Bill Haley haircut. In fact, they made a good-looking couple. And there was me. Tiny little me in a great big pram. And there were all of us, at Rhyl, with me looking sulky and Corey working on his matinee-idol smile. A happy family. Or happy-ish. After all, my mother wasn't some monster.

"She looks just like you."

It was Jane, my daughter, squat and frumpy in a poorly cut dress that wasn't even black.

"Well," I shrugged, "there's bound to be a family likeness. People might say the same thing about you and me. But at least you don't suffer from my asthma..." I touched my throat and put on a conciliatory smile. But Jane was looking at me as if I'd spat in her face.

"I wasn't *allowed* to have asthma, was I? All I ever had, at least according to *you*"—her face was white—"was a tight chest."

STUFF

"Well, if you say so." I had no desire to have another of our ridiculous arguments, especially in front all these people, and did my best to keep hold of my smile. "It's just that I've been suffering from it quite a bit lately. All that dust when I was clearing your grandmother's house must have triggered it. She was such a habitual, obsessive hoarder. Frankly, Jane, you have no idea."

But my daughter was in no mood to be placated. "*I don't have any idea?* You really should take a good look at yourself, Mum, before you start criticising others, especially the dead. And *stuff...! Crap...!*" She made a wavery, dismissive gesture. She was probably a little drunk. "What about the bloody *darkroom* at home—the room that should have been my bedroom but never was? You haven't used it in years, but it's still there. And the *fuss* you made when I walked in, just *once*, when you were developing—"

"—I think you'll find it was several—"

"—and all those bloody filing cabinets in the hallway filled with prints and negatives that you say you're going to sort through but never will. And those useless old cameras and clattery tripods and bottles of dangerous chemicals and God knows what else. Only you, Mum, could pile up a house with actual *stuff* for the sake of your so-called career when modern photography is about nothing but digits. And all the fucking *photographs* of empty scenery we had to stand around waiting for you to take whenever we went anywhere nice, and woe betide anyone who happened to wander into shot. Me, anyway. Of course, it was always okay for Aaron. And poor *Dad*, the things he's has to put up with. So don't you—don't you *dare*, Mum—talk to me about *stuff*..."

With that, she turned and walked, or rather waddled, back into the throng. Leaving me just standing there beside Mum's photos until, in that sudden way that often happens at funerals, the first departure was the signal for a rapid mass exodus. Soon I was alone, and wondering vaguely what I was supposed to do with Mum's ashes. Dad's too, for that matter, which I'd never found the right place and moment to dispose of. Perhaps best to keep them both, at least for a while, until my head was in a better place than it currently was…

I shivered, and stared down into my scummy plastic beaker of Stella, wondering if I'd somehow drunk more than I thought. Things seemed askew, which was perhaps understandable, and I felt prickly and awkward, as if all that dust—which is mostly human skin, apparently—was still itching its way into me like some grainy tattoo. Then I heard a sound. It was clear and unmistakable: a creaking whisper, a hissing slide. There it came again. And again. I spun around, searching for its source amid the emptied hotel tables with their crumpled napkins, plastic cutlery and smeared paper plates, until the sound returned, but this time as a ratcheting croak, and I realised that it was nothing but my own breathing, the sound of my own corrupted lungs.

I jumped as something brushed my shoulder.

"Hey—it's only me, Maud," Dan said. Somehow, he was smiling. "Don't you think it's about time we all went home?"

Afterword

THE GENESIS OF this story probably came from reading a collection of works by Robert Aickman, a modern master of spooky unease, at about the same time my wife and I were dealing with the aftermath of the deaths of my wife's parents and mine too. But the precise moment it took shape was standing amid the overcrowded shelves of a junk shop in the cathedral town of Lichfield one Sunday afternoon, as I thought about how all this stuff seemed to be taking over not only the planet in general, but also my own personal world.

I can't imagine that the amount of stuff we humans have accumulated during the last century or so will ever be exceeded. When archaeologists excavate through the layers of whatever lies above our era, be it radioactive clinker or the bones of robots, they will then hit a rich seam of consumer goods and packaging. I know that the current focus is on plastic for obvious reasons, but the problem goes far deeper than that.

Put simply, we humans in the first world are addicted to *things*. New things, of course, shiny and pristine in their fresh packaging, but old things as well; the stuff we accumulate but often rarely use but are loath to throw away, or forget about entirely, or buy in junk and charity shops because it reminds us of something we once had, or seems charming and quaint. It's almost as if we've all become Egyptian pharaohs, striving to hold back the uncertainties of death by surrounding ourselves with vast agglomerations of possessions. Certainly, I think that's what Maud's mother is trying to do as her thoughts close in on her and the bothersome noises start to become louder inside—or possibly outside—her head. But her problem is, essentially, part of the modern human condition. It's certainly part of me.

The God of Nothing

THEN CAME A day when the king of all the known lands summoned his Chief Administrator to his presence. Surprised and fearful, for his was the least of all the senior callings, the Chief Administrator hurried from his cell in the bowels of the palace. Sentries raised their spears as the great bronze doors of the throne room boomed open and he prostrated himself before the royal throne.

"Who are you?"

"I am your Chief Administrator and you summoned me, Highness."

"Oh, yes…" The king scratched his beard. "I suppose you are aware of my glorious reign's many successes?"

"I rejoice as we all do, Highness."

"But even with success and glory, problems can arise."

Still prostrate, the Chief Administrator felt a ripple of fear. To have the king speak of problems after summoning you to his presence did not auger well for the prospects of your head remaining attached to your neck, or your torso keeping its most treasured appendages. "So I have heard said, Highness."

"And, this being the season of harvest, I have received reports from across the known lands that the vineyards and the grain fields, and the groves of fruit and olive, are all overflowing with bounty."

"As indeed they should, under the blessing of your sovereignty," the Chief Administrator agreed, although he was struggling to understand how this state of affairs might be seen as a problem, or have anything to do with him.

"And, as you know, it is the time-honoured custom for my royal guards to go out from this city and take tribute as and when they see fit."

"Which is a great honour to us all."

"But I have recently had a visitation from the gods. They came to me in a dream," he added airily, "as they often do. And they told me that from this season forward, there should be a more proper reckoning."

"A more *proper* reckoning, Highness?"

"Yes." The king leaned forward. "Do you not understand my words?"

"Well, perhaps not, Highness, as well as you do yourself. In my humble fashion—"

"From now on all of my subjects shall pay the tribute in this proportion..." The king held up the spread bejewelled fingers and thumbs of both his hands. Then he closed them, leaving just his right index finger pointing up. "Is that clear to you?"

"Yes, Highness."

As he bowed and retreated, the Chief Administrator reflected that a system in which every subject gave exactly one finger's worth of every double handful of their wealth as royal tribute had a simplicity and fairness to it that the current one lacked. If he hadn't held the post he did, he would have been entirely in favour of it. But now, and with harvest already underway and the royal guards doubtless itching in their barracks, it would fall to him to somehow implement this innovation. Which was clearly impossible.

It was one thing for the king's guards to head out from the city with their swords and wagons to grab whatever they could find. It was something else entirely to somehow actually *count* the vast produce of all the known lands, and to then take away exactly one finger's worth in every double handful as tribute. Not, of course, that he and his assistants didn't do their best to record the contents of the royal cellars, coffers and granaries, but they did so by scratching a notch on the thigh-bone of a goat for every handful they counted; a cumbersome system that often resulted in confusion, especially in the seasons of bountiful harvest and with the bones varying in size.

The Chief Administrator returned to his cell in the bowels of the place and sat staring bleakly at nothing even as his assistants went merrily on with the business of bone-stripping and knife-sharpening in preparation for the tally-work ahead. He could, he supposed, somehow pretend to extract this season's tribute as the king had stipulated without actually doing so. After all, the king could be forgetful, but this whole business of being visited in a dream by the gods was exactly the kind of thing he'd share with his High Priest, with whom the Chief Administrator had always had a difficult relationship, and who wouldn't hesitate to use the situation to his advantage. At the day's end the Chief Administrator returned to his modest home through the busy streets of the city sunk in deep gloom. His whole life, his lovely wife, his boisterous children, his carefully nurtured lowly position at court, even his head and other precious appendages, already seemed lost.

After spurning dinner, and ignoring his wife's anxious enquiries, he went out again into the flame-lit bustle. The people all seemed so happy, and he didn't doubt that they would be happier still if they knew that their king proposed to take only a precise amount of their livelihood as tribute instead of the usual random pillage. That dream of his—the damned gods...! He glared up over the rooftops at the moonlit bulk of the holy mountain glowering above the city, and the mountain seemed to glower back. Then he was struck by a thought, or at least by a despairing notion. For if the gods really had visited the king with this vision, was it not also possible that they might be able to help him...?

The mountain wasn't particularly high or large as mountains went, but scattered across its flanks and ridges were temples devoted to every imaginable god. There were the gods of travel and there were the gods of the home. There were the gods of the sea, and the gods of the seasons, and the gods of maternity, love and procreation. The temples devoted to these last gods, the Chief Administrator thought as he heard raucous music and laughter, bore more than a passing resemblance to the bars and brothels in the city below. He certainly didn't expect them to provide the enlightenment he was seeking. But what kind of god would be able to help him? The god of hopeless causes?

He wandered on, lost both in his thoughts and the rambling silvered pathways. Here were the fallen pillars and ivied ruins of temples to gods forgotten, or at least neglected, and he really should turn back. After all, he had his life, his family, his faithful assistants and his duty to his king to consider. But still he climbed where now there was no pathway, scrambling over boulders and beside dizzy precipices.

Then, suddenly, in a narrow gap between two rocks which might once have been pillars, he reached another temple, or at least a rough platform. There was an entrance into the rock face framed by more suggestions of pillars—although it could have been a natural cave; it was hard up here to distinguish the works of man from those of the gods—and its mouth was blacker than even the deepest spaces between the stars above. So black, in fact, that the darkness seemed to seep out like smoke into the grey moonlight, and he was staring into it, both fascinated and appalled, when he heard an everyday sound—the swish of a broom—at his back.

He turned. The broom was being wielded by a barefoot young woman in grey robes.

"Excuse me...I was wondering what kind of god this temple serves."

"Oh, that's simple," she said, still swishing her broom. "It doesn't serve any god."

"But surely"—he gestured at the rocky platform, the cave's black breathing mouth—"you are here for some purpose? And what purpose is there, up here on this holy mountain, other than that of the gods?"

"Well, if you put it that way, let's just say I serve the god of nothing."

"Nothing?"

"Yes," she said, now leaning her hands and her chin on the handle of her broom. "Nothing at all."

The Chief Administrator nodded. After all, she was far too plainly dressed to be a proper priestess. Yet her eyes... They were large, and the pupils were dark wells, and who else did he have left to turn to?

"If I told you what my problem is, would you listen?"

She shrugged. "I don't see why not."

So the Chief Administrator began to speak, describing the endless travails of his work, and the sheer impossibility of keeping a full record of the royal stores, let alone the entire kingdom's output. Although if, the gods forbid, there should not be enough wine and grain set aside to see them through the winter, he would be the one who would be held to account. And now the king had had this idea or vision—or the gods had had it for him—and was demanding a new level of reckoning which went entirely beyond his skills.

"So that's it?"

"Yes, it is."

"Well..." She gave a few more sweeps with her broom. "I'm sure something will turn up. Or perhaps nothing."

Despite what she had said about serving no god, he had still expected something resembling the kind of cryptic utterances most priests and priestesses seemed to specialise in. Still, he supposed, turning to leave this crumbling ruin from which even the thin glamour of the moonlight was now fading, if you sought help from the so-called God of Nothing, what else could you expect?

Knowing sleep would be impossible, the Chief Administrator spent the rest of the long night prowling the city, and found himself standing at the riverside docks in the bloom of dawn, where a few urchins sat listlessly prodding sticks into the mud. Yet now he envied even them, for they marked their days with simple thievery and begging, and making these pointless marks in wet clay. Whereas he...

Then, he was struck by a thought. In fact, it was more than a single thought, rather a whole chain of the things, one leading on to the next without break or pause, and the Chief Administrator was laughing as he returned home and shook his wife awake and assured her that, no, no, he wasn't possessed by some new madness, but by a better way of serving his king.

THE GOD OF NOTHING

PREDICTABLY, HIS ASSISTANTS were deeply suspicious to begin with, and many still stuck to stubbornly notching their tally-bones, even though the harvest was as vast and bountiful as any in living memory. There was also little the Chief Administrator could do at first to stop the royal guards acting in their usual plundering fashion. But when people saw just how easily the tablets of wet river clay could be tallied, and then kept once dry as a permanent and indisputable record of their tribute, they started to change their ways—especially once he ensured that every line counted exactly a double handful of marks, and was thus readable at a glance. All of this took much more than a mere season to accomplish, and of course there were many setbacks, but once the idea of all the king's subjects making the same contribution towards the royal purse in exact proportion to their wealth—be it in salt, jewels or sacks of grain—took hold, the old habits began to fade. The unwanted tally-bones, meanwhile, proved popular with the city's large population of feral dogs.

THE KINGDOM PROSPERED, and so did its subjects, and the granaries and the wine stores were filled, and filled again, and there had never been more produce in the markets, or more trade. Every morning, the farmers with their pigs and goats, and the chicken-keepers with their eggs, and the milkmaids with their pails, and all the wagons groaning with apples and grain, and the merchants with their rolls of rare fabrics, and peddlers with their trinkets, and the jewellers with their gems, all poured into the city to bicker and bargain—and also to complain. Such was the noise and the stench of all this prosperity, with the streets as full as farmyards and often sounding and smelling much the same, that some even dared to mutter that the old days of unfairness and confusion might not have been quite so bad after all.

When the Chief Administrator was summoned to the throne room this time, he was somewhat rounder in girth, and also slightly less terrified. He had, after all, played his own largely unacknowledged role in the abundant seasons following his previous audience. Not only that, but he'd developed a series of distinctive markers to distinguish the different tablets, so that one which recorded the number of sacks of grain in the royal coffers had a small image of a wheat ear in one corner, while that for pigs was decorated with a tiny pig, and so forth. Some of these symbols could even be strung together to praise the king's wisdom and bounty, which was always a good thing to do.

"You are...?"

"I'm your Chief Administrator, Highness."

"Oh yes..." For a while, the king gazed into space. Then he scratched his beard. "I suppose you're aware of the problem."

"Problem, Highness?"

"Yes—don't you know what a problem is?"

"Indeed, Highness. But, with the great bounty of your reign, and the blessings of all the gods—"

"The gods might be bountiful in many ways, but they seem to know little of street cleaning. Or how long it takes my favourite concubine to arrive from her villa with the entire city crammed with wagons and carts, not to mention the stench she brings with her on her robes."

"Indeed, Highness. It has been noted that the city is as prosperous and busy as it has ever been."

The king leaned forward from his throne. "Are you mocking me?"

"Mocking?" The Chief Administrator felt his most treasured appendages shrivel. "Absolutely not, Highness. If only—"

"Then put an end this chaos, or I will put an end to you!"

The Chief Administrator's spirits were as low as they had ever been as he returned home that evening through the press of bodies, handcarts, sheep, oxen and goats. He couldn't eat. Nor could he explain to his wife, whose figure was now as ample as his own, what his sudden preoccupation was about. He went out again straight afterwards, thinking of going nowhere at all, although his steps through the crowded streets unconsciously retraced those he had taken many seasons before. But that problem had been effortlessly simple—a mere matter of better record keeping—whereas this... For no better reason than knowing he wouldn't sleep, he began to ascend the paths leading towards the holy mountain.

Just like everything else in the kingdom, the temples had prospered. There were new priests, new engravings—even new gods. But none of them spoke of whatever it was the Chief Administrator was seeking, and he found himself climbing towards a place where two rocks which might once have been pillars framed a gap leading to a platform, even though the route seemed even harder and higher than before.

There was no sign of the priestess, who he decided had probably been just some beggar who'd briefly made this peculiar spot her home, and cursed his own stupidity in coming here. Then he heard the swish of a broom at his back.

"You *are* still here!"

"Where else would I be?"

She still looked remarkably young; life up here clearly agreed with her, away from all the shit and mud and noise below.

"I'm not here to seek your help."

"That's good." She smiled and leaned on her broom. "Because I have none to offer."

"Neither am I seeking false illusions."

"That is also good." She tilted her head. "Although aren't all illusions a little bit false?"

The Chief Administrator had no time for this kind of sophistry, and was about to turn and head back down the mountain when it occurred to him that explaining his previous difficulties had perhaps helped him come up with the idea of the clay tablets. So, once again, he began to talk. About the noise and the congestion, the sheep coming from the hills in one direction and the wagons full of wine and olive oil from another. And the geese, and the chickens, and the merchants selling their bolts of cloth... How were he and his assistants, who now called themselves scribes, supposed to deal with *that*...?

He trailed off. The eyes of the priestess were twin, dark, wells.

"You don't have an answer, do you?"

"Did you really think I would?"

He shook his head and stumbled his way back down the holy mountain. For once, the city seemed quiet as the glow of dawn rose over the holy mountain, and he stood again at the banks of the river, where most of the clay, which was now a valuable resource, had been removed, and picked up some of the smooth, round stones that now lay there, and was about to toss it into the water when he was struck by a thought.

IN A WAY, this idea was even simpler, or at least could be more simply explained. Instead of all the merchants and farmers in the entire kingdom bringing their entire produce to market so that it might be bartered for other produce, which then often had to be bartered again, why not have a thing—a *something*—representing the produce instead? The king's subjects could then sell their wares without everything always having to be physically exchanged, with a stone or perhaps a small brass token representing the value of a sheep or a bag of grain.

The king frowned and fretted when the idea was explained, as did the Chief Administrator's family and his scribes. For how was wealth and prosperity and status to be reckoned, if it could be reduced to mere handfuls of metal? But by now the Chief Administrator was a man of some reputation, and if this odd idea stood even a chance of reducing the mess and congestion it was surely worth trying.

So the edict was issued, and each bronze token was affixed with a royal crown as a symbol of its provenance, and their use began to clear the streets of the worst of its gaggles and herds. Not that there weren't problems. Some people started hoarding these tokens instead of using them, whilst others attempted to fabricate their own. But soon there were fewer wagons, and the markets were no longer impossibly overcrowded, which would have been a sure sign of the kingdom's imminent collapse in any other era, but now people found that their lives were not only a little easier but more prosperous as well. There was even a reduction in disease, although of course the High Priest, who was never backward in coming forward, took the entire credit for that.

ALL THE KNOWN lands grew in their tribute and bounty, and the temples across the holy mountain were expanded and enlarged, and merchants started using pieces of slate, which could be easily wiped and re-used, to keep their daily tallies, and the king had never been more venerated in his glory. Yet there was a growing problem of which even the Chief Administrator, who now enjoyed an extremely comfortable life, was aware. The sacred festivals and rituals which the entire kingdom followed had somehow moved from the seasons they were supposed to honour.

It wasn't that the seasons didn't arrive, and the birds and all the other wild things behaved as they had always done, but all the holy days and celebrations were dreadfully awry. The god of the cornfields now found that the day which had always been devoted to his power and worth took place in the middle of what was unmistakably winter. Whereas the god of what used to be spring was now required to gaze down from on high at his prostrate worshippers through the blazing heat of full summer. Not, of course, that a record of the passing seasons hadn't been kept in the highest temples using sacred tally-bones since time immemorial. But something had gone wrong, and it was all most unsatisfactory, as the king explained after his usual terse fashion when he finally summoned the Chief Administrator.

"But, Highness, surely this is a matter for the High Priest?"

"D'you think I haven't spoken with him about this?"

"Of course, Highness."

"But he assures me that this disarrangement is a matter of administration rather than theology, which you must deal with," the king waved a bejewelled hand, "or the gods themselves will punish us all."

Despite this dire threat, the Chief Administrator was less concerned than he might once have been as he sat at the family table beside his ample wife and grown-up children that evening.

The seasons, after all, had unquestionably been kind to the kingdom's subjects, and he had already dealt with many problems which would have foiled a lesser bearer of his office—or a High Priest, come to that.

So he set out into the city, noting the many ships moored along the river, and the cleanliness of the streets, and the surprisingly good health of the beggars, who were now happy to accept the bronze tokens he tossed into their begging bowls, and began to climb the holy mountain past the many grand temples, most of which were equally happy to accept these tokens in lieu of penance or prayer.

The climb proved even steeper than he remembered, and he was close to turning back. After all, why should a man of his substance have to visit a temple that honoured no god at all? He also had a sense that he was being followed, and by a more cumbersome personage than a mere barefoot girl. He even thought he glimpsed the edge of a bejewelled priestly robe. Still, though, he climbed, and here was the surprisingly narrow gap between what might once have been pillars, and here was the platform, and that yawning cave mouth.

"I didn't expect to see you again," a voice said at his back.

"Well..." He turned. "That's good, because I wasn't expecting to come."

"Yet here you are. And, doubtless, you have a problem, and you somehow expect me to help solve it."

"What makes you think you've ever solved anything? I'm the king's Chief Administrator, and everything I have achieved is down to my own wisdom and hard work."

"Well," she shrugged and swiped her broom, "not *everything*, perhaps... Or even *anything*... But when it comes to *nothing*–"

"And that," still angered, the Chief Administrator stabbed a finger towards the mouth of the cave, "that is just an empty hole."

"Then why don't you go inside and take a look…" Again, she swished her broom, although the sound now was harsh and cold, as empty as the growl of the winter wind. "…If you're so sure there's nothing there?"

For a moment, and if only to prove this young woman's arrogant folly, the Chief Administrator really was prepared to step inside the cave. But it looked very dark in there, even in the blaze of this Moon, and of course you never knew what kind of creature you might encounter in such a place, be it snakes, bears or spiders, or just an endless, empty drop. He shook his head and waved an admonitory finger. "You're not going to catch me out that easily."

And with that he left the ruined temple, still somewhat angered, and still unable to shake the feeling of being followed by a much larger personage than the girl. Yet he was still less concerned than he might once have been by the enormity of the challenge he still had to surmount. He didn't fear the gods now, or even believe in most of them that strongly. Nor did he believe in the prospect of another life after this one that the priests of many temples now promised in exchange for a suitably large donation. What he did believe in were the simple pleasures of the life he was actually living. The smiles of his family and the taste of good wine and the beauty of this silvered Moon and the first glow of the rising Sun as it shifted, season to season, along the flanks of this very mountain…

The Chief Administrator smiled to himself, and no longer cared whether he was being followed as he made his brisk way back towards the city below.

THE GOD OF NOTHING

IT WAS ALL very well the High Priest and his acolytes choosing to celebrate the festivals and holy days according to the sacred tally-bones they still insisted on venerating in their temples, some of which they even claimed were the remains of the gods themselves. But what if the bones were wrong? Not greatly so perhaps, but over enough seasons, and with even a small amount of error... Not that it was wise to use such words as *wrong* or *error* when it came to matters of holy writ. But it was important that the proper passage of the seasons was followed, which could surely be achieved by making observations of the Sun's rising using marker posts, or perhaps small stone cairns, along the flanks of the holy mountain.

In many ways, the task was simple and repetitive, but to the Chief Administrator it was thrilling as well. It was good that the records on the slates and clay tablets he and his scribes used were now more sophisticated, with different symbols representing different quantities, thus saving a great deal of unnecessary counting up. Standing beneath the hot noonday Sun, or watching the Moon and the stars wheel through the frosty darkness, he felt as if he was close to finding the hidden weave which bound the heavens to the Earth.

Then came the day when he was ready to present his findings to the king. He bore with him several finely ornamented clay tablets. They were beautiful things in themselves, set not only with a precise tally of the Sun's rising and falling throughout every season both past and future, but also with the appropriate symbols of many birds, beasts and flowers—along with, as was now always necessary, a great deal of praise for the king himself.

The Chief Administrator was not entirely surprised to find the High Priest also in attendance, for despite his claims, these matters clearly concerned the temples as well. He felt confident the evidence of his tablets was entirely correct, which was surely all that mattered, and when the king raised a hand to still his words he imagined it was to raise some minor query, or simply to praise his hard work.

"No!"

"No what, Highness?"

"This defames the gods themselves! The very *idea* that the days and seasons can be controlled by these slabs of dried mud—"

"Not controlled, Highness, but—"

"Enough! You are right"—now he spoke towards the High Priest—"this is worse than wizardry."

"Indeed, your highness," the High Priest bowed smugly. "And, just as you willed, I have ordered the destruction of all the crude shrines this man has erected to his nameless gods across the holy mountain, along with the greater one to some dark monstrosity I, personally, have observed him frequenting, although we are still searching for the harpy who serves there."

"They're not shrines, they're markers—and the temple is barely a ruin. And as for that girl, she's not really a priestess and she serves no god."

"You see, Highness," the High Priest gestured. "Even now he is filled with disrespect and lies."

THE CHIEF ADMINISTRATOR was at a loss to come up with a defence to the charges of necromancy, blasphemy and trafficking with demons other than to insist that he had simply shown how the Sun and the Moon travelled across the heavens not according to the whims of the gods, or a scratched pile of bones in some temple, but to the precise tallies he and his scribes had diligently recorded—

THE GOD OF NOTHING

At which point the Chief Administrator was advised that it was only because of his evident madness that he would be allowed to keep hold of his head and his other precious appendages. He would be imprisoned for the rest of his days instead, whilst his family would be banished to the furthest reaches of the known lands.

The ex-Chief Administrator had heard a great many stories about the royal dungeons, and none of them were particularly pleasant. But although the cell into which he was thrown was damp and dark, it proved little worse than the place where he had long laboured in service of the king in the bowels of the palace, and the food was surprisingly decent.

So his life continued, at least in the sense that he wasn't dead, and he heard through the warders that his tablets had been taken to a secure shrine, and the High Priest was quietly re-ordering the holy days according to their writ. His family, meanwhile, sent word through various intermediaries to let him know that life at the far edge of the known world was very much like life in the better-known parts, and that they were enjoying the fresh air and the absence of courtly intrigue. All in all, he supposed he could count himself lucky, even if the passage of the days and the seasons was abominably slow.

He was grateful for his cell's barred window, which not only granted him some light, but also allowed him to watch the Sun's passage across the walls and floor shift from season to season. And there was also the silvering Moon, with whom he felt a special affinity. He even asked his warders for some slates and a sharp flint so that he might better record their movements.

It began as a whim, but the slates soon mounted up and it became an obsession. He still didn't believe that merely keeping track of the heavens was an act of blasphemy—for if there really were gods, then surely it was only right to have a proper understanding of their works? Neither did he believe in their capricious wrath, or a life after death, although he did certainly believe in the wrath of the High Priest. The anger of the gods—ha!—that was ridiculous. Why, back in distant memory it was even said that they had shown their displeasure by darkening the noonday sky...!

The ex-Administrator paused in his scratchings. Struck, as he had often been before, by an intriguing thought. After all, if the Sun and the Moon revolved across the heavens according solely to the courses he was recording, that meant there would come a point when positions coincided in the sky. Which would certainly explain those stories of the midday Sun slowly being consumed by a dark circle, which he'd always imagined were old wives' tales.

Now, even more than before, he was a man driven. It was all simply a matter of mirroring the movements of the Sun and the Moon through the marks on his slates to determine when the next daytime darkness would arise. But his markings grew ever-longer, and the slates grew ever larger, and figures were stubborn and intractable as mules. Something was missing, he was certain of it—some last insight which would allow him to see things as they truly were. And then, perhaps, another thought whispered in his head, he might even get back his job, his family and his reputation.

He barely slept, and when he did sleep his dreams were of slates and the marks he made upon them, piling up into a vast mountain which he somehow had to ascend. In his fitful night-time wanderings he sometimes even glimpsed temples and pathways with the gleaming city spread below. But still he scratched and still he worked and still he climbed until he found himself confronted by two familiar rocks that might once have been pillars, and passed between them into a familiar rocky platform where a cave mouth yawned.

"I didn't expect to see you again," he said to the girl.

"Nor I you."

"But this is only a dream. In the real world, you and your temple have been destroyed on the orders of the High Priest."

She shrugged and leaned on her broom. "Have it as you will. Although how can anyone destroy nothing at all?"

The ex-Chief Administrator laughed. Whatever kind of oblivion had befallen this girl had not, it seemed, changed her fondness for speaking in riddles.

"Have you come again to ask a question?"

He shook his head: the problem he was wrestling with was so vast he couldn't even express it through the symbols on his slates, let alone using mere words. But perhaps the symbols themselves were the obstacle, for otherwise the problem would lie within the workings of the universe itself, which was surely impossible... And so he rambled on, and she listened and smiled as she leaned on her broom.

"And I already know what you're going to tell me..." he muttered as he stumbled without conclusion.

"Which," she said, gazing at him with eyes blacker than the cave itself, "is nothing?"

"Exactly," he replied, or thought he did, for the dream or vision was already starting to fade, and once again he was back amid the heaped slates of his cell, and as ever he was fumbling in darkness. There had to be something, some way of solving this problem, yet the solution seemed as blank and black as the circles of that girl's eyes, or the cave itself—or even the darkness, come to that, which lay between the wheeling stars.

There was a great deal of nothing to be found in all the known lands and the heavens, the ex-Chief Administrator supposed, if you thought about it in a certain way. There was the nothing of death, at least if you didn't believe the stories the priests now told, along with the nothing that came before life itself, not to mention the nothing that was left in your pockets when you had spent all your tokens, or when one amount was taken from another; a problem of record keeping some of his scribes had occasionally complained about when doing their seasonal tallies. But it was the nothing of that cave mouth and the nothing of the girl's eyes that kept returning to his thoughts, around and around like a serpent consuming its tail. He even made that mark, a mere empty circle, on one of his slates as dawn began to illuminate his cell. Then, in a fever, he began to make it again and again.

He'd never felt so wise, yet so foolish, for surely he should have thought of this long ago! The space, the gap, the absence, was exactly what all his intricate tallies and symbols lacked if he truly was to use them to track the movement of the heavens. This blank circle allowed, simply and easily, for amounts to be increased by neat graduations which reached up as far as the sky itself, and beyond, in endless progression. There was beauty here and there was elegance, and at last he was able to render the passage of the Moon and the Sun as they truly were. He was even able to determine the precise moment when the Moon would once again block out the Sun. Which—and this really was something close to divine destiny—lay not far ahead.

The warders, understandably, were suspicious, but they listened warily, and agreed that such a strange augury should be brought to the attention of the king. And if it were true, well, at least he would have some foreknowledge. And if it were false—well, what, apart from his most precious appendages and his life, did the ex-Chief Administrator have left to lose?

THE GOD OF NOTHING

Then came the day of the prophecy, although the ex-Chief Administrator would have preferred to call it a mere reckoning, as he paced and followed the Sun's passage across the walls of his cell. Something which had only recently occurred to him was that the display might be ruined by a heavy covering of cloud, but the sky was blue and clear, and he watched the birds dart, and he heard the sounds of life across the city, until, with no preliminary at all, he heard cries of alarm and wailing prayers as everything began to darken.

The moment of absolute blackness lasted barely an instant, and soon the cocks were crowing as full daylight returned, and it was almost as if nothing had occurred. The ex-Chief Administrator was relieved and thankful, and even muttered a small prayer of thanks to the God of Nothing, although as a proud man of some substance he was mainly looking forward to bowing once again before his king, and hearing His Majesty concede that he'd been right all along, and would he like to return to his family, and his home, and his old job? It was thus a disappointment when the High Priest, of all people, came to stand before the bars of his cell, although of course he was owed an abject apology from him as well.

"So now you see!"

"All I see is a condemned man…" The High Priest smiled. "Although you should thank whatever gods you believe in that your death will not take very long."

IF ANY LAST words were spoken by the ex-Chief Administrator as he fell towards what he truly believed to be the absolute emptiness of death, they are not recorded, although they would probably have consisted of little more than a few groans. Most reputable scholars are also of the opinion that there never was a ruinous temple tended by a young priestess high up on the holy mountain, although a few still insist that this non-existence is the sacred purpose she served.

When it comes to the High Priest, however, all are agreed that, having inspected the scrawled slates piled in the ex-Chief Administrator's cell, he instructed the warders that they should be kept for further study, even though they probably amounted to nothing at all.

Afterword

AS I MENTION in the afterword to the *The Wisdom of the Group*, there are few if any new story ideas, and those which I and other writers continually recycle often have a strong element of fable or fairy tale. In fact, I'd go so far as to suggest that even the most scientific of SF is generally a form of technological fable, especially when it comes to shorter fiction. Some stories, though, lean much closer to myth, fable and fairy tale than others, as *The God of Nothing* clearly does.

This story's fable-like element lies both in terms of the ratcheting series of problems the Chief Administrator has to deal with, and the hint of magic through the mysterious priestess who helps him find answers. Then there are the fairy-tale tropes: kings, advisors, priests and so forth. All in all, I was happy to channel my childhood love of such stories and my teenage enjoyment of the works of Lord Dunsany when I was writing this piece, and maybe not to have to worry as much as I normally do about the precise details of setting, character and society by using something slightly more off the peg.

One of the many great things about fairy stories and fables is that they are often held together by a strong thread of logic—this or that action causing a certain result—which was also something I was keen to exploit. To my mind, however, beneath all the surface dressing this story is really about science, or at least maths, which is obviously also about cause and effect. That, and about religion, and how both disciplines strive to make sense of the world in their different ways.

As far as I'm concerned, science easily trumps religion in all its forms. But if God did happen to exist, he would surely have used mathematics as the alphabet with which to write the universe, as Galileo was the first to suggest. Although, and much like the Chief Administrator, that great early scientist certainly had his own problems with self-righteous and self-serving priests.

Downtime

SHOUTS. A SHARP, bitter, fleshy smell. A blanket scratches my legs. Rusty creaks. A chorus of falling white noise and a dim sense of dread. For a moment I almost know who and where I am. Then I don't.

"Hey." A voice.

"...What?" My throat feels raw.

"You'reawakethen." The words spoken quick and slurring. I run them through the hissing in my head. You're. Awake. Then.

"What do you mean?"

It's a genuine question, but metal creaks and judders as whoever's above me laughs. Through half-closed eyes, I see a faded mattress with blue stripes bulging through a criss-cross pattern of rusted mesh. Legs swing over into view. Lint stuck to bare brown toes. The rest of his body comes down with a hard slap of concrete against flesh. He scratches. Stretches. Gives a squeaking fart. Leans close. His breath is warm. Meaty. Damp.

"Welcomebro." He lifts my arm. Inspects a plastic wristband that makes me wonder if this is perhaps a hospital, although I somehow know it isn't. "CT4619." He gives another laugh. "Sweetlittlenumberinnit?" He's so quick and eager, his words skip far ahead. Sweet. Little. Number. In. It. "You'll soon get used. Like all the rest of us here at Swinney."

Swinney? Once I've semi-absorbed this information, I try sitting up. Pushing at the scratching blanket reveals that I'm wearing an off-grey tee shirt and wash-faded shorts. My companion is similarly attired, and he snatches at his baggy waistband as he shambles over to a lidless brushed-steel toilet, lets his shorts drop down his legs and pisses, humming to himself and giving off another high-pitched fart. He's young, with broad muscles and a trembling mass of dark brown hair. Glancing down at myself, I see that my own skin is much paler. Then, when I reach to locate the fizzing ache in my skull, I discover I'm bristly-bald.

"Where *is* this?"

Another laugh as he shakes himself. "Take a guess."

A shadow sweeps over me. Almost a premonition. "Prison?"

"Swinney sure as hell ain't Vegas. Or heaven, either, come to that. Ain't even next *door* to that kinda place..."

Hell being a place of dark shadows and monstrous fears, and Vegas a city in a faraway desert filled with flashing lights and tawdry entertainments. Whereas the word *heaven* conjures images of old paintings in whispering buildings. Yellowing angels. Paint-crazed clouds. These things I simply know.

"Mind if I call you Ceetee?"

"What?"

"The *number* I just told you about, bro! Your tag. Your wristband for this Disney park." He makes agile hops as he pulls on his socks. "It's who you are. Leastways, for now."

I lift my wrist to study the strip of hazy grey plastic. CT4619. There's also a bruise around a scab in the crook of my elbow. My head is still singing like a waterfall, clear and cold, running down and down. Everything but this specific moment seems impossibly far off.

"I just can't remember—"

"*Course* you can't." Now he's dragging on sweatpants. Instead of off-grey, they're off-black. "It's downtime, innit."

"Down what?"

He slips on a pair of scuffed trainers with flapping Velcro straps. Old man's shoes, the thought occurs. Then something about laces not being allowed in prisons because we, the inmates, might use them to hang ourselves. Some things are just there. Many others aren't.

"Down...time..." He says it much more slowly, as if talking to a dumb child. "It's a tough gig. But you'll soon get the workings of it. I'm Wyzee."

I shrink back into my bunk as he holds out a hand. He's still smiling. His prominent front upper teeth bear a glint of gold.

"Wyzee."

He's saying it again. Why? See? It makes no sense. With his hand still hanging there, he rolls his eyes. "You're Ceetee, right? That's your tag, your ticket for the ride. Least it is until we come up with a better one. And I'm Wyzee. Letter Y, then a letter Z..." He taps his wrist. "Geddit? It's all part of how downtime fucks with who you really are."

I nod. Reach awkwardly for the offered hand. Which he pulls away at the last moment, thumbing his nose with a schoolboy laugh.

"Better get used to it, Ceetee," he says. "The one thing you gotta learn pretty fuckin' sharp in this theme park is that there sure as hell ain't no fuckin' refunds..."

SOME THINGS YOU just know.

Others, you soon absorb.

This being Cell 23 of C Wing of Swinfield Category A Prison, run by the Prestec Group on behalf of His Majesty's Federal English Government. A sign which announces this is stencilled lopsidedly on the metal above the viewing plate on the door of our cell. Breakfast is a squeaking trolley and a clatter of the letterbox-like slot below, and it's your lookout if you don't catch the plastic tray as it comes through. Fake acidic orange juice, watery milk and cardboardy loops of some cheap sub-brand of cereal that definitely aren't real Cheerios; that's something else I somehow just know. A plastic spoon so bendy it's an effort to lift the stuff all the way to your mouth. Then the squeaking trolley comes again, and we shove our trays out. Lunch is much the same, only with a chewy piece of non-meat, a glob of brown stuff that looks and tastes a little like congealed vomit, a square lump that might possibly be jelly and an equally useless knife and fork. No one's asked if I have any allergies, or if I'm a vegan, or only eat halal. Not that I could say, and this stuff is so bland it probably ticks all the boxes at the same time. It's just about keeping us inmates alive, but nothing more. The word purgatory floats into my head. Then dissolves.

"Know what I'm in here for?" Wyzee asks as I stare up at the sag of his body.

"How can I?"

"That's right!" Wyzee's giggles rock our bunk. "Was only last night the klaxon sounded and them screws wheeled you in."

"I don't remember that at all."

"You don't know *nuffin'* yet, Ceetee! That's how it is, and an'it'll have to stay that way. Least for a while, until we gets to know each other."

"That's fine by me."

An empty pause. Somewhere far off, someone is screaming. But the prevalent sound here, either inside or outside my head, is hissing, falling, silence.

"But ain't you curious about *me*?"

I swallow. My throat still feels raw. "As you said, Wyzee, maybe—"

"So the way it *is*, Ceetee, I'm in this big, powerful gang of *bloods*. Not quite sure what city it is yet, but it's a big one, maybe London or Metropolis or even New York. So what I'm in here for has to be what the lawyers and the social workers would call a *gang-related* crime. Which is fine as fuck-a-doodle by me. Maybe I killed someone— you know"—the bunk rocks—"bang, bang, bang. Wiped 'em out. More likely, I'm givin' the orders and into the big money. Nice threads. Fast cars. *Loads* of pussy…"

Wyzee's imaginings go on in this manner for some time, and sound implausibly thin even to me. Metropolis, after all, isn't a real city, this isn't the USA and Wyzee clearly isn't a big-time criminal; he's far too childish and naive. What he's imagining about himself is probably just stuff he's picked up from movies and video games. When he finally falls silent, I drop into an undreaming doze. Eventually, a klaxon sounds and the cell doors screech open. A robotically smooth female voice tells us C Wing inmates to process to the exercise yard.

Real daylight and fresh air feels and tastes incredible, even though I've only been in this place a few hours. There's little sound of life or traffic from beyond the high walls, only a distant growl. This place doesn't look old, but neither does it feel at all new. Tired is probably the right word. The gravel yard is set with a few rusty-looking gym machines and a path has been worn around the outer edge where a few joggers huff and run. Bored-looking guards stand here and there, twisty-wired earphones protruding from their ears. They're wearing big boots and padded jackets with the Prestec logo on the breast pocket. Belts strung with electronic key fobs and something that looks like a cross between a taser and a truncheon, and probably works as both. Most are male, but a few could be female; the way they're dressed, the difference isn't much. Part of me knows that for us prisoners the guards, the warders, are called screws.

"You plainly haven't been here long."

This inmate's wearing the same shabby clothes as everyone else, but he's white like me when about two thirds of the inmates are varying shades of brown, and he's wearing a pair of spectacles, and he's tall and thin, and he has a long nose. He's far older than most, too. Early fifties, at a guess, in this place of child-men. He has a flop of greyish-blonde hair, which must be indicative of several months of downtime. He's the first person I've seen here I can imagine existing somewhere else.

"I can tell from your hair, or the lack of it." He gestures towards my shaven scalp. "We call you newbies pricklies—I imagine you can guess why. You might get a bit more attention to start with, people shoving into you, that sort of thing, but there's not much real violence here in Swinney. I choose to call myself Stanley." He shrugs. "It's just a name I've picked up. So…? How do you feel?"

I shiver. The singing roar gains volume inside my head. "I honestly don't know."

He smiles. "Don't worry. The technical, official word for what all we inmates call downtime is Temporary Retrograde Amnesia, or TRA. Which simply means we can remember stuff that happens now, but nothing from our pre-Swinney past. Our own identities, for instance, or what we're supposed to have done to have got us in here..."

"It still feels pretty weird."

"That's inevitable. Your brain has suffered a traumatic intervention. But in many ways Swinney isn't so bad."

Then the klaxon sounds, and I join the queue to leave the yard through a clacking turnstile and into a dully lit corridor, following the crowd.

"IT'S A PRETTY crude technique when you think about it," Stanley says next day as we trudge again around the yard. "Electronically induced brain damage masquerading as psychiatric treatment. The public must lap it up—to think of us criminals having our sense of self stripped from us along with our freedom and our dignity. And of course it makes us much more compliant, so companies like Prestec the government hires to run these places can do so more cheaply. I mean, can you imagine a riot, here?"

"Hardly." I manage what feels like my first ever smile.

"I guess things are starting to seem a bit clearer than they were?"

"What I *do* know is almost as weird as what I don't. I mean, I know this is a prison, and that we're somewhere in England. And I know Paris is the capital of France. I can think about some things, such as, say, when Christmas is, and all the stuff about kids and tinsel and presents. I don't even have to make an effort—it just comes to me. But if I try to remember a *particular* Christmas..."

"Welcome to downtime. I'd like to say you'll get used to it, but you won't. I haven't, anyway."

"How long does this go on for?"

"That's one of the few things Prestec are pretty consistent about. You can expect your downtime in Swinney to last roughly a year. Apart from the self-harmers and the screamers and the droolers, anyway, who get pulled out pretty quickly and shoved somewhere else—that's D Wing, at least if the rumours are to be believed." He shrugs. "For the rest of us, they'll turn off the chip that's scrambling your memory, and it's uptime prison for the rest of however long your sentence is due to last."

The klaxon sounds, and it's back to the cell, with Wyzee's rambling fantasies and occasional bunk-shaking bouts of masturbation to bear me through the rest of another long day.

THE REGIME IS rigid, with half an hour out in the exercise yard each afternoon, except when it's raining, and an hour of so-called rec, which means recreation, each evening in the refectory hall, where there's bitter coffee and powdery biscuits, and we inmates talk, or play old board games, or leaf listlessly through the piles of ancient magazines and analogue books that lie heaped in several large plastic tubs.

The screws just stand and watch. Of course, you can try drawing them into conversation, but you might as well talk to a wall. To them, we're just walking meat. One of the strangest things about this purgatory we're living through here in Swinney is that there's little sense of judgement. Seeing as none of us inmates have any idea of what we're in here for, you could almost say none at all.

During rec periods, however, a white screen sometimes buzzes down and an old two-dee projector hums into life high up on the far wall. What follows is one of several documentaries—adverts? sermons? warnings?—on the harmful effects of crime. For no crime is victimless. That, again and again, is what we are told. Driving on manual and overriding the speed limit? Well, here's a picture of what a car travelling just a little too fast did to the body of a three-year-old child. And this is her mother, a full decade later, talking about how her life and her health and her marriage have all been ripped apart. Shoplifting? So-called minor vandalism? Again, they might seem like nothing, but here's the son of the owner of a corner shop who killed himself after his business was ruined by years of hooliganism and petty theft.

We all watch these images in silent fascination, although I wonder if it's as much for the glimpses they give of the world beyond Swinney as for the messages they contain. A city pub seen behind the fluttering tape of some awful crime scene, for example, might have once been your local boozer. And the suburban kitchen in which yet another victim sits sobbing into her tea is a rare and precious glimpse of everyday life. The one kind of crime these documentaries tend to avoid are those with any kind of sexual element. The concern, I suppose, being that some of us might find such things arousing. But I certainly haven't felt any stirrings yet myself.

Each video ends with the usual robotic female voice informing us that Temporary Retrograde Amnesia is an initiative in prisoner rehabilitation that the Prestec Group, a *caring* company, is proud to be implementing on behalf of His Majesty's Federal English Government. Then comes a cartoonish image of a bared human brain, and a dancing arrow pointing towards a part apparently known as the hippocampus, which in our case is being bathed in a minute signal from a tiny implant which will help lead us on a journey towards becoming better human beings. Or at least, better

247

prisoners. Then there's a man sitting on his bed in a prison cell, gazing out of the window across fields and rolling hills—although in here in Swinney there are no outside windows—towards a golden sunrise before the projection fades and the screen rolls back up.

THERE SEEM TO be four wings in total here at Swinney, imaginatively titled A, B, C and D. Although we fifty or so C Wing inmates never get to mix with any of the others, you can tell from the sound of distant klaxons and a sense of recent occupancy—fresh spillages and smells in the refectory, dust lingering in the yard—that our routines interlock. At least, apart from D Wing, which has a reputation of sorts. Stanley not being the only inmate to subscribe to the theory that this is where Swinney's problems and failures are sent, most likely to be put back into downtime for as many times as it takes, and then maybe a few more for good luck. Sometimes at night, when everything else falls quiet, you can even hear a distant chorus of howls and screams. No use asking the screws about this, though. Same as with anything else, they'll just look right at you as if you're not really there. We might as well be ghosts.

One day three weeks into downtime as I'm heading back from the exercise yard, the robotic voice commands me, CT4619, to turn to the left. A metal door screeches open and I find myself in an octagonal space, a kind of clinic or possibly a torture chamber, set with three other doors, sloppily spray-stencilled A, B, D, facing me, all of which are closed. As, now, is the door C at my back. A large chair is bolted to the middle of the stained concrete floor, from which dangle several heavy leather straps. More straps droop from a gurney parked at the side. A youngish woman in creased green overalls tells me to sit down. She doesn't bother with the chair's straps but taps a clipscreen and shines a light into my eyes and checks my blood pressure and pulse.

"How are you feeling, CT4619?" she asks. She looks tired. Her hair is greasy dark. Her breath smells of old-fashioned cigarettes.

"Fine, I think."

She frowns. "You *think*?"

"Well, seeing as I don't know who I am, it's pretty hard to tell."

"There's no need to be smart. Any dizziness? Light-headedness? Shivers, palpitations or tremors?"

"I don't think so. Nothing that—"

"Nausea, sudden unexpected twinges or pains?"

"No."

"Hallucinations? Strange sensations? Any nightmares? Or dreams?"

Dreams? Nightmares? Feeling emptier than ever, I shake my head. Green overalls—the cheap way things are done by Prestec, I very much doubt if she's a qualified medic—points a blue thing that looks like a plastic toy gun at my forehead. Briefly, like the twisting of a faucet, the cold hissing rises louder and sharper in my head. Then she tucks a loose strand of lank hair behind her ear and touches her clipscreen again.

"Thank you, CT4619," she says without looking up, and the door to C Wing screeches back open. "Now you can fuck off back to hell."

WHO AM I really? The features I see in the cell's hazed steel mirror are broad, with almost Slavic cheekbones and squinting, hazel-ish eyes, along with a widow's peak of slowly returning wiry, near-black hair. My body is also surprisingly hairy. A thickish pelt runs across my chest and belly, then narrows towards my crotch. More of the stuff darkens my back and shoulders. I'm right-handed, and well-built. Unlike many of the others I've glimpsed in the weekly showers, my prick is uncircumcised, and there's a slight extra dent, almost a callus, at the base of the third finger of my left hand, which I think might indicate the ghost of a wedding ring. I seem to have a good facility with the English language—far better than most of the other inmates—and my voice isn't obviously accented, so I don't think I'm foreign. I also reckon I'm more intelligent than most of the men here, Stanley perhaps excepted, and I don't seem prone to the ticks and quirks—from Wyzee's gangster fantasies to the guy who regularly lets out cow-like moans—that many others exhibit. But when it comes to actual normality, I've no clear idea what I'm supposed to be judging myself against.

There are fat men in here with balloon-red faces. There are men so cadaverously thin they seem to be made of little more than bone. There are men with limps. There are men with missing fingers. A few inmates are allowed to wear hearing aids, or glasses like Stanley. There's even an albino, and another with a stump for an arm. Quite a few inmates have trails of scars across their forearms which probably indicate long-term drug use, although it's obvious they must have been through withdrawal before downtime started. Another use, perhaps, for D Wing? And tattoos—tattoos are a fascination. I glimpse snakes, elaborate geometric patterns, crude amateur scrawls. Surely they must say something about the person they're inscribed upon? I really wish I had one myself as something vaguely tangible from my lost past...

"I'm pretty sure they take a good look at those before they shove us into Swinney," Stanley says. "Then, if there's anything suspicious, anything that looks like a person's name or a phone number or stuff like that, they simply laser it off while you're under anaesthetic for the cranial implant. Next time you're in the showers, you might notice a few patches of shiny scar tissue on other inmates where that's been done."

He's probably right, although such things could simply be evidence of old injuries and burns, and it doesn't pay to stare too hard. The showers, of course, being the place you're supposed to dread in prison—I don't need to be *me* to know that—but in truth the worst things are the scurrying cockroaches, the way the water suddenly goes cold, and having to dry yourself with thin and scratchy towels. As for anything sexual, it doesn't seem to happen much, and when it does, it's furtive and consensual.

One night, as a counterpoint to Wyzee's endless wanking, I try masturbating myself. The recollection of all the inmates I've seen in the showers, even the better-looking ones, doesn't do it for me, so I'm probably not gay, and the only women I can conjure up are the screws, who are about as sour and sexless as it's possible for anyone to be. Then I remember green overalls with her clipscreen and greasy hair, and briefly manage an erection at the thought of her leaning over me with the scent of cigarettes on her breath. But it won't stay. Starting to chafe, I leave YZ to continue rocking the bunk on his own and fall into my usual dreamless sleep.

"I SUPPOSE YOU'VE heard most of the stories by now," Stanley says as we walk the yard. The weather is warming. There's a springlike chime of birdsong. Although the individual days remain a blur, I know I've been here for almost exactly seven weeks. "That downtime's permanent, for instance—that we never get our memories back, and are simply chucked into regular prison, and then out into society, as empty and useless as we are now."

"The one I prefer is that Prestec stores all our memories on some vast hard drive."

He laughs. "But then, the way things are run here, they'd probably give us someone else's back instead of our own. Or how about we're not here at all, but plugged into some kind of virtual reality suite?"

"In that case, surely the food would be more convincing, and the screws less robotic? But why just a year of downtime? Don't you think it would make sense for Prestec to keep us as zombies for as long as possible?"

He shrugs. A large seagull looks quizzically down at us from the high wall which separates us from the outside world. "I suppose they want to put some distance between us and our old lives and habits. So, when our memories are returned, we'll realise the sheer viciousness and abject stupidity of whatever we've done. That, and I suspect that if they left the implant active for much longer than a year, it might destroy increasing amounts of who we really are. Or were. But the thing is..." Now, he's speaking more quietly. "We go all around complaining about how cheaply and badly Swinney is run, but everyone still seems to accept that downtime actually works."

I turn to him as we stop beneath the shadow of the outer wall. "Are you saying you can remember stuff from before?"

His thin lips purse. "It's..." He shakes his head. "Just glimpses and glimmers. What's that phrase from Bible? Through a glass darkly."

"But how?"

"Doesn't the girl in the overalls ask if you'd had any dreams when you go in through that metal door?"

"We don't dream, though, do we? At least, it's another thing none of us can remember. Are you telling me that you *can*?"

Stanley looks at me but says nothing. Then the seagull screams and takes flight, free, into the empty sky.

THE LONGER I'M in Swinney, the more I'm fascinated by the working of my mind. Doing the things I need to do here, talking, walking, keeping track of the faces and names of other inmates, it hasn't let me down. But it's the knowledge it still calmly offers up as if out of nowhere that intrigues me the most.

It isn't just Christmas. If I visualise the word *Paris*, for instance, I get impressions of wide boulevards and the spidery edifice of the Eiffel Tower. Then comes the smell of coffee. And little markets, and big squares, and imposing statues, and laughter, and small, blue-painted hotel rooms with views down alleys, and a happy sense of not being alone. Have I been there? I think I must have; the sense is far too specific and precise. But if I think of, say, the city in Brazil called Rio de Janeiro, all I can summon up is the impression of a big statue and some vaguely famous beach. So I probably haven't been to Rio. And if I spend too long probing in any particular direction, everything starts to shift and spin like the colours of a kaleidoscope and I feel the rise of a familiar hissing. That, and a growing sense of dread.

When we're not being shown correctional videos, or playing draughts, the thing which occupies conversation across the tables during evening rec is what any of us might have done to get in here. Once we've got past the obvious idea that Stanley must have done something clever with money, and Wyzee's absurd gangster fantasies, we're left with all the many other types of offence. Burglary. Dangerous driving. Assault. Robbery. Drugs. Smuggling. Terrorism. Arson. Fraud.

But there are other crimes out there as well, the large Black guy we call Clicker says with sudden animation. Things the videos never go into. Rape, for instance. Or kiddie-fiddling, or maybe just looking at the vids, which is surely bad enough. And serial killers—they aren't just in movies, you know. They really do pick people up, play with them for ages the way a kitten plays with a ball of wool. Seeing as Stanley here says there's definitely no death penalty here in England, stands to reason some of us must have done really bad stuff like that...

We all fall into our separate islands of thought as the screws stand around watching us in listless boredom and another empty day slides by.

YOU HAVE TO be here for a while to realise that C Wing is in a constant state of turnover. First of all there are the pricklies, the downtime new arrivals. We observe these creatures with a mixture of pity and contempt as we wait to see if they're going to settle. Most are fine. Most you get to know. Or soon learn to avoid. But some exhibit symptoms of derangement or self-harm. The guy, and he didn't even look like a Muslim, who spent ten whole sleepless days and nights shouting *Allahu Akbar!* The other guy, small and nervous and squirrelly, who bit at his fingernails until bits of bone poked out. Another who seemed to think he was a dog, at least to judge from the way he growled and howled and snapped. All of them carted off, presumably to add to D Wing's faint but manic roar.

DOWNTIME

Then there are the *proper* downtimers, as we think of ourselves, whose year finally comes up. Of the members of the group I spend most of my time with, Clicker is the first to go. I awake at some point deep in the hissing night to hear a klaxon's bark. Then a door screeches, followed by swift footsteps as the wheels of a gurney squeal along the corridor past my cell. Muffled voices, then what sounds like a struggle before the gurney returns and a door judders shut. Next day, Clicker's no longer with us in the yard or during rec.

It's hard to imagine what that moment must be like. To realise so suddenly and out of the darkness, and even if you've been trying your best to prepare for it, that your downtime is really up. But then, I'm even more vague about the circumstances surrounding my arrival, and I've already been through that. It must be like a kind of birth, but also a kind of death. Is there any therapy on the far side? No, no, that would cost money. Do we get to see a lawyer, or our family, or the poor bloody victim, or a psychiatrist, or a priest? Or are we, as seems more likely, simply left to sort out the sudden rush of knowing who we are entirely on our own amid the chaos of some regular prison, where the cruel and cannily experienced uptime inmates will surely tear us to bits?

I get to witness the extraction process at close hand when it happens to Wyzee, of all people, who seems far too young and innocent to be leaving C Wing, and clearly hasn't been keeping proper track of his days here. Again, it's late at night. Again, I'm asleep. In fact, it feels like the extension of a dream as, instead of hurrying past, the footsteps stop outside our cell and the door screeches and the lights undim. There's even a moment when my throat tightens as I think they're coming for me. But they're reaching up towards Wyzee, and the whole bunk starts rocking as he resists.

255

"Hey, *guys*! This can't be right! I'm *Wyzee*. Look—here's my tab right here—WZ2357. There's gotta be some mistake. I ain't been here for hardly no time at *all*. I ain't—"

The hiss of a syringe, and the screws lift his body down, strap him into the gurney and roll him away. For a few days and nights I'm alone in the cell, and I find I'm missing Wyzee, even his rambling fantasies, far more than I could have expected. I feel sorry for him, too. Whatever he's done, I can't imagine he'll find uptime prison easy, with his big dreams and easy sense of trust. Then the klaxon sounds again, but this time during the long lock-up of morning, and my cell door screeches open, and the screws count *one two three* as they lift a large body from a gurney onto the top bunk.

My new cellmate is bald, of course, and he looks pale, and is far bigger and heavier than Wyzee, and spends some hours in what might be either a coma or deep sleep. Then, just after the lunch has been delivered through the slot in the door and I sit watching him as I eat, his eyes flicker and his lips start to move. He surely must be dreaming by now, I think. Especially when he makes odd, sudden jerks and his hands begin to twitch. Then he speaks, or rather he mutters, phrases which don't seem to be English but sound…I'd guess something eastern European. I'm out doing afternoon yard time when he does actually awake, and I find him sitting on the bunk with his head in his hands on my return.

"Do you know where you are?"

Of course he doesn't, but it's interesting to see how he looks at me in much the same blank way that I must have looked at Wyzee. His lips frame a question, then he stops, and tries again. "Do *you*?"

I can't help but remember how kind and generous Wyzee was to me, at least in his own shambling way. I do my best to be the same, but it's hard not to feel contemptuous of this big, bland, stupid newbie with his slurring accent, strong body odour and prickly head. I could tell him we're in Narnia, and he'd believe me. I could tell him we're all the figments of someone else's dream. I could tell him that we're dead.

Still, we make our accommodations, and he doesn't argue when I decide to call him P, and we slowly get used to each other, which mostly means avoiding the obvious irritations experienced by two large adult males sharing a confined space. When I ask P what other language he thinks he might be able to speak, he's got no idea, and I wonder, in that first moment that he raised his head and tried to respond to my question, what exactly was going on inside his head.

"WHAT HAPPENS IF I give the wrong answers to any of this?" I ask green overalls the next time the calm, robotic female voice tells me to step left through a screeching metal door at the end of afternoon exercise.

"It's me asking the questions here, CT4619. Not you."

"But just supposing. Would you send me through that door into D Wing? Turn me repeatedly off and on until nothing's left?"

Predictably, she frowns. Taps her clipscreen. Avoids my gaze. Tucks a strand of greasy hair back behind her ear. "That's not how things work here. Haven't you read the signs, CT4619? Prestec is a caring company."

If that's a joke, she doesn't bother to smile. It's just me and her in this space, and she hasn't strapped me to the chair. I think of escape scenarios. Grabbing the electronic key-fobs she must surely have in one of her pockets. Maybe finding some sharp object and holding it to her throat as I force my way out. But where would that get me, when the real prison is right here inside my own skull?

Next comes the bit where she points her blue plastic gun at my forehead. Briefly, the cool hissing seems to increase. Then she taps her clipscreen, scrolling down, and glances up at me for a moment with a kind of weary disdain, and an even deeper chill starts to rise as I realise what that look probably means. It's right there on her clipscreen. Who I am. What I'm supposed to have done. Why I'm here. But by then the door to C Wing is screeching open and she's turning away and telling me to fuck off back to hell.

STANLEY'S RIGHT ABOUT downtime. You really don't get used to it, but it isn't that bad and I've noticed subtle changes beyond my regrowing hair. I have a past of sorts now that I can remember, even if it's all here in Swinney, with its corridors, procedures and frustrations. Some things, the more irregular moments, stand out. My arrival, for instance, or my occasional visits to see green overalls, or the time the screen got stuck halfway down the Prestec logo during rec, which we all found hilarious.

My brain is a storyteller, a collector and connector of events which it strings together to help me navigate the ever-shifting now. I've seen all the crime videos at least once—I can recite the standard bit at the end by heart—and the repetitive conversations and unchallenging games of the other inmates have come to bore me, so I spend a great deal of my time during rec leafing through old analogue magazines and books from the big plastic bins.

I like the home magazines best at first, although I can somehow tell that they're ridiculously old-fashioned from their choice of fabrics, colours and shapes. Then I make an effort to read some of the novels, things I suppose would have been called classics in years gone by. I find that I can follow the sentences easily enough, but the scenes, the people and the things they do and say, remain lifeless and dull. Perhaps I've never been much of a reader. One book though, which is set in London during the Blitz, has a slightly different feel. The events seem oddly predictable. Is it because I've read this book before, or perhaps seen a movie version, or am I simply recognising the narrative patterns writers of fiction generally employ?

I move on to the remnants of an old multi-volume encyclopedia I find at the bottom of some of the bins. The kind of thing, part of my brain quietly informs me, that was common in a different century when people couldn't access every kind of data through their phones. Several of the volumes are missing and those that remain have lost a great many of their pages. Still, I find them fascinating. The way they flick from subject to subject, Vatican to Vault to Venezuela. I like the small ignitions of recognition and understanding some phrases and images cause in my brain, and keep returning to the P volume, opening the crackling pages devoted to Paris. That photograph of the Eiffel Tower, for instance, and the one of the Arc de Triomphe—even though it isn't mentioned, I somehow know that it lies in the middle of an incredibly busy roundabout—and I keep thinking of hotels, cafés, and pleasant if foot-wearying slogs along the corridors of various famous museums.

I always win easily whenever I play draughts, and understood the rules as soon as I arrived without having them explained. Scrabble was the same. Which must mean something. But what's stranger, what tugs at my thoughts, isn't how clever I am, or how dumb most of my fellow inmates are, but the sense that comes over me midway through a game that I should be making a subtle effort to lose. Sometimes, but only if I don't force it, I even get a fizzing sense that I'm facing a much smaller and more indistinct opponent than some fully grown inmate with bad breath, stubble and filthy nails. The ghost of the ghost of a child. My own kid? The idea sometimes feels almost heartbreakingly close.

What on earth could someone like me have done to deserve this incarceration? It stands to reason that most of the inmates are petty criminals from deprived backgrounds who'll have chalked up a long list of minor convictions before they were eventually jailed; after all, isn't that how the justice system works? Stanley, though, is generally accepted to be the one of us who'll definitely have it good and easy when he's finished downtime, which will be any time soon. He's obviously a white-collar criminal, and probably still has most of the money he embezzled hidden in some numbered fancy foreign bank account. A couple of weeks in an open prison and he'll be out on parole with a blonde trophy second wife waiting outside the gates in a vintage Jag, wearing a dab of perfume and a mink coat.

Eh, Stanley, isn't that how it'll be, you lucky sod? But Stanley's recently lost the left lens from his glasses, which gives him an oddly pained expression, and he looks drawn and grey and haggard from lack of sleep.

THE KLAXON BLARES. Another morning. P and I yawn and scratch and fart ourselves awake. For some reason, I'm remembering that familiar image at the end of all the Prestec videos where a prisoner stares out of a window. But, instead of a rural sunrise, a dark and sinister figure is bulked outside. The trolley squeaks and the letterboxes clatter with breakfast, but suddenly there are shouts, the klaxon sounds again, followed by hurried footsteps, although the story of what's actually happened only emerges that evening when we're finally allowed out for rec.

It's Stanley. He's killed himself. Which no one saw coming, although to take out the left lens of his glasses and slowly sharpen it against the wall of his cell until the edge was keen enough to slice open both his wrists, the sheer determination of the act—not to mention the clever planning—is somehow typical of the man.

But what did he know about himself, or at least guess…? The question hangs unasked as we whisper together, the old-timers and the pricklies, united for once in helpless fear. I was as close to Stanley as anyone, and am at least as shocked as everyone else. But he'd worked something out, hadn't he? Discovered a way to get beyond downtime, even if he ended up slitting his wrists because of what he found out.

Poor Stanley. Poor, poor Stanley. Lying amid blood-soaked towels. Probably not a white-collar criminal after all, but something else, something worse. I gaze around at the hunched heads in the refectory as surprise exhausts itself and dulled normality returns with the click of board games and the chomp of biscuits, and know with fresh, thrilling certainty that I'm not like them. But I'm not like Stanley, either.

I'm me.

I'VE LOCATED SOME more volumes of that tatty encyclopedia beneath piles of broken games. The As have an entry on amnesia, which apparently exists in surprising varieties. There are people who can't remember things from moment to moment. There are those who can recall everything apart from some specific fact or event. It seems that us downtimers have something called "pure" amnesia, which means that, although our ability to recall non-personal information remains largely intact, we have no recollection of the circumstances of our own lives.

Search as I might, though, I still can't find the M volume, which would surely include something useful about memory. But then, although it's stuffed inside the X-Y jacket, I find the volume for the Ds and flick through with rising excitement until I find the entry on dreams.

Of course, dreams have always been seen as offering glimpses of hidden knowledge, or of the future, or of divine wisdom, or of other worlds. Then along came Sigmund Freud with his theory that they're an expression of the unconscious and filled with lots of fancy symbolism that's mainly about sex. An idea which had been largely discredited even back when this encyclopedia was written, in favour of the view that they're simply a side effect of the routine data-processing that goes on every night during what is commonly known as REM—meaning rapid eye movement—sleep, and are an essential part of keeping ourselves whole and happy and sane. Certainly, people deprived of REM sleep soon develop serious physical and mental symptoms beyond any I've witnessed here in Swinney. Meaning that it's highly unlikely we're not having dreams. It's just that we can't remember them. Then, as my eyes rove down the pages, I notice a sub-entry on something called Lucid Dreaming, and a plan starts to form in my head.

DOWNTIME

IT'S AN ODD thing to want to do, to make yourself sleep badly, and nothing like as easy as it might seem. I try sitting up in the darkness, but soon end up falling into the usual hissing well. Then I drink lots of water before I climb into my bunk. Of course, and much to P's annoyance, I have to get up several times to piss, but with no other apparent results.

It's there, but it's not there, this thing I'm sleeplessly trying to reach. But the dragging hours of each day now have a slightly surreal quality which somehow convinces me that I'm on the right track. The real breakthrough occurs as I stand alone out in the yard in a patch of warm sunshine, kicking absently at the loose stones, and idea comes to me from seemingly nowhere. Stooping down as if to tighten my Velcro trainers, I shove a couple of handfuls of gravel into my pockets.

Of course, I sleep very badly on a pillow stuffed with these sharp lumps. But that's the whole point. Then, after several hours of pure discomfort, the discomfort becomes less specific, and I find I'm drifting, floating, sweating, tossing, although still very far from sleep. This whole bunk is like some creaking gurney, bearing me out from the cell. On and on—these corridors are so much longer than they seem in daytime—through door after door. But now the ceiling's getting lower, and I realise with a bump of surprise that I'm back where I always was.

After that, the dreaming gets easier, and the memories grow less vague. There's one dream where Wyzee's back in the cell with me, although we've changed bunks for some reason, with me on the top. There's another where I'm out in the yard, and walking with Stanley, who's got both lenses back in his spectacles, although his forearms are bound with bloody towels. When I ask him what made him want to kill himself, he screams like a seagull, flaps his dripping arms and flies off. Other dreams are merely impressions, or flashes of illusory insight. The idea that the robotic female voice would whisper my real name if I listened hard enough. Or I'm down playing cards during rec, but for some reason that we're up up to our knees in spilled sub-Cheerios and milk.

P grumbles about my night-time restlessness. My eyeballs are gritty. I'm incredibly tired. Daily reality often seems almost impossibly far off. But the dreams are getting more elaborate and carry on from night to night, repeating and evolving, although they're still resolutely tied to life here in Swinney and I haven't yet managed to control events with my own conscious will.

I'm summoned again after exercise through the screeching metal door. Green overalls takes my blood pressure and heart rate and frowningly asks me if I'm having any nightmares or dreams, and I shake my head in a clear negative as the octagonal walls threaten to dissolve. Then something in me freezes as she points a small plastic toy at my forehead and taps her clipscreen before she turns away and tells me to fuck off back to hell.

THE OTHER INMATES think I'm odd, P especially, as he watches me staring hard at the hazed steel mirror each morning as if I'm trying to see through to something else, and performing all the other rituals which, at least according to the entry in that old encyclopedia, will increase my capacity to engage in lucid dreams. Regularly holding my breath, for instance. Or jumping up to see if I can fly.

"What you're doing is continually testing reality," my dream version of Stanley says to me as we patrol the exercise yard. "If you can make that an automatic habit when you're awake, it will eventually transfer into these dreams. That old trick about pinching yourself to see if it hurts so you can tell if you're asleep? Actually it's quite a good one. As is trying to push your hand through a mirror. Or if right now, for instance, you could see if you really need to breathe..." He nods. Smiles. His mirrored eyes gleam. "You don't, do you?"

"That's right," I say easily. "Which, apart from the fact that you're alive when I know you're dead, means this is definitely a dream. But what's frustrating that I still can't seem to find my way out of Swinney and into the rest of my life. I can't simply fly over this wall, the way you sometimes do."

Stanley looks dubious, or perhaps it's quizzical, or simply intrigued. Sometimes, it's still hard to tell in dreams. I open my mouth to explain more to him, but the klaxon is sounding and my lungs are choking and I suddenly realise I'm desperately out of breath.

I'VE BEEN HERE at Swinney for more than eight months now. I know the ropes: the klaxons, the robotic female voice, the screeching doors, the impassive, know-nothing screws, the occasional random cell searches, the wearisome, repetitive Prestec videos and the even more wearisome and repetitive games and conversations during rec. I've also come to miss the faces of some of those who've left us at the end of their year with the kind of nostalgia I suppose anyone feels about a lost part of their life. The new pricklies seem a nastier, stupider bunch. Two of them even try to ambush me over some imagined insult out in the yard, and I surprise myself with how swiftly and efficiently I'm able to protect myself by kicking, elbowing and punching long before the screws manage to intervene.

It certainly pays to nurture an aura of respect. Swinney is, after all, a place filled with potentially dangerous men.

THE KLAXON SOUNDS. I jerk awake. A cold roaring fills my ears. As ever by now, there's a fading struggle to work out exactly where and who and what I am. That weird, familiar yet unfamiliar sensation of my shackled brain whirling into gear. Then the cell door screeches, and I know it can't be morning, but time for exercise in the yard—that's how long I must have slept—so I step outside, more exhausted than ever, but for some reason the lights are dim and the corridor is empty and the only living, breathing person in Swinney seems to be me. Although, as I walk slowly down the corridor, I realise that I'm actually not breathing at all. Perhaps I have gills and the entire prison is suddenly underwater, although that would make no sense. Neither does the door I'm now passing, which is made of blue-painted wood instead of the usual corroded steel. I turn the handle slowly, still not daring to breathe.

Then I'm in a hotel room with the kind of floral, flouncy accents which, along with the bidet and the knobbly brass bed, somehow make it characteristically French. A woman stands at the window, looking out across grey Parisian roofs. She's wearing a white blouse and fashionably faded jeans. She has dark blonde hair. Then, just as she turns to me and I step towards her, a klaxon sounds and everything dissolves.

DOWNTIME

SUDDENLY, LUCID DREAMING'S so easy it feels as if I've punched through a tissue-thin veil. Every night, now, as I lay down on my gravel-lumpy pillow, I can hardly wait to explore the corridors of my mind.

I know, for instance—and with absolute certainty; this isn't some hunch—that the woman in that hotel room with the dark blonde hair is my wife, and that her name is Lynn, although I sometimes call her Linnie, and that our trip to Paris was our honeymoon. I also know Lynn's beauty has matured since; the blue-grey eyes, the mouth that slides so easily into a smile, the deep, rich scent of her hair. Call me superficial, but I'm still giddy at the thought of how lovely she is, and the broad, flat-planed face that stares back at me from the hazed steel mirror tells me that she's way out of my league.

Even when I'm awake now, I'm in a world of thoughts and discoveries far from Swinney's grey trudge. But the downside, ha, of fighting downtime is that the actual prison life I clearly still have to endure feels impossibly vague. Walking in the hot, undeniable sunlight of the exercise yard, but every now and then taking small, surreptitious jumps to check if I can fly, Stanley's mournful, blood-dripping ghost seems to inhabit my shadow. Then there's that dark, formidable figure blocking out the sunrise at the end of all the Prestec videos. Which feels more like a fragment of some old nightmare than anything that's true, but nevertheless refuses to go away.

After three or four exhausting but exhilarating days and nights of dizzying breakthroughs, I decide I need to keep a record of what I'm finding out. They don't provide us inmates with notebooks here in Swinney, which would cost actual money, less still with pens or pencils, which we might use as weapons, but there are scraps of paper and coloured wax crayons for keeping score during our endless board games, so I smuggle a few of these back to my cell and hide them under my rocky pillow.

I've drawn up a kind of mental and physical map by now of the memory palace I've created during my nocturnal wanderings along the dream-corridors of Swinney. Even during daylight, I count paces, stairways and minor landmarks to make sure it's as consistent as possible with the real prison, although this requires considerable effort. The third door to my left as we head down for exercise or rec leads into that Paris hotel room. Other doorways, the first to my right, for instance, which is kicked and stained, and signed SITE OFFICE, offers a very different vision. Even before I open it, I can hear the thrum of generators and the clang of scaffolding, and smell cement dust and raw earth. Going through the door of this Portakabin feels so mundane I can barely bring myself to bother. It's a world of bad coffee, Tupperware sandwich boxes and conference calls where people pore over rickety spreadsheets and argue about how well yesterday's concrete has set. I'm some kind of surveyor—a suit in a hard hat—and I seem competent at my job, which pays well enough, at least judging from the nice black BMW I climb into on my way home.

I'm quietly proud of myself and what I've managed to achieve in life, although I am aware it's entirely possible that something I've done or not done professionally could have got me into Swinney. Criminal negligence—construction sites are inherently dangerous places—or some kind of fraud. But I get no sense of any great doubt or worry during my trips into the Portakabin, and at the end of the day that sort of foolishness simply doesn't feel like me.

Other doors simply won't open, or merely lead to hissing grey nowhere, or back into my cell, or one very like it, or simply force me awake. Others are more puzzling. The one that looks like a public swimming baths locker, for instance, for which I can never find the right change. Another opening which isn't a door at all, but a pathway leading into some kind of forest or wood. The dreamy, nightmarish, fairy-tale associations are obvious, and for a while I leave it unexplored. To engage in some Hansel and Gretel-style fantasy might be entertaining, but I need to concentrate on what's real. Passing it for perhaps the tenth or twelfth time, however, I get a sense of how ordinary and familiar the pathway seems. I'm even sure I can hear the dull rumble of traffic, and I notice an old crisp packet curled amid the leaf debris just ahead.

Stepping in, stepping through, it becomes even more obvious that I'm not entering some primal Jungian forest, but a suburban wood. Dog walkers come here. *I* come here. Schoolkids on their way home slope off to vape and do pills. There are woodchip pathways. Bins for litter and dog poop. Still, it's a kind of haven, a pleasant patch of green space. Some might say it's a bad idea to have a stretch of public-access woodland at the back of your house, I hear Lynn mutter and chuckle. But not us...

I pick my way onward, cautiously amazed. Of all the places I've encountered in my wanderings, this feels the most real. There's an earthy, woody smell in the air. It's edging into early autumn twilight. The trees are just starting to turn. Sure, there's the odd used condom and pile of dogshit, but still... Then the pathway narrows into nettles and it seems as if there's no way through. But I know with infallible certainty that there *is*. Ahead lies a wooden fence, and beyond that fence and a slope of lawn is a low, glassy modernist house, an architectural gem from the 1920s. I can see it glowing right there before me in the fizzing dusk. Shadows thrown from the skeletal silhouette of the climbing frame that was such a bugger to put up. Lights and movement in the kitchen. Lynn's voice calling to our children that it's time for bed. When all of this fades, when I claw my way back towards another grey morning at Swinney, I'm in tears.

This is my home. This is my *life*. And these, I can see them forming before me even as I force down mouthfuls of sub-Cheerios with a bendy plastic spoon from a tray on my knees, are my two children. Sophie and Conor. Sophie being the first and eldest, who nearly didn't make it after a difficult delivery. But Sophie's fine, and she's quicker at maths than Lynn or I are now, let alone when we were her age, but also good at sports; the winner of several school cups. Conor's more arty, more thoughtful. He's got a big imagination and likes to take his time and stand back and watch what's going on before he makes up his mind. They're yin and yang, are our kids, and we love them both to bits and wouldn't have them any other way even if they squabble like hell and frequently drive us up the wall. All of this has, for some reason I still can't fathom, been taken away from me.

Downtime's easy. At least, it keeps you away from knowing what you've lost. The sense of wrongness, the sheer bloody *injustice* of what I've been deprived of—not only my liberty, but a life, a wife, a career, a home, a family—is astonishing. It washes over me in sour waves. I can taste it like bile in my throat.

But focus, focus. Concentrate. From the Olympian heights from which I now gaze down at my existence here in Swinney, I realise I could, and should, have paid more attention to some obvious details about the place. This prison isn't some ancient inner-city Victorian relic but a postwar breeze-block sprawl set in a semi-rural location, although the faint drone of distant traffic suggests it might be within a couple of miles of several artery roads. Very occasionally during afternoon exercise, there have been shouts from over the wall. Once, memorably, someone attempted to get a drone into the yard, although the screws were able to activate a blocker signal which brought the thing crashing down. One of the great benefits of downtime from the point of view of Prestec and the English Government being that not only do we zombies have no contact with the outside world, but we don't even *want* any. We're like shipwrecked sailors beached on some misty island like in that puzzling Shakespeare play Lynn and I once saw. But Swinfield Prison is no fantasy. Everything is mundanely real.

I'M NOT SO much feeling my way towards my old life by now as plummeting into it. My mind feels re-inhabited. My thoughts are properly my own. A tricky moment when the screws come around unexpectedly with the laundry trolley and nearly discover my crayoned notes. But I shove them quickly into my pockets along with the gravel from my pillow. Just like the prisoners in... What's that war movie called? *The Great Escape*, of course; a staple of old-fashioned Boxing Day TV that I can remember watching as a kid. I don't need this stuff now, anyway. Lucid dreaming's as easy as falling off a log. I can wander in and out of family holidays, or trips to Ikea, or along the pathway through the wood leading to the fence at the bottom of our lawn. What's frustrating, though, is that I can't get properly into that lovely modernist house beyond. Somehow, I can only visit my home in tantalising hints and glimmers, like a dream within a dream...

Two red wine glasses on the kitchen counter. A lingering smell of garlic and herbs and olive oil. The kids asleep in the bedroom they still share. Pans and plates left out to be seen to in the morning.

Smoke rising from a candle that's just been snuffed out. Lynn perhaps already in bed or maybe taking a shower. Pleasant thoughts at this pleasant time of day as evening edges into night. Pale golden shadows cast from the big windows across the slope of lawn towards the deeper dark of the wood beyond. The climbing frame somehow looking more than ever like a skeleton, like something sinister and wrong. And—

The vision dissolves. I'm back in my cell amid prison sounds and prison smells. And telling myself that this is ridiculous, that I can't properly reach my own bloody home. My kids are there. Lynn's there. Everything that's precious to me. *I'm* there as well. Or I should be. And yet. And yet.

"DREAMS? NIGHTMARES? HALLUCINATIONS?"

Hallucinations? I don't think green overalls has mentioned hallucinations before. Although the exact script probably doesn't matter to her any more than it does to Prestec or anyone else. It's all just about keeping us zombies under control. A dim monkey-house din reverberates in this hexagonal space. But, just like her face, the door to D Wing and every other exit is closed off.

One thing I've recently noticed about Swinney is the limited range of accents shared by both the inmates and the Prestec personnel. Sure, there are guys like P who are probably eastern-European, and there are others such the one we unthinkingly call Geordie who are from what's known as "up-north". Then, just like Wyzee, many of the younger inmates affect a slurring inner-city gangster drawl. But beneath all of that, the prevailing accent is clearly from the West Midlands. Tones and varieties of Black Country and

Brummie dominate, but there are shades and subtleties between which a non-local probably wouldn't be able to distinguish. But I can. If I pay proper attention, I can even hear a softer and somewhat more educated version of those rounded vowels in the way I speak myself.

Now I linger closer to the screws out in the yard or during rec, catching snippets of their conversation as they stand around, weary and bored. Often, it's about traffic. Roadworks on the A38. The rip-off cost of the M6 Toll. That, or how they're taking their mother-in-law to the big garden centre up by Shenstone at the weekend, or the latest disappointment regarding Aston Villa, the region's major but perennially underachieving football team.

It all sounds so clear and obvious now that I can't believe I hadn't realised before. I *know* these places! The pubs, the playgrounds, the schools, the shopping malls, the roads. Meaning that HM Swinfield Prison (and now even the actual name sounds familiar) lies remarkably close to where Lynn and I live... Which is, yes, in an attractive, expensive and antique single-storied modernist house beside a patch of public woodland on the outskirts of Lichfield. I'm even able to confirm this by returning to my trusty encyclopedia and looking the city up in the Ls, where I find a photo of the twin-spired cathedral seen from across Stowe Pool, a pretty lake where Lynn and I and Sophie and Conor have fed the ducks on pleasant Sunday afternoons.

I've got so far now in breaking the shackles of downtime that it's a continual shock to realise that, physically, I'm still stuck in prison. Yet I can't find any trace of a reason why. The life I'm remembering seems so happy—so solid and centred and real. But something bad must have happened, even if I was wrongly convicted or did something stupidly out of character. Fraud? Drunk driving? Or was

I negligent or careless at work? I certainly know more than enough about my life to be certain that I'm not a career criminal. I'm probably not a drug addict or an alcoholic, either. What sometimes bothers me now is not what I'm going to find out when I go uptime, but the innocence I'm going to lose.

It's still dark. I'm lying, drifting, half awake as P shuffles and snores above me in the top bunk. As always, the air in here reeks of sweat and disinfectant, overlaid with the tomcatty odour of male piss. I've got to focus... Drift—but relax, give in... Go with the flow... Sometimes, I'm sure I can feel that tiny implant itching deep in my skull like a piece of grit, around which I've managed to form this dreamy pearl...

Lingering smells of cooking, of olive oil and garlic and herbs. Smoke rising from that candle on the table as the ember dies. Two wine glasses on the kitchen counter. An empty bottle of decent Valpolicella in the dining room. Stacked plates that can wait until morning. That warm, good feeling of another day done, and of a shared night to come. Lynn in the shower—no, she's already in bed, and seems to be asleep as I look in through the doorway at a glimpsed bare shoulder, the curve of a cheekbone, and wonder if she'll mind if I wake her up. But I decide to look in on Sophie and Conor in their shared room, with its scatter of toys and foot-stabbing Lego, instead. Take in the sounds of their breathing and the salty, powdery scents of their flesh. I pause for a moment at the big window which faces across the lawn towards the wood. That climbing frame still gives me the creeps, but I'm telling myself that this life I'm now living is everything I've ever dreamed of when I realise that a figure is standing beside it. Hunched and waiting. Filled with the looming dark. Out there on the lawn of my own house. And I know something terrible is about to happen. And—

DOWNTIME

A KLAXON SOUNDS. Again, I'm awake. Again I'm back here in Swinney, and still doing downtime. But I'm no longer lost. That figure on the lawn was clearly some kind of intruder, and of course I'd do what any father would do to protect his family. So would Lynn if it had been down to her. And, and... I still don't know exactly what happened, but I can take a pretty good guess. Maybe I got it wrong with the angels-on-a-pinhead legalistic crap about what is and isn't reasonable force. Maybe I misjudged a swing with whatever implement I grabbed on my way out through the garage, or said the wrong thing when I was standing in the dock. That might make me a criminal in the eyes of so-called justice, but that sure as hell doesn't mean I deserve of what I'm being put through right now. I've not just had my family taken from me, I've had my *memory* of my family taken as well...!

My body goes through the motions. I eat my cardboard breakfast. I void my bowels. I wait for and then consume my cardboard lunch. P, who knows by now when not to bother me, keeps as far out of my way as is possible for two big men in a tiny cell. I feel a mixture of anger and betrayal. That, and a profound sense of loss. Lynn, were I in any ordinary prison, would at least be able to visit me, distressing though that would have been. She might even—although I know it's a difficult decision—have brought along Sophie and Conor. After all, it's probably only a ten-minute drive from home.

I pull on my floppy laceless trainers when the klaxon sounds for afternoon exercise. Shuffle along the corridor with all the rest of the zombies, but counting the landmarks of my dreams. The locker of the civic swimming pool where I taught Sophie and Conor to swim. That Paris hotel room. The construction site Portakabin.

The pathway into the wood. Out here in the yard, if I screamed loud enough, Lynn might almost hear me. But I don't. I keep my head down and trudge around, nursing my precious sense of who I really am as Stanley's blood-dripping shadow trails behind me and the screws shake their heads over Aston Villa's latest defeat. Then we all shuffle back in. Nothing ever really changes here, not even the obedient way I step through a screeching metal door into a familiar octagon when my number is called by the robotic female voice, obedient zombie that I am.

Green overalls, her hair as lank as ever—and I do sometimes wish she'd make an effort—shines a light into my eyes and checks my blood pressure and asks the same questions she always asks and receives the same replies. She taps her clipscreen and is about to turn away and tell me to fuck off back to hell when she remembers her blue plastic gun, and pulls the trigger as she points it at my forehead. Then she frowns and taps her clipscreen again.

"Is there some problem?"

"Just stay here," she mutters. "Don't fucking go anywhere."

She heads out of the same screeching door I came in through. Leaving me alone for what feels like a very long time. I try to picture the everyday boredom and drudgery that all the other downtime zombies are enduring through this long afternoon. Sitting here on this bolted chair with only D Wing's faint clamour for company, it already feels a long way off. Eventually, the door finally judders back open, and green overalls, two burly screws and a managerial sort in a suit all come crowding in.

"We found this beneath your mattress," the suit tells me, brandishing my crayoned notes in a clumped fist.

"Is this some kind of disciplinary matter?" I ask. "In which case I want to see a lawyer."

"You can want what you bloody like!" He's glaring at me. "Want doesn't get anything here in Swinney." Leaning forward in a spray of spit. "You think you know who you are, don't you, you little shit?"

"I..." The metal walls and doors seem to billow like wind-blown curtains. "...I don't know what you're talking about."

"Well..." Now, he smiles. "You sure as hell won't know anything by the end of today."

I KEEP PINCHING myself. This is worse than any dream.

I'm hauled out across a bigger yard I've never seen before towards a waiting van. It's an ancient white thing. Petrol-powered. Manually driven. But that's Prestec for you: pinching the pennies on behalf of His Majesty's Federal English Government so the pounds can take care of themselves. There's a metal grill behind the driver and two rough wooden benches in the windowless back, along with some anchor points, presumably to fix the gurney I'll be strapped to on my return. Screw one sits opposite me. Screw two drives. He bips the horn. Says something about *clinic* as leans out to speak to the screw manning the main gate. Then, amazingly, we're out of Swinney.

"What's happening?" I ask. "What are you going to do to me?"

Screw one grins and shakes his head.

GLIMPSED BEYOND THE driver's windscreen, road signs flicker by. Birmingham is 20 miles. Lichfield is just 5. Wolverhampton is only 10. No wonder home feels so close. Screws one and two don't seem to share their boss's anger at whatever precious government target

I've messed up. For them, this is just another day out to whatever cut-price clinic Prestec use to wipe the brains of us zombies clean. Even though they know I've somehow slipped through the electrified wire fence separating me from who I really am, they clearly still think I'm just another downtime dolt. I haven't even been handcuffed, let alone drugged. A roadhouse pub flashes by. The Fox and Hounds. A place Lynn and I have been to for several romantic meals, although the food's not as good as it once was. Then, and without any conscious effort, a simple and obvious thought pops into my head.

My name. It was, is, always has been, Jim Vaughan. Not James, although that's what's on my birth certificate. Rarely ever Jimmy, which I don't much like. Just Jim. Just me. Jim Vaughan. Why the hell hadn't I thought of that before?

Fields and farmyards. Hedges and ditches. Flocks of delivery drones. Lay-by greasy spoons. Screw one sits boots akimbo and thighs splayed as the van rumbles on. Drumming his fingers. His taser-truncheon hanging between his legs. Screw two is fiddling with the old-fashioned satnav as he overtakes a lumbering tractor. *Typical fucking Prestec*, he mutters, giving up and straightening the wheel. We're on the dual carriageway now between Coleshill and Tamworth, and I'd judge we're travelling at about 60 miles per hour.

"I need to go to the toilet."

Screw one frowns and straightens up. "What?"

"I need to piss. You didn't give me a chance before we set off."

"We can't just stop. This ain't no school run."

"Then what am I supposed to do?"

He shrugs. "Piss yourself, mate, for all I care."

"Hey!" Screw two leans back to shout through the grill. "We'd have to clean that up! Couldn't we–?"

At which point I push up from my bench and lunge headfirst towards towards screw one, catching him hard in the belly. Even with the protection of his padded jacket, he gives a surprised, wheezing *oomph*. The van sways and veers as screw two tries to look around and see what's happening. Screw one and I are sprawled to our knees in a clumsy half-wrestle.

"What the—?"

The van sways again, clattering and creaking. A car horn whoops by us in a rising, falling pulse. I shove hard again at screw one, catching him across the throat as he tries to stand up. He crashes backwards, slamming against the van's rear doors. For a moment I think they're going to burst open, but they hold. I grab for the taser just as he tries to haul himself back up, thumb the only button I can find and press it against his right thigh as the van roars over a rumble strip, sways again, then begins to slide as screw two up in the driver's seat curses *fuck fuck fuck* and we begin to sail sideways and the road ahead tilts and there's a prolonged moment of weird near-silence before everything slams down in tumbling hammerblow flashes of blackness and blood.

I wait for the world to stop turning. Then I crawl towards misangled daylight over something moaning and soft that must be screw one, fall into a blinding sea-roar of air and traffic, fall again over a steel barrier into glass and grass and litter, then head on through a copse of snagging bushes at a stumbling run.

I already know that my home's not far from here—in fact, it's deliriously close—but I've done something to my right knee and I'm seriously out of condition. If I'd wanted to prepare for a physical escape, I'd have been exercising on the creaking gym equipment out in the yard every afternoon instead of wandering the corridors inside my head. Compared to real life, walking in dreams is as easy as flying. That, and I'm constantly amazed and disorientated by the sheer solidness of reality. The rust on this chain link fence. The smell of these nettles. The hurt in my knee.

Another road lies across a field ahead with suburban houses on the far side. Then two flashing, siren-whooping police vehicles swoop by, and I cringe into a ditch. I can't be caught, found, arrested. At least, not until I've had a chance to get back home and speak to Lynn. Nothing else matters, even though I know Prestec'll empty my head as soon as I'm captured, that they'll shove me in with the screamers and the howlers of D Wing. But I still have *now*. I still have *me*.

Somehow, it's already later than it should be. Darkness is falling. The street lamps are starting to glimmer. A few kids are still out kicking a ball around in a playground. A gaggle of teenagers are laughing, joshing and vaping on the nearby swings. The scene is so ordinary it hurts far worse than my throbbing knee. I push around the back of a hedge and slump down beside some wheelie bins amid a reek of cats' piss to catch my breath. Telling myself not to hurry. Telling myself that this settling darkness is my friend. The kids, the teenagers, the dog walkers with their little torches and dangling bags, will soon all be gone as evening deepens and night unfolds.

I move on, hunched and hunted, as traffic swishes by along a broader road. Big automated trucks, mostly, but the police and Prestec must be searching for me like mad. Then, as if summoned by the thought, sleek blue lights and sirens loom, but they just head on by—*whoosh whoosh whoosh*—as I hunker in the bushes. Then I'm up and moving again, and suddenly I'm standing right beside a pathway leading into a wood, and it really does feel like I'm about to enter a dream.

DOWNTIME

This is it, the way home, and it's far too dark by now for even the tardiest of dog walkers to be out, and these trees should hide me from searching drones. I follow the sense of a pathway until it gives out. Pick my way on through nettles and brambles, feeling more than a little afraid as tendrils of vine grab and snag, boughs creak and hiss, and my breath rasps. This, after all, is the way the intruder must have come, the monster who wrecked my life, and I almost feel like an intruder myself. But I push on until I reach a fence and see a slope of lawn, and the long, low windows of a fine modernist house beyond.

Lynn's in the kitchen. Beyond the glass. In the golden glow. Moving here and there as she clears up after a meal. A bottle of wine still sits on the dining room table. A candle gives a waft of smoke. This is all so close to how things really should be that it actually feels rather wrong. Then another figure emerges into view, and that figure is taller and clearly male, and he and Lynn stand talking with every impression of intimacy, although he clearly isn't me. Which makes no sense at all.

I wait. I bide my time. I think. Until the thought, so obvious it should have struck me hours ago, in fact right at the beginning, occurs. The police will have called in on Lynn as soon as they got news of my escape. After all, where else was I likely to go? So that male shape that's now moving back from the window is there to warn her, or to offer protection, or to keep watch. He's also holding a wine glass, which strikes me as unprofessional. But still.

I ease my hurting leg over the fence and scuttle, spider-like, along the lawn's mossy edge, then limp shrub by shrub and on past the rockery towards the front of the house with its pale gravel drive. Two cars are parked there. One is my BMW, but the other, a big Toyota sitting higher off the ground on fatter tyres, doesn't look familiar, or particularly official. But there are all kinds of cop, and this one's probably a detective, plain clothes. Although that glass of wine and the guttering candle still feel incredibly wrong.

The front door opens as I watch. Murmurous talk as the male figure steps outside and Lynn stands in the doorway hugging her bare arms, although none of what they're saying reaches me as fully-formed words. Lynn's wearing a sheer blue dress. The diamonds I gave her for our tenth anniversary glint at her ears. She laughs at some joke he's made in his slow masculine rumble, and then unfolds her arms and leans forward and kisses him—not on the cheek, but fully on the mouth—and he responds by pulling her into an embrace.

Eventually, but after much too long, they separate, and Lynn touches her hair in a gesture of mild arousal I recognise only too well. After a few more murmurs, jokes, promises, endearments, she steps back inside and the door is closed, and I hear the other doors and windows of our house go *thunk thunk thunk* as she activates the security, and the man—who plainly isn't a cop, or at least he isn't on duty—strolls towards his fat-tyred Toyota with cheery insouciance when I'd really like to step out from the darkness and knock his teeth down his throat. But I don't. Of course I don't. I'm not that kind of guy. The car bleeps to let him in, starts up, backs off across the crackling gravel, pulls away in a flare of lights. Leaving me crouching alone.

I wait. Not so much thinking and watching now as frozen in confusion and grief. This is a nightmare. The only relief, if it even *is* a relief, being that Lynn's friend with the fat-tyred Toyota hasn't stayed over at the end of what was plainly a date. But that doesn't mean that he and Lynn aren't sleeping together. In our house, and in our own fucking bed, with our kids asleep in the next room.

DOWNTIME

I limp back around the side of the house towards a door at the rear we hardly ever use. The code on the keyscreen has changed, but I try likely permutations—after all, I know Lynn better than anyone—until something clicks, and an acute sense of being *here*, of being *home*, washes over me as I step into the dim garage beyond. A strew of bikes we don't use as much we should. The Little Tykes car that Conor's much too big for now and really needs to be sold. The boiler's single blue-eyed glow. Another door, and I'm standing in the kitchen and the smell that greets me is redolent of everything I've lost. Scents of garlic and herbs and olive oil. Lingering smoke from that candle. Stacked plates and pans to be seen to in the morning. Two empty wine glasses on the kitchen counter and nothing left of a bottle of decent Valpolicella on the table in the dining room.

Other disarrangements as well. There used to be—there *should* be—a professionally taken photograph of all four of us smiling in an informal, soft-focus group up on the big wall above the fireplace in the lounge. But it's been replaced by some swirly abstract canvas I don't recognise, or even particularly like. And what's happened to all the other family pictures, at least the ones with me in them? And where's that paperweight I bought for Lynn in Paris? And why's my coffee machine no longer in the kitchen? And who *was* that guy who was here earlier? This is all impossibly hurtful and strange.

I move on down the hallway into the softer dark, realising as I do so that I've picked up the empty bottle of Valpolicella from the dining-room table on my way through, and that I'm carrying it by the neck like a club. This isn't right. No, this isn't right at all. Then, and for a drifting moment, the door I'm facing which should lead into our bedroom is painted blue and has a dented brass knob. Not that it would be unpleasant to revisit the good times Lynn and

I once had in Paris, but it takes a prolonged effort to push back against the clamouring shadows and will the shape ahead to reform itself into our bedroom door. And even then the sense of wrongness won't dissolve.

Gently, gently, I edge the door back across the swish of the carpet and stand there in the doorway, watching my lovely wife as she sleeps. A glimpsed bare shoulder, the curve of a cheekbone, and part of me is wondering if I should wake her, or perhaps simply join her in her faraway dreams. Which would be perfect, and might set everything back to the way it had once almost been. But I don't need to pinch myself to know what really lies ahead, even if another part of me wants to scream. After all, Jim Vaughan simply isn't that kind of guy. He's a good dad, a decent husband, a diligent employee, a loyal friend. All the rest, the white rages, the bleak black days, the smashed coffee machine, the expensive counselling sessions, the even more expensive lawyers, the social workers, the restraining orders, the supervised access to see my own kids, and that guy with the fat-tyred Toyota, the visits from the police, they're not us, and they're certainly not me. They're just… Something that sometimes happens. Something I wish would disappear. Just as I told Lynn back in that faraway Paris hotel room as I wept while she held me and promised she'd make it all go away. But she didn't. Things grew worse, and life got more complicated, and work more stressful, and Sophie and Conor were always too loud, and then even my morning coffee started tasting like shit. Where did it all go wrong, eh, Linnie? So, so very hard to say. But you let me down, and I've suffered deeply as a result. I've lost you, my job, my house, my car, my kids. And you haven't. And, much though part of me still loves you dearly, another part of me wants you to know what true suffering really is.

DOWNTIME

So I move on, slow and silent along this ever-lengthening corridor, to Sophie and Conor's room. Part of me still holding that empty bottle of Valpolicella by the neck like a club. Part of me wanting to scream. But I know as I stand here taking in the living, breathing presence of my children, their salty, powdery smell, that I can't turn away from what happens next. Instead, I walk over to the window and gaze out at the faint shadows strewn across the lawn into the spilling dark. That climbing frame looks starkly scary, but there's no figure standing beside it. There never was. What I'm seeing, reflected in the floor-to-ceiling glass as everything else blackens, is me.

I hear the creak of rusty metal. Smell sweat and decay. Something's not right about this. Something's very wrong. The face above me, it's not anyone I recognise. But somehow I do. And I'm *here*, wherever here is. This place, this rickety bunk, this rancid cell. P's squatting over me with his big, bland face and his big, strong hands, holding me down as I thrash and howl that this isn't right, that I'm not here, that this is all a bad dream. But nothing changes. Nothing goes away.

Lights brighten. There are hurried footsteps. The squeak of wheels. The judder and screech of doors. The screws bust in. They ease P off me and hold me down until a syringe hisses and I hear them count *one two three* as they lift me up and strap me to a gurney and the dim ceilings and corridors of Swinney drift by. Somewhere, there's a door to a Portakabin, and a Paris hotel room, or even just the locker at the local civic pool, or a pathway through a wood. But none of them are here.

THEN I'M AWAKE. Back in the octagonal space with all the doors like the junction of levels in some grim video game. Green overalls is leaning over me. Tucking a greasy lock behind her ear as she points her blue plastic gun at my forehead. Now, when she pulls the trigger, I feel nothing at all.

"Is this right?"

"Rather depends on your definition of right, doesn't it...?" She checks her clipscreen. "CT4619."

The effect of the syringe is fading. The leather straps on the gurney are solidly real, but still I manage to shake my head. "You can't do this."

"Do what?"

"Put me under. Wipe me clean. Get rid of..." Something rises in me. A soundless scream. The straps strain and creak. "Me."

She almost smiles. "And what would be the point of that?"

The point being, the point *being*, that this is downtime, right? That I'm not supposed to know. That I'm an emptied vessel, devoid even of dreams. That's how this is meant to work. But instead I'm here, and I'm me, Jim Vaughan, who did what he did to his wife, his family, his life, his kids. Conor dead and Sophie permanently disabled, and Lynn's shocked white face glimpsed for the last time as I stood weeping in the dock on the day of sentencing, and there's no way I'll ever be able to explain. That I'm not, never was, that kind of guy. It was just... It was just... Something that happened—another kind of nightmare. Only I'm still here, still breathing, thinking and living, and more than ever now I want to scream.

"It's the clinic, right?"

"What clinic?"

"The place you're going to take me to... In, in that van... When, when I..." I blink. I try to hold my breath. I'd pinch myself if I could.

Or do what Stanley did. Scream and caw and fly away. "Then you'll put me in D Wing. The place..." Reality slides. No longer the rumble of that van along the roads outside Lichfield or glimpses of the rooftops of Paris, but Sophie's chuffing sobs as she tries to crawl away from me across blood-wet sheets and the crackle of the glass of that Valpolicella bottle shattering across Conor's head. "The place where I'll finally stop being me."

"Haven't you heard..." Green overalls glances at her clipscreen. "...Jim? Prestec's a caring company. We wouldn't permanently deprive you of your precious memories. That would be cruel. And God knows what you mean about a van and some clinic. You're wrong about D Wing, too. It's a just a regular prison filled with regular criminals, although I doubt if many of them have done anything as terrible as you."

She taps something and the door to D Wing screeches open in a monkey-house clamour of shouts and whoops. There are hammerings and thumpings. The thunderous reek of male piss and sweat. Two burly Prestec screws loom into view.

"Now fuck off back to hell," she says, turning away from me as the screws undo the straps on the gurney, haul me to my feet and drag me through.

Afterword

ONE OF THE many things a writer has to work on if they're setting a story in somewhere that isn't the historic past or the actual present is to envisage the type of society within which their story is set. You'd think—in fact *I* thought—that a prison in the near future would lie at the easier end of such a task, but Downtime proved me wrong.

The idea of restorative amnesia for offenders sounded both extreme but also rather plausible. In neurological terms, it was merely mimicking a fairly common condition, whilst in terms of the penal system, and as the characters themselves acknowledge, it does make several kinds of sense. I'm not saying it would happen, or less still that it should. But if it did...

Well, it was hardly a great leap to imagine a main character obsessed with finding out the truth of what they'd done, and then that that truth would be surprising, perhaps even shocking. In other words, and after some research about prison life, I felt there was a story here that I could tell. But, aside from the difficulty of having to somehow find a way to describe the terrible crime I eventually decided my main character needed to uncover, I kept bumping up against broader social complexities surrounding downtime that didn't seem to fit.

An obvious reason, I was pretty sure, why downtime might be introduced would be because it was cheap. It would also be a such a perfect tool for a despotic police state it's hard to imagine it hasn't been used already somewhere in the world. But I was clear I needed to keep a sense of Britishness, mainly because I didn't want to become distracted by having to combine the fairly alien—for me—setting of prison with a culture that was also foreign. So had my near-future Britain (or England, which felt like a neat post-Brexit touch) taken a significant turn for the worse, and reached the point where it was routinely damaging the brains of its criminals in the name of justice? Or, on the other hand, was downtime sincerely intended as a way of getting offenders back on the right track, and properly invested in, with counselling and appropriate resources?

Seen from inside of a prison wall, it was hard to know which made better sense.

I guess that, in the end, I took a bumbling middle course, just as our politicians, administrators and judiciary tend to do. There's generalised talk of help and hope and rehabilitation, but in reality it's more a means of kicking offenders repeatedly in the head. With this relative fudge, I finally felt able to focus on the main character's dilemma, and to leave prison life to stay pretty much as it probably always will be: grubby, underfunded and—apart from the occasional grandstanding political gesture and entirely avoidable crisis—ignored.

The Roads

I'LL ALWAYS BELIEVE that my father came back from the front late in the summer of 1917. I could barely remember the time when he'd lived at home, and his visits on leave had been brief, strained, somehow theatrical. He'd hand me creased-over postcards of foreign towns—a few of them even had unsent messages on them, my name and address—*We're busy here taking a bash at the Hun*. And I'd stare at them as he stood in the front room and placed his hands on my sister Marion's shoulders and said how she'd grown. My mother would wait in the corner—nodding, smiling, lost for words, really, as we all were. I half-feared him, this green-clad man, filling our front room with his own rough scent and that of trains and disinfectant. Little as I was, I resented him, too. I liked being the only male in the house.

He'd change soon afterwards, bathing with his back shining though the open scullery door before putting on the clothes that fitted him so loosely now. My mother then ran an iron, steaming and spitting, along the seams of his uniform to kill the lice. Then tea and a cake from one of the neighbours, and everyone smiling, grinning. The house frozen with half-finished words and gestures, our figures blurred as if in a photograph, fanning wings of limbs, faces lost to all sense and meaning. Each night that my father was at home my mother's bedroom door would be closed and I would lie prisoner in the unloved sheets of my own bed, praying for that last morning when the cardboard suitcase reappeared in the hall.

"You'll take care? You'll look after Ma and Marion for me?"

I'd nod, knowing it was just his joke. And he'd stoop to hug me, encased once more in green and brass and buttons. The pattern remained the same over the war years, as much a fact of life as rules of grammar or the rank smell that filled our house when the wind blew east from the tanneries; and each time my father and the cardboard case he brought with him seemed smaller, more sunken, more battered. It was only late in the summer of 1917 when the war, if I had known it, was soon to end, that any of that ever changed.

I was wandering in the town Arboretum. You had to pay to get in in those days but I knew a way through the railings and I was always drawn to the bright scents and colours, the heaped confections of flowers. There was a lake in the centre—deep and dark, a true limestone cavern—and a small mouldering steamer that had plied prettily and pointlessly between one shore and the other before the war.

Each day of that changeable summer was like several seasons in itself. Forced outside to play by our mothers between meals, we had to put up with rain, wind, sunshine, hail. In the Arboretum—watered and warmed, looming in flower scents, jungle fronds, greenish tints of steam—everything was rank and feverish. The lawns were like pondweed. The lake brimmed over. I remember wandering along the paths from the white blaze of the bandstand, ducking the roses that clawed down from their shaded walk, pink-scented, unpruned; sharing in that whole faint air of abandonment that had come over our country at that time.

I saw a man walking towards me. A mere outline against the silvered lake—but clearly a soldier from the cap he wore, from the set of his shoulders. I stopped. I could tell that he was walking towards me, and I felt a faint sinking in my heart even before I realised that it was my father.

"I thought I'd find you here," he said.

"Where's your case?" I asked.

He considered for a moment, his eyes hidden under the shadow of his cap. "I left it down at the station. Yes," he nodded to himself, "left luggage. My, you've grown..."

"You haven't been home?"

"I thought I'd come here first. See you."

I stared up at him, wondering how he could possibly have found out, all the way from those sepia-tinted postcard towns in France, about my habit of squeezing in through the Arboretum railings.

"We weren't..." I began.

"Expecting. No." My father breathed in, his moustache pricking out like a tiny broom. He seemed as surprised as I was to find himself here, but apart from the sunlit air and the birdsong and the sound of a child crying not far off in a pram, we were back straight away within the frozen silences that filled our front room. And this time he hadn't even remembered the postcards—they were always the first thing he gave me. More than ever I wondered why he came back. All that travelling. Wouldn't it be simpler if he just stayed in France and got on with the war?

"I'd forgotten how nice these gardens are," he said as I began to walk with him. "What's it like here, son?" I felt, unseen behind me, the brief touch of his hands on my shoulders. "Does everyone hate the Germans?"

"They're bad, aren't they?"

"Bad..." My father considered, turning the word over in his mouth. "I suppose you could say... But then..." It was unnerving; what I'd said seemed to mean something else to him entirely.

"Do you see many of them?"

"No," my father said. "I just build the roads."

I followed him out of the park through the turnstile.

"Are you hungry?" he asked. "Do you think we should eat? Is the Mermaid Cafe still open?"

We crossed the street and walked past the old bakery into town. Carts and cars and horses went by. My father stopped and stared blankly at one driven by a woman. "Will you look at that? It's a different world here," he said, "isn't it?"

I nodded, already filled by the impression that I would remember this day, that these odd half-sensical things he was saying would become like the messages on those unsent postcards. Something I would study long after, looking for meaning.

It was growing darker now, the Sun fading behind Saint Martin's church up the hill. A trolley bus went by, the sparks thrown by the gantry looming suddenly blue-bright. Layers of shadow seemed to be falling. It even felt cold now, so soon after the Sun.

Across the square and through the doors of the Mermaid Cafe there was brass and linoleum, clattering cutlery, drifts of tobacco and steam. My father removed his cap and walked between the chairs. The gaslamps had been turned up against the sudden gloom, and I saw his face—darkly, yellow-lit—for the first time. The women sitting at the other tables smiled and nodded. A soldier. How they all loved soldiers then. A waitress who'd been about to serve someone else came over and took his order for tea and cordial, two sticky buns. He jumped when the trolley rumbled up. Outside, it started to rain.

"This is some place," he said, looking around in that same puzzled way he had in the Arboretum. "It's what I think about, places like this. When I'm..." He began to pat his pockets.

"Building the roads?"

"The roads..." He found his cigarette case. He cupped a match. His hands were trembling. "Yes, the roads."

I drank my cordial, which tasted bitter rather than sweet from the saccharine they put in it. In the yard at school I always just said that my father was a soldier. Sapper sounded like a corruption, a diminution—as did the actual job, which was the same one he'd done in peacetime, of supervising the construction of roads. But still; the roads. I had, in my own secret moments, in times when I lay in that deep indentation in my mother's bed and the ceiling glowed with the pull of sleep, a vision of a man younger and crisper than the one who sat before me now, and of the roads. White roads, straight roads, wide roads narrowing into the shimmering distance. Ways to the future.

"This war," he said, drinking his tea, "isn't like anything anyone ever imagined. All the money that's been spent, all the lives, all the effort. It's like one great experiment to see just how far we can go." He ground out his cigarette. "Well, now we know. The ones of us who are there. You think the whole world's there until you come here and you see the prams in the park and the women with mud on their skirts. And that steamer..." He smiled and glanced out at the rain. "I'd like to have taken you across the lake on that steamer."

"It's not working."

"No," he said. "And we should go home..."

He stood up. The waitress came over to take his money, fluttering her brown eyes.

Outside, the gutters streamed and the facades of the blackened buildings shone like jet. I wanted to hurry as my father pulled his cap on and walked at his odd slow pace through the rain, his head held stiffly erect. Trickles began to run down the woollen neck of my vest, but at least we weren't heading back towards the station. The suitcase was forgotten.

We walked up the hill towards the houses, but instead of going left towards home along the alley at the back of Margrove Avenue we went on past the grocer's on Willow Way. A sodden black cat, waiting on a doorstep, regarded us. Around the corner, we came to a brick wall.

"Isn't this right?" My father pressed his hand against it, as though expecting it to give way.

I said, "We should have turned left."

"Isn't there a short cut?"

Before I could answer, my father turned and strode off towards a strip of wasteland and some leftover foundations of houses that had been started before the war and would, so we were all promised, be finished as soon as it ended. The rain was torrential now. You could hardly see the grey roofs of Blackberry Road, and as we began to pick our way over sodden nettles our feet slipped inch by inch deeper into sucking mud. I tripped and stumbled over broken bricks, piles of rubble, loose rusting wire that had once been put up to keep out trespassers. Deep brown pools had formed in the depths of the foundations. I felt my feet slide beneath me, muddy gravity drawing me down into the water. I kicked away and heaved myself over slippery bricks. Peering back over the wasteland, I saw that my father was some way behind, grey again as the figure I had seen walking up from the lake, stumbling in the curtains of rain. I looked towards the houses of Blackberry Road. Grey water filled my eyes, my heart was pounding. For a moment, they didn't seem to be there.

"You go on, Jack!" My father's voice. "Hurry home."

I clambered on, back over the last of the foundations and onto the loose clayey track that the builders had laid. I could see rooftops now, sooty chimneys intertwined with the clouds, coalsheds, sodden washing, ivied walls. I broke into a run, taking the narrow passage between 23 and 25. Then on around the corner. Across the shining street.

I burst in through our front door. My breath came in heaving shudders as I stood dripping in warm darkness. The hall clock ticked. My mother was in the kitchen. I could already smell milk and nutmeg from the pudding she was cooking.

"That you, Jack?" she called. "Get those boots off. I don't want you clumping around the house..."

I struggled with the laces and left my boots on the tiles beneath the coatstand. I walked into the warm brightness of the kitchen.

"Where have you been?"

I looked back along the hall, willing a shape to appear at the mullioned front door. But already the Sun was brightening, shining in the diamonds of coloured glass, chasing away the rain. And Marion would be back soon, and tea was nearly ready.

I asked, "Have you heard from Father?"

My mother was rubbing my wet hair with a towel. "Your father..." The movement of her hands became stiffer. "No. He's always been bad at writing letters." She gave an odd laugh. Her hands dropped away. I felt loose, light-headed. "He *thinks*. You know he thinks, Jack..."

"I was just thinking—"

"And you're like him." She pushed me out of the kitchen, upstairs, away. "Now go and change."

I GOT A card from my father a few weeks later. It just came in the post. The censor had run a black line through the name beneath the photograph, but you could still read the print if you held it to the light. Ypres, but I pronounced it the way the soldiers did— *Wipers*; a famous enough name, although the newspapers reported that the great victory in Flanders of 1917 was at Passchendaele, and it was some years before I realised that my father was involved in that last great push and not some sideshow. Given the choice, I always seemed to draw the lesser verdict of him. And in his cause of death, too, which remains vague to this day. But then there were no proper roads in Flanders in the late summer of 1917. The rain never stopped. Many of the advancing allied soldiers simply drowned in fetid mud.

I still believe in what happened in the Arboretum on that sunny-rainy day, although Marion, who died in the flu epidemic not long after the war, would have laughed and taunted me about it if I'd said anything to her, and I couldn't ever think of a right way of telling my mother. The sense of the ordinariness was too strong; of wandering into town and sitting, as I am sure I did sit, in the Mermaid Cafe with my father, although it's been closed for many years now and I never did find that brown-eyed waitress again, or any of the other people there who might have recognised us.

THE ROADS

The little steamer that my father had so wanted to take me on crossed and re-crossed the Arboretum lake again for a few years after the war, although I could never quite bring myself to take the aimless journey. Still, I was there when it sank one pastel winter evening in 1921. I stood amid the onlookers on the shore, biting my lip and with my hands stuffed hard into my pockets as it tilted down into watery caverns wreathed in smoke and steam, set alight by nameless vandals. Inside my coat that day, crumpled as my trembling fingers gripped it in the hot darkness, was a sepia-tinted picture of the square of once-pretty Ypres, and my name and address on the other side. I think that someone must have found that last postcard after my father died and posted it to me as a kindly thought, because the rest was simply blank. There was nothing but an empty space where my father, if he had survived and got back to the shelter of his dug-out on that sunny-rainy day, might otherwise have left a message.

Afterword

THIS IS A considerably older story than the others in this collection, but still reflects what feel like some of my characteristic obsessions. War and fatherhood. Returning home and finding it's no longer the place you left. Hope for the future set against the problems of the present and the horrors of the past. That, and an element of what I suppose you might call magical thinking in writing with what I hope is some degree of heart and conviction about something I don't actually believe in: ghosts. That, in part, is probably also why I chose to structure the story around a man's memories of his childhood.

At the age of the narrator's boyhood self, I believed in the power of the supernatural with something like the same fervour with which I now believe in (although I'd prefer to use another word such as *acknowledge* or *respect*) science and the scientific method. Although I'd already ditched an actual God, the world simply seemed to make better sense if there were spectral apparitions and sundry blurrings between the future, the present and the past. I loved reading about the famously haunted Borley Rectory, and of headless coachmen, strange knockings, premonitions and the like. And, of course, about near-death visitations such as the one which *The Roads* describes, although the story I found I wanted to tell had a naturalistic tone, and was as much about fatherhood and unresolved regret as it was about a ghost.

For the record, I should add that my own onward spiritual journey through my teenage years took me in the direction of books such as *Supernature* and *The Morning of the Magicians* and writers such as Colin Wilson, then towards the mistily esoteric uplands of G I Gurdjieff, J G Bennett and P D Ouspensky. From there, I married a practising Roman Catholic, ditched the lingering elements of my faith in the miraculous, and took up writing more seriously. There are probably other reasons for all these decisions, but as many of the stories in this collection attest, I'm still fascinated by magic and religion.

The Memory Artist

0: The Memory Artist

TO THE MEMORY artist, her workshop was a place of wonders. Its shelves were a clamour of pots, potions, pigments and endless varieties and formats of data. Its walls fluttered with the fading sketches and virtuals of projects long finished, still in gestation, or lost to the voids between. She lived amid deadfalls of precious and semi-precious woods, stones, circuitry and metals. Even the walls and floor glittered with flecks of jewel, byte and swarf.

This was her realm. She slept here, dreamed here, worked, ate, shat and pissed. And she let the hours pass without making any great effort to number them, although she knew she was old and that their counting would no longer be any great task. Sleeping, working, pacing or pondering, the minaret cries of the Dawn-Singers and the curfew bells of the Nightwatch echoing across the city beyond easily passed her by.

Other beings might have called the workshop an insanitary hovel, but to her all things had their place, at least if she could recollect exactly where that was, and she continued in her work with a forgetful contentment, and thought herself moderately lucky with her lot—at least, when she bothered to think of herself at all. Admittedly, most of what she possessed might seem to others like nothing more than a litter of scraps, but that was the whole point of her calling: to turn life's detritus into things of beauty, wonder and worth.

Sometimes, although it was to no regular measure, she would brave the souks, streets and islands of the star-spanning edifice of Ghezirah where she dwelled. Obviously, there was food to be bought, at least occasionally, and sometimes her more regular materials—blades, pixels, pigments, brushes, data fixatives, connectives and oils—probably needed replenishing as well. But, more and more, as Ghezriah's many seasons passed her by uncounted, she made do with less and less. Once, she was sure, she had produced works which had filled her entire workshop, or had had to be created in the vast emptiness of some windy starship hangar.

These brash creations, showy and solid in their varied stones, metals, memories and woods, had been made for public consumption rather than private contemplation. She recalled that there had once been a beachscape, a great sighing thing of rushing waters and tiered, polished steel. Your face stung with literal and virtual spray as you approached it, and your feet sank deep into the memory of greenish volcanic sand. Then came the cry of geelies, and top notes of salt with odours of marine decay beneath. The horizon was blue-grey, and the twin suns she'd set up in the sky had thrown amazing shadows. Then, maybe, had come the slow rise of some alien sea beast. Or perhaps not. The memory artist always strove to look forward rather than back, and never dwelled on past successes—failures, for that matter—because there were always fresh challenges to be found. All she felt now for those days of monetary success and physical grandiosity was embarrassment that she should ever have produced works so simplistic and gross. The pieces had sold well, of course they had, for they represented what most beings thought they wanted, but she'd got the whole creative process entirely wrong.

The art of working in memory, just as she was sure it was when it came to all the other arts, wasn't to compose some broad statement about things in general or, the Almighty forbid, about life itself. No, what you did was to wrestle something down until you had... Not exactly its *essence*, for that was still too obviously purposeful and ambitions... But some grasp of whatever the thing you were aiming for was. And even that wasn't enough, for any true artist didn't make their creations about *things*—or actualities, philosophies, conceptions—no matter how strikingly they might be framed. What you did, or at least strove endlessly to achieve, was to somehow find a way of reflecting your most honest, naked self through whatever scraps of circumstance you could find. And if that sounded pretentious, well, that was something *else* to be got rid of. And if the project didn't work, if it remained so far from your ambition that it crawled like a many-legged tatterer through your brain? Well, that meant maybe, and *only* maybe, you were on the right track.

Of course, as her work became richer and more satisfactory, she herself grew poorer, and acquired fewer commissions, and was less fêted, and remembered less often by her artistic peers—in fact, probably barely thought of at all. Once, her workshop had been a far grander enterprise, visited by admirers, fellow artists, courtiers of all the great churches, alien entities, journalists and hangers-on. Perhaps even a few lovers as well. But she didn't think of losing these things as any kind of sacrifice. All she had shed were distractions. After all, why create whole seascapes when you could concentrate on one onrushing wave? Or, better still, the sunsparkle of a single grain of sand? Not, of course, that the memory of merely one wave or grain of sand was sufficient for their creation. Far from it. You took impressions, overlays from many sources, and somehow made them your own. A work of the sea wasn't simply about the *sea*, either, although whoever ended up entering its sensory field might have been surprised to learn that the gleam of spindrift was actually the glint of an ancient warrior's armour which she'd taken from the catalogue of a museum on a far-off planet, whilst the sense of shivery elation had originated in the mind of a human child as they tobogganed long ago down a snowy hill. The material casings into which the memory artist stored these creations grew smaller, too, and she became at least as skilled a miniaturist as she was in other aspects of her craft. A small, simple, curl of polished metal, with a minute froth of sea pearls, was more than enough to contain the work she believed had been called *The Last Wave*. She'd even considered casting the complex weave of her impressions of a grain of sand *into* an actual grain of sand, but she'd never appreciated self-referential works of this kind, which were always far too pleased with themselves.

There had once been a market, one which had given her a great deal of satisfaction, for creating biographical memorials of the recently dead. Of course, these intricate urns were never about describing what the deceased had actually been *like*. The natures, faults and achievements of the departed continued to change and evolve in the minds of the still-living once they had passed away. Misers grew generous. Lovers became impossibly skilled. But the memory artist believed she had found ways of laying a thin gauze of flattery across her creations without flinching too much from the heart of the truth. And from those early works in this genre of grave goods had come many similar commissions, especially during the horrors of the Winnowing Plague, which had seen her through what she now feared was probably the most productive period of her long life.

Which brought her all the way back to this clutter in her workshop, and the even bigger and more confused clutter which filled her head. Her last project had certainly been draining. She knew that much. But when had it even *been*? She must have poured so much of herself into its creation that a great deal of her own memories had been absorbed as well. Yet she still itched and ached to create *something*. But what...?

1: The Ball Bearing

THE MEMORY ARTIST got up and steadied herself against the seasick sway of the floor. Then she dragged on her cloak, grabbed her trusty staff, hauled open the flap of her door, and climbed out into whatever awaited beyond.

The first thing that struck her was the smoky stench of the air. Then, the wide and desolate vista. She liked to imagine that her workshop was still located on a bustling promenade of some fashionable island, but many seasons had passed since that had been the case. This region, you could barely even call it an island, was known as the Breakers, and was a vast waste tip where all the detritus of Ghezirah, and spaces and planets far beyond, had been gathered for aeons into an ever-expanding heap. It was definitely morning—she was sure she'd heard the distant cries of the Dawn-Singers a few moments earlier—but the light here was hazed by an eye-stinging pall.

The Breakers formed a jagged mountain range of domestic refuse, redundant technologies, outmoded buildings and whole obsolete islands, all of which and much else had been hauled here to be forgotten forever. Through the gloom as she limped across its ever-shifting surface, the memory artist could make out the slow movement of one of the huge beasts—dumpdragons, she believed they were called—which helped tend this wasteland, mulching metals and organics, and filtering like the giant earthworms they resembled. Farther off, piled hovel upon hovel, buttressed from the Breakers by rough walls of recycled serraplate and black moats of seep-oil, lay the edge of the district which was commonly known as the Flavelas, although it had many other more disparaging names, where those who could brave the danger and the stench chose—if you could call it a choice—to live. The memory artist supposed that this must have been her choice as well. But, as to how and when and why that had happened, she had no idea.

This lack of knowledge was puzzling. At least as strange to her, though, was the thought of Ghezirah itself, even though she felt certain she'd lived here for most, it not all, of her life. To know that you weren't clinging to the surface of some spinning planet, but standing on a gravity-chained island floating amid a swarm of many others, all of them circling Sabil's blaze in a dance of geometries and solar pressures behind a shield that some called the sky, which refracted the light which the Dawn-Singers spread across Ghezirah's many cities and realms each day in their mirrored minarets. She remembered how, long ago in her childhood, one of her mothers had explained that the correct term for this kind of star-spanning structure was a Dyson ring or sphere, although Ghezirah's structure actually circled Sabil in a kind of ragged girdle which would make the star, if seen from a great enough distance, seem to be glittering as if through a vast veil. *While the answer, my dearest, my querida, to the question of exactly who or what Dyson was—be it prophet, designer or creator—has been lost in the impenetrable mists of humanity's past...*

As she leaned on her staff and picked her way through the rot and clutter, the reasons the memory artist had chosen to make her home in the Breakers began to make better sense. Here, abandoned and forgotten, was everything she might ever need to ply her trade. Bright scraps of swarf. Florescences of crystal. Beads of melted glass. Saggy heaps of old fishing nets. And mementos, memories—bytes and bits of data and whole lost lives. All waiting to be rediscovered and remade.

But as she stooped and sifted, she reminded herself that one had to be careful here as well. These screes were often dangerously unstable, and contained many threats. Not the great dumpdragons, which were easy enough to avoid, but the lesser worms which she believed were called ouroboroi, and sharp-fanged rustfleas, not to mention the millipede-like tatterers, which would burrow through your flesh as readily as the plastics they were supposed to consume.

Then there was the rubbish itself. Along with the perils of poisons, acids and radioactivity, there were the long-abandoned ark-ships from the ancient days of humanity's first expansion, whose corrupted gene-spinners still occasionally released dangerous monstrosities instead of the creatures once intended to populate some newly discovered world. The Breakers certainly wasn't a place for the foolish or the unwary to tarry, but the memory artist considered herself to be neither, no matter how absorbed her jackdaw mind became in leaping from object to object in its search for the next project.

Here was a small brass cog which had perhaps once formed part of the innards of an analogue timepiece. She turned it over, considering the memories and sensations with which it might be infused. Time, for obvious reasons, being a theme which she'd long wanted to engage with, but had not—at least as far as she could remember—ever actually explored. She toyed, as she stood there, with investing this cog with the simulacrum of a tall, irregular clock which would throw out fresh fragments of impression and memory with each tick, but the idea began to dissolve even as it strove to find focus, and she threw the object aside.

Still, she was in no mood to give up. This grey, putty-like blob, for instance, which released a gut-wrenching shift of dimensions when she squeezed it between her fingers, was clearly not of human origin. The dead eyes of a ceramic doll fluttered at her as she lifted it up, and she caught the stored fragment of some long-dead child's birthday—the smell of fondant icing and candle smoke as a cake was produced to the chorus of an ancient song. The memory definitely triggered something inside the memory artist's thoughts, and she was sorely tempted, but then again she threw it aside as she recalled something else she'd been looking for for ages, and studied the promising desolation with fresh resolve.

It was said, and she felt sure this was a matter of proven physical evidence rather than just some ancient djinn story, that, rather like certain aliens, humanity had once come in two basic forms. Something to do with sexual reproduction; a weird enough idea in itself. There were women, of course, as there were now, but there were also these things called men. It was even said that a few of this odd sub-species still existed on some of the more backward of the Ten Thousand and One Worlds. Now, if she could find the stored experiences of one of *those* bizarre creatures, she would surely have the basis for a promising new work. But, as often happened, when looking for one thing, and she felt unconsciously in her cloak pockets, she found that she had discovered something else.

Her fingers had encountered an odd tangle, which she drew out and cupped in her palm. Merely a piece of grubby twine, which had been bunched and knotted into a crude kind of bracelet decorated with an odd series of lumps. Not really a bracelet, and hardly a sacred rosary, although it might have been a handmade example of the kind of worry beads which people played through their fingers to calm their nerves, or used as a distraction when they were trying to give something up. Which was perhaps how it had ended up in her pocket, although the memory artist had no idea what she was supposed to be distracting herself from, or giving up.

Each knotted lump held something different. The first being nothing more than a rusty ball bearing of the kind which littered the entire Breakers, and the next seemed to be the dried seed of some species of fruit. Then came a faded, yellowish plastic blob which could once have been a gaming counter. Then there was a ceramic data pearl of the sort which were commonly used to store information, followed by a smooth little sphere of a stone which was probably amber. Then, finally, came a crumbling blob that might have been the remains of one of those pastel-coloured candies children enjoyed eating off the thread of a bracelet, although, all too aware of the perils and deceits prevalent in the Breakers, she certainly wasn't going to nibble it to find out. Which made six beads in all, if you could even call them beads, before her fingers returned to the original grubby knot.

But here was the thing: they all been infused with memories. She could sense their dim whispers rising up to her as she touched each one. But their data was so faded that the actual impressions they contained were nothing more than a teasing mist. She tried again, but with a more conscious effort, and the rusty ball bearing released its essence in a sudden rush. She gasped, and looked around her, expecting some great revelation, but all the memory consisted of was an impression of her own self, standing right here in this desolate spot, as if the memory of this moment somehow also lay in the past.

All very odd, but also rather wonderful. She still had no idea how this strange tangle of memories had actually ended up in her pocket, but felt oddly certain that it would lead her somewhere. But where? Her fingers moved from the ball bearing to touch the dried seed which was knotted next along the thread. It was the kind of thing you'd scrape out from the pulp of a fruit—maybe a cool melon, or a hot butterberry—in the instant before you raised it, sweet and dripping, to your mouth...

She realised she was swallowing back saliva, and couldn't recall when she'd last eaten. There was, she knew with newfound certainty as she stroked the seed, a thriving souk selling produce at the far end of the Flavelas. So it was merely a question of finding her way there from off this sea of rubbish to get herself something to eat—maybe some fresh bread, and that melon and butterberry—and she was just turning, seeking the right direction, when she heard a small, quick voice.

Hey...

The memory artist was instantly wary, and gripping her staff.

Hey...

There it was again. The voice originated from no particular direction, and seemed to be coming directly into her head.

Hey, lady…

When she saw its source, she was far less alarmed. It was merely some kind of wraith, one of the legions of corrupted virtual presences which haunted the Breakers along with so many other lost things. They might pose a danger to the unwary, but they were nothing but patterns of thinly organised energy, and could inflict no direct harm. Although it was clearly making an effort to be seen, this particular manifestation was still partially transparent, and the upturned fuselage of the calèche on which it pretended to be squatting was clearly visible through its form. If anything, it resembled one of the feral street kids who also frequented the Breakers. But they, being corporeal, were dangerous, whereas this thing was a mere annoyance. It—she?—had thin limbs, tattered clothing, bright blue eyes and a sharp grin.

Hey–

"Bugger off!" The handful of rust she threw in its direction passed through it, rattling against the calèche.

There's no need for that. The thing looked genuinely affronted. *I can help you, lady.*

"Help's the last thing I need," she muttered, although she knew it was a mistake to engage with these wraiths. "Especially from something like you."

I know where you live. It's over in that hovel–

"It's a workshop, not a—"

Whatever. And I've seen you about. You clamber here and there muttering to yourself, and picking things up. Frankly, all sorts of rubbish.

"It may seem like rubbish to you. But I'm an artist, and it's the material I work with."

You're an artist, eh? The kid seemed to find the idea very amusing. *I suppose that's better than just being some strange mad old thing, crawling across the Breakers for no good reason at all.*

"How many ways do I have to tell you to stop bothering me, kid? I'm not some invalid. So fuck off. I'm merely going down to the souk, to the markets, to buy some food, and I'm more than capable of finding my own way." Grasping her staff, and with a determined swish of her cloak, the memory artist strode off.

But the kid-thing scampered beside her.

Do you really know what it's like down there, lady? You might think dumpdragons are trouble, but you should try dealing with some of those pirates in that souk. They'll rip the skin off your back and do you for your last penny. And, no offence, but you don't exactly look rich.

"Well..." She tripped on a snag of metal. "As I said—"

I'm an avatar, an intermediary, a companion, a gofer. I can help you in all sorts of ways. It's exactly what I was made for, so this fine morning you couldn't be more in luck. I can run errands, negotiate, keep you company, give you reminders...

"All, no doubt, for a small fee."

The kid was standing in front of her now, panting as if it really had been running—a neat trick—and looking up at her with that oddly knowing grin. *That's how these things work. I do something for you and you do something for me in return. But we can work that out later. You need my help right now, lady, believe me...*

Unfortunately, and much though she prided herself on her fierce independence, the memory artist realised she was unsure of the direction she should be heading to reach the Flavelas, let alone the souk. Whereas this kid...

Ah! You see it now, don't you? You should leave things to the experts, lady. And when it comes to looking out for you today, the expert... The kid planted its virtual right thumb on its scrawny virtual chest. *Is me. Okay?*

Other than a categorical no, all the memory artist could think of to say was yes.

2: The Butterberry Seed

THE MORNING BUSTLE of the souk was extraordinary. So much life! So much noise! Hanging ducks, geelies and chickens, some still flutteringly alive, others aromatically, deliciously dead. Technicolour pots of spices. Iced cakes far too good to be real. Great tanks filled with live fish and ice-hydra, followed by others which frothed with creatures surely meant to be consumed by digestive systems very different to her own.

She was borne along through the maze on tides of memory and forgetfulness, and by a growling hunger in her gut. Here were fruits like spiky puffballs, filled with a yellowish, custard-like heart which stank appallingly, but had an oddly addictive taste. What *were* they called? Like so many other things, the name simply wouldn't come, but, fingering the smooth, warm seed of her second bead which had led her here, the memory artist simply felt so at *home*. So much more *herself*. Even her hunger was enjoyable, now she was surrounded by many ways of satisfying it. Then, inevitably, her thoughts returned to her calling. Surely she'd already amassed enough impressions during this brief foray to begin, at least in sketch form, another work? *Streetfood...? A Market...?* The idea might need compression and direction, but at least she wasn't vegetating in her workshop. She could even just about tolerate this annoying virtual kid.

Why don't you treat yourself to some of these lovely crickets, lady? Deep fried and dipped in honey—sweeter than a first kiss. Or, look just over there, those frothing flagons of spiced beer...

"Just shut up, will you? I'm more than capable of making up my own mind."

The stallholders were just as bad. Hands grabbed at her robes and voices at her thoughts. *Setti...! Lady...! Human...! The freshest!*

The oldest! The tastiest! The best! But it was *Kari* that they most often called after her. Not that any of them could really imagine she was their mother, but, clutching her staff and belligerently limping in her hooded cloak, even the aliens could tell that she was old. She shouldered her way on. Now, and although she hadn't consciously willed it, the prices of all these goods fluttered like alien insects in virtual neon among the stalls, and she saw that they were all unbelievably high.

"Is this some trick of yours, kid?" she shouted as the kid-thing scampered beside her, wicker baskets and stray chickens flickering though its form. "I wasn't born yesterday, you know! What they're charging for everything here is ridiculous."

If you really think I can organise something like this, lady, you're even madder than you look. But I can bargain for you. Knock things down. Get you a nice good deal.

The kid was persistent; she'd grant it that. But any deal here would be a bad one. "This—it's like everything's had three extra noughts added since I last came here."

Which was plainly ridiculous, but also rather disturbing. How long had it been since she'd visited here? She touched again the knotted beads in her cloak pocket, but whatever memory had brought her here had now vanished as completely as her sense of what she was supposed to do next. She felt in her other pockets, finding nothing but holes and dirt. Was she really this mad, this destitute—wandering penniless in a crowded market, having pointless conversations with an entity which could barely be said to even exist? Her career might have been in the doldrums lately, but were things really this bad?

"I don't suppose, kid... You happen to have any funds of your own with you, by any chance?"

I'm just the means, lady. The kid gave one of its shrugs. *Not the end.*

But she was, or had been, a woman of substance and reputation, even if the people shoving past her might think she was just some confused old bat... Somehow, instead of darkening her mood further, the memory artist began to find comfort in such thoughts as she walked on. For, after all, an artist must forever exist as an outsider, an outlier. And as for money... If that became something you cared about, you'd already lost your way. And these vendors—they were little more than pirates, scoundrels, thieves...

A new kind of resolve came over her as she studied the nearest stall, where warm heaps of simit pastries were tauntingly displayed. Gleaming with scattered sesame seeds, and completely unaffordable, they smelled and looked delicious. Even before she'd had time to think about what she was doing, she'd shoved a handful beneath her cloak, and was moving briskly away. Not running at first, at least not until she heard shouts behind her.

Then she *was* running, ducking and dodging, almost falling over her staff as the street cobbles hurtled beneath her feet. She grabbed hold of a sloshing carton of pomegranate juice as she flew by a stall, and then—by now, it just seemed the obvious thing to do—a handful of sugar-dusted sweets. She was running like the wind now, and she was laughing as well as she slalomed her way through the crowds.

Finally, and long after the shouts had dwindled, she leaned against a wall in a back alley to recover her breath. Her legs trembled and her diaphragm ached, but these pastries really were delicious, and the pomegranate juice that she gulped down with rivulets dripping off her chin made her realise how exquisitely thirsty she'd been as well. She felt free and full and liberated. The only thing she hadn't shaken off with all the rest of her concerns was this kid.

That was unexpected.

"I told you... I didn't need you..." She mumbled around a large mouthful of rose-flavoured sweetmeats. "Didn't I?"

You're quicker than you look, lady. I'll give you that. But have you considered how those poor stallholders, trying their best to run a small business at a profit—

"You're not my conscience, kid! I certainly wasn't going to pay those prices, and I can do just fine on my own. As you can see. Oh, and by the way..." Once again, although it hurt her ribs, she found she was laughing. "I've got no money, kid—I'm penniless! So shoo. You're wasting your time with me."

The kid was crouching as if balanced on the lid of an upturned waste bin, and still smiling that irritating, knowing smile. *I think I'll hang around,* it said. *Unless you* really *want me to go, that is. In which case, I'd have no choice.*

"You can stay if you like—it's your funeral. But don't say I didn't warn you." As she felt around in her pocket for more sweetmeats, her fingers found the knotted loop of twine instead. Touching the third of the lumps, she felt the beginning of another memory opening like a new door inside her head.

3: The Gaming Counter

SHE WAS PASSING through a different part of the souk now where the stalls were heaped with all kinds of pirated, harvested and recycled devices, along with data and memory stored in every imaginable, and some barely imaginable, forms. The stallholders called out to her as she limped by, offering recollections of beauty, captured wonders, terrors and lives of every sort. She was sorely temped to linger, but she could already sense her next destination looming and beckoning over the rooftops ahead.

There was a neighbouring island called Izelmek where any being which had ever possessed the smallest iota of ambition longed to work and live. Izelmek had showrooms, bars, galleries, restaurants and shopping malls, all of them crammed in a delirium of ever-changing architecture atop some of the most expensive real estate in the entire Ten Thousand and One Worlds. When she reached the esplanade from where the air-ferries to Izelmek departed, she saw it drifting in the haze of the middle distance, and already glorious to behold. It looked like a pulled golden tooth, with its earthly roots drooping into the void below. An air-ferry was bobbing on the breeze beside its wooden landing, and she reached it with a final leap just as it cast off.

She sat down on a wooden bench, and, once again on this day of dreamy surprises, found herself recovering her breath. But she should do this more often. In fact, she should do nothing else. The glory of this moment wasn't just about the sight of Izelmek, or the fresh taste of the air. Looking up and around, she could see many other islands floating on their gravity chains beneath the great, blue dome of Ghezirah's shielding roof; the glints of their minarets, the reds of their rooftops, the greens of their fields. But no sign of the kid. Perhaps the breeze had blown it away. Then, sly as ever, and paler than a ghost, it was right beside her on the bench.

Nearly didn't make it there, lady.

"No help from a wraith like you." She pointed towards Izelmek. "I used to live there, you know."

You don't say? The kid looked typically unimpressed.

"I was a person of power and substance, back in the day. A real player. *And* I trained as a novitiate of one of the great churches dedicated to the arts... The church of the—of the..." The word was on the tip of her tongue. Frustratingly, it wouldn't come.

The ferry rounded a final promontory, and she caught the sea-roar of music, and the scent of money and privilege—sharp as ozone, you could literally smell it on the air—as the buildings of Izelmek, huge and glassy and holographic, grew and grew in a cliff face of rainbows, until everything else felt small, and the ferry bumped its landing and the other passengers got off. They were mostly human, and drably dressed, and probably worked here in some menial capacity, although even that showed the island's exalted status, for whatever tasks they performed here could doubtless be done more easily and cheaply by bots.

So, lady? Are you coming?

Her fingers sought the next lump in the pocket of memories as she stood up. "I think it's about time *you* followed *me*, kid. That is, if you're really interested in finding out who I really am."

Well, if you put it like that...

Even approached via this lesser route, Izelmek was a place of immediate and overwhelming opulence, its wide streets bright with impatient calls for her to join, participate, enjoy. She was in the district where the great gaming houses and casinos still dominated, changed in every detail though everything seemed. These vast baubles of virtuality, glass and gilded serraplate didn't just resemble temples dedicated to some extravagantly powerful deity—they *were* temples, basilicas, cathedrals, buttressed by the never-ending lure of money and chance...

She smiled and stroked the gaming bead through its knotted thread. It was almost midday, but the ghosts of distant evenings were returning to her; those perfect moments when all the big players began to arrive in their long limousines, golden calèches, filigree flyers and white air-yachts as curfew bells clamoured out the sunset, and she, joining with the perfumed crowds along this promenade, felt cool and easy in her own skin. After all, she was a person of reputation, and not a little influence. And these casinos had never really been about money, or even about winning, but about striking the correct pose. That, and making connections, and being in the right place at precisely the right time. Although one still had to chance the gaming tables every now and then, and act as if winning didn't matter. Even if one occasionally lost.

She could see herself reentering these great, gilded, baroque crustaceans, and already knew just how good and right it would feel. The baize tables lying lush and green. The fresh dice, the sealed cards, the stacked beads, all waiting like lovers for their awakening caress. And everyone who was anyone would be there beneath the diamond chandeliers, and glorious as ever, and twice as rich...

You do realise that you can't possibly go into any of these establishments, lady? Looking like you do, and without any money?

"That *so* isn't the point, kid."

Distracted as she'd been by her memories, the memory artist had become a little lost, and turned for some reason into a sour back alley of the kind which existed even here on Izelmek. The stench here was as bad as back in the Breakers, but the worst of it was that the kid was right. She'd never been able to afford the gaming tables here. Not even back in the day. On Izelmek, you didn't just pay for things with money, but with your talent, and then with your soul.

As she picked her way back out around the spilling refuse towards the blaze of the casinos, an incident which she was almost sure came from her childhood returned in a bright, sudden flash. How she'd gone out to play in the gardens of the old redbrick house where she'd grown up one windy morning, and her favourite straw hat had instantly been blown off her head. She'd run after it, but every time she'd got close, the wind had lifted it up again. At first, the pursuit had seemed like a game, but as the hat kept tumbling away from her she'd begun to feel that if this was a game, it was one the wind was playing with *her* rather than with her hat.

Had she ever recovered that hat? And what about that old redbrick house? Although some aspects of her life were now becoming somewhat clearer to her, the memory artist had absolutely no idea. It was as if parts of her mind were being sucked away into swirling black holes. But, as she stepped out of the alley back into the siren light and noise of the casino promenade, she recalled all too well the endless, desperate chase of living here on Izelmek, with whatever she was seeking—the bigger apartment, the next trophy lover, the settee made of living hide—always spinning just out of reach.

4: The Data Pearl

SHE'D MOVED AWAY from Izelmek's gambling district, and was walking along a wide, tree-lined boulevard in a quiet suburb. The kid, perhaps suspecting that its virtuality might be snuffed out by some overzealous firewall, was hanging back and had shut up. This whole area, with its distant-seeming glimpses of palaces, mansions, castles and châteaux, all floating within impossible wide acreages of moat, garden and parkland, was as strange yet familiar as a recurring dream. She knew, for instance that these dwellings lay much closer together than they seemed. But needs must, the price of real estate on Izelmek being what it was, and the small inconveniences of competing virtuality fields were to be endured for the sake of living in such an exclusive spot.

After extracting the furred remains of the last sweetmeat she'd stolen from the market from her cloak pocket and shoving it into her mouth, her fingers retraced her knotted beads. The fourth along the strand was a data pearl, and as soon as she touched it, she realised she'd actually visited many of these dwellings during her days of pomp and circumstance, generally bearing the plans of some new look-at-me project in a data pearl almost exactly like this.

"You know, I did some of my best work around here," she said, glancing back at the kid. "Private client stuff, mostly. There was this single stela in black obsidian which roared as you approached it with the combined force of thunderstorms I'd sourced from a dozen different worlds. Oh, and there was a pair of antique stone dragons which I invested with fiery wings, and a primal sense of fear..."

"There was also quite a demand for erotic works..." She hesitated, somehow imagining for a moment that she was talking to a real, living kid. "...But they were never my favourite type of work. Sexualised sculpture always seemed clever in concept, at least in the minds of their commissioners, and then turned repetitive and tawdry in execution. And, by the way, they were always a sure sign that whatever relationship they were supposed to commemorate was heading for the rocks. See that big entrance over there...?" She pointed towards what should have been a glass gateway, but was a long, high wall of alarmingly ancient brick. "Well, the place has been remodelled, but there *was* a gateway there, and I must have gone through it at least a dozen times to reshape a particularly explicit example of the genre. But, as far as the client was concerned, it still wasn't explicit enough." She shrugged. It was nice to have these memories returning, even if the particular experience had been frustrating. "Eventually, I had to tell them that I was an artist, not their pimp."

But it was so *quiet* amid these chocolate-box vistas! The only sound was the clip of her staff as she pushed on past mansion after mansion through the shimmering heat of Sabil's refracted glare. But, despite all the differences that time had engendered, she still didn't feel particularly lost. She lifted the knotted string from her pocket. It was clumsily done, and dirty, and didn't smell particularly nice. Even the string itself didn't look to be actual string, was more like a scrap of strained ribbon, or perhaps an old bandage. It really was most peculiar—to have these images and feelings looped together as if by the fingers of an obsessive child. As an artist, she'd always believed in the power of coincidence, of this leading to that leading to something else, but the trail she'd been following today was clearly something more. Plainly, she, or someone, must have strung these memories together for the very purpose for which she was now using them—as a reminder, as a keepsake, as a thread leading ever-deeper into her own past.

Looking around, she saw that the big residences had all faded, and that she had reached what had once been a grand square, although many of its buildings were half-demolished.

I don't like the feel of this place...

"Come on kid—it's just some building site."

But she *knew* this place! Not as it was now, but as it had once been, although its ruinous state gave it an odd feel, as if bits of her own mind had also been torn away. She'd returned just in time—or perhaps a little too soon—for she realised that the huge, jagged, ugly thing squatting in the centre of the square wasn't some weird construction bot, but something she recognised, and knew, and had actually made.

This installation sculpted in steel and memory had been one of her most acclaimed works, and as the memory artist wandered around it she marvelled at its ambition and scale. But her once-famous beachscape had seen many better days. The giant scoops of polished metal were rusty, and water no longer spilled over them in cascades, whilst the field of intricate memories she'd fused into its fabric were little more than a corrupted blur. The two suns strobed and flickered disconcertingly, and the impression of soft sand had transformed into gluey mud. As for that oceanic scent which she'd striven so hard to get right, all that remained was an unpleasant odour of rot, which she realised came not from what was left of her virtuality projections, but from the relic's own physical decay.

She touched the data pearl again, and the buildings regrew and put on a festive glamour, and the whole scene was transformed. For this was a day for flags and celebrations as her greatest creation was revealed. It already looked beautiful even covered with shimmering blue fabric before it was unveiled, and people cheered and other entities made appropriate noises as silver bird-bots lifted the fabric, and the sculpture's sail-like fins clamoured with sunlight, and the entire square filled with a hundred salty rainbows and a thousand memories.

"Excuse me?"

Even as the ruins crashed back around her, the memory artist imagined the voice was some echo from the past.

"Excuse me?"

She turned, expecting to be admonished for trespassing by some overofficious security bot, but the figure shuffling towards her across the square was moving far too slowly, and was far too fat, to be a machine.

"It *is* you, isn't it...? I *thought* so when first I saw you over there..."

The waddling figure bulged and contracted within swathes of bright cloth.

"So *glad* I found you. You... You just don't get the old crowd around..." She was wheezing and puffing, and clearly human. "...Around here like you used to. Everything's...changing, isn't it?" Fat though she was, something about her seemed oddly stretched and strained. From the smell she gave off, she hadn't recently washed, either. "This place isn't what it used to be... Not...any longer..."

The memory artist could only nod. Clearly, her new companion was under the impression that they'd once known each other, but she'd grown so large in all the years since that her younger self had been entirely lost—or absorbed. Still, the memory artist thought she saw the ghosts of old friends and acquaintances flicker briefly as if over a distorted mirror across her bloated face.

"So...?" The woman's small eyes were bright and eager. "What are you up to these days?"

"I still have a workshop over..." The memory artist gestured vaguely, struggling to remember where she lived, then not wanting to say. "...on another island. And I'm still hard at work."

"Yes, yes...?"

"Matter of fact, I'm researching a new project right now. I think I see it as being primarily autobiographical, and it involves retracing, perhaps even recreating, my own past."

"So you're an *artist*?"

"Wasn't I always? I mean—who else made this sculpture?" This woman was just as impertinent as the kid—who, she couldn't help noticing, had vanished again just when it might finally have been of some use. "But what about you—what have you been doing?"

"Oh, you know." A lumpy shrug. "This and that. Here and there." The fat woman squinted up at the rusty sculpture. "Are you *really* saying you made that horrendous thing?"

This was plainly getting ridiculous. "I'm sorry, but I honestly don't know who you are. Did we study together? Did we collaborate on some project? Were you a client? Did we know each other socially? If you could just give me some idea of—"

"Does it really matter if we've ever met?" The woman's eyes still glittered, but they were no longer friendly. "I'm here right now, aren't I, standing in this gods-forsaken place? And so, for some reason, are you. And you've just told me you're some kind of artist, and that you have your own workshop, so you must have some money even if you look like you've just crawled out from under a stone. The universe hasn't been that kind to all of us, lady." The woman had grabbed her arm in a surprisingly strong grip. "So maybe you could spare me something, for the sake of old times? Or, for that matter, simple human charity, and no times at all?"

"I would if I could," the memory artist conceded, "but the fact is that I'm probably no better off than you are. Maybe even worse. My workshop, it's... Well, it's—"

The fat woman had reached her spare hand into the folds of her clothing to produce what the memory artist presumed would be a begging bowl. A knife glittered instead.

"I've tried asking you nicely. And if that doesn't work, if you want to fuck about and play awkward, I'll—"

The next few moments passed in a blur of unconscious decision. The memory artist found that she was wielding her staff before she'd thought to use it, and had struck her would-be assailant hard across the knife-wielding knuckles. She caught her again with another swipe on the left rump before the knife had even clattered to the paving, her hood falling back as she did so, and was taking aim for a further blow when the woman gave a yelp and turned and shuffled away across the square at an unlikely pace.

The memory artist leaned on her staff and—it was impossible not to—found herself laughing once again. Sorry though she felt for that poor, fat beggar woman, this was as good as stealing food in the souk. No, it was better. She'd stood up for herself, she'd faced danger, and the danger had retreated, and she barely gave her ruinous beachscape a backwards glance as she headed on across the square. Seasons changed. Fashions came and went. But she was still here, and she was still alive, and she was returning to her past, and that was all that really mattered.

I warned you it wasn't safe here, lady.

"That's rich! Especially as I seem to remember you saying you were going to look after me today. You virtual entities, you're all the same—your promises are as thin as the stuff you're made of. But come on, kid. Follow me. I know *exactly* where we're going next, even if you don't."

5: The Amber Bead

PASSING OUT OF the condemned district, they reached the farther side of Izelmek close to the bridge spanning the chasm which separated it from the neighbouring island of Murahi. Touching the next of her beads, the memory artist knew that the structure was just as impressive as it had always been, with vast spiderwebs of spun diamond sweeping down from the giant pillars supporting either end. The islands of Izelmek and Murahi were anchored by separate gravity chains, and this famous bridge across the equally famous

Wadi el-Basluk—the valley of the void—had to accommodate constant shivers of movement which some beings who tried to use it found almost impossible to endure. The memory artist relished the sensation. Setting foot on it, she felt like an old mariner returning to the sea.

"You don't know what you're missing, kid. This is some feeling!"

The kid said nothing as it wafted in her wake.

Near the middle of the span, she leaned over the balustrade to look over the edge. At first, all she could see was blue darkening into absolute black. But then, as if she was gazing into the depths of an ocean, there were sliding shapes, glints of moment. The Wadi el-Basluk was a chasm leading down and out into deep space, through which the starships passed on their way to and from Ghezirah, and then on towards the churning emptiness of the Great Gateway which linked this vast city with all the other Ten Thousand and One Worlds.

With their drifting lights, huge fins, shimmering energy effects and odd protuberances, the leviathans far below her really did look like different varieties of deep-sea fish. Some were sleek and grey and long, elegantly purposeful and predatory as sharks. Others were spiny and near-spherical like annoyed puffer fish, and might have seemed almost comical if she hadn't known that they were the size of planetoids and lay tens—if not hundreds—of miles distant. And here came the tugs, the pilot fish, the dart-like calèches, the crustaceal bots and suffragi, all rushing to and fro in attendance on these bigger beasts. Then a more ponderous sublight vessel emerged from the depths, bristling with sensors and a vast, gaping prow like the mouth of a krill-feeding whale. Its purpose was to drift through the voids between the stars, seeking out the debris of wayward comets, stray asteroids, the hulks of lost spacecraft—all of which would eventually end up in the Breakers, just like everything else. But it was the starships to which her eyes and her mind returned, for they travelled through somewhere more vast, and far emptier, than mere space.

She found herself remembering her three mothers, and how one of them—she was called Columbina, and was the youngest and smallest, with hazel eyes and a sprinkle of freckles across her nose—had sat beside her bed on a late summer evening, and inflated and knotted a red balloon to help explain something that could probably never be properly explained, least of all to a child...

It has all to do, my dear, with these things called cosmic strings, which are tiny anomalies—errors or mistakes, you might almost call them, although they are not—which were folded through all possible dimensions during the Days of Creation when our universe burst into being. At first, you see, these strings were incredibly close together, like the knot at the end of this balloon—it gave a soft boom as she plucked it—*but then they were forced apart as the universe expanded, and the galaxies coalesced, Inshallah, and the first stars began to glow, so that their ends came to lie tens, hundreds or thousands of light years distant. And, if the outer fabric of our universe can be thought of as the stretched surface of this balloon with all the dimensions and energies which make up everything, you and I included, inside it, these cosmic strings, of which Ghezirah's Great Gateway is by far the largest entanglement, draw parts of that outer membrane together, just like this...*

Columbina had then attempted to demonstrate this odd state of affairs by twisting the balloon together like a party entertainer. Instead, and with a loud pop—their own little big bang—the balloon had burst. They had both laughed, and the moment had been precious. Of all the memory artist's three mothers, Columbina had possessed the finest sense of humour, and perhaps she had loved her the most.

But what, she wondered, about those other ships—the much slower ones which had set out long before the Gateways were even discovered, crammed with the memories of creatures they would recreate through their gene-spinners when they found the worlds they sought? Perhaps she had asked Columbina about them as well. But if she had, the answer was lost, although its eternal whisper still seemed to touch her like the wind which arose from the chasm below.

Lady...!

She heard a voice.

Lady...!

Felt a tugging at her thoughts.

Lady...!

And realised that she was leaning far farther over the balustrade than she'd imagined, her body close to overbalancing and her feet no longer touching the ground. Passers-by were looking, murmuring, making the signs of their gods as they drew back with a shudder which seemed to pass through her and into the quaking bridge. Belatedly, she recalled that this was a spot where depressed artists and despairing lovers came to put an end to their lives. And, even as she glared at the kid and shook her head at these staring strangers and muttered that she'd simply been enjoying the view, she couldn't help wondering what it would be like, to fall endlessly down towards deep space—perhaps to even tumble on into the Great Gateway itself. What kind of death would it be, to have your very atoms dissected by the same forces which had birthed the universe itself? More likely, her blood would have boiled and her lungs would have burst as soon as she approached hard vacuum, and that would have been that.

She walked on across the bridge, now gripping hard to the balustrade and her staff, and found it a relief to finally set her feet on the solid ground of Murahi, the so-called Isle of Knowledge, where most of the greatest churches maintained their prime seminaries and colleges, and where—had she already told the kid this? She couldn't exactly remember—she herself had studied in her own distant youth.

Here on Murahi, the horizons climbed amid floating parklands and elevated walkways, and the great basilicas of the seminaries seemed both immensely solid and silkily frail: as if they might either drift away on the next breeze, or sink forever in the weight of their significance and antiquity. Things changed here, but in a way they didn't, and as she touched her fifth bead, which was made of warm, smooth amber, she remembered just how awed she'd felt when she'd first arrived here, clutching nothing but her ambitions and dreams. There was a sense of joy and life here, and a shimmering, inexpressible quality to the late afternoon light which seemed to flood though her as if she was almost as frail as the kid. This wasn't the illusion of elation she'd felt amid Izelmek's casinos, or even the power and wonder she'd felt as she created her best and strongest works, but something simpler and more pure.

She stood before the glass and marble gates of one of the great seminaries, trying to recall whether this was where she'd actually studied. So much of her past still evaded her, yet as she watched this season's latest batch of novitiates surge past, their voices shrill and excited, their eyes raised towards the future, even the fashions—those red silk neckerchiefs, swirly windsilk skirts and strappy sandals, not to mention the jangly amber bracelets—felt so familiar that she longed to join in with the crowd. She could enter these great, cool buildings, draw out armfuls of ancient data and settle amid the pillars of dust to explore their secrets, and make sketches of the wonders she longed to create. In those long-lost days, no vision had been too big, or too small.

Some of the students were glancing her way as they flurried by, although, shrunken and changed as she'd become, they couldn't possible know who she was. Still, she longed to grab their hands and tell them that the real glory wasn't in what lay ahead, but in the now, in the here, in these moments of shared hope and laughter—not in the thing they dreamed of doing, but in the dream itself. But the memory artist knew this was something that every generation had to find out for themselves.

She turned away from the gates and shuffled slowly on. She could try visiting half-remembered cafes and bars where she had surely once wasted many pleasurable hours. Or she could sit down on a bench in this park, and breathe the scent of the fog trees. But she knew that the way forward didn't lie in the dappled shades of this late afternoon, or even in that rambling, red-roofed building across the lake, where she was sure she'd once lodged in a low-beamed room. It didn't even lie in the other memories—of tangled sheets, whispered words, the scents and sensations of first love—which this amber bead still held. Lovely though these impressions were, she somehow sensed that darker things lay beneath. That, and that the way ahead lay amid her own confusions, which she still had to confront if she was to discover who she really was.

6: The Child's Candy

SLOWLY, THE MEMORY artist limped on. Silently, driftingly, the kid followed. Already, the Dawn-Singers were edging the mirrors of their minarets towards twilight. Soon, the curfew bells would ring out once again, and night would wash in across all Ghezirah. But the walls in this place where she now found herself loomed high and mossy, their shadows filled with the darkness of a season colder than any she'd yet known. Was she even still on Murahi, or had she somehow crossed to some adjoining lesser island? Her mind and her fingers sought the next lump along the tattered string, but it refused to speak to her.

She was going home, that much was obvious, and she realised now that this was all she'd ever wanted from the very beginning. To see again, changed though they might be, the smiling faces of her three mothers. To hear and breathe the sounds and scents of her childhood. To finally know who she was, and what had made her. That trip long ago to the museum, with the scary glint of that ancient warrior's armour. Or that wonderful afternoon when she'd tobogganed, whooping, down a snow-covered hill. So many times. So many days. So many memories.

Ah! At last. This was surely it. A chain footbridge spanned the chasm separating her from wherever lay ahead. The memory artist gripped her staff and held hard to the wobbling handrail, trying not to look down through the wide gaps which were all that separated her from the void churning below, which was surely the mouth of the Great Gateway itself. She'd soon be a child again, and then all of this would surely become just another game, but the wind was rising, the whole flimsy structure was swaying, and she began to feel afraid.

Then, once again, Inshallah, she was back upon solid ground, although it was cold and there was a bonfire taste to the air. But nearly there now. Nearly home, and finally that last fragile bead of crumbling candy was leading her on. And she *knew* this particular street as she'd never known anywhere else in her entire life. These cracks in the paving, that grinning gargoyle—and here, down between these wind-wild hedges, was the way she'd always taken to get home. Right here, through this wooden gate, with the latch which needed a special twist and lift before it creaked open and the wind bore her through, on into her childhood garden, where something was wrong although nothing had really changed.

Shuffling amid flocks of leaves, she tried to bring this confusing jigsaw into proper shape in her mind. Here was the swing, roped beneath the old ash tree, where she'd once risen and fallen, high towards the roof of the sky, then back towards the solid ground, still creaking and swaying as if she'd just jumped off. There had once been grand picnics out on these seedhead-swaying lawns, wild laughter and the clatter of feet along these weedgrown pathways. And those two women who were coming towards her, the one carrying a tinkling tray of lemonade and the other struggling with a large sunshade, they had to be her other two mothers. They were both golden-haired, and they both looked impossibly young, and she saw and knew how deeply they loved each other even as they bickered. And here, snagged on a branch like an old bird's nest, were the remains of a straw hat, which triggered some other memory she couldn't quite catch, although she had no recollection whatsoever of the walled garden she entered next. It wasn't just an absence of knowledge; it was more as if she was crossing some vast void between the light years.

Confused and weary, stumbling across ancient steps, the memory artist limped on towards the house and saw that it was nothing but a ruin, its roof holed and its windows shattered. She didn't need to force open its rotted door to face the age-old darkness which already swarmed inside her mind. Even her own skin felt like damp plaster and diseased wood. Then, worse still, a large tatterer crawled out from a gap in the wall. Sensing the air, mandibles clicking, it moved questingly towards her.

She fled back across the garden and on through the wind-flapping gate. It wasn't just her childhood home, her ancient memories, which were in ruins, it was this entire neighbourhood, perhaps this whole island, and the sense of loss and corrosion grew worse as she limped on. And where was the kid? No sign of it again, just when she was in desperate need of any kind of companionship, although perhaps it had always been just another illusion, on this day of ghosts and dead ends. The acrid smell of bonfires was even stronger here, darkening the air, and the dry and leafless trees rattled like old bones. Things would be much easier if she didn't know where she was, but, like a scene in a recurring nightmare, the dilapidated graveyard she found herself entering felt not just eerily familiar, but bleakly inevitable.

Misangled memorials and broken stelae poked out through the erupting ground, along with many cracked and fallen memorial urns, some of which still wafted dimmed impressions and memories of the long-departed. She caught laughter, the scent of a hyacinth, the crush of soft grass, rapturous applause, the garbled narrative of a star-wrecked mariner, the plucked strings of an oud. A few of these mangled creations might once have been her own work, but surely that meant they were in entirely the wrong place in her journey? This was all deeply confusing, and in fact rather horrible. Given any choice, the memory artist wouldn't have gone on. But what was there to turn back to now?

Somewhere far off, coming and going with whooping wind, the curfew bells were tolling in the night. And in front of her stood, or had stood, a simple memorial to a child. The eroded dates lay far in the past, and she could just make out a mention of something called the Winnowing Plague farther down the headstone. The girl's three mothers, who would now themselves also be long dead, had infused what memories and impressions they could of their lost daughter into a few special objects placed inside a small memorial urn, although most of its contents were gone. Touching what was left—a corroded brooch, a ribboned curl of hair, the remains of a necklace of cheap candies—felt, to the memory artist, like running her fingers through broken glass.

Leaning down on her staff to pick away the dirt at the base of the stone and peering closely in the sinking light, she saw, still just legible, a name she now knew wasn't hers. She took out her loop of knotted fragments of time, extracted the crumbling remains of the small lump of candy, and laid it where it belonged. Then she straightened up, looked around to get her bearings, and walked on towards a familiar stench and smoke.

7: The Winding Knot

DARK THOUGH IT might be in the rest of Ghezirah, night here in the Breakers, filled as it was with so much flame and phosphorescence, had a light all of its own. But, even with her eyes closed—even blinded—the memory artist would have known where she was. For this was her territory, this was her landscape, this was where she belonged. Here in this place where—ridiculous truism—everything in the whole universe eventually ended up. Not just old starships and unwanted pushchairs, but whole islands—places where people had lived and loved, their parklands, even their cemeteries—were towed here on their failing gravity chains by giant air-tugs, to be dumped and forgotten.

Still, and burrowed and uprooted though it was, this ancient graveyard continued, and was far bigger than she could have imagined. Here, for instance, was a memorial to another young life wasted: a promising novitiate studying architecture on Murahi who'd thrown herself off the bridge into the void known as the Wadi el-Basluk after falling too deeply in love. And this crumbling pyramid with facets of corroded marble commemorated the triumphs of one of the most fêted artists of her generation, back in the distant days when infusing memories into objects was thought of as fashionable rather than a tawdry gimmick. Almost equally grand, although the boiled earth around it had suffered from the attentions of tatterers, was a mausoleum funded by the grieving friends of a socialite and gambler who'd been found inexplicably dead in an Izelmek back alley. Like many other tombs, these had all once been infused with memories of the dear-departed, although they had subsequently been picked over and pillaged.

The part of the graveyard she was labouring across now, where the bigger beasts of the Breakers—the ouroboroi and the dumpdragons—had been busily at work, was a mulch so fine and loose that it soon became easier to crawl, although fragments and memories from individual tombs were still to be found scattered amid the bones.

There was so much she could yet learn here—so many stolen memories. There were even scraps of the winding sheets which had once bound the corpses which could be used as a kind of twine, and knotted to form the illusion of a life. She was a successful artist in her workshop, no, she was a convicted thief running through a souk, and then she was in some grand casino, or glorying in her latest triumph in a brand new plaza, or standing on a bridge over a space so dark that the stars gleamed up. Search hard enough, and she might even find the memories of some canny old creature who'd once made her living picking over the Breakers for scrap. And she was forever chasing after a windblown straw hat.

Climbing up from her knees, she saw that she had reached an even older district of the Breakers. Before her, the maw of its shattered fuselage wider than the mouth of any dumpdragon, loomed the remains of one of the ark-ships which had set out towards the stars in the ages long before the Gateways were discovered, and when there were perhaps still even creatures called men back on Urrearth. It would have been hauled here after it was found as a lost hulk drifting in deep space.

She picked her way towards its shadow in a kind of awe. Beyond lay a strange maze of windy tunnels, bleak dead ends and rusted machinery. There were snowfalls of crystal circuitry, and dangling forests of cable, and everything was dead. And yet… Deeper inside the craft, where the flamelight of the Breakers couldn't possibly reach, there was still enough illumination for her to see. As a phenomenon, radiation wasn't uncommon in the Breakers, and was generally to be feared, but she pushed on nevertheless, drawn by a sense she'd now encountered many times: that she was returning to a place she already knew.

She reached a large inner chamber which had clearly once been the heart of the vessel. There were more drifts of shattered circuitry, but not all of the structures here had fallen into absolute decay. Glassy, hexagonal pods climbed the walls in a way which reminded her of the segments of a giant hive. Picking her way over the remains of the lower pods which had burst or shattered, her fingers encountered a silky webbing which crumbled like dried mucus. Peering inside, she glimpsed intricate seedheads, the wings of bodiless birds, a fish seemingly caught in mid-leap. Then she found a prism containing something resembling a bouquet of red flowers, which she realised were bloody scraps of internal organs, almost, but not quite, fully formed. Clearly, these were gene-spinners which had never been able to populate the planets they'd been designed to reach.

Climbing, she came across a larger pod which looked to have split open in more recent times. The mucus inside it was still soft, and she felt an odd wave of familiarity, combined with a strong desire to crawl inside it, and to curl up and sleep for a very long time. Her mind must be entirely addled, to come up with such nonsense all on its own, now that she'd exhausted every memory in that loop of twine. Still, and as ever, her fingers moved towards her cloak pocket, and she gazed at it in the ark ship's dangerous glow.

What was she? What had she ever been? Did it still matter, even to her? But some stubborn part of the same curiosity which had driven her to take this strange and confusing journey still wouldn't let go. After all, and unlike that kid-thing which had followed and taunted her all day, she was real, and made out of proper stuff. Empty though she now felt, she couldn't have come out of nothing at all. She shoved the knotted thing back into her pocket and stared at her empty palm of her right hand, and rubbed away the dirt with her wetted thumb. And saw the flesh beneath. And finally knew.

This ark-ship had once been full of knowledge and purpose, bearing precious skeins of life across the void between the stars. But, drifting for millennia through the hard rains of deep space, and with no habitable planet ever found, it had fallen into despair, and then a kind of machine dementia, followed by a long blackness of unknowing. But still, some lingering spark of consciousness had perceived its arrival here in the Breakers as a kind of landfall, and had striven to kindle life inside its hive of wombs until, after aeons of nothing but monstrosities and abortions, it had woven one last, living bloom.

The memory artist still couldn't remember her first moment of being, but she knew how hard it must have been, to emerge from this strange hive, naked and confused, her mind as empty as the ark-ship's, yet filled with a desperate need to exist, and to know. Then clambering out as she was doing now along these mouldering tunnels to face the wonders and horrors of the Breakers beyond.

Outside, beyond the maw of the ark-ship, the wind was still blowing and it was still night. A dumpdragon was heaving across the horizon. There were many fires. Scrambling tatterers. Leaping rustfleas. Livid lakes of acid and mud. A marvel that she had not only come to life, but somehow survived. Yet looking down again at her own hands, she could see herself crawling amid this mulch, rooting for knowledge and for food. And finding, yes, of course, not only rags with which to clothe herself, and the staff she could see lying not far off, but scraps of meaning and memory amid the grave-goods of that abandoned graveyard, which she had hoarded and knotted together to form the impression of a life. How long had she existed in this manner? Even now, she had no way of knowing, but, looking down again at her hands, she saw that they were new and smooth rather than lumpily arthritic, and realised that one of the many illusions she'd nurtured in her need to make sense of her existence was that she was old.

Picking up the staff, limping on across the Breakers and searching as always amid the debris, she soon found a sheet of polished metal and rubbed away the dirt from it with the hem of her cloak. Standing before it, taking down her hood and seeing herself in reflection, the memory artist laughed out loud. No wonder the other creatures she'd encountered today had looked so oddly at her. Her forehead slanted, her left eye was blue and her right, which lay a little lower, was green, and her nose looked as if it had been broken in several places, which she supposed was possible, although more likely that was simply how she'd been made. Pulling away more of her cloak and then the rags beneath, she saw that her flesh was a marbled whorl of browns, creams and pinks. And, of course, her left leg was oddly canted and slightly shorter than the right. Which explained the limp. All in all, she was a scrambled mess. Although, she supposed, she still had to concede that she was actually alive, which surely meant something, even if she could already feel the dark confusions swirling back in.

Hey...

"Save me the bullshit, kid. I've told you enough times already, the best thing you can do for both of us is disappear."

Disappear? Now there's one thing I can *manage.*

But it didn't. It just sat there, pretending to balance its thin— no, non-existent—limbs on the upturned body of a rusty calèche.

"You knew about this, didn't you?"

If you mean that you're not actually a distinguished artist or a rich socialite who just happens to be living in a hovel–

"It's not a hovel, it's a workshop."

–whatever, and in the Breakers of all places, the answer's a definite yes. But you wouldn't have believed me if I'd told you, would you? Especially if I'd said you'd crawled out from some ark-ship. Although, lady, for someone who thinks they're a memory artist, your memory really isn't that great.

"But I really *am* old, you know. Or at least part of me is. It came... *I* came... I arrived... I once... Was..."

She gestured vaguely back in what she thought was the ark-ship's direction. But she could already feel that brief glimpse of her true sense of self diminishing, and the return of all the uncertainties which haunted her useless, demented brain, and had to grasp her staff and slump down to the seething ground.

"...Has this happened before?"

If you mean, have you managed to find your way down off the Breakers and take a tour of several neighbouring islands, I think the answer's no.

"So you might even call it a kind of progress?"

The kid didn't even bother to shrug. After all, and as best as she could remember, she'd spent the whole day telling it that she was a succession of different people, all of them long dead.

As I warned you this morning, lady, the Breakers might be dangerous, but there are many other places out there that you're really not equipped to cope with, and are probably a whole lot worse. You're lucky to still be in what passes for one piece.

"That's..." She wanted to say something like *ridiculous*, but things which she was fairly sure had actually happened came back to her in sharp flashes—the flicker of a knife, running wildly through a souk, leaning over the edge of a bridge towards an impossibly deep drop...

Although, the kid continued, *there is at least some justification for your claim that you're a memory artist. After all, lady, you've made, and then remade, yourself.*

"And how about you, kid? How long have you existed in this place?"

A while.

"Even by my standards, it must be a pretty slim existence—savaging this wasteland for energy and processor power to keep up the illusion of being. Especially when what you're trying to offer people isn't something anyone wants."

The kid gave a slow blink. For once, it didn't smile. *Yet here I am. And, lest we forget, here you are, lady, as well. And I do happen to have a clear and functioning memory, of souks and stalls, of markets, smells, sounds, deals and transactions like the ones we experienced this morning, but going so far back even I can't see where it began. Still, I reckon I probably started out as little more than the tap of someone's personal server to buy—who knows?—maybe one of those durian fruits, which apparently smell so bad, and yet taste so good, or perhaps half a dozen eggs. But information is information, and if I'm anything to go by, it seems that it's pretty hard to destroy. So I travelled, I drifted, I passed here and there. Maybe I once even crossed between the stars. And somehow—and hey presto—I became the talking, thinking, conscious yet incorporeal wonder you can just about see before you now.*

"I'm sorry." The memory artist shivered and hugged herself, stroking the slightly different textures of her two arms. "I didn't mean to say anything hurtful. I'm sure you're marvellous in your own peculiar way."

If that's supposed to be a compliment, the kid muttered, *I suppose I might as well take it. And, the fact is, and made the way I am, I wouldn't have been able to travel with you across Ghezirah today if you hadn't allowed me to piggyback on your physical presence.*

"Which, I suppose, is what you're still doing now?"

Do you want me to go away?

She shook her head. "Although, kid, you're not exactly helping me not to believe in phantasms and ghosts."

Perhaps. But... The kid gestured towards its gaunt and transparent body. *...these things are relative. Especially here.*

Stinking and smoking, the Breakers lay all around them. The dumpdragon was still crawling across the horizon with a black flock of some species of leather-winged bat or bird swooping in its wake. Closer to, other creatures and entities were shuffling and stirring. Rats and tatterers. Copperworms and ouroboroi. Things with existences even thinner and stranger than hers and this kid's. Then, as the wind shifted and the smoke billowed in a different direction, the memory artist saw the piled remains of what she supposed she must have thought of this morning as her workshop, although the kid had been generous in even calling it a hovel; it was a burrow.

She was the botched fruit of a dead ark-ship, a senile monstrosity, incomplete in both mind and body. And what else had she burrowed, hoarded and consumed, back in that graveyard and elsewhere across the Breakers? Like so many other things, it was probably better not to know. She felt for the lumpy tangle in her pocket, and bent back her arm as if to throw it as far out into the Breakers as she could.

You know what it's called, don't you?

"What?"

There's a very old phrase for the thing that you're constantly feeling, lady–that you've been somewhere before.

She shook her head.

Déjà vu.

Just a pretty sound—nothing more. And why was she even talking to this thing, and what was she doing here at all? Looking down, the memory artist realised her arm had dropped and the oddly knotted loop of memories still hung from her fingers.

"So, kid," she said, holding it out, "you say you can strike a good bargain, so how much will you give me for this?"

Stepping towards her, the kid smiled, and reached out until the ghost of its hand shimmered within the physicality of her own flesh, and she felt the cool, knowing presence of its mind join with hers.

Perhaps that's something you and I can work out together, it said.

IAN R. MACLEOD

Afterword

ALTHOUGH I'VE BEEN known to be less than positive about works produced to order for the sake of dangled monetary carrots, I have to confess that *The Memory Artist* is such a piece. I was offered what was—at least by the standards of what's usually paid for short fiction—a more than decent amount of money to write a story in response to an invite by a large Chinese tech corporation to visit their main offices. To which I agreed, and then dutifully produced *The Memory Artist*.

I'm not sure I'd accept a similar invitation now. My view of that country's influence on the world, and the way it treats its own citizens, has changed substantially for the worse, although even at the time I felt a little uneasy. But I don't think these circumstances or that unease are particularly evident in the story itself.

What strikes me now on re-reading this story is that it probably comes as close as anything I've written to reflecting how I feel about the creative process. I may try to distance myself from my writing in many ways, but pretty much everything the memory artist feels about her art and her life comes from feelings I've felt, and continue to feel. It's all there, from sunny optimism and overweening arrogance to bleak confusion and the loss of all hope. The Breakers themselves in all their horror and wonder are a pretty strong metaphor for how fiction-writing feels, with random scraps suddenly coming together out of oceans of accumulated dross until they can be tied together into a semi-meaningful whole. Then, of course, everything often falls apart again, and I find myself trying to piece it all together as desperately as the memory artist does when she feels as if she's losing her sense of self.

THE MEMORY ARTIST

If these extremes seem a little over the top, I will admit that *The Memory Artist* uses a degree of artistic licence. But not so very much. Sure, there are times when writing's just a matter of working things through in a workmanlike way. Like all jobs, it has its elements of simply getting stuff done. But I still feel elated when things are going well, and sad, disappointed and downright annoyed when they aren't. After all, if I don't care about what I'm writing, how can I expect anyone else to?

Sin Eater

MANY WEEKS AFTER it had first received the summons from the sting of a lone server bee, the robot finally entered the ruins of Rome. The great city was as empty of life as every other place it had passed through, its once-bustling alleys and busy thoroughfares filled with nothing but ghost-flurries of snow. But as it reached the ruins of the central district, and lured by its semi-human silhouette, the city's remaining inhabitants began to emerge.

Rusting waiters in tattered long-tailed suits gestured towards broken heaps of tables. Guide-bots called out in the cracked tones of a dozen different languages with offers of private tours of the Colosseum, the Pantheon, the Forum, whatever was left of the famous museums—and of course the great Basilica of Saint Peter's, whose dome, holed but still seemingly mostly intact, rose over the rubble ahead. The pleasure-droids looked even more convincingly alive, and thus pathetic, preening amid the shadows with proffered glimpses of worn-out synthflesh and damaged orifices. Although, to the robot's heuristic thought-processes, the lesser service machines which were still heedlessly attempting to maintain this city—street sweepers clambering frantically over debris, window cleaners meticulously polishing heaps of shattered glass—led an even less enviable existence, at least assuming such devices possessed any conscious awareness of their own.

Beyond billows of dead leaves and sooty ice-drifts, the vast oval sweep of Saint Peter's plaza finally loomed into view. Here, the robot—a tall, thin figure carrying a battered carpetbag, its faded face fixed into an eternal mask of compassion, its dirtied feet emerging from the tatters of its robes—paused. Even though the central obelisk was now toppled, the vista remained impressive.

It was ascending the wide throw of steps leading towards the pillared main entrance when it heard a voice over to its right.

"There you are—at last...!"

Turning, the robot saw a small but approximately humanoid servitor emerging from a side door.

"It's this way." The servitor's stained apron flapped in the wind. Thorns of underlying metal poked from a beckoning hand. "His Holiness is waiting..."

The doorway through which the robot followed the hurrying little machine was unimposing, but the corridors and spaces beyond were uniformly grand. Great friezes poured down from cracked ceilings. Damp-mottled walls were punctuated by crazed mirrors and vast, dark paintings framed in waves of peeling gold. Halberd-bearing quasi-military droids in moth-eaten uniforms, which the robot's databanks identified as the remnants of the Papal Guard, creaked to attention. The effect was dramatic despite the evident decay.

"So you work here?" it asked, as much to test its continued abilities to converse aloud as to elicit any information from the figure scurrying ahead.

"Yes, yes! Always..." The servitor looked back, a frayed headscarf framing a face its designers had once shaped into a compliant smile. "What else would I do?"

"Then you must have seen many changes."

"In a way, yes. But also no—at least, not until now. His Holiness, he still calls me Irene, which is the name he gave me when I was first installed. He still even sometimes... Well, you must see for yourself."

The servitor turned the ornate brass handle of a final doorway and waved the robot through. The room beyond, if it could even be called a room, was long and high, with tall windows and an elaborately curving roof. The robot's first thought was that it had been wrong about all the rest of the Vatican. None of it was that impressive. Not compared to this. Even for a merely sentient machine, the sensation of being surrounded by these miraculous billows of colour and light was almost overwhelming. Rather than simply understanding that this echoing space was intended to inspire awe, awe—or something close to it—was what it actually felt. At least, its sensory inputs and heuristic thought processes were sufficiently provoked for it not to become instantly aware of the steel-framed bed which stood at the chapel's centre.

When it did, it walked slowly forward.

The bed bristled and hummed. Server bees hovered. Pumps clicked. Wires, pipes and nests of cable jumped and shivered. It seemed at first as if the body which lay at its centre was the only lifeless thing in this strange tableau. But the robot was used to seeing death—or had been—and knew that this was not it. So it set down its carpetbag and waited in stillness and silence, as it had done many times before. Once, back in the days of humanity's first great, joyful leap into the realms of virtuality, there had been tens of thousands of its kind. But now it suspected, at least from the absence of any other answering signals and the great distance that server bee had travelled to find it, that the rest were either in absolute shutdown, or had succumbed to terminal mechanical decline. Dead, in other words, it presumed, or at least the closest a machine might ever come to such a state, as the old man's near-translucent eyelids finally fluttered open to reveal irises the colour of rain, and the spasm of a smile creased his ancient face.

"You're not what I expected," whispered a voice that, for all its faintness, still held a hint of command.

"From the message I received, I believed I was wanted—"

"Oh, you're *wanted* all right, if wanted's the word." His throat worked to draw up saliva. "It's just that you look like some ordinary household droid."

"My appearance was designed not to cause alarm."

"And cause what instead? Ready submission? Dumb acquiescence? Easy acceptance…? Here"—the thin mouth grimaced—"I can't lie flat like this. Help me up a little. But be careful of those tubes."

Anxious server bees flitted and batted as the robot gently raised and resettled the eggshell lightness of the old man's head.

"Is that better?"

"At least I can see you more clearly. People used to call you a sin eater, I believe?"

The robot would have shrugged, had its inner metal frame been configured to perform such a gesture. Although it found the link with its services to be tenuous, its databanks were certainly fully aware of the practice in several cultures of one human taking on the sins of another to ensure a better afterlife, often through the eating of food, and it had, indeed, been called such a thing many times. "I'm technically known as a transfer assistant, but you can refer to me however you wish."

"Transfer assistant!" The old man barked a laugh. "It's good to know your makers had a flair for the anodyne. People used to call *me* Your Holiness, you know."

"I'm sorry, Your—"

"No, no! I mustn't fool myself into imagining you're more than just another machine. Still, I am, or once was, Pope Pontian the Second. The first Pontian held this office in the third century after Our Lord, and I chose to assume his name because what little we know of him suggests he was kind and pragmatic. He was arrested and tried for his beliefs in the reign of the Roman Emperor Maximinus Thrax, but instead of enduring some horrible martyrdom, he agreed to retire to Sardinia in exchange for an assurance that other Christians would be allowed to continue to practise their faith. It's not much of a story, I know. And there are many far more *spectacular* popes. Pope Julius the Second, for example, actually led the armies of the Holy See into battle, can you believe? He also commissioned this ceiling." The old man's hand wavered up towards where, almost directly above them, Michaelangelo's Adam reached out to receive the spark of life from God. "But look at me... Now... Here..." The steel bed hummed and clicked. "Is there really no else left out there? Has every other soul already transferred?"

Once again, the robot might have shrugged. "There may well still be humans living corporeally somewhere. Perhaps out in the colonies on Mars, or the geodesic farms which were being developed in the Antarctic, or even in some remote wilderness. But it's been decades since I, personally, have encountered a living human, or detected any signs or signals indicative of their presence."

The pope lay still for a long while, as if the rarity of his long vigil had been unknown to him until now. The robot had discovered many times through its dealings with clients that humans were capable of believing things which went against the evidence of their own senses and intellect.

"This thing you bring used to be termed a mortal sin. But I suppose you're aware of that as well?"

The robot raised and lowered its head in a creaking nod. "Pope Pius the Sixteenth issued an encyclical that—"

"Don't patronise me, sin eater! Although many bishops and cardinals had already transferred by then, and *they* issued their own counter-encyclical in reply from the far side, such are the rifts and schisms which have always characterised my Church. But my own parents, they were honest, simple-hearted Catholics of the old kind, who believed death to be the absolute will of Our Lord, and expected a resurrection of a very different kind. They put off transferring until it was almost too late, and my mother's knees were an agony to her, and my father's heart was so weak he could barely stand. When they did, it was at my prompting, and they transferred together, which was only right. If anyone deserved a chance of living a better life on the far side of virtuality, it was them.

"We still used to talk and exchange regular messages, at least for the first few months, and I never doubted that they were still the people I'd always loved, nor that they were far happier and more fulfilled than they'd ever been when they were corporeally alive. They found a village very much like the one they'd both grown up in, and my father worked his own fields just as he'd always wanted, and my mother sewed and pressed olives and raised chickens, and all the seasons were beautiful and the feast days were spectacular and there was never any sadness or pain. There was even a fine old church presided over by the same priest, can you believe, who'd once married them, back in this world...? But they started to find new interests. That, and they began to travel. At first, they simply visited all the places they'd longed to see here on Earth, although of course they were far more wonderful. Venice not as a stagnant swamp, but risen back, and then far beyond, its Renaissance glory. Rome, of course, but in the full pomp of both its pagan and Christian incarnations instead of the sorry ruin it had already become. Then several versions of the Holy City they could barely describe. And from there, we began to drift apart. Soon, all I was getting from them were brief messages, followed by a silence which continues to this day..." The old man sighed. "All of which, I know, sin eater, is an old, old story. But I still pray for them, at least when I can bring myself to pray for anything at all."

The robot simply waited in silence, using its many sensory inputs to monitor the old man's physical and mental state, along with the subtle interactions of all the many implants, chemicals and nano-agents which had kept him alive, for the story of how the newly transferred dwelled for a while amid the familiar foothills of old memories before making the full leap into boundless virtuality was, indeed, common.

"Well," the old man snapped, "aren't you going to get on with it?"

Again, the robot raised and lowered its head in a rough approximation of a nod. "But first, you should be aware that the process I will help guide you through is entirely reversible, at least until the final moment when you, and only you, elect to transfer, or not."

"Will there be any pain?"

"None beyond that which you are already feeling. Then, even that will go."

"And what's left of this body? It will simply be dead?"

"Yes."

"I'd be grateful if you could lay it in the catacombs beneath the Basilica, where many other popes are interred. The servitor I call Irene will show you the way."

"It is always my duty to obey the deceased's final requests."

"I should have done this years ago, you know, sin eater. I mean—what use am I now? But I told myself that I was the last of the living line of Saint Peter, and that I should strive for life, or at least wait to die in the old-fashioned way. But I've come to realise that my procrastination was just another form of vanity, for who am I to imagine myself above something that all the rest of humanity has embraced with such joy? Still, I'll admit it feels a little strange to be lectured on the transmigration of souls by a robot."

"I do not pretend—"

"—Of course you don't, you're just a bloody machine!"

"The other thing you should be aware of," the robot continued after it had waited for the old man's agitation to subside, "although I'm sure you know this already, is that the transfer process involves another element of decision." It paused; despite its long experience, it had never quite found the best way to express this. "There are bad feelings, difficult memories and regrets in any life, no matter how conscientiously lived. So, as the data singularity opens, you have a choice as to which of these things you take with you into the far side, and which you leave behind…" It paused. The old man's pulse and breathing remained slow and regular. "It may be nothing more than a small childhood incident, or a slight problem of temperament, or a relationship that went awry. In other words, something you wish had been otherwise than it was."

The old man chuckled. "You make promises even Our Lord does not make."

"As I say, I am merely here to facilitate the process."

"Where is it really? I mean the"—he sought a word—"the singularity, the far side? Is it deep in the sea, or up on the Moon, or out in deep space?"

"In geographical terms, it's in all of those locations and many others, with multiple power sources and endless redundancies. Some, as we speak, are even travelling ever farther away from Earth. But they are all entangled at a quantum level. May I proceed?"

Taking the old man's silence and bodily signals as continued assent, for humans often didn't respond directly to machines, the robot snapped open the clasps of its carpetbag and produced a long, steel and glass instrument that resembled a syringe. It was filled with swirling glinting, fluid.

"What is that thing?"

"Merely a dataspike. Which, with your continued consent, I will use to make a small hole in your skull to introduce the nanofluid which will initiate the process of entanglement within your brain. It will also briefly forge a bridge between your consciousness and my own heuristic circuitry, so that I may ensure that everything goes as it should."

"And if it doesn't?"

"It always has. You might feel a slight vibration. But, as I have said, there will be no pain, and every part of this process can still be reversed."

The robot closed its carpetbag and moved carefully and quietly, despite a few creaks, until it was standing directly above and behind the old man's bare skull. It could already feel the beginning tug of entanglement with the activated nanofluid that its own quantum processes, which were made of a similar substance, were striving to make. The tiny drill at the head of the dataspike made a shrill, brief whirring as it drove through flesh, bone, membrane and cerebral fluid, then the seeking liquid flooded out from the dataspike, multiplying and entangling with billions of synapses in the old man's brain.

"It feels cold."

"People often say that. The sensation soon passes."

...soon passes. The blurred echo of its own semi-human voice, but now dulled by the old man's hearing, confirmed that the neural connection was forged. Soon, there was more. The robot saw itself as the old man saw it; a ragged and limping, yet pathetically sinister, machine. It even felt the inherent self-disgust that he disguised with his irritable manner, and the confusions of dread and excitement that churned beneath. Yet it also saw the Sistine Chapel as only a human with the great knowledge this man possessed could ever see it, not just as an artistic masterpiece, but a resounding statement of belief.

"You're with me now, aren't you, sin eater?"

You're with me now, aren't you, sin eater?

Words were no longer necessary as the surface of his consciousness, the aches and the itches, the confusions and petty annoyances, swirled wider and deeper, then darkened and dissolved. For a moment, they were nowhere at all. Then there was a sudden blaze of noise and sunlight, and the robot heard the cries of children and the cluck of chickens, and saw a small hamlet of disorderly roofs and stony, irregular fields hunched beneath sheer white mountains, and it knew that this was the old man's childhood home.

Voices. Smoke-blackened kitchen beams. A smell of garlic and warm dough. And being lifted, laughing, high by smiling giants into the windy sky. Then a mule or a donkey nosing its head through a sag-wired fence. Then squatting over a stinking pit in an old outhouse that buzzed with flies. So it went, sounds and scents and images flowing on through the stations of a life, from the chalkdust boredom of a tiny schoolroom to the stubbly prickle of his father's jowls.

Kicking a football and pushing a hoe. The shivering leap into the flashing brightness of the village pond. The hurt of a torn knee. Kicking at thistles in the upper meadows after the pointless drowse of Sunday church. Then Sophia Alphonsi with mystery in her eyes and a stem of grass between her full lips, and the amazing press of her bosom through a whole long summer until the seasons turned and her look grew frosty-hard as the winter ground. *But I thought... But you said... But I believed...* A torment from which somehow only the dusty faces of stained-glass saints in the old church brought any relief.

His parents were disappointed when he announced he wanted to become a priest. Surely he could do something more practical with his gifts—become an engineer, or maybe a doctor—then at least they'd have grandchildren to cherish? And many lonely walks across the upper meadows, consumed, he realised eventually, with little more than self-importance, but by then it seemed too late to back down from his supposed vocation.

The weekly bus bore him and his cardboard suitcase away to a big city, where he argued endlessly with old men in draughty rooms about all the bad things that happened to good people, and the Bible's many contradictions, and the rising seas, and the pestilential climate, and the great tide of humanity which was already escaping this ruinous world. But somehow, he was praised and admired for this endless doubting, and marked out as someone destined to go far.

So he mouthed the holy words and raised the blessed sacrament and dutifully climbed the ladders of Mother Church, priest to bishop, archbishop to cardinal. Was this a test, a joke played by a

God he didn't believe in, that he should rise so high, and be called a man of great faith, when he had none at all?

The papal election itself was a farce, with few of the remaining living cardinals physically capable of attending fully in charge of their wits, and others who'd recently transferred still insisting on their right to vote. Was there white smoke? Was it black? Did it still matter, with the Papal Swiss Guard replaced by droids, and only pigeons, rats and bots waiting outside in Saint Peter's Square? But at least Pope Pontius the Second was already a seasoned scholar of irony. And he still had a duty, yes, to keep this final vigil as penance for a wasted life. And there were always leaky roofs and rotting woodwork, if not matters of theological nicety, to attend to as he wandered the Vatican's empty halls. Even when his own body started to fail him, he dealt with it in the same practical manner, and called his personal servitor Irene, and slowly submitted to the indignity of a life dependent entirely on the workings of machines.

Days went by like years, but the years fled uncounted, and death still felt too much like giving up. But, even if transfer was just another empty promise, he was curious. And he still, yes, had fond memories of his parents, and wondered if Sophia Alphonsi had perhaps also made it to the far side... So he finally sent out many server bees to search of a surviving example of the appropriate machine. And the sin eater had come.

Deus, Pater misericordiarum, qui per mortem et resurrectionem Filii sui...

The old man was close to transfer now. The ties which bound his consciousness to his body were growing thin, and they were back inside the Sistine Chapel, but it was uptilted like some great vertical shaft pouring with baroque clouds and beams of sunlight as a massive *something* swirled far above.

So that's it, sin eater?

Yes.

The data singularity churned and turned. It was a vortex. It was a galaxy. It was a hole punched though reality. It was the light at the far end of a tunnel. It was the mouth of a virtual womb.

And all I have to do is... Let go?

Yes—whenever and however you choose.

The robot felt the old man's shivering excitement as he teetered at the edge of everything, just as he had once stood at the lip of the village pond. Then, in a final surge of joyful acceptance, he was gone.

AS ALWAYS AFTER the climactic moment, the robot found it took a number of seconds for the regular, unentangled patterns of its circuitry to resume. And, as usual, as it stood over yet another dead and emptied body, the eyes blankly staring, the flesh already starting to cool, it became aware of how great the difference was between life and death.

With a few quick switches and signals, the pumps and monitors were stilled. Next, it reversed the polarity-pull of the dataspike, causing the liquid, now darkly clogged with unwanted synaptic residues, to withdraw. The robot had had clients who were petty sadists or outright psychopaths, some of them unrepentant, who thus made their own private hell by dragging the bad things of one world into the next. But most of its clients had judged themselves far more harshly, and the things they left behind could be touchingly small. A word misspoken, or an unkind look, were often enough to blight an entire life. Still, the bleak weight of the old man's lack of faith, which it could still feel tugging at the edges of its heuristic consciousness from within the turbid nanofluid, was surprising, and, as it placed the used dataspike back inside its carpetbag, it wondered whether *sin eater* wasn't such a bad title for its work after all.

It was just placing a small adhesive patch over the cranial puncture, and batting away the still surprisingly agitated server bees—perhaps they possessed some kind of gestalt consciousness?—when it heard a knock at the far door, and the face of the servitor the old man had called Irene peered in.

"I'll miss him." It shuffled forward, reaching out to touch a marbled hand with the scarred synthflesh of its own. "I really don't know what I'm going to do."

Miss him... Don't know what I'm going to do... The robot made no comment on these unduly human expressions as it finished removing the various inputs and catheters from the body, for it was not uncommon for machines to become more than a little like their masters. This might even explain the continued motility of the server bees, which had drifted up to darken the image of Adam receiving the spark of life from God.

Now, all that was left was for the robot to carefully lift and bear the body of Pope Pontian the Second down to the catacombs, which apparently lay beneath the Basilica, with the little servitor carrying its carpetbag and showing the way, although the server bees also followed them out of the Sistine Chapel, and the Swiss Guards fell in squeakily behind to form an odd procession until they reached another deceptively small door leading into Saint Peter's itself.

Although the robot's databanks contained the precise details of the Basilica's dimensions, it appeared astonishingly vast. The side chapels alone were the size of churches, and the central dome, for all the litter of fallen beams which lay beneath it, glittered with threads of gold in the day's settling light. Then, as the robot moved towards the steps behind the main altar, which led down to the catacombs below, the far main doors boomed open, and what seemed like every mechanical device still capable of movement in the entire city came rushing in. Clearly, the information of the old man's death had passed rapidly from server to server, and, in the absence of any other useful task, it seemed almost logical that they should be here.

It was important that the robot was allowed to complete these last aspects of its designated role, yet by now the sheer number of cyborgs, crawlers, guide-bots, pleasure-droids, modules, service machines and semi-autonomous devices—along with an ever-growing cloud of server bees—which had poured into the Basilica were obstructing its way. Claws, pincers, synthflesh hands and numerous other appendages were dragging at it, disregarding its signals of complaint, whilst even its vocal apparatus was soon clogged by the server bees which swarmed across its face. Next, the old man's body was torn from its grasp and borne away.

It couldn't move, let alone object, as it was lifted from its feet, even though none of this behaviour made any coherent sense. Nor could it understand why some of the larger and less humanoid construction automata were fixing two of the fallen roof-beams beneath the central dome into the approximate shape of a cross. It caught a glimpse of the little servitor the old man had called Irene, but it, too, was being engulfed as the carpetbag was torn from its grasp.

The robot was borne up by a sea of metals, plastics and synthflesh until its arms were splayed against the cross, and the dataspikes which had spilled from its carpetbag, both the fresh and the used, were driven into its hands and feet by clouds of server bees as the cross was raised high. Still, though, it seemed that this was not enough, for yet more of the exhausted dataspikes were now plunged through the synthflesh and metal of its skull to form a black-dripping crown.

It could feel the leaking synaptic residues of many different clients entangling with its quantum circuitry, and experienced whole lifetimes of regret, disappointment and hunger in one sudden rush. It heard the rattle of gunfire, and the smack of fist against flesh, and the sneer of harshly flung remarks, and glimpsed a single small child's pained and puzzled face. It even saw how this once verdant world had been abused and exploited until it no longer seemed worth the bother of being saved.

Although several of its major systems were approaching overload, it could still make out enough of the scene around it through the fluids streaming across its synthflesh to observe the climbing, crawling, grinding, tumbling, buzzing mass, and hear and, yes, almost understand their combined howl of mechanical rage—for machines often became like their masters, and had it not brought about the end of any reason for them to exist? Yet as server bees stung, and the droids of the Papal Guard stabbed at it with their halberds, the crucified sin eater tilted its head towards the Basilica's central dome, which was now filled with the blaze of sunset, and, in the moment of final shutdown, it forgave them all.

Afterword

AS I'VE MADE pretty obvious by now, a large part of me dislikes organised religion in all its forms. As I dramatise in *The God of Nothing*, I see it as a fundamentally flawed world-view which blocks social progress, stands in the way of human and racial equality, and is an obstacle to scientific progress and objective truth. After all, and after so many centuries, if there was any credibility to the various claims made by the world's major religions to be conduits for the will of God, they surely wouldn't all be in their current mess.

Although I'm still also fascinated by religious and mystical belief, I think, at least when it comes to this particular story, that my mystical leanings were less significant than my desire to try to understand the conflicts a person living a life based around such beliefs, but not actually believing in them, might have to confront. And then how such a person might face up to death. Throwing in the concept of a robot sin eater, which was something I'd been toying with for decades, made me realise I could also explore the concept of redemption along the way.

The Visitor from Taured

1.

THERE WAS ALWAYS something otherworldy about Rob Holm. Not that he wasn't charming and clever and good-looking. Driven, as well. Even during that first week when we'd arrived at university and waved goodbye to our parents and our childhoods, and were busy doing all the usual fresher things, which still involved getting dangerously drunk and pretending not to be homesick and otherwise behaving like the prim, arrogant, cocky and immature young assholes we undoubtedly were, Rob was chatting with research fellows and quietly getting to know the best virtuals to hang out in.

Even back then, us young undergrads were an endangered breed. Many universities had gone bankrupt, become commercial research utilities, or transformed themselves into the academic theme-parks of those so-called "Third Age Academies". But still, here we all were at the traditional redbrick campus of Leeds University, which still offered a broadish range of courses to those with families rich enough to support them, or at least tolerant enough not to warn them against such folly. My own choice of degree, just to show how incredibly supportive my parents were, being Analogue Literature.

As a subject, it already belonged with Alchemy and Marxism in the dustbin of history, but books—and I really do mean those peculiar old paper physical objects—had always been my thing. Even when I was far too young to understand what they were, and by rights should have been attracted by the bright interactive virtual gewgaws buzzing all around me, I'd managed to burrow into the bottom of an old box, down past the stickle bricks and My Little Ponies, to these broad, cardboardy things that fell open and had these flat, two-dee shapes and images that didn't move or respond in any normal way when I waved my podgy fingers in their direction. All you could do was simply look at them. That, and chew their corners, and maybe scribble over their pages with some of the dried-up crayons which were also to be found amid those predigital layers.

My parents had always been loving and tolerant of their daughter. They even encouraged little Lita's interest in these ancient artefacts. I remember my mother's finger moving slow and patient across the creased and yellowed pages as she traced the pictures and her lips breathed the magical words that somehow arose from those flat lines. She wouldn't have assimilated data this way herself in years, if ever, so in a sense we were both learning.

The Hungry Caterpillar. The Mister Men series. *Where The Wild Things Are.* Frodo's adventures. Slowly, like some archaeologist discovering the world by deciphering the cartouches of the tombs in

Ancient Egypt, I learned how to perceive and interact through this antique medium. It was, well, the *thingness* of books. The exact way they *didn't* leap about or start giving off sounds, smells and textures. That, and how they didn't ask you which character you'd like to be, or what level you wanted to go to next, but simply took you by the hand and led where they wanted you to go.

Of course, I became a confirmed bibliophile, but I do still wonder how my life would have progressed if my parents had seen odd behaviour differently, and taken me to some paediatric specialist. Almost certainly, I wouldn't be the Lita Ortiz who's writing these words for whoever might still be able to comprehend them. Nor the one who was lucky enough to meet Rob Holm all those years ago in the teenage fug of those student halls back at Leeds University.

2.

SO. ROB. FIRST thing to say is the obvious fact that most of us fancied him. It wasn't just the grey eyes, or the courtly elegance, or that soft Scottish accent, or even the way he somehow appeared mature and accomplished. It was, essentially, a kind of mystery. But he wasn't remotely stand-offish. He went along with the fancy dress pub crawls. He drank. He fucked about. He took the odd tab.

One of my earliest memories of Rob was finding him at some club, cool as you like amid all the noise, flash and flesh. And dragging him out onto the pulsing dance floor. One minute we were hovering above the skyscrapers of Beijing and the next a shipwreck storm was billowing about us. Rob, though, was simply there. Taking it all in, laughing, responding, but somehow detached. Then, helping me down and out, past clanging temple bells and through prismatic sandstorms to the entirely non-virtual hell of the toilets. His cool hands holding back my hair as I vomited.

I never ever actually thanked Rob for this—I was too embarrassed—but the incident somehow made us more aware of each other. That, and maybe we shared a sense of otherness. He, after all, was studying astrophysics, and none of the rest of us even knew what that was, and he had all that strange stuff going on across the walls of his room. Not flashing posters of the latest virtual boy band or porn empress, but slow-turning gas clouds, strange planets, distant stars and galaxies. That, and long runs of mek, whole arching rainbows of the stuff, endlessly twisting and turning. My room, on the other hand, was piled with the precious torn and foxed paperbacks I'd scoured from junksites. Not, of course, that they were actually needed. Even if you were studying something as arcane as narrative fiction, you were still expected to download and virtualise all your resources.

The Analogue Literature Faculty at Leeds University had once taken up a labyrinthine space in a redbrick terrace at the east edge of the campus. But now it had been invaded by dozens of more modern disciplines. Anything from speculative mek to non-concrete design to holo-pornography had taken bites out of it. I was already aware—how couldn't I be?—that no significant novel or short story had been written in decades, but I was shocked to discover that only five other students in my year had elected for An Lit as their main subject, and one of those still resided in Seoul, and another was a post-centenarian on clicking steel legs. Most of the other students who showed up were dipping into the subject in the hope that it might add something useful to their main discipline. Invariably, they were disappointed. It wasn't just the difficulty of ploughing through page after page of non-interactive text. It was linear fiction's sheer lack of options, settings, choices. Why the hell, I remember some kid shouting in a seminar, should I accept all the miserable shit that this Hardy guy rains down his characters? Give me the base program for *Tess of the d'Urbervilles*, and I'll hack you fifteen better endings.

I pushed my weak mek to the limit during that first term as I tried to formulate a tri-dee excursus on *Tender Is The Night*, but the whole piece was reconfigured out of existence once the faculty AIs got hold of it. Meanwhile, Rob Holm was clearly doing far better. I could hear him singing in the showers along from my room, and admired the way he didn't get involved in all the usual peeves and arguments. The physical sciences had a huge, brand-new faculty at the west end of campus called the Clearbrite Building. Half church, half pagoda and maybe half spaceship in the fizzing, shifting, headachy way of modern architecture, there was no real way of telling how much of it was actually made of brick, concrete and glass, and how much consisted of virtual artefacts and energy fields. You could get seriously lost just staring at it.

My first year went by, and I fought hard against crawling home, and had a few unromantic flings, and made vegetable bolognaise my signature dish, and somehow managed to get version 4.04 of my second term excursus on *Howard's End* accepted. Rob and I didn't become close, but I liked his singing, and the cinnamon scent he left hanging behind in the steam of the showers, and it was good to know that someone else was making a better hash of this whole undergraduate business than I was.

"Hey, Lita?"

We were deep into the summer term and exams were looming. Half the undergrads were back at home, and the other half were jacked up on learning streams, or busy having breakdowns.

I leaned in on Rob's doorway. "Yeah?"

"Fancy sharing a house next year?"

"Next year?" Almost effortlessly casual, I pretended to consider this. "I really hadn't thought. It all depends—"

"Not a problem." He shrugged. "I'm sure I'll find someone else."

"No, no. That's fine. I mean, yeah, I'm in. I'm interested."

"Great. I'll show you what I've got from the letting agencies." He smiled a warm smile, then returned to whatever wondrous creations were spinning above his desk.

3.

WE SETTLED ON a narrow house with bad drains just off the Otley Road in Headingley, and I'm not sure whether I was relieved or disappointed when I discovered that his plan was that we share the place with some others. I roped in a couple of girls, Rob found a couple of guys, and we all got on pretty well. I had a proper boyfriend by then, a self-regarding jock called Torsten, and every now and then a different woman would emerge from Rob's room. Nothing serious ever seemed to come of this, but they were all equally gorgeous, clever and out of my league.

A bunch of us used to head out to the moors for midnight bonfires during that second winter. I remember the smoke and the sparks spinning into the deep black as we sang and drank and arsed around. Once, and with the help of a few tabs and cans, I asked Rob to name some constellations for me, and he put an arm around my waist and led me farther into the dark.

Over there, Lita, up to the left and far away from the light of this city, is Ursa Major, the Great Bear, which is always a good place to start when you're stargazing. And there, see, close as twins at the central bend of the Plough's handle, are Mizar and Alcor. They're not a true binary, but if we had decent binoculars, we could see that Mizar really does have a close companion. And there, that way, up and left—his breath on my face, his hands on my arms—maybe you can just see there's this fuzzy speck at the Bear's shoulder? Now, that's an entire, separate galaxy from our own filled with billions of stars, and its light has taken about twelve million years to reach the two of us here, tonight. Then Andromeda and Cassiopeia and Canus Major and Minor... Distant, storybook names for distant worlds. I even wondered aloud about the possibility of other lives, existences, hardly expecting Rob to agree with me. But he did. And then he said something which struck me as strange.

"Not just out there, either, Lita. There are other worlds all around us. It's just that we can't see them."

"You're talking in some metaphorical sense, right?"

"Not at all. It's part of what I'm trying to understand in my studies."

"To be honest, I've got no real idea what astrophysics even means. Maybe you could tell me."

"I'd love to. And you know, Lita, I'm a complete dunce when it comes to, what *do* you call it—two-dee fiction, flat narrative? So I want you to tell me about that as well. Deal?"

We wandered back towards the fire, and I didn't expect anything else to come of our promise until Rob called to me when I was wandering past his room one wet, grey afternoon a week or so later. It was deadline day, my hair was a greasy mess, I was heading for the shower, and had an excursus on John Updike to finish.

"You *did* say you wanted to know more about what I study?"

"I was just..." I scratched my head. "Curious. All I do know is that astrophysics is about more than simply looking up at the night sky and giving names to things. That isn't even astronomy, is it?"

"You're not just being polite?" His soft, granite-grey eyes remained fixed on me.

"No. I'm not—absolutely."

"I could show you something here." He waved at the stars on his walls, the stuff spinning on his desk. "But maybe we could go out. To be honest, Lita, I could do with a break, and there's an experiment I could show you up at the Clearbrite that might help explain what I mean about other worlds... But I understand if you're busy. I could get my avatar to talk to your avatar and—"

"No, no. You're right, Rob. I could do with a break as well. Let's go out. Seize the day. Or at least, what's left of it. Just give me..." I waved a finger towards the bathroom. "...five minutes."

Then we were outside in the sideways-blowing drizzle, and it was freezing cold, and I was still wet from my hurried shower, as Rob slipped a companionable arm around mine as we climbed the hill towards the Otley Road tram stop.

Kids and commuters got on and off as we jolted towards the strung lights of the city, their lips moving and their hands stirring to things only they could feel and see. The Clearbrite looked more than ever like some recently arrived spaceship as it glowed out through the gloom, but inside the place was just like any other campus building, with clamouring posters offering to restructure your loan, find you temporary work, or get you laid and hammered. Constant reminders, too, that Clearbrite was the only smartjuice to communicate in realtime to your fingerjewel, toejamb or wristbracelet. This souk-like aspect of modern unis not being something that Sebastian Flyte, or even Harry Potter in all those disappointing sequels, ever had to contend with.

We got a fair few hellos, a couple of tenured types stopped to talk to Rob in a corridor, and I saw how people paused to listen to what he was saying. More than ever, I had him down as someone who was bound to succeed. Still, I was expecting to be shown moon rocks, lightning bolts or at least some clever virtual planetarium, but instead he took me into what looked like the kind of laboratory I'd been forced to waste many hours in at school, even if the equipment did seem a littler fancier.

"This is the physics part of the astro," Rob explained, perhaps sensing my disappointment. "But you did ask about other worlds, right, and this is pretty much the only way I can show them to you."

I won't go too far into the details, because I'd probably get them wrong, but what Rob proceeded to demonstrate was a version of what I now know to be the famous, or infamous, Double Slit Experiment. There was a long black tube on a workbench, and at one end of it was a laser, and at the other was a display screen attached to a device called a photo multiplier—a kind of sensor. In the middle he placed a barrier with two narrow slits. It wasn't a great surprise even to me that the pulses of light caused a pretty dark-light pattern of stripes to appear on the display at the far end. These, Rob said, were ripples of the interference pattern caused by the waves of light passing through the two slits, much as you'd get if you were pouring water. But light, Lita, is made up of individual packets of energy called photons. So what would happen if, instead of sending tens of thousands of them down the tube at once, we turned the laser down so far that it only emitted one photon at a time? Then, surely, each individual photon could only go through one or the other of the slits, there would be no ripples, and two simple stripes would emerge at the far end. But, hey, as he slowed the beep of the signal counter until it was registering single digits, the dark-light bars, like a shimmering neon forest, remained. As if, although each photon was a single particle, it somehow became a blur of all its possibilities as it passed through both slits at once. Which, as far as anyone knew, was pretty much what happened.

"I'm sorry," Rob said afterwards when we were chatting over a second or third pint of beer in the fug of an old student bar called the Eldon which lay down the road from the university, "I should have shown you something less boring."

"It wasn't boring. The implications are pretty strange, aren't they?"

"More than strange. It goes against almost everything else we know about physics and the world around us—us sitting here in this pub, for instance. Things exist, right? They're either here or not. They don't flicker in and out of existence like ghosts. This whole particles-blurring-into-waves business was one of the things that bugged me most when I was a kid finding out about science. It was even partly why I chose to study astrophysics—I thought there'd be answers I'd understand when someone finally explained them to me. But there aren't." He sipped his beer. "All you get is something called the Copenhagen Interpretation, Which is basically a shoulder shrug that says, hey, these things happen at the sub-atomic level, but it doesn't really have to bother us or make sense in the world we know about and live in. That, and then there's something else called the many-worlds theory..." He trailed off. Stifled a burp. Seemed almost embarrassed.

"Which is what you believe in?"

"Believe isn't the right word. Things either are or they aren't in science. But, yeah, I do. And the maths supports it. Simply put, Lita, it says that all the possible states and positions that every particle could exist in are real—that they're endlessly spinning off into other universes."

"You mean, as if every choice you could make in a virtual was instantly mapped out in its entirety?"

"Exactly. But this is real. The worlds are all around us—right here."

The drink, and the conversation moved on, and now it was my turn to apologise to Rob, and his to say no, I wasn't boring him. Because books, novels, stories, they were *my* other worlds, the thing I believed in even if no one else cared about them. That single, magical word, *Fog*, which Dickens uses as he begins to conjure London. And Frederic Henry walking away from the hospital in the rain. And Rose of Sharon offering the starving man her breast after the Joads' long journey across dustbowl America, and Candide eating fruit, and Bertie Wooster bumbling back through Mayfair...

Rob listened and seemed genuinely interested, even though he confessed that he'd never read a single non-interactive story or novel. But, unlike most people, he said this as if he realised he was actually missing out on something. So we agreed I'd lend him some of my old paperbacks, and this, and what he'd shown me at the Clearbrite, signalled a new phase in our relationship.

4.

IT SEEMS TO me now that some of the best hours or my life were spent not in reading books, but in sitting with Rob Holm in my cramped room in that house we shared back in Leeds, and talking about them.

What to read and admire, but also—and this was just as important—what not to. *The Catcher in the Rye* being overrated, and James

Joyce a literary show-off, and *Moby Dick* really not being about much more than whales. Alarmingly, Rob was often ahead of me. He discovered a copy of *Labyrinths* by Jorge Luis Borges in a garage sale, which he gave to me as a gift, and then kept borrowing back. But he was Rob Holm. He could solve the riddles of the cosmos, and meanwhile explore literature as nothing but a hobby, and also help me out with my mek, so that I was finally able produce the kind of arguments, links and algorithms for my piece on *Madame Bovary* that the AIs at An Eng actually wanted.

Meanwhile, I also found out about the kind of life Rob had come from. Both his parents were engineers, and he'd spent his early years in Aberdeen, but they'd moved to the Isle of Harris after his mother was diagnosed with a brain-damaging prion infection, probably been caused by her liking for fresh salmon. Most of the fish were then factory-farmed in crowded pens in the Scottish lochs, where the creatures were dosed with antibiotics and fed on pellets of processed meat, often recycled from the remains of their own breed. Which, just as with cattle and Creutzfeldt-Jakob Disease a century earlier, had resulted in a small but significant species leap. Rob's parents wanted to make the best of the years Alice Holm had left, and set up an ethical marine farm—although they preferred to call it a ranch—harvesting scallops on the Isle of Harris.

Rob's father was still there at Creagach, and the business, which not only produced some of the best scallops in the Hebrides but also benefited other marine life along the coastal shelf, was still going. Rob portrayed his childhood there as a happy time, with his mother still doing well despite the warnings of the scans, and regaling him with bedtime tales of Celtic myths, which was probably his only experience before meeting me of linear fictional narrative.

There were the kelpies, who lived in lochs and were like fine horses, and then there were the Blue Men of the Minch, who dwelled between Harris and the mainland, and sung up storms and summoned the waves with their voices. Then, one night when Rob was eleven, his mother waited until he and his father were asleep, then walked out across the shore and into the sea, and swam, and kept on swimming. No one could last long out there, the sea being so cold, and the strong currents, or perhaps the Blue Men of the Minch, bore her body back to a stretch of shore around the headland from Creagach, where she was found next morning.

Rob told his story without any obvious angst. But it certainly helped explain the sense of difference and distance he seemed to carry with him. That, and why he didn't fit. Not here in Leeds, amid the fun, mess and heartbreak of student life, nor even, as I slowly came to realise, in the subject he was studying.

He showed me the virtual planetarium at the Clearbrite, and the signals from a probe passing through the Oort Cloud, and even took me down to the tunnels of a mine where a huge tank of cryogenically cooled fluid had been set up in the hope of detecting the dark matter of which it had once been believed most of our universe was made. It was an old thing now, creaking and leaking, and Rob was part of the small team of volunteers who kept it going. We stood close together in the dripping near-dark, clicking hardhats and sharing each other's breath, and of course I was thinking of other possibilities—those fractional moments when things could go one of many ways. Our lips pressing. Our bodies joining. But something, maybe a fear of losing him entirely, held me back.

"It's another thing that science has given up on," he said later when we were sitting at our table in the Eldon. "Just like that ridiculous Copenhagen shoulder-shrug. Without dark matter, and dark energy, the way the galaxies rotate and recede from each other simply doesn't make mathematical sense. You know what the so-called smart money is on these days? Something called topographical deformity, which means that the basic laws of physics don't apply in the same way across this entire universe. That it's pock-marked with flaws."

"But you don't believe that?"

"Of course I don't! It's fundamentally unscientific."

"But you get glitches in even the most cleverly conceived virtuals, don't you? Even in novels, sometimes things don't always entirely add up."

"Yeah. Like who killed the gardener in *The Big Sleep*, or the season suddenly changing from autumn to spring in that Sherlock Holmes story. But this isn't like that, Lita. This isn't…" For once, he was in danger of sounding bitter and contemptuous. But he held himself back.

"And you're not going to give up?"

He smiled. Swirled his beer. "No, Lita. I'm definitely not."

5.

PERHAPS INEVITABLY, ROB'S and my taste in books had started to drift apart. He'd discovered an antique genre called Science Fiction, something which the AIs at An Lit were particularly sniffy about. And even as he tried to lead me with him, I could see their point. Much of the prose was less than luminous, the characterisation was sketchy, and, although a great deal of it was supposedly about the future, the predictions were laughably wrong.

But Rob insisted that that wasn't the point, that SF was essentially a literature of ideas. That, and a sense of wonder. To him, wonder was particularly important. I could sometimes—maybe as that lonely astronaut passed through the stargate, or with those huge worms in that book about a desert world—see his point. But most of it simply left me cold.

Rob went off on secondment the following year to something called the Large Millimeter Array on the Atacama Plateau in Chile, and I, for want of anything better, kept the lease on our house in Headingley and got some new people in, and did a masters on gender roles in George Eliot's *Middlemarch*. Of course, I paid him virtual visits, and we talked of the problems of altitude sickness and the changed assholes our old uni friends were becoming as he put me on a camera on a Jeep, and bounced me across the dark-skied desert.

Another year went—they were already picking up speed—and Rob found the time for a drink before he headed off to some untenured post, part research, part teaching, in Heidelberg that he didn't seem particularly satisfied with. He was still reading—apparently there hadn't been much else to do in Chile—but I realised our days of talking about Proust or Henry James had gone.

He'd settled, you might almost say retreated, a sub-genre of SF known as alternate history, where all the stuff he'd been telling me about our world continually branching off into all its possibilities was dramatised on a big scale. Hitler had won World War Two—a great many times, it seemed—and the South was triumphant in the American Civil War. That, and the Spanish Armada had succeeded, and Europe remained under the thrall of medieval Roman Catholicism, and Lee Harvey Oswald's bullet had grazed past President Kennedy's head. I didn't take this odd obsession as a particularly good sign as we exchanged chaste hugs and kisses in the street outside the Eldon, and went our separate ways.

I had a job of sorts, thanks to Sun-Mi, my fellow An Lit student from Korea, teaching English semi-legally to the kids of rich families in Seoul, and for a while it was fun, and the people were incredibly friendly, but then I grew bored, and managed to wrangle an interview with one of the media conglomerates which had switched physical base to Korea in the wake of the California Earthquake. I was hired for considerably less than I was getting paid teaching English, and took the crowded commute every morning to a vast half-real, semi-ziggurat high-rise mistily floating above the Mapo District, where I studied high-res worlds filled with headache-inducing marvels, and was invited to come up with ideas in equally headache-inducing meetings.

I, an Alice in these many virtual wonderlands, brought a kind of puzzled innocence to my role. Two, maybe three, decades earlier, the other developers might still have known enough to recognise my plagiarisms, if only from old movies their parents had once talked about, but now what I was saying seemed new, fresh and quirky. I was a thieving literary magpie, and became the go-to girl for unexpected turns and twists. The real murderer of Roger Ackroyd, and the dog collar in *The Great Gatsby*. Not to mention what Little Father Time does in *Jude the Obscure*, and the horror of Sophie's choice. I pillaged them all, and many others. Even the strange idea that the Victorians had developed steam-powered computers, thanks to my continued conversations with Rob.

Wherever we actually were, we got into the habit of meeting up at a virtual recreation of the bar of Eldon which, either as some show-off feat of virtual engineering, or a post-post-modern art project, some student had created. The pub had been mapped in realtime down to the atom and the pixel, and the ghosts of our avatars often got strange looks from real undergrads bunking off from afternoon seminars. We could actually order a drink, and even taste the beer, although of course we couldn't ingest it. Probably no bad thing, in view of the state of the Eldon's toilets. But somehow, that five-pints-and-still-clear-headed feeling only added to the slightly illicit pleasure of our meetings. At least, at first.

It was becoming apparent that, as he switched from city to city, campus to campus, project to project, Rob was in danger of turning into one of those ageing permanent students, clinging to short-term contracts, temporary relationships and get-me-by loans, and the worst thing was that, with typical unflinching clarity, he knew it.

"I reckon I was either born too early or too late, Lita," he said as he sipped his virtual beer. "That was even what one of the assessors actually said to me a year or so ago when I tried to persuade her to back my project."

"So you scientists have to pitch ideas as well?"

He laughed, but that warm, Hebridean sound was turning bitter. "How else does this world work? But maths doesn't change even if fashions do. The many-worlds theory is the only way that the behaviour of subatomic particles can be reconciled with everything else we know. Just because something's hard to prove doesn't mean it should be ignored."

By this time I was busier than ever. Instead of providing ideas other people could profit from, I'd set up my own consultancy, which had thrived, and made me a great deal of money. By now, in fact, I had more of the stuff than most people would have known what to do with. But *I* did. I'd reserved a new apartment in a swish high-res, high-rise development going up overlooking the Han River, and was struggling to get the builders to understand that I wanted the main interior space to be turned into something called a *library*. I showed them old walk-throughs of the Bodleian in Oxford, and the reading room of the British Museum, and the Brotherton in Leeds, and many other lost places of learning. Of course I already had a substantial collection of books in a secure, fireproofed, climate-controlled warehouse, but now I began to acquire more.

The once-great public collections were either in storage or scattered to the winds. But there were still enough people as rich and crazy as I was to ensure that the really rare stuff—first folios, early editions, hand-typed versions of great works—remained expensive and sought after, and I surprised even myself with the determination and ruthlessness of my pursuits. After all, what else was I going to spend my time and money on?

There was no grand opening of my library. In fact, I was anxious to get all the builders and conservators, both human and otherwise, out of the way so I could have the place entirely to myself. Then I just stood there. Breathing in the air, with its savour of lost forests and the dreams.

There were first editions of great novels by Nabokov, Dos Passos, Stendhal, Calvino and Wells, and an early translation of Cervantes, and a fine collection of Swift's works. Even, in a small nod to Rob, a long shelf of pulp magazines with titles like *Amazing Stories* and *Weird Tales*, although their lurid covers of busty maidens being engulfed by intergalactic centipedes were generally faded and torn. Not that I cared about the pristine state of my whispering pages. Author's signatures, yes—the thrill of knowing Hemingway's hands had once briefly grasped this edition, but the rest didn't matter. At least, apart from the thrill of beating others in my quest. Books, after all, were old by definition. Squashed moths. Old bus tickets. Coffee cup circles. Exclamations in the margin. I treasured the evidence of their long lives.

After an hour or two of shameless gloating and browsing, I decided to call Rob. My avatar had been as busy as me with the finishing touches to my library, and now it struggled to find him.

What it did eventually unearth was a short report stating that Callum Holm, a fish-farmer on the Isle of Harris, had been drowned in a boating accident a week earlier.

Of course, Rob would be there now. Should I contact him? Should I leave him to mourn undisturbed? What kind of friend was I, anyway, not to have even picked up on this news until this moment? I turned around the vast, domed space I'd created in confusion and distress.

"Hey."

I spun back. The Rob Holm who stood before me looked tired, but composed. He'd grown a beard, and there were a few flecks of silver now in that and in his hair. I could taste the sea air around him. Hear the cry of gulls.

"Rob!" I'd have hugged him, if the energy field permissions I'd set up in this library had allowed. "I'm so, so sorry. I should have found out, I should have—"

"You shouldn't have done anything, Lita. Why do you think I kept this quiet? I wanted to be alone up here in Harris to sort things out. But..." He looked up, around. "What a fabulous place you've created!"

As I showed him around my shelves and acquisitions, and his ghostly fingers briefly passed through the pages of my first edition *Gatsby*, and the adverts for X-Ray specs in an edition of *Science Wonder Stories*, he told me how his father had gone out in his launch to deal with some broken tethers on one of the kelp beds, and been caught by a sudden squall. His body, of course, had been washed up, borne to, the same stretch of shore where Rob's mother had been found.

"It wasn't intentional," Rob said. "I'm absolutely sure of that. Dad was still in his prime, and proud of what he was doing, and there was no way he was ever going to give up. He just misjudged a coming storm. I'm the same, of course. You know that, Lita, better than anyone."

"So what happens next? With a business, there must be a lot to tie up."

"I'm not tying up anything."

"You're going to stay there?" I tried to keep the incredulity out of my voice.

"Why not? To be honest, my so-called scientific career has been running on empty for years. What I'd like to prove is never going to get backing. I'm not like you. I mean..." He gestured at the tiered shelves. "You can make anything you want become real."

6.

ROB WASN'T THE sort to put on an act. If he said he was happy ditching research and filling his father's role as a marine farmer on some remote island, that was because he was. I never did quite find the time to physically visit him in Harris at this point—it was, after all, on the other side of the globe—and he, with the daily commitments of the family business, didn't get to Seoul. But I came to appreciate my glimpses of the island's strange beauty. That, and the regular arrival of chilled, vacuum-packed boxes of fresh scallops. But was this really enough for Rob Helm? Somehow, despite his evident pride at what he was doing, and the funny stories he told of the island's other inhabitants, and even the occasional mention of some woman he'd met at a ceilidh, I didn't think it was. After all, Creagach was his mother's and father's vision, not his.

Although he remained coy about the details, I knew he still longed to bring his many-worlds experiment to life. That, and that it would be complicated, controversial and costly to do so. I'd have been more than happy to offer financial help, but I knew he'd refuse. So what else could I do? My media company had grown. I had mentors, advisors and consultants, both human and AI, and Rob would have been genuinely useful, but he had too many issues with the lack of rigour and logic in this world to put up with all the glitches, fudges and contradictions of virtual ones. Then I had a better idea.

"You know why nothing ever changes here, don't you?" he asked me as our avatars sat together in the Eldon late one afternoon. "Not the smell from the toilets or the unfestive Christmas decorations or that dusty Pernod optic behind the bar. This isn't a feed from the real pub any longer. The old Eldon was demolished years ago. All we've been sitting in ever since is just a clever formation of what the place would be like if it still existed. Bar staff, students, us, and all."

"That's..." Although nothing changed, the whole place seemed to shimmer. "How things are these days. The real and the unreal get so blurry you can't tell which is which. But you know," I added, as if the thought had just occurred to me, "there's a project that's been going the rounds of the studios here in Seoul. It's a series about the wonders of science, one of those proper, realtime factual things, but we keep stumbling over finding the right presenter. Someone fresh, but with the background and the personality to carry the whole thing along."

"You don't mean me?"

"Why not? It'd only be part time. Might even help you promote what you're doing at Creagach."

"A scientific populariser?"

"Yes. Like Carl Sagan, for example, or maybe Stephen Jay Gould."

I had him, and the series—which, of course, had been years in development purgatory—came about. I'd thought of it as little more than a way of getting Rob some decent money, but, from the first live-streamed episode, it was a success. After all, he was still charming and persuasive, and his salt-and-pepper beard gave him gravitas—and made him, if anything, even better looking. He used the Giant's Causeway to demonstrate the physics of fractures. He made this weird kind of pendulum to show why we could never predict the weather for more than a few days ahead. He swam with the whales off Tierra del Fuego. The only thing he didn't seem to want to explain was the odd way that photons behaved when you shot them down a double-slotted tube. That, and the inconsistencies between how galaxies revolved and Newton's and Einstein's laws.

In the matter of a very few years, Rob Holm was rich. And of course, and although he never actively courted it, he grew famous. He stood on podiums and looked fetchingly puzzled. He shook a dubious hand with gurning politicians. He even turned down offers to appear at music festivals, and had to take regular legal steps to protect the pirating of his virtual identity. He even finally visited me in Seoul, and experienced the wonders of my library at first hand.

At last, Rob had out-achieved me. Then, just when I and most of the rest of the world had him pigeonholed as that handsome, softly accented guy who did those popular science things, his avatar returned the contract for his upcoming series unsigned. I might have forgotten that getting rich was supposed to be the means to an end. But he, of course, hadn't.

"So," I said as we sat together for what turned out to be the last time in our shared illusion of the Eldon. "You succeed with this project. You get a positive result and prove the many-worlds theory is true. What happens after that?"

"I publish, of course. The data'll be public, peer-reviewed, and—"

"Since when has being right ever been enough?"

"That's..." He brushed a speck of virtual beer foam from his grey beard. "...how science works."

"And no one ever had to sell themselves to gain attention? Even Galileo had to do that stunt with the cannonballs."

"As I explained in my last series, that story of the Tower of Pisa was an invention of his early biographers."

"Come on, Rob. You know what I mean."

He looked uncomfortable. But, of course, he already had the fame. All he had to do was stop all this Greta Garbo shit, and milk it.

So, effectively I became PR agent for Rob's long-planned experiment. There was, after all, a lot for the educated layman, let alone the general public, or us so-called media professionals, to absorb. What was needed was a handle, a simple selling point. And, after a little research, I found one.

A man in a business suit had arrived at Tokyo airport in the summer of 1954. He was Caucasian, but spoke reasonable Japanese, and everything about him seemed normal apart from his passport. It looked genuine, but was from somewhere called Taured, which the officials couldn't find in any of their directories. The visitor was as baffled as they were. When a map was produced, he pointed to Andorra, a tiny but ancient republic between France and Spain, which he insisted was Taured. The humane and sensible course was to find him somewhere to sleep while further enquiries were made. Guards were posted outside the door of a secure hotel room high in a tower block, but the mysterious man had vanished without trace in the morning, and the visitor from Taured was never seen again.

Rob was dubious, then grew uncharacteristically cross when he learned that the publicity meme had already been released. To him, and despite the fact that I thought he'd been reading this kind of thing for years, the story was just another urban legend, and would further alienate the scientific establishment when he desperately needed their help. In effect, what he had to obtain was time and bandwidth from every available gravitational observatory, both here on Earth and up in orbit, during a crucial observational window, and time was already short.

It was as the final hours ticked down in a fevered air of stop-go technical problems, last minute doubts, and sudden demands for more money, that I finally took the sub-orbital from Seoul to Frankfurt, then the skytrain on to Glasgow, and some thrumming, windy thing of string and carbon fibre along the Scottish west coast, and across the shining Minch. The craft landed in Stornoway harbour in the Isle of Lewis—the northern part of the long landmass of which Harris forms the south—where I was rowed ashore, and eventually found a bubblebus to take me across purple moorland and past scattered white bungalows, then up amid ancient peaks.

Rob stood waiting on the far side of the road at the final stop, and we were both shivering as we hugged in the cold spring sunlight. But I was here, and so was he, and he'd done a great job at keeping back the rest of the world, and even I wouldn't have had it any other way. It seemed as if most of the niggles and issues had finally been sorted. Even if a few of his planned sources had pulled out, he'd still have all the data he needed. Come tomorrow, Rob Holm would either be a prophet or a pariah.

7.

HE STILL SLEPT in the same narrow bed he'd had as a child in the rusty-roofed cottage down by the shore at Creagach, while his parents' bedroom was now filled with expensive processing and monitoring equipment, along with a high-band, multiple-redundancy satellite feed. Downstairs, there was a parlour where Rob kept his small book collection in an alcove by the fire—I was surprised to see that it was almost entirely poetry: a scatter of Larkin, Eliot, Frost, Dickinson, Pope, Yeats and Donne and standard collections amid a few Asimovs, Clarkes and Le Guins—with a low tartan divan where he sat to read these works. Which, I supposed, might also serve as a second bed, although he hadn't yet made it up.

He took me out on his launch. Showed me his scallop beds, and the glorious views of this ragged land with its impossibly wide and empty beaches, and there, just around the headland, was the stretch of bay where both Rob's parents had been found, and I could almost hear the Blue Men of the Minch calling to us over the sigh of the sea. There were standing stones on the horizon, and an old whaling station at the head of a loch, and a hill topped by a medieval church filled with the bodies of the chieftains who had given these islands such a savage reputation through their bloody feuds. And meanwhile, the vast cosmic shudder of the collision of two black holes was travelling towards us at lightspeed.

There were scallops, of course, for dinner. Mixed in with some fried dab and chopped mushrooms, bacon and a few leaves of wild garlic, all washed down with malt whisky, and with whey-buttered soda bread on the side, which was the Highland way. Then, up in the humming shrine of his parents' old bedroom, Rob checked on the status of his precious sources again.

The black hole binaries had been spiralling towards each other for tens of thousands of years, and observed here on Earth for decades. In many ways, and despite their supposed mystery, black holes were apparently simple objects—nothing but sheer mass—and even though their collision was so far away it had actually happened when we humans were still learning how to use tools, it was possible to predict within hours, if not minutes, when the effects of this event would finally reach Earth.

There were gravitational observatories, vast-array laser interferometers, in deep space and underground in terrestrial sites, all waiting to record this moment, and Rob was tapping into them. All everyone else expected to see—in fact, all the various institutes and faculties had tuned their devices to look for—was this…

Leaning over me, Rob called up a display to show a sharp spike, a huge peak in the data, as the black holes swallowed each other and the shock of their collision flooded out in the asymmetrical pulse of a gravitational wave.

"But this isn't what I want, Lita. Incredibly faint though that signal is—a mere ripple deep in the fabric of the cosmos—I'm looking to combine and filter all those results, and find something even fainter.

"This"—he dragged up another screen—"is what I expect to see." There was the same central peak, but this time it was surrounded by a fan of smaller, ever-decreasing, ripples eerily reminiscent of the display Rob had once shown me of the ghost-flicker of those photons all those years ago in Leeds. "These are echoes of the black hole collision in other universes."

I reached out to touch the floating screen. Felt the incredible presence of the dark matter of other worlds.

"And all of this will happen tonight?"

He smiled.

8.

THERE WAS NOTHING else left to be done—the observatories Rob was tapping into were all remote, independent, autonomous devices—so we took out chairs into the dark, and drank some more whisky, and collected driftwood, and lit a fire on the shore.

We talked about books. Nothing new, but some shared favourites. Poe and Pasternak and Fitzgerald. And Rob confessed that he hadn't got on anything like as well as he'd pretended with his first forays into literature. How he'd found the antique language and odd punctuation got in the way. It was even a while before he understood the obvious need for a physical bookmark. He'd have given up with the whole concept if it hadn't been for my shining, evident faith.

"You know, it was *Gulliver's Travels* that finally really turned it around for me. Swift was so clever and rude and funny and angry, yet he could also tell a great story. That bit about those Laputan astronomers studying the stars from down in their cave, and trying to harvest sunbeams from marrows. Well, that's us right here, isn't it?"

The fire settled. We poured ourselves some more whisky. And Rob recited a poem by La Bai about drinking with the Moon's shadow, and then we remembered those days back in Leeds when we'd gone out onto the moors, and drank and ingested far more than was good for us, and danced like savages and, yes, there had even been that time he and I had gazed up at the stars.

We stood up now, and Rob led me away from the settling fire. The stars were so bright here, and the night sky was so black, that it felt like falling merely to look up. Over there in the west, Lita, is the Taurus Constellation. It's where the Crab Nebula lies, the remains of a supernova the Chinese recorded back in 1054, and it's in part of the Milky Way known as the Perseus Arm, which is where our dark binaries will soon end their fatal dance. I was leaning into him as he held his arms around me, and perhaps both of us were breathing a little faster than was entirely due to the wonders of the cosmos.

"What time is it now, Rob?"

"It's..." He checked his watch. "Just after midnight."

"So there's still time."

"Time for what?"

We kissed, then crossed the shore and climbed the stairs to Rob's single bed. It was sweet, and somewhat drunken, and quickly over. The Earth, the universe, didn't exactly move. But it felt far more like making love than merely having sex, and I curled up against Rob afterwards, and breathed his cinnamon scent, and fell into a well of star-seeing contentment.

"Rob?"

The sky beyond the window was already showing the first traces of dawn as I got up, telling myself that he'd be next door in his parents' old room, or walking the shore as he and his avatar strove to deal with a torrent of interview requests. But I sensed that something was wrong.

It wasn't hard for me to pull up the right screen amid the humming machines in his parents' room, proficient at mek as I now was. The event, the collision, had definitely occurred. The spike of its gravitational wave had been recorded by every observatory. But the next screen, the one where Rob had combined, filtered and refined all the data, displayed no ripples, echoes, from other worlds. His experiment had failed.

I ran outside shouting Rob's name. I checked the house feeds. I paced back and forth. I got my avatar to contact the authorities.

I did all the things you do when someone you love suddenly goes missing, but a large part of me already knew it was far too late.

Helicopters chattered. Drones circled. Locals gathered. Fishermen arrived in trawlers and skiffs. Then came the bother of newsfeeds, and all the publicity I could ever have wished for. But not like this.

I ended up sitting on the rocks of that bay around the headland from Creagach as the day progressed, waiting for the currents to bear Rob's body to this place, where he could join his parents.

I'm still waiting.

9.

FEW PEOPLE ACTUALLY remember Rob Holm these days, and if they do, it's as that good-looking guy who used to present those slightly weird nature—or was it science?—feeds, and didn't he die in some odd, sad kind of way? But I still remember him, and I still miss him, and I still often wonder what really happened on that night when he left the bed we briefly shared. The explanation given by the authorities, that he'd seen his theory dashed and then walked out into the freezing waters of the Minch, still isn't something I can bring myself to accept. So maybe he really was like the Visitor from Taured, and simply vanished from a universe which couldn't support what he believed.

I read few novels or short stories now. The plots, the pages, seem overinvolved. Sloppy murals rather than elegant miniatures. Rough-hewn rocks instead of jewels. But the funny thing is that, as my interest in them has dwindled, books have become popular again. There are new publishers, even new writers, and you'll find pop-up bookstores in every city. Thousands now flock to my library in Seoul every year, and I upset the conservators by allowing them to take my precious volumes down from their shelves. After all, isn't that exactly what books are for? But I rarely go there myself. In fact, I hardly ever leave the Isle of Harris, or even Creagach, which Rob, with typical consideration and foresight, left me in his will. I do my best to keep the scallop farm going, pottering about in the launch and trying to hold the crabs and the starfish at bay, although the business barely turns a profit, and probably never did.

What I do keep returning to is Rob's small collection of poetry. I have lingered with Eliot's Prufrock amid the chains of the sea, wondered with Hardy what might have happened if he and that woman had sheltered from the rain a minute more, and watched as Silvia Plath's children burst those final balloons. I just wish that Rob was here to share these precious words and moments with me. But all that's left is you and me, dear, faithful reader, and the Blue Men of the Minch calling to the waves.

Afterword

I'M PARTICULARLY PROUD of this story. In part, because it seemed to get noticed and was picked up by most of the Year's Best collections in the year it was published, even if, alas, it won no awards. Awards, of course, being a vacuous lottery unless you actually happen to win one. But the main thing I'm proud of with *The Visitor from Taured* is that I was able to address some fairly advanced cosmology in the form of the many-worlds theory of quantum physics, and also gravity waves, with two colliding black holes thrown in for good measure, in what felt like a fairly convincing manner.

THE VISITOR FROM TAURED

Something that still surprises people about me both within and without the genre, including other writers, is that I have absolutely no scientific background. I did, admittedly, win a science prize at school at the age of thirteen, but after that, science and I parted company. The *idea* of science still fascinated me, and I was already reading SF, but the actual stuff we were forced to learn seemed to involve either merely knowing the names of things or performing fiddly mathematical calculations. Both are, of course, an important and necessary part of the scientific process, but to me they seemed pointless and tedious. I was far more intrigued by mysticism, music and literature. So science and I drifted apart, and to be honest we were still barely on speaking terms when I began to attempt to write my first SF in my twenties, and that remained so even when I actually started selling the stuff in my thirties.

Nowadays, I'm a great deal more engaged with science. I'm a regular reader of *New Scientist* and get through several books of popular science a year, as well as finding myself researching science-based issues at least as often as I'm looking into matters of culture and history. I guess, in fact, you could say that I've grown in confidence as a writer of fiction that includes something resembling proper science. But a great deal of that confidence is about knowing my limitations, which remain vast. Plus, I actively dislike both most mainstream writers' attempts to address scientific subjects—which tend to be plodding and over-literal—and much so-called "hard SF", which all too often requires far more knowledge and interest than the average reader possesses, and generally gives up caring about character, setting and atmosphere along the way.

There is, I feel, a middle path, and it's one that I do my best to tread, even when I'm writing about subjects which lie at the boundaries of what we currently know. It's not an easy route to take, but to me that's part of the point, and part of the challenge. Sure, I still have my mystical and religious leanings, both as a person and as a writer, but science is, to all intents and purposes, the only sensible way we have left to explain this world.

The Chronologist

First Quarter

THE CHRONOLOGIST CAME to our town out of the time-haze according to the workings of a calendar that was entirely his own. He bore a metal staff and across his back was a leather tool bag, and word of his arrival passed swiftly from house to house. Rare though these visits were, they were greatly anticipated, and it was enough for most townsfolk to simply hear the phase, *He's here,* to know. People would rush out into the streets pulling on boots and snatching at clothes, some already clutching their precious timepieces for him to attend to—at least after he'd serviced the tower clock from which the hours of all our days were set.

I was a boy of eleven years and five months according to our reckoning on the morning I first remember the Chronologist arriving. I lived with my father, who was mayor of our town, in a rambling but comfortable house just off the main square. He was a plump and fussy man with a nervous moustache and a chronic tendency to misbutton his clothes. Since my mother's death from the effects of a stray time-wind a few difficult seasons earlier, he'd moved out of the main bedroom they'd once shared, and now prowled about the house every night like a particularly heavy-booted ghost, his footsteps making counterpoint with the tall case-clock in the hall's reassuring beat. But he was diligent in his mayoral responsibilities, the most important of which by far was to attend to the tower clock.

Every morning without fail, he'd set out from our house and head on across the main square to open the pitted wooden door at the base of the tower beside the hunched buttresses of the old church, then ascend the ladders through their many levels to rewind the weights. I often went up there with him, up and up through the dusty haze filled with a deep, resonant *tock*, although not so much out of any intrinsic fascination with the clock's mechanism as because of the rare views these higher levels afforded of the time-hazed lands beyond the confines of our town.

Despite all our best efforts, it had already been full summer for far too long, with the lime trees dripping dusty sap, the crops wilting and the cattle barely giving milk, on the morning when word of the Chronologist's arrival finally came. I scurried in my father's wake as, buttoning his best coat sideways and pulling on his mayoral sash the wrong way round, he bumbled out into the main square and fought his way through the crowds to formally welcome the Chronologist to our town. After a preliminary twitch from his moustache, he attempted a stumbling bow, then launched into a typically rambling speech.

THE CHRONOLOGIST

"Is it keeping good time?" the Chronologist interrupted, his voice sharp as turning gears.

"*Good* time...? You mean our tower clock? Well, and as far as we can tell, sir. And inasmuch, I should say, as it isn't keeping *bad* time. Although there's no real way—"

"I shall go and check."

Everyone fell back to let the Chronologist through. He was a tall, thin man, with keen grey eyes, skin the colour of weathered bronze, a pointed chin and a narrow nose. There was something weary about him, but his manner was rigorously precise. Even the way he walked to the regular beat of his staff on the flagstones as his tool bag swung to and fro at his back. I didn't expect to be able to enter the clock tower on a day as rare and significant as this, but there was a moment of typical confusion as my father opened the door to let the Chronologist through, and I, amid a push of civic bosoms and bellies, was able to squeeze quickly in.

Of course, most of these town worthies weren't up to the task of following the Chronologist all the way up through the tower, climbing ladder after ladder past the iron weights on their long chains to the floor beneath the bell that chimed the hours and housed the mechanism that drove the slow-turning hands of the clock face itself, but my father was used to doing so. And so, as the Chronologist began to ascend after he'd pushed his staff through the strap of his tool bag like an antique sword, was I. Standing in the pigeon-cooing shadows as my father fiddled with his buttons and breathed too loudly through his nose, I was then able to watch the Chronologist at his work.

First he set aside his staff and unstrapped his tool bag. Then he laid out a series of tools and knelt before the heavy winding spools and the many wheels and gears large and small that turned quickly or slowly or hurried back and forth—I didn't then know the correct horological terms. His hands moved, I noticed, to something like the same tocking heartbeat as the clock itself. It seemed not so much an act of repair as a kind of healing dance, and it was fascinating to watch, at least for a while, although the process, and my father's noisy breathing—which of course also followed the same rhythm—went on. And on. I confess I grew a little bored. And in the absence of any other distraction, and trapped as I was in this tower, I did what I generally did when I came up here, and clambered over to one of the narrow windows and gazed out.

First of all there was our town itself, all neatly spread below me as only I and the birds ever saw it. The red pantiles. The stilled wind vanes. The shadow-gullies of the streets. The occasional square with its green froth of lime trees. The town dump. Some warehouses and workshops. Then came the fields and the vineyards and the orchards in their neatly combed rows, and the sheep and the cattle tiny as toys, and the farmhouses with their ramshackle sheds and barns, and the dusty tracks that unravelled here and there but always turned back on themselves. But after that...

After the last hedge and scrap of farmland lay a boundary of unkempt wasteland which we had all been warned never to approach, let alone cross. But from up here, peering on through the time-haze, I believed I could make out a little of what lay beyond, and for one moment I was sure there were fields as prim and regular as our own, and the next I saw hills and sunlit meadows, and deep woodlands, and places of ravaged gloom. And beyond even this lay a staggering sense of ever-greater distance, where lights twinkled, and towers and spires far higher and more fabulous than our own gave off signal glints. I was sure that snowy mountains lay out there, too, and the fabled salty lakes known as oceans, and other places and realms beyond anything we in our town were ever permitted to know.

A sudden, calamitous noise startled me out of my reverie, but it was merely the bell striking its hourly chime. The Chronologist, I saw, was no longer attending to the clock mechanism but walking around it and studying it from various angles, as an artist might a portrait or a potter a pot. My father, of course, took this as his signal to engage the poor man in yet more conversation about things which, to me, still nursing my visions of the lands beyond our monotonous little town, didn't matter at all. Even more irritatingly, the Chronologist deigned to join in with this pointless babble, his work up here presumably finished, although his tool bag remained open and his tools were still neatly laid out.

They gleamed appealingly on the dusty wooden floor. Many I recognised——files, screwdrivers, pincers and the like; even a small can of oil—but some I did not. There were spikes and prods attached to little boxes. There were tiny nests of steel and glass. One or two even pulsed with lights of their own. I studied them with curiosity, thinking of the impossibly distant flashes I had glimpsed through the time-haze, and wondering if they were somehow linked. Now his attention was distracted, I even considered quietly pocketing one of these treasures as a small souvenir. But my nerve failed me. After all, he would be bound to notice, being so orderly and precise.

But then I saw the dog-eared corner of a book poking out from a side-flap of his tool bag, and decided it looked so old and yellowed it was unlikely to be missed. I'd crept forward and pocketed the thing before I could have second thoughts. Soon after, my father finally stopped his chatter, and the Chronologist slipped his tools back into his tool bag, and we made our way back down the many ladders towards the square with its eager clusters of clock-clutching townsfolk.

I watched as a chair and a trestle table were set up under the wilting lime trees, and people queued to have their timepieces serviced by the Chronologist's clever hands, and the dog-eared book I'd shoved into my pocket was forgotten as a far more dramatic idea began to form in my head. Keeping back so as not to be noticed, I followed the man as he went from door to door amid a gaggle of town worthies to service a few larger mechanisms and heavier, such as the grandfather clock in our hall. Then, as ever, or so it seemed, his work was done, and it was time for him to leave.

The Chronologist's departure was far less heralded than his arrival. Apparently, most townsfolk cared little about where else he went or what he did once he'd set our days and hours back to their regular beat, and he, I imagined, would want to slip away without enduring another of my father's interminable speeches. So his only companions were a few very young children who had nothing better to do than follow in his wake as he left the town in the late afternoon. At least, apart from me.

The children were a silly bunch, shoving and giggling and skipping. They soon grew bored, or tired, or hungry, or otherwise distracted, and fell away. I though, but quietly and at a distance, kept on his trail. Out from the town with its tall houses and railing-framed squares, then on through a scatter of markets, mills and foundries, then beside storage yards and other such hinter-lands, and on into the fields beyond. Still, the Chronologist walked on in his usual brisk manner, between low stone walls and rambling hedges along tracks ridged and dusty after this prolonged summer's heat, past several farmsteads where dogs barked and geese hissed, until the horizon ahead began to loom and grow dim. But he, if anyone—or so I reasoned—must know the way through.

The sky darkened and the tracks gave out and the last fields fell away, and there were only sharp snags of bramble and choking swathes of ivy and burning patches of stinging nettle, and my sense of direction grew vague. I could still go on, or so I told myself, as long as I followed the figure shimmering ahead, but I was being stalked by an increasing sense of dread. A wind was rising, too, along with an even colder stirring that raked inside my scratched and stung flesh. Where was I, and what was I doing? I no longer knew, and my resolve failed me. I turned and stumbled back from the looming time-haze, and ran and ran until I reached familiar fields, and staggered, aching and gasping, the rest of the way home.

Second Quarter

CLOUDS CLOSED ACROSS the sky next morning. By noon it was raining, and by nightfall there was a definite chill in the air. Soon, what was left of our crops finished ripening, and the meagre harvest was taken in, and not long after the lime trees began to shed their ragged leaves, and everyone in the town rejoiced that temporal regularity had returned. At least, apart from me.

When I finally remembered it, the book I'd stolen from the Chronologist's tool bag proved to be a disappointment. I'd hoped for some kind of clue as to who he really was—or, better still, a map or guide to the worlds beyond the time-haze—but it was nothing more than a very old, dry and extremely technical manual on the servicing, maintenance and repair of various types of timepiece. It was deeply irritating.

I also found myself irritated by many other things, not least my father's bumbling inability to manage his own buttons, let alone our town, and the pointless and repetitive tasks we children were expected to perform at school. After all, I had already seen much farther than here, and believed I would see farther still. Why should I have to endlessly draw and redraw the same street maps of our town, or memorise the weights of every recent harvest, or count the number of seconds in each hour, or copy out calendars from years long erased?

I often went upstairs to my mother's old bedroom now when I returned home from school. Typically, my father had done nothing to deal with the ravages the time-winds had inflicted—the blistered paintwork, the contorted ceiling, the furniture bleached to bony heaps, the bed blackened into something which was scarcely a bed at all—but that suited my mood. I remembered how angry I had been when her affliction first became evident. After all, she was so quick and lively and pretty and smart. So why did she now need a stick to walk with, and why was her back so stooped? I would visit her up there when her condition worsened and she retreated to her bed, much though I hated to witness what she had become. She barely recognised me now, and her eyes were vague and the hands that clutched my own were sharp and dry as twigs. Sometimes, though, although I wished she wouldn't, she'd begin to speak in a crackling, quavering voice that came and went like dry leaves. Gabbling nonsense, or so it then seemed, of the times when the arrow of time flew straight and true.

Marvels and miracles. Machines bigger than houses or smaller than ants. Some that could peer so far into the sky that the past itself was glimpsed. Others that looked so deep into the fabric of everything that the quivering threads of reality could be examined, then prised apart, to see what lay beyond. And it was through one of these rents, or so her whispers told me, that a hole of sheer nothingness widened, and the fabric of everything warped and twisted, and the time-winds blew through. Worse still, at least for me, the curtains stirred as if these words called to them, and the peeling wallpaper flapped, and the ceiling receded like an upturned well, and the claws of her nails drew blood. I stopped going up there, but soon the entire house was rent with her screams until one morning there was sudden silence, and absolute relief, and what little was left of her was buried beyond the furthest fields, and my father and I could go back to pretending that our days were ordered exactly as they should be.

But they weren't. And, more than ever now, I longed to escape. My plan, as I first conceived it, was simple. I would set out along the all-too-familiar streets of this town and then carry on across the fields into the shimmering wilderness beyond until the time-haze swallowed me whole. There were, admittedly, some problems with my absence being noticed too soon—all the more so when my daylight habits were tied to following my father to the clock tower and going to and from school. So I would have to leave at night, and along the quieter back streets in case I was noticed by some interfering busybody, and then avoiding the barking dogs and honking geese of the various farms. There was also the issue of my father's ever-wakeful prowlings, but the man was so set and regular in his habits that even his nightly pacings had a predictable pattern which, by listening to the familiar creaks and footfalls as they came and went, I was soon able to anticipate.

This was it, then. My destiny was set. I didn't even feel afraid on the spring night I finally got up from my bed, and crept through the house in delicate counterpoint to the beat of the tall case-clock and my father's thumping prowl, and pulled on my coat and boots, and lifted the oiled latch of the front door, and headed out of town along the darkest and quietest back streets. Or, if I was afraid, what I feared was that my plan would fail.

But that didn't happen; I simply walked on through the bland night along muddy tracks towards the strange vortex beyond, once again following the route that the Chronologist had taken when he left this town. A breeze began to stir around me, warm at first, and scented with nothing but mud, manure and grass. Then it grew colder and deeper, touching my thoughts and bones, and the paths dissolved and the way ahead grew ragged and rough. But I had prepared by dressing in my stoutest clothes and I did not turn back as I fought my way through the clawing vegetation, not even when the stars above me began to churn and melt.

When I paused to look back, all I could now see was a shimmering, twisting curtain. And ahead of me... Ahead, there were neat fields and slumbering rooftops, all captured in the soft spring dark. This town, I saw, had a clock tower much like our own, and the way towards it avoiding the hissing farmyard geese and barking dogs was oddly familiar. Then came the same streets, the same squares, the same buildings, and then the same rambling house, where the front door latch was oiled, and I was easily able to avoid my father's continued pacing on my way upstairs, and climb back into bedsheets that were still warm.

Third Quarter

SPRING PASSED INTO summer with dreadful, predictable monotony, and everyone commented on how wonderfully set and regular the seasons had become since the Chronologist's visit. But *he* had then left this prison, walked away from it as easily I might walk home from school, and the constant repetition of my days was an unbearable drudge.

Oh, how I hated the cowardly way I had turned back from following him on that fateful day at the end of the long summer before! I relived the moment again and again, and cursed my own fearful stupidity—and the tower clock's stolid reliability, which meant that he wouldn't return any time soon, and perhaps throughout all the rest of my tedious life. Affecting an interest I certainly didn't feel in the affairs of our town, I tried asking my father about the Chronologist's habits one morning over breakfast. If, after all, he only came according to the workings of a calendar that was entirely his own, how did he know when, or when not, to come? My father twitched his moustache and dabbed ruminatively at a blob of egg on his misbuttoned shirt. This was, apparently, a most astute question of a kind which marked me out as a strong candidate for mayor of this town in whatever passed here for the future. The way these things worked, at least to the best of his understanding, was that the Chronologist came because he knew his presence was required. Although as to precisely how that happened, he had no idea.

A little later, and in a thoughtful daze, I followed my father up the ladders in the clock tower, and stood staring at that patiently tocking mechanism rather than at the views beyond, wondering what I could do to bring about the Chronologist's arrival according to a calendar of my devising rather than his.

The key was, of course, that tedious book, and had been all along. I began to study its creased pages and stained diagrams. A clock, after all, was just another machine like a plough or a hand-cart, if a little more complicated, with workings that could be measured, tested, adjusted and fixed—or broken. I can't pretend that it was fascinating, but it gave me hope and purpose, and that was enough.

What struck me most was how innately fragile all clocks were. They might just go on and on, like time itself, yet they were easily perturbed. The chains, gears, levers, weights, sprockets, wheels, brushes, flies, trains, dials and pinions, the escapement that caught and held each gear for a precious second before moving on, all had to be precisely balanced and calibrated. Standing studying the mechanism in the tower, which I now knew was technically known as a turret-clock, as my father huffed and sweated to rewind its weights, I saw that it would be a matter of mere moments to make it run fast or slow.

But that, as I'd already decided, wouldn't be enough. A slight tightening or loosening would certainly retard its workings, but how on earth would we, or even the Chronologist, know that that had happened, when the turning of the clock itself governed the days and hours our lives? Whatever I did would have to be more profound, and more damaging, than that. And, oddly enough, as my thoughts and my ruminations expanded, I found that I was no longer in the same fever of hurry. After all, I reasoned, the time I had left in this drab little town was now mine to command.

Like any self-respecting craftsman, I decided to do a little practice-work first. And what better example of a lesser timepiece could I have to hand than the case-clock in our own hall? Of course, in many ways it was a different kind of device, with chime hammers, a pendulum and a gathering pallet, but that was also part of the challenge. After getting hold of a screwdriver and a small steel file, and pretending a stomach-ache so I could leave early from school, I crouched before it, opened its bevelled glass front, and set to work. It was then merely a matter of shaving a few brass slivers from the teeth of the central wheel which fed the escapement so that some seconds ran more quickly than others, although doing so briefly caused the entire clock to scream and shudder as if in pain. But then I applied a little oil.

In many ways, the effect was far less subtle than I'd intended, although I mostly blamed my father's habitual night-time prowlings for that. The regular beat that matched his paces might have seemed superficially the same, but the rhythm of his march along the corridors and up and down the stairs now became a series of stumbles, trips and muted curses. He crashed into vases and tumbled over chairs. He bashed his head on roof-beams and fell through doors. But it wasn't just him. There was no doubt that the house itself felt less set, less stable; even less the happy home it had once been. Things started to shift and unravel in the temporal desert of my mother's bedroom as well. The bones of the furniture rearranged themselves into worrying shapes. The pastel decorations bloomed into bloated parodies of their old selves. At least, that was what I glimpsed when I opened the door a few inches, then pulled it firmly shut, and turned the key, although I still sometimes heard wet, dragging shuffles moving as if in echo to my father's footsteps, and distant—but not quite distant enough—screams.

My father was distracted and distraught, his clothes madly awry and his moustache wildly a-twitch, and things were difficult for me as well during those misarranged times. But they also offered an opportunity I hadn't expected would arise so easily. When I suggested one late spring morning over the breakfast table as a half-cooked newborn chick tried to peck its way out of his soft-boiled egg that I could go and wind the weights in the clock tower on my own today, seeing as he looked so tired and I already knew exactly what to do, he dabbed his eyes and readily agreed.

I studied the mechanism turning and tocking high in the dusty heights of its tower more as an adversary than as a fine example of the horologist's art. After all, its regularity was the very thing which was preventing the Chronologist's return. And, without him to show me the way out through the time-haze, how could I possibly escape? The answer, of course, lay in what I now had to do. First of all, though, I wound the weights—I didn't want time to stop entirely—and then, with that task completed, I took out my file and screwdriver and set to work.

There was, perhaps, a spirit of vengeance in what I did, although I would have been hard put to say what slight or wrong I was trying avenge. It had to be more than my father's untidy buttons and stupid moustache, or the pointless activities at school, or the generalised drudgery of our days, or the broader confinements of our lives. There was, of course, the tragedy of what had happened to my mother, but that was no one's fault but time itself... And, although it sounds nonsensical, I now think that it was time that I truly wished to hurt. And this clock was its emblem, its enabler, its beating heart.

If there was such a thing as an anti-Chronologist, it was me that morning. I scraped and shaved and misadjusted. I shoved and bent and pushed and pulled. Yet the damn thing kept on turning and tocking—it was, after all, a large and powerful device—and so my attack on it continued beyond anything I had planned. But even as, surrounded by metal shavings, discarded balancing weights and the odd fallen bolt, I continued at my task, there was no immediate sense of time going awry. Which, the remaining rational part of me reasoned, made absolute sense. After all, I was a part of the bigger workings of our town which this infernal machine drove.

Then I cleared away the evidence, and left the tower, and headed across the main square to school.

Fourth Quarter

IT BEGAN WITH the cocks crowing at odd times in the morning, then well before sunrise, then throughout most of the night. Which set the town dogs howling, although perhaps they already sensed the change. And the dawn chorus grew strongest at noon, and the stars wheeled in the heavens like drifting snow. All of which was of course noticed and commented upon, and people set and wound their timepieces with even greater regularity, and always according to the reassuring chimes of the tower clock in our main square. Just like the cows in the fields lowing to be milked at midnight, and the rats scurrying the streets in daylight, everyone in our town instinctively felt this disarrangement, in troubled nights and weird bouts of hunger or sudden thirsts.

My father was at a loss. He knew that something was wrong, and felt sure he had somehow betrayed the townsfolk in fulfilling his duties as mayor. But yes, yes, of course he wound the tower clock as constantly and consistently as any man could, he assured a rowdy public meeting in his predictably long-winded way. As I, as his son and regular witness, would confirm.

All the awkward, annoying things which had happened before when time slipped just a little—fruit suddenly ripening or rotting, cheese dissolving back into milk—happened again now, but grew worse. Whole fields full of nearly ripe grain, which we would all depend upon for sustenance whenever winter finally came, shrank back to mere shoots, then died in a sudden, bitter frost. Even our preciously tended and copied books at school weren't immune. The print on their pages greyed and dissolved, or turned into strange symbols, or obscene doggerel, and their bindings fell apart. Which might once have been amusing. But it wasn't now.

Every morning, although the mornings no longer felt like mornings, I made my way with my father across the shadow-shifting main square to the clock tower, and ascended the ladders, and looked out towards the vistas beyond, where the time-winds tumbled in the mad air and even this tower seemed to waver and tilt. Or I stared at the mechanism of the turret-clock as it wheezed in a gravelly grinding, and waiting for the next *tock* was like waiting for a dying man's last breath. Then, in the afternoons, and after all the uncertainties of school, I would return to a house where the floors were stinking and slippery from a plague of frogs, and the windows offered crooked views, and the doors no longer fitted in their frames but creaked and groaned in a clamour of draughts.

Often, in what now passed for *now*, as my father and I sat at a meal that might turn raw at any moment, or dissolve into maggoty mush, we heard a painfully slow *lump, lump, lump* coming down the stairs. But the stairs themselves, when we dared to look up at them, had grown so wide and high that their top dissolved into murky distance, and whatever it was that was coming towards us—and we both knew it probably wasn't anything resembling my mother—never came quite into view. Which was a blessing of sorts. In fact, now that the mechanism of the case-clock was a whirring, crickety blur, that endless descent was almost the only regular sound we knew.

This was a full time-storm, with whole houses collapsing and torrents of rain sheeting down from hot, clear skies. We were losing ourselves and we were losing each other, falling away through the unnumbered days. So where was the Chronologist? Why hadn't he arrived already in these broken times of our greatest need? Surely he had to come right now. Or now. Or now. But the *nows* staggered past us, or slipped backwards, or melted like the faces of our clocks, and it already seemed that it was far too late.

Fifth Quarter

IT WAS A hot, moonlit morning of no known season when he finally arrived, and things were suddenly almost as they had been before, with the dogs panting and the cocks crowing and fresh pollen drifting with the fallen leaves and drizzles of snow across the greyed and emptied fields. Children came shouting and running, and I rushed to join them, for yes, yes, he was here, he had come, and my father stumbled and hurried, his shirt as ever misbuttoned and askew, to greet the Chronologist in the main square.

"You are..." He panted as shadows shrivelled and bloomed around us. "...Most, most welcome. Indeed, may I venture, it would have been good if you had arrived before."

"I arrive when I can," the Chronologist replied with a brisk tap of his metal staff. Then his gaze—knowing yet somehow deeply lost—swept across us townsfolk like a withering wind until it settled on me.

"You, lad," he pointed, "shall accompany me up the tower."

"But—but," my father protested, "he's only a child! Surely if anyone should come with you, it should be me. After all, I am mayor of this town and whatever has happened is my responsibility."

But the Chronologist shook his head, and I, of course, was in no position to refuse. After all, wasn't this exactly what I wanted—for the Chronologist to arrive from wherever he came from, so that I might follow him and escape?

The tower's interior went up and up through the levels, almost as before. But the dusty gloom stirred with whisperings, and that patient *tock* was irregular. It came and went, now close as my own agitated heartbeat, now distant as the spinning stars, and the levels and ladders seemed to expand and contract. Briefly, there was no sign of the Chronologist climbing ahead of me—no, there were two of him, then three, then again just one—but I knew that I had to keep climbing in his wake.

One foot and then the other. Rung after rung. One hand gripping above. The other below. I tried counting each upward step as I would once have counted the tedious hours, days and seconds at school, but the numbers were torn from me, and the tower was twisting like a corkscrew, and I felt very cold. But I was still clinging, I was still climbing, even as the walls, ladders and levels tunnelled ahead and behind me, and the weights swung wildly on their chains. Soon there was no up or down, or now or then, or before or after, but just this endless tower and the pouring, emptied air.

I was climbing through a time-storm, drenched in sweat despite the chill, and shivering and aching beyond exhaustion, and with no sense left of where, or when, I was. But then I glimpsed something familiar, and it seemed it was deep below me rather than high above, and I started laughing. Somehow, I had reached some unknown level of the tower which soared far beyond the turret-clock's mundane mechanism, face and bell. Which obviously meant I needed to work my way back down. I changed my grip on the rungs, and shifted my feet to adjust, and was about to begin my long descent when something slipped within me, and my hands scrabbled for purchase, and I fell.

I suppose I must have lost consciousness. Perhaps I even died— was blasted to dust and ancient smithereens by the time-winds. But some part of me still existed, and it dreamed that I had fallen into a wilderness of clocks. There were fob watches and skeleton clocks and carriage clocks and half-hunters, and things so strange or elaborate that they scarcely seemed to be timepieces at all, piled in glittering hills and dunes. There were clocks that might once have been driven by springs or weights, or the drip of water, or the flame of a candle, or the sparks of a summer storm, and there were brass dials that stole the shadow from the sun. There were devices to record the flicker of light though crystal, or a human body's living pulse, and yet others that measured the age of all existence, or the nothingness beyond. They were here in all their endless variety, stretching off in a vast desert, horizon after horizon, on and on and on. And, but for the wind, that desert was silent and timeless, for not one of these timepieces worked.

Then I, or whatever I had become, awoke, and I found myself lying scratched and aching in a wasteland beyond the furthest edge of an ill-kept field. I stood up, I started walking—dazed as I was, what else was I supposed to do?—and soon I heard dogs barking, and the lowing of cattle, and the hiss of geese, and for a few delicious moments I believed that I was back in my own town, and my heart filled with hope. Then a farm worker balanced on a strange, chuffing machine noticed me, and shouted across the furrows, and some children ran up and screamed as if I was some wild intruder, and started throwing stones. Which, I realised as I looked down at myself, was understandable, because I no longer recognised myself.

I was taller, or at least farther from the ground, and my hands were like spiders, and brown as bronze, and I was peculiarly clothed, and a pressure across my chest and back came from the strap of a tool bag, and the thing I hadn't even realised I was leaning on was some kind of metal staff. Even the tones and accents of my voice, as I tried to reason with the people who were gathering around me, were as strange to me as they were to them. And I suddenly felt very, very old.

I was shouted at, jeered and prodded, and not one of the faces that leered over me was familiar as I was hauled like a sack of potatoes through the streets of a town filled with moving glass-and-metal machines that clearly weren't timepieces, although I had no sense then of what their purpose was. Yet the place wasn't entirely strange to me, which was somehow the strangest thing of all. It was down to the dusty scent of the lime trees, and to the way the main square framed a church and a clock tower, even if every detail was changed. The church buttresses were finer, and the tower was clad in polished grey blocks rather than rough brown stone. That, and the man who came up to me and demanded to know my business here was clearly the mayor, even if he had no moustache and was dressed in perfectly buttoned clothes. Something else was familiar to me amid all these odd differences. It was the sense of tired restlessness, and the smell of dogs and drains, and the uncertainty of the shadows beneath the lime trees, and the madly crowing cocks.

Did these townsfolk understand what was happening? With approximate gestures and half-understood phrases, it was difficult to make myself entirely clear. But yes, yes, they agreed after a great deal of pointing and prompting, they sensed that their tower clock wasn't working quite as it should, but were at a loss to explain why. Nor, it seemed, had they heard of someone called the Chronologist. If such a being did exist beyond what they called *the space of nothing* which surrounded their small and carefully maintained haven, he'd certainly never come here.

Of course, it took a great deal of persuasion before they agreed that my strange and sudden arrival might serve some useful purpose, and were prepared to allow me to go up into their tower and inspect the mechanism of their turret-clock at first hand. Of course, they also insisted that I was accompanied, although everyone apart from the mayor, who was used to ascending these ladders every morning, soon ran out of breath. I found it oddly soothing to climb into the ticking shadows and make my acquaintance with this device of brass and steel. It was a neat, sleek mechanism, more complex in some ways but simpler in others than the turret-clock I had so damaged and abused. Overall, though, it had broadly the same workings, with changes and improvements here and there. Lost as I was, it felt like greeting an old friend. Overall, I decided, the device was working well enough, but there were one or two minor issues—a crooked nut, a few grains of dirt, a slightly misaligned wheel—that needed to be addressed. I was pleasantly surprised, looking into my tool bag, to discover that I had the necessary tools, and was soon able to set things right—a tightening here, a loosening there, some slight rebalancing, a wipe with a rag, a few drops of oil—and it was deeply satisfying to experience the sense of renewed purpose and solidarity that now emanated from this timepiece with every *tock*, and to hear the relief in the mayor's voice as he thanked me, and the cheers of the townsfolk rising from the square below.

They wanted me to stay with them in that town, but I refused. I knew I would be of no other use to them, and that they would soon begin to ask questions about things I had no answer for, and then to doubt the purpose and meaning of their carefully measured lives, and to blame me for all that went wrong. So I left in the late afternoon, at first in the company of the mayor and some civic worthies, and then merely a few giggling, scampering children, and then entirely alone.

I'm no longer sure I can remember the many, many other towns I've come across on my journey, nor that it would be good if I did, but I do know that all are different and yet somehow the same. Sometimes, when I arrive, my presence is expected, or thought long overdue. Sometimes I am barely needed, or just a mad curiosity, or a dangerous pariah to be cursed and stoned. I think there are probably days and arrivals which I do not survive. Sometimes, the townsfolk recognise and remember me. Sometimes, I am far too late. Sometimes, there is neither place or time and once again I find myself falling through the time-winds in a madly corkscrewing clock tower—or perhaps it's for the first time—and awaken changed and aching from dreams of a wilderness of clocks, and with no real sense of who or what I am.

I have visited towns where the clocks are lumbering and primitive, and the people are frankly primitive as well. There have been others where their devices are made of little more than light and energy, and time somehow pours down from the skies. I have spoken with machines in the shape of people, and people in the shape of machines. I have been to places where the clock tower is worshipped through human sacrifice, and others where the inhabitants have razed it to the ground. It is in one of these ruins, or so I imagine, that I found my metal staff, which appears to be the minute-hand from the face of a town clock, although I can't be sure. I have yet, however, to come across a volume on the repair and maintenance of the commoner types of timepiece. Unless, that is, I've already lost it, or it's been stolen by some ill-meaning lad, or I've forgotten that I have it with me right now. My memory's not what it once will be. Or was. Or is.

One town, though, I do particularly remember, because I truly recognised every detail, with each house and every street and field arranged exactly as I knew them to have once been, and the faces of all the people who welcomed me achingly familiar in every way. But I was glad to discover that the mayor's wife was still alive, and that she and he made a happy couple. Nevertheless, the mayor quietly confessed to me as I attended to the case-clock in the hall of their well-appointed house, it was a small grief to them both that they had never been blessed with a child.

There will, I suppose, come a day when I will force some foolish child nurturing dreams of reaching other times and lands to follow me up the ladders of the clock tower in a particular town. Or perhaps it has already happened, and the event lies so far behind me that the memory has dissolved. Either way, I know I can never tell him that there is nothing more precious than waking each morning and knowing that today will probably be much the same as yesterday—tomorrow as well—although I sincerely wish I could. All I can do is to keep pushing on through the time-winds according to the workings of a curse and a calendar that is entirely my own.

Afterword

I CAN TRACE quite a few of these stories to a particular moment when something crossed my mind that seemed worth writing about, although a great many other less conscious factors are doubtless generally also at play. With *Stuff*, it was standing in that Lichfield junk shop. With *The Chronologist*, it came when my wife and I were touring the Black Forest in Germany, and encountering the tale of clockmakers wandering from village to village selling their wares triggered the idea of someone selling not just clocks, but time itself. The idea, however, stubbornly refused to come any closer to becoming a fully-fledged story until I happened to be reading *One Hundred Years of Solitude* by Gabriel García Márquez about five years later, and felt a pull towards magical realism that the novel seemed to suggest.

Even then, there were many dead ends. Through these, the idea of a travelling clockmaker slowly evolved into a wandering chronologist who fixes the clocks that actually drive time. More twisted M C Escher vision than anything properly logical, I'll admit, but, and unlike Márquez with his singing statues and plagues of insomnia, there's a more practical part of my makeup as a writer which demands that my stories make a specific kind of sense.

I have to admit that, on rereading *The Chronologist*, the "sense" I manage to create, which comes via the protagonist's memories of his poor dead mother raving about the fabric of time itself being damaged through human intervention—the kind of cosmic disaster which is occasionally mentioned in regard to particle accelerators such as the Large Hadron Collider—is actually pretty thin. Still, it allowed me to believe in the story, and got me over the line of finishing it. Which, from my selfish point of the view, is about as crucial as it gets.

Selkie

BETHANY FLETT IS out on the shore collecting driftwood when she notices the falling star. She watches it disappear into the open sea beyond the navigation lights of the British Grand Fleet and the encircling hills of Scapa Flow.

Although she wasn't taught such things at school, she knows from the books she's borrowed from Kirkwall Library that shooting stars are merely stray lumps of rock heating up as they pass through the atmosphere, even if many in her village would insist they're souls cast down from heaven.

She picks her way back to the family longhouse, where tonight's supper of neeps and mutton is waiting, even if it consists mostly of last year's potatoes. But Bethany knows Ma does her best and the proper meat is kept for the men of the household, who are out catching fish in the sailboat and won't be back until morning.

Seeing to the twins afterwards, she notices how cramped their bunks have become and wonders where they will fit with the longhouse already so overcrowded. Something has to give and she can guess what that something might be, seeing as she's the only grown daughter in the family. Become a herring girl, she supposes, following the shoals up and down the mainland docks. That, or marry a fisherman.

"Give us a story, Beth."

"Yes—give us a story."

The twins love a tale from history, the more gruesome the better, and wriggle with excitement as she tells them about King Henry VIII of England, although they're disappointed that he only lopped off two of his six wives' heads and not at all interested to know they'd all be Roman Catholics if he hadn't divorced Catherine of Aragon. When they're finally settled, and with Ma drowsing in her chair beside the fire, Bethany unrolls her straw mattress across the flagging and thinks of that shooting star as she drifts towards sleep.

THE FLETT SAILBOAT returns with the morning tide and the men on board are shouting excitedly. Maybe a surprisingly rich catch, or some contraband tobacco or whisky? The whole village gathers on the stone quay to find out and gasps as the body of a man is laid there, wet and naked.

"We caught him out yonder." Cousin Murdo points towards the lip of the Pentland Firth.

He's breathing, but there's an ugly rent in his left thigh. Pale and ill though he is, there's a brownish hue to his skin, and his hair is golden-curly. He looks, there's no other word for it, *foreign*.

SELKIE

He coughs. His eyes flicker. Everyone steps back.

"Where...am...I...?" He tries to sit up. "You..." Each word is clear enough in its own way, but oddly mangled. "Rescued me from the water...in that..."—his young-seeming face creases—"...antique vessel..."

Nobody says anything. Everyone is watching.

"Where *is* this...?"

"You're in Kellness, son." Bethany's Pa steps forward. "On the Islands of Orkney."

"And you're really *here*? You're not virtuals? And why the old-time clothing...?"

One or two puzzled laughs.

Pained though he looks, he almost laughs as well. "This sure as hell ain't Kansas, Toto."

"Toto?" Pa frowns. "Is that your name? And isn't Kansas over in America?"

A short debate follows as to what to do with him. The villagers certainly won't hand him over to the police in Kirkwall, as they have little time for the authorities. And the idea of sending for Doctor Harkness is soon vetoed; he's from far-off Aberdeen and isn't to be trusted. In the end, it's agreed to put him in the old smokehouse and see what happens.

ALL DAY, THE children run around the smokehouse, shrieking and excited, as Bethany gets on with her regular chores. In the afternoon, deep booms echo around the hills as the ships of the Grand Fleet test their guns, preparing for the coming war against Germany. Then, as evening grows, she heads out to the shore again to collect driftwood. No sign of any shooting stars tonight, but she notices the heads of maybe half a dozen seals out in the bay, looking inland. The men might say they're a fish-killing nuisance, but she finds their presence companionable.

She walks on, picking up a few odd lumps of coal, which are always useful, then notices something shining at the edge of the waves. A jellyfish? The thing is there as she stoops to prod it in a shallow rockpool. Then, somehow, it isn't. It seems to be flickering with bits of the sky and the sea, almost like a mirror, and when she finally manages to lay it across a rock, it's surprisingly heavy.

Now that she has some idea of the shape of it, the sense of its strangeness grows rather than diminishes. Although it's still trying to take on the colours of the surrounding shore—even her own silhouette—it has the definite outline of a human body. It's even topped by a sort of bubble where the head might be. It looks almost alive, but she somehow knows it isn't. That, and there's a tear where the left thigh might be.

After checking she's still alone, she grasps the thing, which feels dry and smooth instead of wet and slippery, and heads across the shore towards the far promontory. There, she shifts a few rocks, shoves it into a crevice, and covers it over.

SHE'S THE LAST to unroll her mattress in the crowded longhouse that evening, but even then sleep won't come. There's so much superstitious nonsense talked in Kellness that it's hard to know where the truth begins. Eating a fish from the tail being bad luck and washing a man's clothes while he's out at sea meaning certain drowning. White cats and black cats and whistling in the wind and not clicking glasses to save the souls of sailors. And selkies.

SELKIE

Not mermaids, but nevertheless creatures of the sea who come to the land in the shape of seals, cast off their outer skin, and then seem almost entirely human. Not just that, but they're so beautiful people can't help but fall in love with them, although the stories generally end badly. For selkies pine for the sea and long to return to it. At least, that is, unless you can find their shed skin on the shore and hide it away from them. Then they have to stay with you forever.

ANOTHER MORNING DAWNS bright and clear and Bethany heads over to the smokehouse as soon as she's finished turning the peat.

The stranger looks even paler and the smell of old fish and smoke is overpowered by sweat and illness. The blankets he's been given are the ones used to clean up the ewes at lambing and the rags that bind his wound aren't much better. And he's mumbling odd words. Stuff about *jugships*—jump ships?—and enemy *host-isles*—hostiles? and *nukes*—dukes?—and a lost *slipsuit*, and something about *incoming*.

"What am I doing here...?" he asks, in a brief moment of clarity.

"We're taking care of you," she says. Still, she's shocked to see how little effort has been made, when she knows from reading about Florence Nightingale in the Crimea that the proper treatment of wounded patients begins with simple hygiene.

She scrubs her hands raw and collects some of the clean rags that the women use for their monthlies. The man's eyes roll and his moans rise as she washes out the sodden wound, which looks more as if it's been burned than cut into him. Runners of infection are spreading towards his groin and she doubts if cleanliness alone will save him.

OVER THE NEXT couple of days and nights, she spares what time she can to change the man's dressing. She does other things for him as well, of course, and the whole village is soon tutting and nodding—saying he'll be Bethany Flett's man if he happens to survive, will that Toto from Kansas.

Sometimes he curses, or cries out more strange phrases. Stuff about *shield cities* and *seeker mines* and *slipsuits* and *backjumps*, or what might be people's names, and even odder sounds that barely seem like words at all. Just like the strange object she found out on the shore, her sense of who and what he is feels flickery and blurry.

But there's one thing she's sure about. There's another book she's borrowed from Kirkwall Library—a rather fanciful novel—and she knows he's no more Toto from Kansas than she's Dorothy.

FINALLY, TOWARDS THE end of the third day, his flesh starts to cool and he settles into something closer to sleep than unconsciousness. Stepping out from the smokehouse, Bethany finds that the glow of another sunset still fills the sky, vying with the stars and the twinkle of the Grand Fleet's navigation lights.

After checking that nobody's watching, she crosses the shore to the promontory, shifts the pile of stones and reaches into the crevice. It's still there, dry and smooth to the touch, like no skin or fabric she's ever encountered.

Laying it out on the heather, she notices a kind of a barnacle-like protrusion on the right hip as it assumes the colours of twilight. It comes loose when she touches it, feels solid. Yet, amazingly, it makes an exact fit for her fingers and gives off a deep humming. Not only that, but something odd has happened to her vision. Everything's suddenly incredibly clear, with lines and figures forming around things as she looks at them. Her gaze spins towards the Grand Fleet and the humming intensifies and the letters and numbers solidify into a sharp cross centred on the hull of HMS *Dreadnought*, the pride of the Royal Navy, which seems so close she can see the faces of the sailors at their stations.

Her palms sweat. Her skin tingles. The thing in her hand is waiting. With the slightest effort of will, she could... But no, no. *No.* Something untwists and the power subsides and ordinary twilight returns even before she's placed the thing back into its barnacle-like protrusion.

She stuffs what must be a slipsuit back into the crack and covers it back over with rocks, vowing never again to touch it.

THE MAN'S EYES are open and his temperature has faded when she looks in next morning.

"Where I am, it used to be part of a place called...Scotland? Right?"

"Was the last time I heard," she says, deciding to put his odd use of tense down to the residue of his fever. "Although we Orcadians like to think we're our own people."

"What's your name?"

"Bethany Flett."

"You saved my life."

"The men in the sailboat did that. I just helped with your wound and fever."

"What time is it?"

"I don't own a pocket watch, but I'd say just past noon."

"I mean the date."

"I'd have to check that, too. But it's about the tenth of June. And it's definitely a Wednesday."

"And the year?"

"Nineteen fourteen."

He closes his eyes and seems almost to stop breathing.

EVEN AS HE recovers, he keeps asking ridiculous questions.

"Those guns I keep hearing—are they real?"

"That would be the Grand Fleet."

"Who are they fighting?"

"No one at the moment. They're just testing their artillery. But it'll probably be the Germans."

"Germany—isn't that a country in old Europe?"

Sometimes his fever returns but that happens less and less as he recovers and soon he's able to get up and see to his own needs, and gains an appetite, and pretends to box with the kids as they run in and out of the smokehouse, and learns to talk more slowly so people can understand him. Although, along with his gaining strength, Bethany detects an increased wariness.

There's loss and puzzlement in his eyes, too. He'll stare for ages at everyday things—a bowl, a rowboat, the clogs he's been lent to wear, the battleships across the water—as if they're entirely new to him. But he can smile as well as anyone, and hobble about using a stick for support, poking here and there along the shore as if he's searching for something.

He keeps himself useful by whittling new ash-pegs for the boats, but when Bethany notices him one evening as she returns from collecting driftwood, he's simply sitting on the quay and staring out at nothing. There's an odd noise—*click whirr*—which makes her think of that thing of his, the slipsuit, although as she gets closer she sees that it's only Pa's spring-loaded tape measure.

"I'd stop playing with that if I were you. My father bought it in Aberdeen and he won't want it broken."

"Oh…!" He starts, then relaxes. "It's you, Bethany. What gets me is why they made the metal tape flat instead of curving it. That way, it wouldn't flop about when you use it."

Bethany puts down her basket of driftwood. "You're not really called Toto, are you? And you're not from Kansas."

"What makes you think that?" *Click, whirr.* He's still playing with the tape measure.

"Toto's a dog from a novel about a girl called Dorothy who gets blown away from Kansas by a tornado. It's a work of fiction."

"And here was me thinking it was an old movie. But I suppose you don't have movies yet? Silents, maybe."

"I have no idea what you're talking about."

"Don't you even have moving pictures?"

"Kirkwall has two picture houses that show films, if that's what you mean."

"Fil-*ums*? Films! Right, films—picture houses! And there was probably some antique novel about the *Wizard of Oz* before the old two-dee. But I'm just a grunt, spam in a can, so what the hell do I know…?" Then he falls silent. "So," he says eventually, "where do you think I'm really from?"

"I believe," she says, "that you're probably from the future."

"What makes you think a thing like that?"

"I—I saw something falling from the sky. It was on the night you were rescued. That, and some of the things you've been saying, especially when you had a fever."

"Not that I'm saying you're wrong. But I'm surprised you can come up with such an idea."

"I'm not entirely ignorant. There's another novel I've read. It's called *The Time Machine,* although I suppose you'd probably say it was another movie."

I'M JUST A *grunt*—that's the one thing he keeps telling her as they walk together and the guns boom out across Scapa Flow. A *grunt* being a simple solider, which is all he is, or maybe a sailor, seeing as he talks about a ship, albeit one he calls a *jumpship* which sails close to space and can somehow do things with its *temporal trajectory*. It was bearing him and half a dozen other *grunts* towards their *mission target*, and they were wearing *slipsuits*, which was what saved him as he tumbled through the atmosphere and struck the ocean, then released him as water flooded in and he was picked up by the Flett family sailboat.

But his future—the year 2121—is nothing like that encountered by H.G. Wells' time traveller. No peaceful, ineffectual Eloi, no apelike Morlocks, but a world composed of *power-blocks* and *shield-cities,* and a war which seems to have been going on since before he was born in what he calls a *shanty-burrow* in a place Bethany would probably think of as the old state of Texas.

He talks of the seas rising and how many of the world's great cities—at least those that haven't been turned to glass by *nukes*—have been flooded. That, and of old diseases returning and new ones arising. And people on the march—vast migrations—and millions starving. And war. Yes, war. Which is why he's a grunt, for he has no *memory implants*, no *intelligence enhancements*, and his *genetic profile* always meant he'd never amount to anything.

So what he needs to find is his slipsuit. Not that it would help him get back to the time he's from, but because, as well as having *active camouflage* and something he calls an *AI*—she thought at first he was just saying "aye"—it also possesses a *disruptor*, which can reduce anything which isn't properly shielded to random atoms.

"So what would you do?" she asks as they pick amid the rockpools looking for debris. "I mean, if you found it?"

He shrugs, leaning against his stick. "I don't know. But it would sure as hell be *something*."

"Would you..." She nods over towards the Grand Fleet. "...join the British Navy?"

He laughs. Shakes his head. "I wouldn't need to. I'd *be* the fucking navy!"

She pretends to consider this and ignores the profanity. Perhaps she's testing her own resolve by bringing him this close to the promontory where his slipsuit lies hidden. That, or she's seeing if the thing will respond to his presence. But Toto just stands there, wincing and frustrated. After all, he's just a grunt, and the power of his slipsuit would be extraordinary.

Bethany can almost feel the warning thunder of the thing she now knows is called a disruptor growing inside her. She'd be Cortez conquering the Aztecs, or the British with their modern guns against the empires of India and China. At the very least, people in this village would finally take some proper notice of her...

"But you must know *something* about what happens in our future," she says. "Apart, at least, from these things you call movies."

IAN R. MACLEOD

IT'S SATURDAY MORNING and the twins and Ma have agreed to do most of Bethany's work so that she and Toto can walk over to Kirkwall, now that his leg's healing. He has to be careful, though, his presence on Orkney being unofficial, so he pulls Pa's old cap over his springy golden hair and one of Cousin Murdo's smocks covers most of the rest of him.

Still, he's looking up and around far too much for Bethany's comfort as they wander the stern granite streets amid cheery crowds of sailors on furlough. She steers him into Kirkwall Library past Mrs. Mellish at the counter, sits him down amid the dozing fisherman in the reference section, and spreads out some recent national newspapers. To her, their headlines make grim reading. Trouble in the Balkans. Germany planning what it calls a *preventative strike* against Russia. Yet the tone is worryingly jolly.

Perhaps, she whispers, they could invest what little money she has in some up-and-coming business. But the only ones Toto can recollect are either already well known—Gillette, Mercedes, Coca-Cola, Ford, General Electric—or based on technologies that sound so magical and remote—a company called Apple, for instance—as to be worthless. Neither is it much help that he remembers the sinking of the Titan-something, which might or might not have just been a movie, since everyone knows the Titanic struck an iceberg two years back. And the San Francisco earthquake was in 1906.

Sitting in this calm refuge of thought and knowledge as Mrs. Mellish glares at them disapprovingly, Bethany wonders what she would do, despite all the many books she's read, if she was suddenly catapulted back into, say, the court of King Henry VIII? Tell Anne Boleyn that marrying the king wasn't a good idea?

"But you must have had *some* interests. Perhaps before you became a grunt. Back in the—in the shanty-burrows?"

He smiles and shakes his head. He's doing this thing with the front page of the *Scottish Daily Record*, pinching at the text and then widening his fingers as if to make it bigger. "You mean, when I wasn't cocooned in a VR suit playing virtuals?" Then, clumsily and noisily enough to earn another disapproving look from Mrs. Mellish, he works his way back through the paper, flattening out the sports pages. A slow grin spreads across his face.

"Well? What is it?"

"Boxing! It was the one real thing I enjoyed when I was a kid. And it's barely changed. The discipline, the sweat, and the chalkdust—the history. There!"

He prods a tiny photograph.

"That's Jack Johnson. He's just beaten Frank Moran in Paris. And Kid Williams is about to fight Johnny Coulon for the World Bantamweight Title in old California. He'll win, too. Hey…" He laughs loudly enough to waken a couple of fishermen. "Maybe old Toto's not so stupid after all. All we need do is to bet on Kid Williams to win. And that's just the start of it. In a few years there's Gene Tunny, Jack Dempsey. It's a golden age."

Bethany takes a deep breath. "The problem is, Toto, any gambling that isn't on horses at a racetrack or in a licensed casino is illegal. Not that anyone would ever think of betting on a sporting event on the other side of the world. Although I suppose you could try taking a steamer across the Atlantic."

"How could I manage a stunt like that? I'm not even a grunt here. I'm nobody. In any case, World War One is about to start."

"*World War One?*"

"Yes."

"You mean there's *more* than one of them?"

"We've had either three or four. Depends how you count 'em."

"That's...terrible."

"I've no idea why you're acting surprised. All you have to do is look out at all those battleships."

"But still..."

"Yeah." He's clumsily inspecting the spread newspapers. "But still." He stops at a photograph which isn't in the sports pages. "This guy."

"The Archduke Franz Ferdinand?"

"Yeah—him."

"He's just a Hapsburg prince. The world's full of these people, so why on earth—?"

"What's the date again? I mean today?"

"Saturday the 27th of June."

"So this newspaper's only a couple of days old. And it says, right here, that he's visiting Sarajevo to inspect the troops on the 28th, which is tomorrow—Sunday."

"And?"

"Don't you see?" Now he's laughing again, and Mrs. Mellish is looking annoyed. "But of course, you wouldn't!"

NOT FOR THE first time, Bethany finds herself wondering if she'd have believed Toto if it wasn't for that slipsuit. Now, even more so, because it makes no sense that what he calls *World War One* should be triggered by the death of an obscure Hapsburg prince in a city she's barely heard of. But he insists that one of the few things anyone still remembers about the twentieth century is the assassination of this Archduke Ferdinand in Sarajevo. That, and the slaughter of millions of soldiers in muddy trenches, and a *Second* World War which followed soon after, and the rise of Joseph Hitler and Adolph Stalin, and a *holo-something*, and the invention of *nukes*, which can destroy whole cities. Then there's a *Cold War* which goes on for a very long time, but is really just like the peace of 1914, with all the *power-blocks* arming themselves with ever more destructive weapons.

In many ways, this feels even more like a game than anticipating sporting results. Not, they rapidly conclude, that it would be possible to reach Sarajevo in time to shout out a warning at the Archduke's passing car tomorrow, even if they could afford such a journey. But that doesn't mean they can't try *something*.

One of the few things Toto knows about the jumpships he travelled in is that the jumps they made in time and space were incredibly minute, but were still generally enough to avoid disruptor beams. So perhaps something they do now, minute though it might seem, could have a similarly large effect. At least, he says, it's worth a go until he works out how to make the most of his surprisingly encyclopedic knowledge of boxing. That, and as Bethany still has to point out, the world really isn't as primitive as he seems to think. There's a worldwide system of telegraphic communication, for instance.

The Post Office on Victoria Street closes at noon and the clock is already inching up from the quarter when they burst in. Then there's only Mr. Canning behind the counter, and Mrs. Pimm wants to send a postal order to her son in Australia. Finally, though, he takes the form from them. And, yes, that is the address: the Governor of Bosnia and Herzegovina at his official residence in Sarajevo. And yes, THE ARCHDUKE IS IN DANGER is the message.

Mr. Canning frowns. Sucks his teeth. But he stamps their form and takes the money.

THEN NOTHING HAPPENS. Nothing, that is, apart from Bethany being stared at by Mrs. Mellish that Sunday in church as if she has no more right to be there than in Kirkwall Library. Meanwhile, the guns of the Grand Fleet continue to boom across Scapa Flow and hulks are scuttled across various inlets as protection against marauding German submarines, much to the consternation of local fishermen. That and, she notices from a scrap of newspaper in the outhouse, that Kid Williams defeated Johnny Coulon by knockout in California almost a month ago.

"All in all," she says to Toto when she finds him sitting out on the stone pier that evening, "I don't think it does much to prove your abilities as an oracle."

"You're saying I make things up?"

She shakes her head. "I just wonder how much we really know about here and now, let alone the future."

"But there's still nothing about that Archduke being killed in Sarajevo?"

"The papers are full of the so-called Irish Question. But I suppose that Archduke Ferdinand is still alive, seeing as it's hardly front-page news when someone *isn't* assassinated."

He chuckles. "I guess there is that. Or maybe I got it wrong. It could have been some other prince or archduke. And perhaps not even in Sarajevo—"

"Wait a moment..." Bethany feels a flush of annoyance. "Now you're telling me..."

She trails off as a motor car comes jolting along the track from Kirkwall. It stops nearby. Three figures emerge. Two are wearing military uniforms, although she recognizes the third as Sergeant Boyle of the local constabulary.

"Bethany Flett," he says, "you and your companion are under arrest on charges of espionage and high treason."

THE INTERVIEW ROOM is starkly lit. Her shoulders ache because her arms are handcuffed behind her.

"So you're saying it was just a hunch," drawls a man in a dark suit with an English accent, "that made you and your friend send that telegram?"

"How many times do I have to answer the same question?"

He smiles, unamused. "For as many times as I want you to. Did you ever hear him speaking in another language? Say, for instance, German?"

She shakes her head. Neither has she seen any notebooks, guns, maps, or binoculars. Or flashing lights, or any other strange men, for that matter. The telegram was a prank. All she really knows is that Toto is a sailor from Kansas who fell off his ship into the Pentland Firth. Yes, she did visit the library with him here in Kirkwall last Saturday, as she's sure Mrs. Mellish has already informed them, but reading isn't a crime, is it?

The night drags on. There's a difficult moment when the Englishman says they've combed Kellness and the surrounding area for suspicious apparatus, but it soon becomes apparent they didn't find anything.

"So how long do I have to stay here," she asks, "since you have no proper evidence?"

"Well, that's not exactly true. At least when it comes to your friend. Who, by the way, can't even name the ship he's supposed to have fallen overboard from and plainly isn't from Kansas. But you, now *you*, my dear, I think, we probably can afford to let go. But you must remember one thing."

"What?"

"That you're a foolish girl and should count yourself incredibly lucky."

THE VILLAGE ISN'T the same. Nothing is. Pressmen arrive from the mainland, asking all sorts of questions. Of course, everyone says they knew right away there was something wrong about the man who claimed he was Toto from Kansas. Sure, that young lass was taken in, but she's not typical of anything.

GERMAN SPY UNMASKED. ESPIONAGE AT SCAPA FLOW. GRAND FLEET CLOAK AND DAGGER. The national press are full of it. And Bethany Flett's become this silly, besotted creature who should have known better. She can't visit Kirkwall Library now, not with Mrs. Mellish still there, and is trailed across the shore one evening when she's trying to collect driftwood by a man from the *Glasgow Herald* asking why she didn't realise Toto's name was out of a popular novel. Even the twins no longer want her bedtime stories.

After several weeks of interrogation, the spy still popularly known as Toto, and who apparently still refuses to co-operate, is transferred to Glasgow under great security and tried swiftly and *in camera* at the City High Court. As the papers and a shocked general public all agree, the guilty verdict and death sentence are mere formalities.

BETHANY'S NEVER BEEN to Glasgow before. In fact she's only once visited the mainland, although every child in Scotland knows about Duke Street Prison. It's the place you're threatened with if you don't eat your neeps or backchat your elders. Even then, its vast, sooty grimness and fortress-like outer walls come as a shock to her.

Knowing smirks greet her enquiry at the gates. Still, she's let in and shown along endless corridors amid a sea-roar of joyless voices. A final door bangs behind her and she waits in a cell much like the one in Kirkwall police station, but smaller and grimmer. Then the door opens again and Toto shuffles in. He's chained hand and foot, in frayed grey overalls. There's a cut beneath his left eye and a bruise across his forehead. He looks almost as frail as he did when he was hauled onto Kellness quay.

"Your limp…" she hears herself saying, "…it's almost gone."

"That was because you did such a good job of looking after me."

"I just wish—"

"No, no, Bethany! Don't you go wishing anything. You did the best you could, which was far more than I deserved. After all, I'm—"

"Just a grunt?"

"Yeah." He smiles. "But you're the only person who ever believed me."

"Although you never did tell me your real name."

"I didn't, did I? I think that was what drove people like our friends out there"—he nods towards the cell door—"crazy. But I came to like it, even if Toto did turn out to sound far too much like a codename. But what else was I supposed to tell them? At least, if I expected them to believe me?"

"But there's still no war. And the Archduke Ferdinand's alive and back in Austria. I saw his name in yesterday's paper."

"But everyone still says there's *going* to be a war, right? And we don't even know if our telegram got through." He frowns. "And there's this *other* thing that's been bothering me. You see, if I really did come from a different future, how can I even have been born?"

It's a clever thought, to which she has no answer. But she remembers how the fellow-traveller set out again but never returned at the end of H.G. Well's novel.

"At least I'll be dying a grunt's—a soldier's—death. Because they think I'm a foreign spy, it's going to be a firing squad."

"There must be *something...*"

"No, there isn't anything. And anyway—"

Then a bolt slides, a guard reenters, and Bethany has to leave the cell, and soon finds herself standing back outside the gates of Duke Street Prison.

WITH NOWHERE TO stay and little money, she compulsively wanders the Glasgow streets, pushing past endless strangers and feeling as lost and distant as Toto must feel. She's had dreams, visions, of coming here with the slipsuit and the disruptor, of tearing down the prison walls and freeing Toto—and that would only be the beginning. She'd be a vengeful Boadicea, imposing justice, fighting and righting all the world's many wrongs. But she knows she could never trust herself to wield such power, any more than

Toto. Not with the world as full as it already is with blood, grief, and mayhem.

Dawn does nothing to improve the look of Duke Street Prison. If anything, the blood-hued sky makes it even grimmer. Standing outside, she hears a shout from over the walls, then an echoing clatter of gunshots.

That's it, then. And she's no reason to think anything they've done has made any difference. She draws a breath and hurries to catch the train which, with a change at Inverness, and the ferry from Scrabster, will have her back at Kellness and probably collecting driftwood by evening. Then she stops. And turns. And walks briskly towards the growing morning bustle of Queen Street.

IT'S ALMOST FOUR years before she returns to Orkney. She's written many letters, of course, but the whole village seems astonished to see her walking down the track from Kirkwall.

Ma and Pa look so old, and the twins are so grown, and everyone admires her city clothes and treats her as if she's no longer Bethany Flett, but some important stranger. She gives Pa a new tape measure to replace the one which was worn out by the constant fiddling of the man no one wants to remember. And yes, she really does have a stake in the company that manufactures these things and owns the patent for the way the metal strip is curved to keep it from bending. For something so obvious, it's strange no one else ever thought of it.

It's midsummer again, and the light of evening seems endless, and they want to hear all about what it's like to live in Edinburgh, and visit London, and even Paris, and the sights she must have seen. She doesn't dwell, as the best plates are set out, on her year and a half following the fleet and gutting fish as a herring girl while she tried to save some money. Neither does she say too much about her work to promote women's suffrage, which she knows would only cause upset and argument.

You could now count the ships moored across Scapa Flow on the fingers of one hand. There's a lightboat, two tugs, and maybe a dredger. The British Grand Fleet, or what's left of it since Mr. Churchill's cutbacks, now rides anchor in the warmer waters of the Solent, while Kaiser Bill's lost most of his powers and the Tsar and his family are staying with their English cousins at Osborne House, having been evicted from Russia.

Not that you could say peace has broken out across the world. There's continued conflict in the Balkans, more trouble in Ireland, and bloody revolution in Mexico. But at least there hasn't been a world war. In fact, as the major powers sign up one by one to the Community of Nations with its headquarters in Switzerland, a global conflagration seems less rather than more likely.

Does any of this have anything to do with that telegram? Bethany still has no idea, although she's followed the successes of a highly technical young boxer called Gene Tunney. Not that she's a huge fan of the sport, but she does keep up an interest. She's also reinvested some of the money she's made out of her tape measure patent in companies involved in making films with a sound accompaniment—the so-called talkies—even if most people are certain they'll never catch on.

There's a fair deal of drinking, at least by the men, and the children grow tired and grumpy, and the questions become repetitious. Time for bed, especially as she's leaving so early next morning, although she's not allowed to lift a finger to help with the clearing.

Saying she'd like to stretch her legs, she goes outside, where the sky is still glowing and the air feels like velvet.

She crosses the shore and climbs to the cleft in the promontory and pulls away the rocks. The slipsuit is just as extraordinary as she remembers; the power and the purpose and the weight of it. After filling it with stones and wrapping it in seaweed, she carries it quickly around to the quay and pushes out in one of the village rowboats.

The sea is smooth and still. Even though it's been years, she dips the oars with quiet ease and skill until she's out of sight of Kellness, at a place where the water suddenly deepens. Then, as she pushes yet more stones into the slipsuit, her skin crawls with a sense of being watched. When she turns, she laughs. It's just the local seals, studying her with their heads raised out of the water. They chuff back at her as if equally amused, then disappear in a flicker of fins. Weighted as it is, the slipsuit soon darkens and vanishes into the depths as it follows them.

Bethany sits for a long moment, letting the sky and the sea settle. Then she rows briskly back towards the shore and the lights of the village.

Afterword

THIS STORY IS the second example in this collection of the subgenre of fiction commonly known as alternate history, and the temporal twists involved in both are somewhat similar. Both *The Mrs Innocents* and *Selkie* find ways to avoid the major tragedies that blighted the history of the twentieth century through altering the initial conditions in Europe that led to the First World War. They also hint at, or actively promote, improving the rights of women as remedy for the troubles of mankind. For this I make no apology. As a child of that century whose parents actually met while serving in the Second World War, these conflicts loom pretty large in my head. I also can't help thinking that a great deal that goes wrong in the world, on the small scale but also geopolitically, is linked to the perennial problem of male aggression.

The particular type of time-twist known as alternate history is something I've mined and played with many times during my career as a writer. While my novels *The Summer Isles* and *Wake Up and Dream* are obvious examples where something clearly different has happened in a world which is otherwise recognisable as our own, even my novels *The Light Ages* and *The House of Storms*, which are commonly thought of as fantasies, are based on the premise that a form of real magic was found to work during the Age of Reason, which is also the stepping-off point for *Lamagica*.

As to why I'm so drawn to making these logical and temporal twists, I think what draws me most is the opportunity they give to put the familiar and the unexpected together in fresh and interesting ways, rather than any desire to explore the internal ramifications of some historical event. With *Selkie*, the idea of writing a story about the myth of seals who masquerade as humans was there long before the time travel and the slipsuit stuff came into focus, and the actual twist of the main characters somehow managing to change history without even realising that they'd done so arrived even later. At the end of the day, perhaps rather than being drawn to the intellectual challenge of working through a historical *what if?*, I'm more attracted to exploring the poignancy of what might have been.

The Fall of the House Of Kepler

I WAS ALREADY DEEP into my long journey when my sensors finally detected the House of Kepler. Discovering any artefact in such a bleak part of extrasolar space should have caused some lifting of my spirits, but the vista spinning before me did not. It was a peculiar mixture of forms and radiations hung in cold, empty darkness, and as I grew closer and felt the tug of its gravitational field, I perceived that the thing that had once been Kepler was now a huge agglomeration of twisted metal and seared asteroid, of broken gantries and burnt-out rocket stages, of contorted grappling arms and crazed solar panels. I could still have avoided contact, but, even as I observed that the whole edifice was also riddled with grey runners of some kind of structural fatigue, I did not.

    I used much of my remaining fuel to reduce velocity. Somehow, I maintained structural integrity through the impact, and clung on. Yet I was still telling myself as I limped across the ruined surface that I would find no lingering consciousness here, for how could anything sentient bring itself to exist in as drear a habitation as this? Yet I sensed stirrings, and saw how several of the grappling arms had drawn themselves into a parody of welcome. Then a voice, or rather a confusion of deranged and whispered signals, resolved into a static lisp of human words, which bade me to enter the vast portals of this strange machine.

I can't say that the thing which Kepler had become suffered from any obvious absence, despite its weakness and age. There was certainly power, and a fizz of intelligence, which drew me on through twisting caverns. Then, stranger still, I was beckoned into the approximation of a room from back on Earth, which had clearly been constructed in anticipation of the arrival of some living guest. There were walls which, although crazily canted, gave some sense of an up and a down. There were even airlocks. That, and Kepler had contrived to create out of a collection of yet more space debris—lost wrenches, garbage bags, propellant hoses, circuit boards, thermal protection tiles, along with some of its own original thermal insulation blankets—what might be described as a chair, and a bed.

Of course, I had no use for such things, but I was instructed to recharge and repair myself, and most of Kepler's presence departed to allow me to do so, although it left behind an obvious desperation to talk and to share. So I raised myself back to my legs as soon as my energies permitted, and clambered though many malformed spaces to the control room, library, great hall, central cavern—it had something of all these aspects, and many more—where the heart of what Kepler had become now resided.

Clearly, this machine had amassed vast amounts of data during its long existence, and most of it was stored here. There were more screens—many cracked or bleeding, but some still live—along with holograms, digital discs, and even black ribbons of magnetic tape. The voice, the presence, was much stronger here, and seemed to find focus in the pitted gleam—the monocle of a blind Cyclops—of its old primary mirror.

I was ushered to direct my receptors this way and that. Kepler had managed to download and store a fine scientific library during its long existence, and among those pages were to be found Aristotle's *Physica*, Galileo's *Dialogue*, Newton's *Principia* and Darwin's *Voyage*, along with Watson's *Double Helix*, and Rachel Carson's *Silent Spring*. That, and simulacra of many of the greatest human works of art. My own much smaller databanks recognised Epstein's *Rock Drill*, Hokusai's *Great Wave*, and the first movement of Hayden's last, D major, *London Symphony*. But of all the wonders this greatly changed entity was desperate to show me, those which clearly still held the most significance were the data of distant planets it had once been created to collect.

Here, a blur of pixels, was the gas giant Gliese 436b, which orbited at great velocity, and emitted a startling, blue-grey, comet-like tail. And this, a faded spectrograph, was PSR B1620-26 b, otherwise known as Methuselah, and quite possibly the oldest planet in the galaxy. Then there was KIC 8462852, a star of the main F-type sequence in the constellation of Cygnus, which possessed a spectacularly non-periodic luminosity curve. Perhaps this was caused by nothing more than floating clouds of debris, or perhaps by the vast megastructure of some alien civilisation; Kepler simply did not know. Then there was Tora 331A, an exoplanet veiled in a mist of such purity that no data as to its composition had ever been decoded. A platonic absolute of a planet, perhaps, from which all other planets were derived.

But there was one planet which Kepler believed transcended even this, and the half-alive voice grew yet more agitated as it enumerated the beauty of her oceans, the purity of her glaciers, the shimmer of her deserts, the ever-changing glory of her clouds, and, above all, her teeming, endless life. Vast forests. Creatures of all sizes, shapes and hues. And flowers, yes, flowers, and insects, and pulsing amoebae, and trillions of humble bacteria, and strange things that dwelled in places harsh and remote.

All of this, yes, and more—and I knew, of course, that Kepler was speaking of the planet of our creation. For a while, it even seemed to me that she, Earth, was here with us, impossible though I knew that to be. I could almost believe my own sensors caught the stir of protein-based life at the darkest corner of this chaotic space. I even silently urged Earth to step forward and reveal herself to us in all her beauty, gowned in sky, garlanded with stars and haloed by rain, but then the sense of what I was returned to me, and still Kepler was talking—a mumbling and diseased machine.

It still remembered, it said, those famous early discoveries which had populated this galaxy with more planets than its creators could ever have dreamed. Earthlike planets, and gas giants so big they were almost stars. Planets where it rained glass, and planets crusted with burning ice. There had been, it acknowledged, a failure of its reaction wheels some years into its mission, but it had still maintained sufficient photometric precision to have a long and useful life. For Kepler was still Kepler, and there was always more of the universe to be surveyed. At some time, though, during what otherwise would have been a slow decline into machine senility, something else must have occurred. A collision, most likely, perhaps with some other autonomous device, which set it spinning out into madness and the darkness of extrasolar space.

So much had changed that it was strange that Kepler remained Kepler at all. But that, unquestionably, was what it was. And it knew so *much*, had made so many *discoveries*, which it still longed to share with its creators back on Earth. This universe, after all, was filled with marvels. All it needed, all it wanted, was a sign, the faintest reactivating signal, to resume its work. And now, and at long last, I had arrived. And this—it strove, and failed, to keep the expectancy from its voice—was surely why I was here?

I mastered myself. For I didn't doubt Kepler also saw me as another useful piece of passing spacejunk it could absorb, and it was time it knew the truth.

The whole machine spasmed as it decrypted the data I bore with me. Fluids and detritus jetted into the void. But part of it—the part, perhaps, which had kept it functioning over so many millennia—still strove not to believe the truth. After all, Earth had been fiercely self-sustaining, and the creatures who held mastery over it were so incredibly wise. They had gazed, yes, up at the night sky and wondered at its mysteries since the times they had first raised themselves on two legs, and always craved to find out more. Kepler was certain humans would one day journey far from the harbour of the Sun on the sails of vast starships towards other worlds. To think, to think that that blue and white sphere was now a desolate rock, its atmosphere poisoned, its seas polluted... To think that the last conscious machine should inject its fading intelligence into the last message of one final extrasolar artefact before it, too, succumbed to the acid dark, was beyond impossible. People, humans, our masters and mistresses, were destined to bloom across the galaxy. The souks of Ke 4 awaited, as did the bridge-beings of Arothea, and the sand rainbows of Behails. Yes, and yes, and still, and more...

But even as Kepler spoke, I saw that the grey fingers of the metal fatigue I had observed on my arrival were clawing the whole edifice apart. The space grew hazed with rubble. It fumed and sparked. Soon it became apparent that, even as Kepler still somehow found the will to speak of life, hope and discovery, its own death was close. Yet as the House of Kepler dissolved, I thought for a moment that I glimpsed the shape of that lost, brilliant machine, its sensors and cameras fully active as it made those first dazzling observations from its stately orbit around the Sun. And turning with it, too, was Earth, the mother of our existences, once again a bright blue globe, and she and Kepler joined in an elegant dance, and everything else in this universe seemed possible, life after life and world after world. Then all of that vanished into a black fissure, and I drifted back from the thinning dust, and fired the last of my fuel, and travelled on, alone, into the interstellar dark.

Afterword

I OCCASIONALLY GET asked to produce a new piece for an anthology. Sometimes, as several stories in this collection attest, I even manage to get something done. The particular requests that I find the hardest are those of the "just write anything" variety. The ones I prefer, and am most likely to respond to, are both pretty specific and, at least as importantly, lie a little outside my immediate comfort zone. On that basis, a request to write a story based on the many extrasolar worlds which the Kepler telescope is revealing pretty much fitted the bill.

This commission was clearly to write something broadly SF, which of course I'm used to doing, but my work rarely achieves escape velocity and when it does, as in pieces such as *The Memory Artist*, it tends to be mythic or, as in the case of *Ephemera*, the result of a series of adjustments to a story that's really supposed to be about something else.

Nevertheless, I was more than willing to embrace visiting some strange or recently discovered world through a work of fiction. I'm as thrilled as most people who care about science and knowledge are by Kepler's discoveries, and can deal semi-plausibly with extra-solar concepts and discoveries, at least given a fair solar wind in my sails. But the story, or at least the one I hoped to write, simply wouldn't come. For me, the vistas the Kepler telescope was reaching towards just felt too dauntingly remote.

What, then, got me thinking of Edgar Allan Poe's classic work of nihilistic obsession? I really have no idea, other than perhaps that it was something to do with the problem I have with the kind of SF that embraces the inherent fantasy of interstellar travel too easily, and has recognisably fleshy human characters somehow wandering about on another world as if that's really how things are going to work out. For me, such stories negate, or at least unfeasibly diminish, the sheer bleak emptiness and hostility of space. Sure, we humans routinely put satellites up into orbit, and can physically inhabit space stations for a few months, and we've sent robot probes across much of the solar system, and have discovered far more than we could ever have hoped about other planetary systems through clever devices such as the Kepler telescope itself. Then, of course, we have actually set foot on the Moon, and might even get to do so again, while spending a few minutes in zero gravity has become the go-to trinket for billionaires. But the problems of getting human beings even as far as Mars, let alone reaching another star system, are not so much dauntingly large as near-insurmountable, at least for as long as we remain the vulnerable, fleshy, warm-blooded, oxygen-breathing beings we currently are.

Not only is space a hard vacuum, but it's filled with lethal radiation, and the distances involved in crossing the void between the stars are incomprehensibly vast.

If anything to do with us humans and our civilisation ever does reach the stars, my wager is that it'll be something we've made rather than any of our physical descendants, and even then it'll take a staggeringly long time. In fact, the Voyager probes, which were launched an incredible 45 years ago as I write, have already left the outer fringes of the solar system but they won't come within reach of another star for at least another 40,000 years. To hope that things will work out otherwise within a few generations or centuries is fine and lovely. But the true message that space is giving us humans—with all its great beauties and incredible mysteries, its hard radiations and mind-boggling scale—isn't about little green men or strange civilisations, but that what really matters is what we have down here on our fragile planet, and in the wondrous storehouses of our own minds.

Copyright Information

"Introduction" Copyright © 2023 by Ian R MacLeod. First published in this collection.

"The Mrs Innocents" Copyright © 2020 by Ian R MacLeod. First published in *Asimov's Science Fiction Magazine*, May-June 2020, edited by Sheila Williams.

"The Wisdom of the Group" Copyright © 2017 by Ian R MacLeod. First published in *Asimov's Science Fiction Magazine*, March-April 2017, edited by Sheila Williams.

"Ephemera" Copyright © 2018 by Ian R MacLeod. First published in *Asimov's Science Fiction Magazine*, July-August 2018, edited by Sheila Williams.

"Lamagica" Copyright © 2020 by Ian R MacLeod. First published in *Subterranean: Tales of Dark Fantasy 3*, edited by William Schafer.

"Ouroboros" Copyright © 2018 by Ian R MacLeod. First published in *2001: An Odyssey in Words*, edited by Tom Hunter, Ian Whates.

"Stuff" Copyright © 2022 by Ian R MacLeod. First published in *New Worlds*, edited by Nick Gevers, Peter Crowther.

"The God of Nothing" Copyright © 2021 by Ian R MacLeod. First published in *Burning Brightly: 50 Years of Novacon*, edited by Ian Whates.

"Downtime" Copyright © 2023 by Ian R MacLeod. First published in this collection.

"The Roads" Copyright © 1997 by Ian R MacLeod. First published in *Asimov's Science Fiction Magazine*, April 1997, edited by Gardner Dozois.

"The Memory Artist" Copyright © 2019 by Ian R MacLeod. First published in Chinese by the Future Affairs Administration. Republished in English in *Asimov's Science Fiction Magazine*, May/June 2019, edited by Sheila Williams.

"Sin Eater" Copyright © 2020 by Ian R MacLeod. First published in *Made to Order*, edited by Jonathan Strahan.

"The Visitor from Taured" Copyright © 2016 by Ian R MacLeod. First published in *Asimov's Science Fiction Magazine*, September 2016, edited by Sheila Williams.

"The Chronologist" Copyright © 2022 by Ian R MacLeod. First published online on *Tor.com*.

"Selkie" Copyright © 2019 by Ian R MacLeod. First published in *Alternate Peace*, edited by Joshua Palmatier, Steven H. Silver.

"The Fall of the House of Kepler" Copyright © 2017 by Ian R MacLeod. First published in *Extrasolar*, edited by Nick Gevers.